M000196431

THE
VAMPIRE
OF
WESTERN
PENNSYLVANIA

a novel by Steven M. Greenberg

INKSLINGER
PUBLISHING

This story is a work of fiction. Names, characters, places, and incidents are the products of the author's imagination or are used fictitiously.

Text copyright ©2015 Steven M. Greenberg
All rights reserved.

Published by Inkslinger Publishing

Cover and interior design by Catherine Adams, Inkslinger Editing LLC

Print ISBN: 978-1-943723-06-5
eBook ISBN: 78-1-943723-07-2

No part of this book may be reproduced or transmitted in any form by any means, electronic, or mechanical including photocopying, recording, or by any information storage and retrieval system without permission in writing from the author or the publisher.

FOREWORD

No truly successful novel should need an introduction, and the presence of one here should tell you something.

Not that this won't turn out to be a successful novel; not that it isn't a good one, or a terrific one: I wouldn't put my name on a piece of writing I didn't think was pretty darn terrific—But then, every mother thinks her child is beautiful, or *ought* to, so an author's opinion on his writing can safely be ignored.

But as to the introductory statement herewith presented (and feel free to skip it right here, right now and go on to the story if you like), the very title of the book (or e-book) in your hands requires a bit of explanation from an author hitherto accused of producing somewhat pedantic and overly literate text—so here goes:

Vampires—Now what right does a literate author have penning a novel about vampires? The concept, after all, is ridiculous in the extreme. I mean—fangs? wings? caskets for nightly bedding? turning to dust from daylight? Give me a break, first of all. Then 'splain me the how or why of *that*. Neither rhyme nor reason to it, is there? And if there is no rhyme or reason for a story—well, hell—why try and write the goddamn thing at all?

OK, point made; can't say I disagree so far—But what if a novelist can make some logic of the illogical? I think I did just that with some success in *Incantation*; and if a magic incantation can be made at least somewhat believable, then is the concept of a guy who kills for blood (sans fangs and wings, admittedly) all that far a stretch?

Having gone through a lengthy education in science, and subsequently in medicine, I felt I had both the knowledge and the grounding in scientific fact to tackle the challenge of making the unbelievable not that tough to swallow. I'll talk about the reason I took on the challenge, and about my overall literary philosophy in general, in a postscript at the end....

But for now, dear reader, please delve in. I hope you like my effort; I write these novels solely for my own enjoyment and (thank goodness!) I don't really need to make a profit. But the validation of having a reader's approval (and therefore taste) coincide with my own—that makes all the effort of writing and tedium of editing worthwhile.

So please, suspend your logical disbelief as you take this flight of fantasy; fasten your seatbelts, brace yourself for bumpy ride ... and read on.

Written this twenty-second day of May of the year after the events in this book actually took place....

Or not—

The author.

THE
VAMPIRE
OF
WESTERN
PENNSYLVANIA

A Novel by Steven M. Greenberg

Acknowledgments

To the people of Western Pennsylvania, who helped inspire the plot and characterization of the novel, such as it is. You have provided me with the best of patients in my tenure as a doctor, and with the best of readers in my tenure as a writer. I humbly thank you.

And a special thanks to Catherine Adams (Inkslinger Editing LLC), the quintessential editor and literary adviser. If this book exceeds the skeptic reader's novelistic expectations, that achievement is entirely owing to her.

PRELUDE

Father's hand is cold, his lips are cracked and pale, and his pulse....

"Do you feel it, Radu? What is the frequency? Count it by the clock."

"Rapid, Father. Very rapid and very...."

"Faint?"

"Slightly faint, yes, but not inordinately so."

"And my breathing: What do you hear in the sound of my breathing? Listen, son. Listen carefully and describe."

"A harshness, Father, a.... I hear a sort of stridor."

"Yes, yes, but be more specific. What exactly is the nature of the stridor? You know this well by now, I taught you these things long ago. Tell me what you hear. Say it with precision. Identify. Specify. Characterize."

"I hear the rattle, Father. I begin to hear the rattle."

"Exactly, my son. The death rattle. Believe your sense perceptions; accept them; use them. Never let emotions cloud your objectivity. A good physician must always be observant and objective; and I expect you to be the best physician the world has ever known. If you fail to rise to that, all my tutelage has been in vain."

"Yes, Father, I know that. I understand."

"Remember this and heed me well: You will need the skills I taught you if you want to stay alive. And you *must* stay alive; it is *imperative* that you stay alive."

"Yes, I fully understand."

"And it is vital also that your sister stay alive. You must do that for me too. Promise that you will."

"Yes, Father, I shall do as you say, as I always have. But Sister may not be afflicted with the disease."

"She will be, though. All the offspring of Originals have been afflicted, even those who coupled with the others. Your half-sister has my traits; she will be afflicted just the same as all the others of our kind have been."

"And if she is, then yes; I shall care for her."

"Do so; swear to me that you will do so. If she survives you, she must be instructed just as you have been. Do you understand?"

Radu nods in silence, kneels beside the deathbed, and holds his father's hand in his. The pulse is faint, fainter than it was a little while before; the pallor has increased; and Father's voice is halting, scarcely audible unless he turns and bends his ear to very near the pallid lips.

The room is dark and quiet; no sounds beyond the doors. King George has left the palace, and his entourage departed in his company for London and the end-of-year festivities. Beside the bed, one on either side, two candles flicker low. The velvet curtains of the canopy are pulled aside, and past the open curtain of the far side, past the second candle, a narrow table can be seen in the scanty amber light. Atop the table lies the body brought here yesterday by two ragged men in cloaks, men well paid for their labors. Twenty guineas: a sum enough to purchase truly anything at Hampton Court when the courtiers have moved on and gratuities are scarce. And the bag of shiny Queen Anne sovereigns was quite enough to purchase this, though the effort was in vain. A faint obnoxious scent pervades the room, a scent of death, albeit rather recent death, decayed but not quite gone to rot, incompletely masked by the perfumed coverlet that hides all but a chalky dangling arm, hanging down below the cloth.

The lengthy silence ends: Father, having paused in speech long enough to spare his failing breath, resumes:

"All right, my son, it is time for us to make our farewell dispositions."

"But … Father—Father!—is there no remedy at all? Should we … can we try another dose of marrow, or…?"

"No, my son; no. The marrow has gone bad by now, and even if the corpse were fresh, no treatment can possibly avail this time. Look: Look at my fingernails—Do you see the lines?"

"I see white, Father; striations of white. Is that important? What does it mean?"

"It is something I have never shown you before; but remember it. If you see it again in a patient, be scrupulous in examining his food."

"The food? Is it a poison? You have not been given poison, Father! We have eaten together—always—and…."

"All right; no matter, Radu. Prepare your own food and beverages henceforth. Trust no others to prepare anything you consume. *No* one, I say; trust no one at all. For now, however, ask no further questions, my son, just do as I say. There." Father lifts his palsied hand to point. The fingernails *are* banded white, all of them.

"My trunk," gasps Father's rasping voice. "Open the trunk and bring the box."

Radu goes to the trunk and lifts the lid. The box is at the bottom, beneath the courtly vestiture of cloth of gold, beneath the medical devices, beneath the ancient books and manuscripts, buried deep in the place a precious relic would be stored. And to look at it, to touch and smell it, the box does seem precious. Radu has seen it before on the rarest of occasions: an intricate casket of sandalwood, carved by his father's fingers long ago, years before *he* was born, before the four of them migrated from the east to Hanover and then from Hanover to their present English home. The sacred paper rests inside.

"This will go with you. Wherever you are, wherever you chance to travel, keep it close, but keep it safe."

Radu nods obediently. He cannot speak, what with the stricture in his throat.

"This will be your purpose, your duty, as it has been mine. Open the box and carry out the instructions it contains— But only do so when the time is right. I have translated the text into English for clarity, so that Sister, if need be, can readily understand."

"Yes." Radu chokes the words by force of will. "But— you say when the *time* is right—How am I to *know* when the time is right?"

"Listen, Radu; come close and listen; my voice is growing weak. When mankind can communicate with the distant-most stars; that will be the time. When that condition comes to be—the words come hard, so listen close—when that condition comes to be, then open the box and read the paper kept within. It will instruct you what to do."

"Yes, but—the *stars*! How can human converse with the stars be possible? How far distant are the stars from us? Will mankind *ever* have ability to do that?"

"Yes, my son, it will come to pass eventually; all such things do. The course of life is ever upward. Think of Leibniz, think of Newton! Things that seem impossible, inconceivable,

3

can happen in the twinkling of an eye. Stay alive, keep your sister alive—protect her if you can—keep the box safe and yet accessible, and you may one day do what I cannot live to do.... Now embrace me one last time and leave. You must not be present when the corpse is found."

"I cannot leave you, Father, not until...."

"'Until,' my boy, is immanent. The box is in your hands. You and it are the only reasons I would wish to live beyond my allotted time, if there were any way to do so—Now take the box and go.... And ... and...."

"Yes, Father—what? I can scarcely hear you." Radu wipes his eyes and swallows down the dryness in his throat. "It is hard to understand. Try to whisper louder if you can."

"Beware, my son."

"Yes, Father—But ... but of what? Beware of *what?*"

"Stepmother. Half-sister. Beware. Take nothing from their hands, not food, not drink. Be vigilant, be circumspective, and you will live, so that maybe, possibly, hopefully, someday you ... will ... will ... will...."

1

She was weak, and frail this afternoon—For, after all, she had gone so long without. Nearly forty days now, Wilson calculated, thinking back; way too long a time.

And so the weakness had set in—though what another man might label weakness in such a thing as Madam, would have been unimaginable power in any other creature of her shape and kind.

But relatively weak just now she clearly was, for the infusions generally sapped her strength. And so her voice was faint and feeble when she said to Wilson, pointing past his shoulder with that crooked finger, bent to nearly double at its distal joint: "You will dispose of that by evening, Wilson," phrasing this, despite the meager volume of the sound, not as a question, nor even as a command, but as a simple statement of fact; as though she knew beyond a shadow of a doubt that Wilson would perform the very text and letter of her bidding without the need for being asked.

And Wilson answered in his subject's voice, a voice obedient and meek and just as hushed in tone as her debilitated voice had been:

"Yes, Madam. By evening certainly; as you wish."

"Then get me up now. Help me up the steps. I need to watch my movies for a while—To fortify my strength, you know; my strength of will, at least; I think you understand."

So over he stepped accordingly and pulled the IV tubing from her arm. The finger she had pointed with twitched a little when the plastic catheter came out. A scythe-shaped finger, so dramatically askew that, while the claw-like hand had clearly pointed toward the body known as Corwin in the corner—that meddlesome David Corwin with his cameras and his questions!—the fingertip itself had pointed someplace to the right of it—*her* right—toward a small, high basement window, through which suffused a slender shaft of muted light: An ancient crooked finger, withered amazingly, though powerful enough when she needed it to be.

Wilson helped her rise, supporting her wiry weight beneath the armpits. She could stand well enough and walk with reasonable stability given a little bit of help; particularly now, with that supplemental dose of red cells in her veins. Wilson helped her to the stairs and held her from behind as she ascended. Up she went, step by plodding step, up to the open cellar door, and through it, and past the cherry-paneled hallway into the sitting room of the big old Victorian mansion where she had lived since many, many years preceding Wilson's time.

Then on they moved conjointly, across the darkened room, and over to her favorite seat, a huge Queen Anne wing chair set snug behind an ottoman. And there she sat—Wilson helped to lower her until she sat, for she was still as helpless as a newborn pup and would be so until the morning when the full effect of her infusion kicked in. Fully forty days now; long enough for the deficiency to really get her down—she'd seldom had to go that long.

Ah but tomorrow, as the day progressed, she would grow stronger by the hour, until by evening all of the formidable force in that deceptive, shriveled form would be restored once more, and she would be a phenomenon of nature, just as she had always been before.... And as that fleeting thought flowed unemotionally through Wilson's vivisected brain, he heard her sharp voice order him to:

"Give me the remote, Wilson. Over on the table there. Hand it to me, and then you can attend to what you need to do."

"Yes, Madam; here; I'll set it on your lap."

"And clean it up down there as well. It smells like a butcher shop, you hear? Make sure you scrub the floor until you get it clean."

"I will, Madam, as I always do."

"All right then, go. Do the tasks required of you. You may be excused."

So Wilson went, accordingly; he bowed and turned about and went without an instant's more delay: Through the paneled hallway, down the basement steps again, and over to the corner where the body limply hung. There was a little pool of blood beneath the corpse of Corwin and he mopped it up. Not too much expended in the dagger's tremulous work, but a bit, a little bit. She'd gotten the bulk of what she'd needed of it in.

Then he pulled the body down. Not as heavy as when he'd put it up, not by quite a lot, what with a good bit of the fluids gone. He hauled it over to the sturdy stainless table at the far end of the room; hauled it easily, for he was strong—He'd been selected and deemed suitable partially *because* he was strong, as Madam often said.

Then he cut the corpse of Corwin into manageable parts, severing the joints neatly, as he'd been taught so well to do. Madam's handsome brother had taught him this, after the operation. Brother was a nice man, as he remembered: kind to him, even considering the surgery that he'd undergone at Brother's hands. A pity that Madam had done what she'd done to Brother. But Brother had survived that day—or so Madam seemed to think, referring to it furiously when she brought the subject up—which was rather often, actually; even after all these many years: "I'll kill him next time, Wilson. Next time no one will intervene."

The various body parts went into the hopper one by one. No blood left, beside the wasted leakage in the chest—so no annoying mess. Chop it up and scatter it on the grounds once the mincemeat chopping had been done; that's what Madam had instructed him from the very first to do: The rats and crows and ravenous bacteria would see to all the rest. A month from now the last molecular remnant of this prying thing called 'Corwin' during life would be eaten by the worms and there would be another one to come—a 'Lewis' or 'Bingham' or 'Dworski'—as there'd been a different one each few weeks before, ever since that memorable day when Brother had been stabbed. These were far from beneficial lives, no doubt, and Madam needed what they offered more than they had ever done, so everything had gone, as always, to an apt and proper end.

Wilson fed the body parts into the hopper bloodlessly; and as he fed, the light slipped through the slender little window Madam's finger had unintentionally pointed to. Out beyond the six small panes, autumn leaves swirled round in the considerable breeze. There was a storm coming up; the TV weatherman had said so. Up from the south it came, warm air intersecting with a shaft of Canadian cold. The leaves flew aloft in it, many did. One sere leaf, reduced now to a scanty thread of veins, rose higher than the rest. Up into the sky it went, borne aloft by some weird tornadic current of air the sudden storm front gave rise and purpose to.

7

Up it flitted, up, up, spiraling skyward swiftly; upward toward the gathering clouds, rising in its feathery weightlessness to outcrop height ... then skyscraper height ... then, as it blew along east-northeast sucked up in the vagrant storm, up the leaf got lifted to the towering height of West Virginia's tallest hills.

Up, up, and over them it went in turn, swept along by the ever-present wind. East-northeast over a sliver of southwest Ohio terrain, and on over the forested hillocks of Pennsylvania. Over the Ohio River then, in turn, churning westward stormily; up along the Allegheny as it flowed due south, and across its restless waters with the wind, to waft aloft above the rolling forests of the counties north of Pittsburgh. Through the moonless night, a hundred miles of Pennsylvanian acreage was overpassed by the leaf-enfolding wind ... until, with dawning day, the peculiar sky-drawn shaft of moving air began to settle down.

The storm front stalled, the cooler air displaced the sullen clouds, and the little leaf sank lower with the breeze's morning death. From a thousand feet up, it wafted groundward in the lazy air. Down, down, onto shaggy land below: riverine valleys; hills with multicolored forest growth, growing somewhat foliage sparse as the autumn rains denuded them of leaves.

Downward swirled the shriveled leaf. Down, down, and ever farther down at last amidst the cloudless air, now finally settling lazily toward a hilltop, bare at its grassy brow....

And near the hilltop, winding toward it on a narrow path, a solitary open vehicle, loud, grumbling, with a wind-blown rider at its helm: a sun-browned man with frizzled hair, a beaten leather jacket, the yellow hint of a bandanna on his neck. Down toward this solitary rider, on a solitary vehicle, on a lazy Sunday morning, the little leaf terminally fell.

Distracted, however, by a blackish cloud of something a whole lot more curious than a single falling leaf, the grizzled rider couldn't possibly have noticed its fluttery,

feathery

fall.

2

Smoke.

A LOT of smoke.

An *awful* lot—Damn!

Roger pulled his ATV up short beside the path atop the hill. Thick smoke; black smoke, gathering upward from the valley high above the treetops to the north. Impressive smoke. *Unnerving* smoke. The kind of smoke that oughtn't to be here.

For there was not much tinder in the forest that would burn that way, this being public land, Pennsylvania State game land. Not much out here otherwise: no farms, no residential settlements. And as wet as it had been this autumn—no real chance of a brush fire or any natural sort of blaze. Of that fact, Roger felt assured.

He stared across the scenery and scratched his head. Roger knew smoke, all right, and the various kinds of fires that sent it up—after all, having been a volunteer firefighter *himself* back in those carefree days before he started cutting timber for the mill—And the specific type of fire that put out *this* variety of smoke had to be a big one—a *bad* one.

But what was down there that could burn this way?— *What?* Roger searched his mental map of the terrain—for he had roamed this region since he was a wee one, first on foot, then later in his grumbly ATV—He scanned his memory, traced the wandering pathways of his youth, though coming up with ... zilch—For there was nobody actually living this far south of Stanleyville, a good eight miles from town, no homes, no businesses, no hunting camps ... not a one—except for....

Except for—Yes! Of course!—Except for old man Jenkins's place! He'd clean forgot about the Jenkins property till now: The legendary Harold Jenkins, dead these thirty years and more, who'd drilled the county land back in the Fifties and made a hefty bundle selling coal and gas and petrol to the Pittsburgh big boys with the megabucks. His place was down there, his old abandoned hunting lodge, deserted thirty years ago by the family heirs and heiresses who moved away from Stanleyville for the city life and fed off the millions Jenkins's efforts had put by.

Yes, of course!—Old Harold Jenkins's compound! Roger had tooled around the boundaries of it lots of times in his ATV: A couple of hundred acres or more of shaggy virgin forestland all fenced off from the surrounding woods: too vast an area for anyone to see much of the property past the multitude of trees— Why, scarce a hint of the house itself was visible to any passerby short of hopping the ten-foot fence; and nobody Roger knew had ever dared to hop *that* formidable fence, not with all the rusting razor wire and crimson-colored warning signs around.

The place was derelict, as far as Roger knew; most of the periphery sure looked it, anyway—the unkempt grass, the overgrowth of trees. But there were rumors about, these past few years—maybe a dozen years or more, now that he got to setting his mind to focus on it—vague talk among the local residents that someone had bought the property and might be living there. All this was gossip, sure enough; and Roger had never been the kind of guy to gossip or to listen to the gossiping of others. But the fellows at the lumber mill had talked from time to time, and you couldn't help but overhear.

And Karen too: His wife had mentioned something, come to think of it—Some hazy something she had said a year or two ago about a weirdo rich dude who'd bought the Jenkins property ten or twenty years back. Whoever she'd heard it from had called the fellow 'weird'; though why they'd called him weird, Roger had no clue. He hadn't really asked, of course; stuff that wasn't Roger's business simply wasn't his concern.

But now, today, just possibly it *was* his concern; that smoke down there had *made* it his concern. If the Jenkins home was burning and untenanted, well, that was one thing, but if burning and *inhabited*—Jeez-oh-MAN!—whoever or whatever was in there was likely in a fix!

Roger didn't think an awful lot after that idea got rattling in his head. A fireman doesn't do a lot of good by thinking— even a fireman fifteen years removed—he needs to act.

And that's what Roger did, precisely that—Back up on his ATV, scrambling on the seat, he revved the little engine and flew. Straight down the dusty bypath to where it branched a lazy right he flew, then along the right-hand branch in turn, out to the tar-and-gravel Hanleytown road.

Which part-paved road, when he reached it a good half-mile forward of the branch, was over-arched with a canopy of trees—meaning that the smoke was pretty near invisible for mostly all the way—But when he made it to the acreage of the property itself—as indicated by a freshly graveled drive he hadn't ever paid much notice to before—he could see the sky above the land ahead beclouded by the rising sooty column straight above. The house would likely be—hmmm—just about there, right below the place the pall of smoke was drifting skyward from: say, a couple hundred, maybe three hundred yards dead ahead, and maybe a tiny swivel of the driveway to the left. Whew!—Quite a *lot* of smoke, thought Roger; way, way more than was apparent from the summit of the hill: No long-abandoned residence would burn that way: Somebody was living there for sure!

DO NOT ENTER! said the posting at the driveway's hither end, a neatly printed sign nailed firmly to an ancient hemlock on his left. NO TRESPASSING! glared a second sign, admonished from a maple on the right. OK, point made, whatever hand had made it—But hey—does a fellow heed a warning sign if human life might be at risk? If you see a place on fire, with maybe someone trapped inside, you gonna pay much heed to signs?—No sir! No way!—You get your butt in gear—and move!

So Roger moved. He shrugged and revved his grumbly double-cylinders, pulled back the shifter knob to first, popped the clutch in stomach-churning haste.... And away past the signs, through an unresisting chain that snapped with minor impact, and on down the freshly graveled driveway—or, rather, *up* it, toward the whatever-the-heck catastrophe awaiting him—he sped.

Hmm, thought he midst rapid transit, as the gravel chips got scrambled by the tires and the branches of the party-colored maple trees flew by: A weird guy, was it? What had Karen said exactly about the guy that made the locals call him weird? He searched his faded memory, regretful that he hadn't listened closer or asked a little more. No expression—yes!—that was what she'd told him, he remembered now: A dull-faced guy who moved and talked just like a robot. Nobody since had had much contact with the fellow, so little more was known.

But then there was that Melanie too—Melanie or Melody, some singsong moniker like that—the girl who worked on Karen's hair: She was the one who seemed to know the most. Her house was out this way, a couple of miles past the game lands down Hanleytown Road. Melanie, so the gossips rumored, had actually *seen* some fellow round about the place: Some dude out running down along the woods from time to time. *Running*, she said—not jogging, but running full out, fast, like a top-condition sprinter. Not the weird guy, apparently, but a different sort of fellow, with a face not flat, but handsome. A regular hunk, she said, built like a Pittsburgh Steeler running back.

All right—whatever!—whatever crusty old half-balding bachelor dude with a robot face, or whatever religious nutcase-of-a-shut-up family, perhaps—or even if it really *was* some young, cool stud in actuality, fit, trim, handsome in actual truth—whoever might be stuck inside that burning building needed help. And he was here to give it. So here's old firefighter Rog on his off-road chariot, whizzing down the last of the freshly graveled driveway, bringing beneficial sustenance toward the smoky clearing dead ahead, seeing the hazy shaft of morning sun between the branches up above, smelling the looming stink of soot now: of burning plastic, melting rubber maybe, kindling finely finished wood; lots of someone's nice possessions going up in flames ahead....

And once the trees were cleared now from his straight-on view and the smoky sunlight thinly yellow on his face—at last—There. Dead on, fifty yards ahead of him. Well, HO-LY hell! but there the damn thing WAS!

Fire! *Man*! DAMN! There in the upper-story window. And down beneath it too, forty feet sideways to the right, in the big two-car garage: flickering flames!—*Ho-ly-moley*—If there's a car in there with its gas tank full—Jeez-oh-MAN—she's gonna friggin' BLOW!

Gasoline—*MAN*—Go up like a regular atom *bomb*! Oily smoke seeping from the window up above there too, over the garage, and flames aplenty just below—Damn! But ... but....

Oh, damn it all to hell! He sped right up to the place, popped the clutch, spun the wheels, flinging up a terminal spray of gravel drive, and flat-out, quick-as-a-bolt-of-lightning *sped*; right smack up to where the upper floor was belching smoke and glowing brilliant flames.

Fast!

Up a ten-yard strip of blacktop drive, then left onto the lawn. There was a big, wide wraparound porch with a couple of steps leading up to it, spread all along the frontage of the place, from far left of him on the one side to where the garage commenced on the other, fifty feet or so to the right; and Roger parked with his right front tire a couple of inches from the lower step, one rear wheel in a pretty little bush, and hopped atop the porch. Big windows, *nice* windows, expensive, double-pane, relatively new—the whole place with the look and feel of being costly, renovated, once-old-now-new, an expanded spiffed-up sprucely gilded rural house—the Jenkins place redone much finer than its finest days—though clearly and regrettably … in flames!

Flames—YES!—above and over to the right. And here, below the flames and smoke, outside the lower floor, through those unlit windows with their vacant double-panes and costly blinds pulled up, Roger peered with his scratchy, smoke-filled eyes and dimly saw....

Well, not a whole lot of *anything*, really. The downstairs of the house looked pretty much unoccupied—desolate, dark—and there was no fire to be seen at all, not that he could discern from where he stood out on the porch, at any rate: no glow, no buckling of the ceiling, no smoke down here in the front room— only upstairs and over to the right in that garage—But the inside lower floor seemed pretty safe just now from the looks of things, so....

He tried the door. Gingerly at first, then with a decent bit of force, shoving with a knee first try, then a shoulder after that—But it was locked; locked up tight—burglar-proof deadbolt and all. Well, naturally; what's a guy like him to expect? Nothing too damn easy, ever—is there? Hell, nothing ever comes too easy to a dumb som'bitch who climbs tall timber for a living, lopping limbs off like some amputating surgeon of the skies—Which is OK, nodded Roger to himself, the stuff they pay a fellow seventeen an hour for, plus tons of overtime: the high-risk, high-wage nature of the game.

So the door was pretty firmly fastened up, as Roger would pretty much have expected it to be, locked up tighter than an old maid's—well, anyway, he didn't like to cuss that much; so he forgot about the comparison, and went ahead and pounded on the wood. Pounded hard! Pounded hard enough, and loud enough, to wake the living dead.

But … nothing. Zero. Zilch.

OK, thought Roger, chill out a sec and think: What if they're…? What if somebody's…? The place, he thought, was pretty surely wasted anyhow, not a hell of a lot to be lost or gained by much of nearly anything anymore.... So ... Roger stepped to the nearest window—four feet, roughly, to his left— and kicked his muddy boot clean through the glass.

Crash! The outer pane went clattering, and then the inner. Crash! Clink! Tinkle! He kicked the pointy shards away to make the passage safe for human transit—namely his—then stuck his head clear through and hollered, emptying his lungs— loud; bellowing! Echoing across the soundless, not-too-smoky room.

"Hey! HEY! Anybody IN there? Anybody HOME?"

Nothing.

Cell phone: Damn it, but he'd left it on the coffee table in the living room at home, right beside his Steelers mug. Karen always told him ... He ought to listen to her more, sensible as she always was about such things. "What if you get stuck someplace, Rog? What if you...?" But he *never* got stuck, did he? Why would he need it? It'd only fall out of his pocket, get dumped beneath some bushes in the woods and lost forever—Dammit! *Damn*! DAMN!!

Smoke really pretty light inside, though—downstairs, at least, it was—That's what he figured, having sniffled up the air within. So he squirmed his bulky shoulders through, and then most of the skinny rest of him. He hadn't been a firefighter these fifteen years past, but, hell, you don't forget this kind of stuff. All those years with the VFD, from high school on, until old Pete Boskin called him from the Mill, the routine's pretty much ingrained: First clear the place of people, then pets, then last of all you can worry about the stuff. By the time the pumper got here, the stuff was likely gone. Pets made a lot of noise; you'd hear 'em from the road, most like. Folks, though, what with the smoke and all: There could be someone in here still, overcome, unconscious, trapped inside a room—And if there *was*...

He didn't think; didn't really take the time to think. His instincts took over. So in he went, all the remnants of the rest of him, legs and boots and all: Flop! Onto the floor, crunch! on the glass, but no big deal in that; he had his leather jacket on, tough as carbon-tempered steel.

Not too bad inside right now, not yet: a trace of smoke, not a lot of heat. He covered his nose and mouth with the bandanna that he'd wrapped around his neck for sweat. There was a subtle crackling up the staircase to his right; and a sickly glow from there as well. Warmth too; an impending glow of heat, radiating down the stairwell: No doubt what that meant, Roger knew, as to the limited amount of time....

That phone—Dammit! He should have listened to his wife for once. Karen always knew. There had to be a phone inside, though; someplace in these rooms there simply had to be. Enough light now seeping through the windows, what with the rising sun and brilliant day.

The living room, where he stood right in the center of a big-ass oriental rug, was something wondrous to behold; a gorgeous picture from a magazine. Exquisite furniture, splendid paintings on the walls, expensive-looking lamps and all the rest of the accessories you'd see in a super-rich man's home. Not the kind of stuff you generally find in country houses in the woods, even in rich-man Jenkins's day—No sirree: Someone had made this place a veritable palace of a home.

Good lord! Who lived in this house, anyway? Somebody who could afford a stinkin' *telephone* at least; *that* was for sure; though Roger found nary a trace of one, however hard he looked: Not on a wall, not on a table, not friggin' *any*where, as far as he could see.

The kitchen was just beyond the dining room, the latter with its own expensive dining-room table and six expensive dining-room chairs: inlaid hardwoods, a museum-treasure of a set. No phone in the kitchen either, when he got to looking there, exploring there in every drawer and cubby hole he could think of opening up and poking around in. Gorgeous stove, though; huge refrigerator, enormous freezer, stainless steel: megabucks, no expenses spared. You'd have thought these rich-ass honchos could afford to buy a goddamn *phone*, at least—Hell, what did they use to call in orders for their caviar and quail? Or maybe the running servant went and picked them up—Maybe the handsome guy that Melanie had seen along the road was one of their high-wage, fast-paced gofers. Yeah, maybe some Arab sheikh had sent the fellow out this morning on an errand: "Here, take the checkbook, Jasper; bring back a couple of twenty carat diamonds and a Rolls. And make it fast, too! Move them skinny buns!"—Cripes! What kind of people LIVED here, anyway?! Right now, from the looks of this deserted burning house, who the hell could even guess?

OK, OK, think a little now, Roger; so Roger paused a little bit and thought: Back into the living room, he started up the stairs ... But no: there wasn't any use in that at all—Suicidal recklessness to even try. The house was all but wasted now. Nothing he could do—nothing much that *anyone* could do, in truth. Hell, nobody could possibly stay alive in all the smoke and flames up in the rooms above: asphyxiated, incinerated, turned to ash and dust. Whatever remained upstairs was toast; the downstairs doomed to follow pretty soon. He'd seen a door adjacent to the kitchen that looked as though it ought to lead down to a cellar, so maybe there? A penned-up pet, perhaps? The flat-faced robot or the handsome runner trapped below somehow? Fallen down the stairwell with a busted leg? Unconscious maybe from the smoke? He ought to check before he left; a conscientious firefighter would, of course. At least he ought to poke his head in there and check. He still had a little bit of time: Not all that much, for certain, but at least a little bit.

So back into the kitchen he went and sprang the door that led down to the basement and called again, down into the hollow, silent dark: But nothing. A bit of an echo from his hollering, a bit of a funny sort of smell: A strange smell, borderline offensive in a nonspecific way; scientifically medicinal, but unsavory somehow: what you might call an antiseptic kind of rot. Not exactly foul or noxious, no; but ... well, almost like a fresh-killed deer when you went to dress it in the field: Dead, that is, but freshly dead. Flesh, not living, but not quite yet decayed: Whatever it was, it sure as *anything* smelled strange.

Roger turned away to leave, but then...? Whew! Then the funny odor drew him back. It really *was* pretty truly odd, its distant familiarity piqued his curiosity: hmm—dead but not that long dead. He ought to check; he really should. The smoke was getting to him now, wafting down the stairwell round the corner to the kitchen, penetrating the bandanna, needling at his eyes— The place was growing threatening and quickly getting worse. Much worse—*way* worse for sure—But, he sort of, kind of reckoned, he still had a teensy bit of time.

The stairs down to the basement were.... Strange to find them in a place like this, but these were no ordinary rural residential steps, even for a spruced-up zillion-dollar home. They were—well, solid, concrete sorts of things with chrome-and-rubber-covered treads. They looked like, felt like ... hmmm: kind of like the staircase over at the hospital when he went in for that busted arm, let's say; or up to the maternity floor where Karen got taken when she went to have their kids....

Impressive-feeling things, that is to say, *expensive*-feeling things, those steps, that let him off twelve feet down onto a basement floor that was—just as strangely, just as obviously costly—a clinic type of flooring, a hospital type of flooring. And the walls too, the little he could see of them in the scanty daylight from the kitchen windows glancing from above: The walls were.... Hmmm: He looked off to the right, into the musty dimness from whence the funny odor seemed to come. His eyes saw not too much at first; but then, after they'd had a moment to adjust....

"Holy *shit*!" said Roger to himself—But loud—LOUD! as if to wake the anesthetic dead again. "HO-LY FRIG-GIN' SHIT!" he said, forgetting for that instant that he didn't like to swear. "Ho-ly frig-gin' SHIT!!"

He scrambled up the concrete stairway, tripping in his haste, stumbling back a couple of steps down again before he finally made it all the way up top. Through the cellar door he dashed, around the kitchen wall; then headlong through the dining room and front room, breathless, choking on the shock and the terror and the smoke.

Then out the broken window, shoulders first, diving flat out to the porch, then finally stumbling toward his vehicle in wait.

He made it. Barely, scarcely made it, just as the front room ceiling started to buckle, crack, and hiss; and flew, four wheels blazing, down the driveway, goose bumps on his neck, the bandana fluttering off behind him in the wind; the wheels scattering gravel chips, accelerating like a Nascar racer heading toward the Hanleytown Road.

He'd wave down the first car or truck or biker he saw along the way—Anyone!—Whoever!—

And hope to hell the som-bitch had a friggin' *phone*!

3

He ran.

Through the autumn brush he ran, flat out, wide striding, catlike, slipping here and there on the newly fallen leaves, but righting himself with the elegance and poise and deftness of a leopard, for he had that sort of graceful, inattentive gait. A peculiar sight to see, if there'd been folks around to see him; but he kept to the shaggy forest hillsides; and was invisible, for all intents and purposes, to the sleepy-eyed awareness of the Sunday morning world.

But *had* he been visible, had he run with such a smooth and feline elegance back *toward* the town of Stanleyville rather than away; had he jogged through the business district of the Borough this lazy Sunday morning, so that folks could glimpse him through the windows of their cars or from the sidewalks as they scurried into church; had he loped down Main Street to be noticed and remarked the way he jogged this morning through the footpaths of the woods: to be noticed and regarded and stared at, not from recognition, no indeed; for none of the local residents had the slightest inkling of his presence hereabouts these twenty-odd years past, since he'd first come to this part of the country—of that utter anonymity he was absolutely sure— and few area residents had so much as glimpsed his loping stride on the roadsides from as close to him as a hundred yards away....

But what the folks out strolling would remark this autumn Sunday, if there were eyes around to see here in the forest where he ran: What they would remark and comment to their friends about the next day would be his handsome features, and his manly sculpted form, and—most of all—his inappropriate sort of dress. For he ran this Sunday morning in what he had hastily thrown on just an hour or so before: A scanty pair of gym shorts with nothing underneath, a hooded cotton sweatshirt hanging loose, and the functionless footgear of wingtip dress shoes of a muddy golden brown: costly shoes when they were new, and remarkably elegant in fit and finish only ninety minutes earlier when they were clean, but just now sullied from pointed toe to bow-tied laces by the forest's sticky mire.

He limped a bit in his inattentive sort of way; for his knee had jammed against a metal chair. From twelve feet up he'd jumped, onto the flagstone patio out back. No time to dangle or slither down a post—Scarcely time to even *think*.

And he really *hadn't* thought too much; just reacted, for his instincts had invariably been sound. By the time he came awake, he knew for certain that Finotti was no more—whether it had been the sounds of Finotti's dying gasps that roused him, or the smoke, or the heat, or the rumble of that vehicle out front— of the specific thing that brought him to, he wasn't absolutely sure. But he knew from the smoke that seeped beneath the door, and the heat that radiated through, and the scent of burning flesh that accompanied the smoke and heat—He knew from all that noxious evidence that he could just now barely save himself—and *just* himself—by jumping. And so he'd grabbed the shoes and clothes at hand, and staggered to the opened window, and thrust one leg across the sill, and then the other, dangling for an instant, and … jumped.

There'd been that awful twinge of agony when his leg had hit the chair, then a snap, and a plenitude of pain at first. But minor strains and sprains and injuries like that were not too great a problem to such a man as he: The knee would heal up readily enough; his minor cuts and bruises always did—Even fractures did—always—a matter of hours often, rarely extending to days—though it took a week or two for that tibial break two years ago that he'd had to set himself.

And now, particularly now, what with the red cells and the stem cells fresh on board since late last night—Why, within an hour or two from now—by mid-morning, say; by early afternoon at the very farthest out—he knew as well as anything that he'd be sound as a teenage athlete fresh from lengthy rest by then; be able, within that hour or two or three, if he really felt the need, to run full out at speed, long stride, interminably; hours and added hours on end. A perpetual eight-minute mile if he had to; six in a pinch; five for shorter sprints if some pursuer were coming up behind. He'd need to stop, of course, for a bite of food, if and when it could be found, but, not requiring rest, bodily refueling would be the utmost of his needs.

Yes, food, the physical imperative of food: That would be a problem at the present pace, figuring a hundred and fifty calories a mile; figuring his liver stores of glycogen would be depleted after—what?—probably ten miles, more or less—Then after those hepatic glycogen reserves had been consumed, the myogenic glycogen would get burnt up in eight or nine miles more—the muscles only held so much—and then the little fat he had. And after that, once the fat reserves were all metabolized, he'd be burning muscle protein up. He hadn't had a bite to eat since early evening yesterday—before the sedative mixed in with the infusion knocked him out—his stomach cramped and pled— Yes, but he'd get through this present little wrinkle one way or another. He always had—a hundred times and more in fixes a whole lot more dire than this.

And besides, starving or sated, hurting or numb, just now the path ahead was smooth enough and getting smoother still with every passing yard. Ninety percent downhill from here on in; the tallest of the tallest peaks were done: There, dead ahead, downslope, flowed the creek; five minutes past the summit of the Bradley rise. He'd stopped back on the topmost height to glimpse the cloud of smoke far off behind—Hard to make it out that far away, but someone surely would have seen a burning house by now and made their call for help. Why, some sharp-eyed stranger might have spotted smoke this morning early before he'd woken up—that vehicle he'd heard out front could well have been the very one. And that sharp-eyed driver of the grumbly car would have made the urgent call. Even now, there could be fire trucks on the way, and the sheriff's men besides, and....

That's the anxious thought that had popped into his head back at the summit when he stopped to take a look; and so he'd turned ahead again and scurried on, at a somewhat faster pace—Past the sloping meadow on the hill and down, down, six miles past the fire now, maybe eight, maybe more; hard to estimate precisely—Angling downward at the trickiest of grades, slipping on the leaves and tripping on the vines, descending toward the creek in placid wait below.

Halfway down the hillside, just around a lengthy run of evergreens, he glimpsed the river glancing gold beams toward the sun. Not a warm day—not quite yet, despite the valiant efforts of the sunshine: far from a comfortable temperature right now, with just those skimpy gym shorts on. But the sun was getting brighter every minute, a couple of hours shy of overhead by now. And with the mild exertion of the run, and the sun above, and the sheltered air on the lee side of the hill ... he found, to his amazement, that he had worked up something of a sweat—That really gnawing twinge of hunger too, though there wasn't too much likelihood of staunching that—not for a while, at any rate; and not without a decent bit of luck.

No, not much chance of finding food out here; the berries and the hanging fruit long gone to feed the birds—Ah, but as for thirst, the water being near and relatively clear and reasonably inviting as it bubbled downslope through the rocks: When he finally made it to the creek-side in a couple of minutes more, the bank all slick with water vegetation and multicolored leaves, he plodded through the mire in those inappropriate shoes of his, and crouched low on his haunches, panther-like, to rinse his face and wet his neck and cup his hands to drink.

The water wouldn't hurt him; that he knew from past encounters with the very filthiest of puddles perilous for normal men to drink. He was immune to microbes, though; immune to all the illnesses that humankind had ever known: protected, resistant, given the bulk of antibodies he'd habitually taken in, replenishing the lot of them bimonthly—and replenishing too the stem cells that churned them out—as was his body's need. Even such as AIDS would be no threat to him, he'd surely been exposed and immunized long since; cholera as well, and typhoid, and the dread bubonic plague.

The water here would likely harbor parasites, but he had no dread of them. He drank his fill of the earthy-tasting stuff— amoeba, giardia and all—microbes and toxins and mother earth herself embedded in those waters, examining the riverbank downstream with an educated eye as he tossed the chilly fluid down: From here on out the path ahead was obvious. He knew the terrain, not at all from personal experience, cautious and homebound as he'd been, but well enough from a Methuselean lifetime of logic and learning and acquired abilities of every varied kind.

He knew, for one important thing, that the creek would flow inevitably downstream into a river of considerable extent, and that there would be a town near the junction of the creek he'd picked to follow, as it branched into the larger river at its end. This was the way to Paxton, more or less; along the Southbend Creek south by east—He'd glanced at a regional map a while ago and remembered. And if he followed the flowing water, circumventing the populated places for safety's sake, cutting across the channel's snaky loops by a route along the hilltops to save a bit of time: then he'd be there by ... well, by sunset at least, at the outskirts of Paxton before dusk. And he could linger there until the sun went down entirely, and maybe finally find a bit of sustenance then, and a restless sort of rest.

So he wiped his mouth on the sweatshirt sleeve and retied his loosened shoes, too floppy at the heels without a pair of socks. And further on he jogged, catlike, sliding here and there along the slippery bank, stumbling on the pebbles, crossing downstream a mile or two up, on an old, deserted trestle-of-a-bridge—Out in the boondocks, no one saw him; no one likely would—Then up again, scrambling up the upslope of an intervening hill—a regular mountain-of-a-thing this time, making him pretty nearly pant for wind by the time he reached the top—and finally down the farther side, now a precipitate declivity, out of the sunlight of the hilltop's dome into the shadows of the nearly noontime sun. He'd come a dozen miles at least by the time he saw the creek again; for it was just past midday by the angle of the sun when he glimpsed its golden light upon the water. And once he made it downslope to the creek this umpteenth time, once his footsteps reached the river and he chanced to glance out dead ahead.... Well, what do you know, but there and then, straight out smack in front of him, lit brightly by the noonday sunshine blazing down, he unexpectedly, and hopefully, and really *ravenously* set eyes upon ... the camp!

A hunting camp—Not what one would think of as a 'camp' from a city-dweller's point of view, but what the folks out here in the woodlands called a 'camp.' These rural 'camps' were solid structures, more or less elaborate, sometimes built of brick and stone—*His* place, once thought of as a camp, had been faced with stone before the major renovations, though now the ancient remnants of that stone would be merely charred and crumbling hulks.

The house in front of him was smaller and less elaborate than his own had been by far, but not all that much different in its functional intent. People built these sorts of backwoods dwellings and used them through the year, even when the game laws kept the critters safe from harm. This one looked untenanted, though neatly trimmed and recently maintained. No cars out back in the graveled parking flat; and he knew full well that people never came to so remote a site as this without a heavy-duty vehicle to haul them there and back: The way out here was not the kind of access path you'd care to walk or drive a fancy car along. For the unkempt trails that branched out from the secondary roads to such deserted spots as this had ruts that would tear the very tanks and tailpipes from a sport or luxury sort of ride.

No vehicles though, not here, not now; not rugged or sporty or otherwise: Which meant—he'd hardly dared to hope for such a lucky find—that the place was pretty certainly unoccupied just now…. It *probably* was, *likely* was—but far better for his security if he took the time to check. And so he halted here, fifteen feet upslope from the creek, and crouched within the forest brush invisibly in carefully attentive wait.

Half an hour he waited thus, rigid, frozen, until the sun had inched on ten degrees beyond its peak—so now most likely one o'clock or one-fifteen or so—And once the time was past and still no sign of movement could be seen, then up a little from the muddy bank, creeping slowly toward the covered porch that opened toward the water, he took his guarded steps.

The place was quiet still: No rustle of a curtain, no curious face behind a pane of glass observing; no sign of life, no sound, no hint of human presence; emptiness, solitude and nothing more. So up onto the little porch he leapt, graceful, catlike, spry despite the knee-sprain—which, in fact, had already—scarcely four short hours since the injury—had already begun to heal.

The door was locked: Of course it was; he would have fled like a startled sparrow if he'd found the latch undone. He could have broken the door in bodily if there'd been the slightest need; he had that kind of strength. He could have shattered a deadbolt easily, torn the sturdiest hinges from the strongest jamb. But there was no necessity for that at all, for up above the porch he'd noticed a window that promised entry: up top, above an overhanging rooflet that gave cover to the porch: a slightly open window right above, providing likely access to a silent room upstairs.

His eyes were like a cat's eyes; like an eagle's: focused faultless whether far or near. And from the ground below the porch, having stepped back down to let himself inspect, he could see quite clearly that the upper sash was lowered half an inch from the adjacent frame. He got atop the rooflet like an acrobat, leaping to a handhold on the gutter twelve feet up, then chinning himself onto the shingles the way a top Olympian might do so deft a thing, wriggling, climbing, grasping, clambering with lizard-like dexterity and poise. Up he sprang and slithered, the slightly tender knee grabbing a dubious leghold on the roof, then grasping firm to let him scramble up the incline toward the window that would finally let him in. He slid it open with a push: And in he climbed, warily; sore knee first, agile body trailing just behind.

Good! The place was soundless once he'd made it in; as desolate as a tomb. It smelled of abandonment, of odorlessness; of weeks and weeks of solitude and settled dust.

He stood then in a sparsely furnished bedroom lit brightly by the open window at his back: Two stacked bunk beds devoid of linen, an empty closet gaping wide; and finally, a doorway standing open, leading outward to a wooden-paneled hall.

So into the hall, on cat feet still; listening for nothing and hearing the nothing he was hoping to hear. There was another bedroom, right-hand down the hall, with one lone double bed, its mattress bare, beside another empty closet and knotty pine-clad walls. No one had been inside this place for months, from the look and feel of what he'd found so far—Which meant he could relax: Safe enough now to head downstairs, and down he flitted in an instant … and didn't have to prowl around for long before he found the very things he'd wished, but scarcely hoped, to find.

Food!—loads and loads of food! Cans, cans, a precious couple of dozen cans of everything a famished runner's groaning gut would long have longed for: Potted meat and Boston beans and tins of ready-to-be-heated pasta of every scrumptious kind. He opened the beans and scrounged a spoon out of a drawer and shoveled the whole cool lot of them down greedily, the way a dog would gulp the mealtime refuse tossed offhandedly into his bowl. Glucose level pretty close to nil by now, glycogen pretty nearly burned up too—even the best of healthy stem cells couldn't manufacture fuel—But the beans and all the other stuff would fix him up with calories enough—if only for a while.

Five minutes' effort in the kitchen fulfilled his nutrient deficiency entirely; no place for gourmet dining now. Cold SpaghettiOs, two four-ounce tins of tuna, some Spam, a sardine cocktail for dessert, and then a ten-ounce can of sugared fruit to raise the carbohydrate level in his blood—He'd need the energy for the many miles that lay ahead.

All right, then, topped off now till evening anyway, like a race car with a brimming tank of fuel; his sweatshirt's moisture drying in the tepid air; feeling reasonably safe and sated now—finally—thankfully—he took a couple of leisure minutes to explore.

On the dining-room table he found an envelope, addressed to a man in Pittsburgh—the owner of the camp, he guessed. This he folded and slipped into the stomach pocket of his sweatshirt top. Then, back in the kitchen, in another cabinet across the sink from the cupboard with the food—Eureka!—There, stuffed into a sugar bowl behind some mismatched coffee mugs—he came across a little cash.

Not all that much, admittedly—but it was welcome. To a man who'd had access to untold millions just the day before, forty-seven bucks and change wouldn't normally have meant a lot. It wouldn't get him far, but if it got him fed again and helped to buy a less abrasive pair of shoes, that would be enough. He stuffed the cash into the sweatshirt's tummy pocket with the envelope and headed toward the door.

He was just about to spring the lock and make his way outside—But then … just on the slightest chance, the faintest odds-against-it possibility that….

There: to his right beside the exit door: that one remaining place he hadn't felt the need to look. One never knew, though: Some little inkling struck him that it wouldn't hurt to check: He hadn't really thought of downstairs closets—not after finding the empty ones upstairs: He'd come in search of food most urgently, and thankfully he'd got his fill—But what if…? What if…?

He moved his hand to the closet door. A turn, a pull, and…. Yes! *More* luck—Amazing luck *indeed*! There, on a shelf above some empty hangars—he reached and pulled them down—two pairs of neatly folded jeans: worn and faded, sure enough; but sturdy and laundered and fresh—

All right, when he spread them out and held them up across his waist, they turned out way too big: A circus costume, pretty much, two double-legged tents. But, OK—everything considered, a whole lot better large than small: He might have found a pack of diapers in that closet, honestly—So jeans too big were plenty good indeed…. Besides—even *better* than the jeans—

There, dangling on a hangar in the recess to the right, off to the side in the shadows—a thermal parka, worn threadbare at the neck, and tattered at the elbows, true enough; but plenty of the material left to keep a chilly fellow warm.

Back in the kitchen one more time, he found a bit of rope and cut it with a steak knife, then stuffed the knife inside the tummy pocket of his sweatshirt with the cash and envelope—you never knew but that might come in handy too. The rope would keep the jeans up pretty well. As baggy as a kilt, for sure, but they slid up pretty neatly past the gym shorts once he'd pulled the makeshift belt up tight. The cuffs a trifle high above the shoes, if you wanted to get critical; but if he wore them down around the hips just so—like that (he knotted up the rope again, adjusting)—they wouldn't slow his running all that much, and the look was pretty good.

That extra pair of jeans he'd found he tied off at the cuffs and filled the legs with another dozen cans of food—Sure; put them on the tab; he'd pay the fellow back with compound interest once he had the means—Then, fashioning a sling with another piece of rope to drape the 'extra jeans and foodstuffs down across his neck, he started out. He'd made it almost out the doorway when he remembered that open window he'd slithered though upstairs.

So up he went—for this was benefactor's property, after all, not wantonly to be abused. He shut the window tight, fastening the latch on the lower sash this time to keep its lock secure. Then back downstairs again and out the door, pushing in the door-lock button to keep the next intruder out. And straight along the creek he started out again, a whole lot more comfortable now, and in better spirits too.

All right, then: On to Paxton tonight, then to West Virginia within the next few days, whatever it took to get there. He'd gather up the things he'd need: The gold and cash he'd stashed there for just this type of contingency; and the new ID he'd have to have to build another life.

His father's papers too—That box was the most important thing of all. Someday he'd open it and take a look inside: some distant evening when the time was ripe, though up till now that ripening time had always seemed a million years away. 'The stars,' Father had told him, communion with the distant stars. Back then it seemed a fable, a fantasy that never could come true. But now? Radio astronomy, laser beams, galactic probes: In ten years? Twenty? Fifty? Who could really say?

The box: He'd keep it with him now forever; Sister was beyond the point of ever following the instructions. Deranged even twenty years ago, how competent would she be by now? Still angered and resentful, she'd be on the lookout for any sign of him undoubtedly. But he'd had worse threats than even Sister in his all-too-many years of life: plagues, shipwrecks, earthquakes, and all the rest.

And if he were watchful—which he'd surely learned to be these many years—and did what he must do as expeditiously as possible, he'd make it in and out of Charleston safely with that precious box and the other things he'd need.

Then on to a new life, in a new home, and with a new Helper to replace the flawed but faithful servant who had burned himself to death.

Poor Finotti: The last sad relict of the most beloved family he had ever known.

4

"And what the hell am I supposed to do with *this*?" asked Agent Braman in that gravelly, grumbly voice of his, a snarling low-pitched utterance poised between a mumble and a growl.

He was slumped down in his chair, as Sidney was generally seen to be when some bold co-worker found the guts to sneak a look. Good for concentration, he'd explained one day when Audrey Hamblin chanced to ask: Slumping takes the blood flow from the backside and feeds it to the brain. Must be working pretty admirably, too, everyone concluded, every awestruck agent in the place:

For Sidney Braman was a bright one, all right. Smartest fellow in the Pittsburgh office by a football field and then another hundred yards to boot. Undergrad degree from Princeton, *summa cum laude*: that's what the lengthy blurb in *Who's Who* proclaimed. And then that top-of-his-class distinction at Harvard Law and all the rest.

Sidney was rich too, way up in the untold millions, if you cared to tote the total assets up. All the other agents had wondered mightily what the holy hell the guy was doing here for six measly G-notes a month—Six grand a month for a finance prince like Sidney?—Hell that was penny ante chump change when it came to a potential zillionaire like him: After all, scion of one of the best known families in the universe; only son, moreover, of the doting dad who'd originally earned the cash: Young Sidney had been the pride and hope and future of the whole darn Braman clan—And the whole darn Braman clan was frankly nothing, if not filthy stinking rich.

Jacob Braman—THE Jacob Braman, that is—Sidney's illustrious dad—was that celebrated Braman who presided over, and had originally founded, the Pittsburgh conglomerate of Bramancorp, a firm that Sidney joined and subsequently ran himself—quite skillfully it seemed—those first two years fresh out of Harvard Law.

Then came that awful business with his wife, two years after their marriage and his starting at the firm. Sidney never talked about his wife. Never talked about *anything* much of a personal nature, not in the ten long years he'd been slumped down at that desk shunting blood flow to his brain. Never said a non-professional syllable to *anyone*, so far as was known and remembered by all: That's what the people whispered when they ran out to the Neptune Diner or down to Papa Angelotti's for a quick spaghetti lunch.

But the story was, getting back to the story again, that lovely Jodi Braman had been kidnapped two years into her husband's directorship of the firm, ten years or a little longer back from the present day. The story was, continuing, that the ransom for this lovely spouse of just about the richest zillionaire in town had been paid in full, on time, no questions asked or answered—several millions in unmarked bills, as it was rumored, though there were no public facts to back those rumors up.

And then, the money paid, the secret kept—so the story went—the guys who'd grabbed her had gone and killed her anyway. Brutally too, according to the rumors, and according to the two-inch-thick UNSOLVED dossier back on the archive shelves. The locals came across her SUV down a side street near their home, and found her body segments in a dumpster way across town, all done up in fancy plastic wrap. No prints, no leads, no suspects; just a horribly dismembered wife and a prominent family who seemed entitled amply to their just revenge.

The local Keystone Cops were stumped, and readily admitted they were stumped, and lateraled the slippery football to the FBI: Apparently there'd been another similar slaying in Ohio, a second in Kentucky, a third one someplace else; and the Bureau could justify interstate authority to intervene—Serial murders generally call for that. But after a lot of time and work, the Bureau investigation came up empty-handed too. Not infrequently complex cases did that here in Pittsburgh, back in the old days before Sidney Braman joined the team.

But it was a notorious crime, all right, and so outrageously demonic that the agents had seemed a little sheepish about no credible suspect ever being charged. Years later, several years after the bereaved husband had undergone his training and become a member of the Pittsburgh branch himself, one of the office secretaries, who'd gotten a trifle curious, went back to the archives on her own. She'd pulled out the UNSOLVED file, sifted through, and stumbled on a photo—so the gossip went—then run out of the archive room and promptly lost her lunch. Nobody ever bothered from that day to the present to open up the Jodi Braman file again.

Certainly Sidney never did. All the other unsolved cases made it to his desk eventually, after the requisite amount of time—he being the top-gun agent here practically since the day he'd started out; the one guy everybody turned to when they needed a little help, a little reasoning ability, a whale of a lot of knowledge and analysis and intellect: the mainstay problem solver ever since he'd finished training, ten years back, a year or so after dumping the Bramancorp management back in the careworn keeping of his dad. He'd dropped out for a year or so, the rumors said, traveled the backroads of the world, disappeared completely for a while, shuttered up that enormous Tudor palace-of-a-home.

Then he'd wandered back to Pittsburgh again, sold the splendid house, bought an inexpensive condo, had his dad redeem the necessary due bills and make the necessary calls; he got a GI haircut, shopped for J.C. Penney suits, went away for the required training and background checks ... and got inducted in the FBI—the last thing in the universe anybody dreamed a brilliant zillionaire like Sidney Braman might ever conceivably do.

But he did, he actually did; and, once accepted and inducted and seated in that sway-back chair, bright Sidney did his customary top notch work as always: First in his class at Quantico, just like at Harvard and Princeton not long before; Director's Award, of course; meetings with the big-name brass up in the hierarchy—even *without* another phone call from his dad. He put in a request for Pittsburgh and they gave him what he'd asked, though he probably could have stayed and got a top-notch management position at Quantico or in the political division in DC.

But here he'd ended up, back here in Pittsburgh again, slumping limply in that chair: A long, tall string-bean-of-a-fellow of thirty-six; darkly handsome in a grimly featured way; glowering ominously with those onyx-blackened eyes: A man who looked for all the world as though he'd battled his godforsaken straight-line path through every wrenching second of his life—That was Sidney Braman in a nutshell—the way he sounded and the way he looked ... on that quiet Monday morning when the sheriff's call came in.

And when nice Miss Hamblin approached him at his desk with an inch-thick folder in her hands on that memorable Monday morning in the fall, what she saw a couple of feet below her from where she was standing a couple of feet above, smiling down in his direction—What she saw was a frowning fellow with close-cropped military hair, not as yet inclined to gray; a metallic-slate complexion where the shaven beard made efforts to poke through; and then a swath of olive skin above the beard-line, up to the low-brow hairline—A fellow dark and gloomy of mien and manner, in short: That was what nice Miss Hamblin likely saw and would have likely thought, if she had judged him from appearances alone.

And as for words—well, Sidney's words could be just as intimidating as that warrier's body and that that razor-sharpened mind.... Ah yes, but Audrey Hamblin knew her fellow-worker Sidney quite as well as anyone in the office ever had these nine years past—since she too had come here fresh from undergrad— And she was not all that intimidated when she answered his grumpy question in her sweet, melodic voice:

"It's the file you asked for, sir. The Kelson file: Wasn't that the one you requested me to get?"

"And where's the *rest* of it, Miss Hamblin? When I ask you for a file, young lady, what I require from you is...."

"The rest is coming, sir. Linda went to get the evidence carton from archives; I assumed you'd want it with the regular material, as you generally do. She'll be back with everything we have on the Kelson case in just a bit."

He nodded silently and took the file and shuffled through it in that meticulously purposeful way in which Sidney Braman seemed to do everything in life. The Kelson case was.... But what does it matter, truthfully: These dreadful case files that finally found their way to the regional Bureau branch here in Pittsburgh were not your run-of-the-mill domestic crimes; and the ones that came to Sidney's desk were a darn sight more heinous than the rest. This was the big-time, sports fans: serial murders, mob hits, despicable offenses that crossed state lines or jeopardized the General National Good. The bleakest cases dealt with homicide, the very bleakest *multiple* homicide, all-too-often brutal—And that's where Sidney Braman invariably came in.

But it isn't quite accurate to say he merely 'came in' to such disastrous cases. For Sidney pretty much ran the whole division here in Pittsburgh—not just in homicide, but in all the rest of the awful stuff as well. Oh, there was a Supervisor, all right, some political appointee who schmoozed with the appropriate bigwigs and signed his name obediently to the field reports when they were done. But he left the handling of the investigations to the men who did the brain work and the foot work. And the guy who did the lion's share of brain work and directed all the most important aspects of field and foot work—at least in the very worst cases of homicide he did—was Sidney Eliot Braman, Pittsburgh's Go-to Agent Number One.

So when that memorable call came in—some Hicksville sheriff up in the boonies north of the city who needed, as he blurted on the phone line, 'a little feder'l help'—well it was naturally to Sidney that the call got transferred in the end. And it was Sidney, fiercely grumbling, archly glowering, who had to set down the perplexities of the Kelson file just when he had it pretty nearly figured out (even in the absence of that carton of evidence which hadn't yet arrived)—It was Sidney who peered harshly up into that gentle unintimidated face, staring veritable daggers at it, when nice Miss Hamblin respectfully stepped over once again, mere moments after the Kelson dossier had been delivered, and told him:

"Agent Braman? The Chief wants you to pick up on line one."

"Sheesh, Audrey! What the devil is it *this* time? Can't you see I'm busy with this cockamamie Kelson business that they dropped on me? Holy Moses! Don't you people realize that—?"

"Yes, but…. It's from the Chief, sir. He said just answer it—please? … But if you want to, though—the Chief told me to tell you—if you really want to, you can just talk to the fellow for a minute and politely brush him off."

So Sidney grumbled, as was his standard way, and picked up the remote, and clicked the button for the appropriate line. That's all the other agents and the several secretaries in his vicinity happened to see, including Audrey. He said a couple of words to the caller, then just sat and growled a bit and listened, slumped down deeply in his chair.

Then he got up, set down the phone, and left.

He didn't say a thing. He very rarely did. Sidney had unlimited discretion in this place, and didn't need to sign in or out, or say where he was going, or give the slightest indication why.

And he *didn't* sign in or out or say a thing or give the slightest reason to account for what he finally *did* get up and do. If any of the workers had looked out the window of the Third Floor office five minutes later, they would have seen him speeding down Sixth Avenue toward the Freeway entrance leading northbound in his government-issue silver Chevrolet.

5

When he woke, there was sunlight in his eyes—though whether it was the light that finally woke him, or the mere sweet plenitude of sleep, he couldn't really say.... And as he came around a little ... and then a little more ... he didn't quite remember....

But then he did—Yes! The memory flowed back again, and up he got, straight upright on the seat, and reached down for the parka that he had stripped off midway through the night and rolled into a cushion for his head—Though he didn't quite remember doing that; only that his head had felt more comfortable with something soft and cushiony folded down against the panel armrest—which had seemed to him, he distantly remembered, a trifle hard.

He didn't quite remember pulling off the shoes either, or wrapping that toilet tissue carefully around his feet to soothe the blisters, though he sensed this morning that the blisters had begun to heal. And the knee as well: Why, it was a whole lot better too; pretty nearly back to normal now when he prodded with a finger; scarcely any soreness left. So the good long night of rest and sleep—well, factoring the stem cells into the equation too, of course—had done him an inordinate amount of good.

He yawned and stretched and slipped the parka on, for it was slightly chilly in the car, regardless of the valiant efforts of the sunshine to warm things up. Then the shoes came next, pulled gingerly over the tender skin, first stuffing the heels with that extra wad of tissue in his pocket that he'd had the foresight to scrounge up from the BP restroom late last night.

He had staggered out of the woods into the outskirts of Paxton in the dregs of evening just as it was growing dusk. That was sometime after seven, judging from the angle of the sun below the hills. And he had waited there, just beyond the boundaries of the town, propped against an old oak tree in the darkening air, consuming the last four cans of his little stash of food hungrily, feeling a pretty urgent pang of thirst as well, for he hadn't had a sip of anything refreshing since he'd left the creek bed several miles behind.

He must have dozed then—from physical exhaustion, more than any other thing—and when he'd come around again, it was full dark. No way to estimate the time now: That pretty watch he'd had Finotti buy for him last summer was likely lying in a heap of cinders at the moment.

During the daytime, in his sprint along the creek and up across the hills, he had estimated the passing hours by the moving sun: A hundred and eighty degrees of sky, divided into twelve hours of daylight—for it was right around the equinox, just into October now—so roughly fifteen degrees of solar transit for every passing hour. That was in the daytime though; but now at night, after having dozed who knew how long, there was no practical way to estimate, other than the temperature. And it was growing pretty chill.

Safe enough to move by then, dark enough to walk along unseen beside the main road, which would be the most immediate route. Not *on* the road per se, no; but along it, the way he'd run along the creek. From his woodland vantage by the ancient oak, he could hear the nearby sounds of traffic on the blacktop: the two-lane principal route that passed from Stanleyville up north to Paxton here twenty-five miles of asphalt to the south. So he followed the hiss of tires and growl of engines for a quarter-mile or so by ear … until, catching the glow of headlights past the rubble of a stubbly field of corn, he came gradually and wearily to the tar-and-gravel shoulder of the road.

Yes, but he hadn't thought it safe to skirt the road too near the traffic, even in the dark. He'd be a curious sight to see, no doubt, with that threadbare parka and the baggy jeans and the filthy fancy shoes: A vagrant sure as anything, destined to be stopped and frisked and questioned by the law—So better not be caught in a headlight's passing glare: And anyway, word might well be out by now; the local authorities on alert.

And so he'd taken a path along the highway, but not too visually close; twenty yards or thirty yards: out past the fence of a dairy farm for a bit—the cows were long asleep—then down some residential side streets running parallel to the road a block away; and then across some tended lawns and cluttered alleyways replete with weeds and mud and trash; then lastly through a bit more forested terrain that abutted on the center of the town itself … until he came to the garish lights of an intersection with a bustling Wendy's on the far side and a service station on the near—a quiet green and gold BP.

He'd gotten hungry again by then, and nearly desperate with thirst. Twenty-five miles to Paxton if you drove it straight by road: That was the total he had come from A to B—the way he might have flown if he had been a crow. But following the river through the upland woods, then straddling the many farms and villages along the way, when the hilly land grew flat; staying out of sight—That had added another five miles to the trek at least, maybe a whole lot more.

So it was over thirty miles that he had run. Two thousand calories to keep a fellow sentient and alive, just lounging around in bed; and then another—oh, say five thousand more to negotiate that much terrain at a decent pace. Those cans of food he'd happened on: the luckiest of finds, all right; but maximum four thousand calories when you toted the whole of the grocery list up. And since he was ravenous for the couple thousand deficit; and had those forty-some-odd dollars in his pants; and since the Wendy's on the far side of the roadway had a whole lot more cars in the lot, and seemed therefore a good deal more populous and hence less safe, it seemed appropriate at the present juncture, to toss the dice and hope for the best and take his chances with the green and gold BP.

It was empty in the place, at any rate: silent bordering on the vacuous: No one in the convenience shop, no vehicles fueling at the pumps. Just the clerk, a skinny twenty-something fellow with a metal thingy in the pinna of his ear and a paisley neck tattoo, who nodded when he entered, then went back to shuffling though a girly magazine. His name tag, once you got up close enough to read it, gave his designation as BP Phil. The BP portion of the title seemed likely to be extraneous.

"Excuse me—Phil, is it?—Those hot dogs turning on the rollers there: Are they cooked enough to eat?"

"Yup. Them dogs is allus cooked. We keep 'em goin' night and day."

"OK—two for a dollar? Is that really what you people charge? It sounds a little cheap to me."

"Yep, jus' like that sign there says, my man: sixty-nine cents fer one, a buck fer two. We sell a heck of a lot of 'em, mister, I'll tell ya that. The sign there says all beef, but the package don't, so I ain't too sure what's in 'em, 'zackly—but they're pretty decent when they get cooked up. I eat à lot of 'em

—myself I do—and there's this one old dude comes in prack'ly every day I'm here and…."

"OK—Uh, what time is it exactly, Phil—do you happen to have a watch?"

Phil pulled his BP-issue shirtsleeve up to have a look. There was an intricate design across his forearm to complement the ornate pattern on his neck.

"Time? Yeah, sure; I got it. It's, um … 10:47—So—did you wanna get that dog then, man, or…?"

"I do. I'll take—how many have you got there that are cooked enough to eat? Can you make me four?"

"*Four*, man? You sure you want four? Wow! Oh, OK—you wanna, like, get 'em wrapped then, right? Like wrapped up in a bag to go?"

"No; no need to wrap them. I'll eat them here. Listen, I'm going to go and use the restroom for a little while, all right? I'll take the hot dogs when I'm done."

They were just above room temperature when he'd finished with the toilet and the sponge bath; but he was ravenous as a lion from the scent of heated food and wolfed them down, one after another in immediate succession: Mustard, catsup, relish, mayo—everything with calories dumped on—Sloppy to eat, not a pretty sight to look at, he figured. But young Phil was busy with his magazine again, and seemed ecstatic, once he got it, with the couple dollar tip. The fountain drink was a dollar or so more—all the yellow dye and adulterated glucose that any empty stomach dared embrace—and he tossed three generous cups of the sweet concoction down, thus adding another eight-hundred-odd calories to the deficient blood stream fill. Then a bag of chips for one final dollar more—he'd lost a lot of sweat and would surely need the salt—and he was sated enough to pat young Phil on the shoulder with compliments from gourmand to master chef, and head through the door into the overhead fluorescence and thence along his way.

"How far to Paxton, Phil?"

"Hey, you're there, man. You're in Paxton right now, dude. This here's the reg'lar city line."

"OK, sure; I figured that, but how far to the center of town?"

"Oh—mile and a half straight on down the road. Thataway. Follow them cars." Phil gestured with a thumb in the southerly direction, from which the whitish headlights emanated, and toward which the reddish taillights flared.

So out the door and straight toward Paxton he'd set off, plodding on, keeping to the parallel side streets, a short block's distance over from the main route leading into town. Sunday night late, merging into Monday morning, and the side-street he was trudging down was silent, with its muffled street lights and darkened homes and leaf-strewn cars moored sleepily along he curb. Half a mile or so straight on, the side street opened into the recess of a seedy parking lot; fissured pavement adjunctive to a shopping plaza with a boarded-up K-Mart that had likely been its magnet store in better days. He stumbled into the lightless lot at its store-ward end, fifty yards back of the highway, close by a shuttered gift shop with its lamely stuttered sign—*Hag-erty Co-l-ctibles*, it said—

And right straight ahead of him, dead on, at the lot's far end, beneath a fading street lamp and a barren clump of maples bordering the pavement, nestled beneath the blanketing of autumn leaves the weary trees had lately shed … sat the big, old rusted car.

He hadn't thought about a car, really. If he'd thought at all about a place to sleep that night—*last* night—he'd probably pictured an isolated park bench somewhere, or, if push had led to shove, some quiet grassy clearing underneath a tree.

But a car! A big, old rotting behemoth-of-a-car parked in a derelict lot, dimly lit and desolate! The idea hadn't even slipped into his mind before, but: hmmm…. If there was a way to pry the lock up, working around the rubber of the window seal: a hanger he could locate, say; a piece of wire he could twist; maybe some pointed metal object lying in a pile of refuse back behind the shops, or in a bag of trash left in some neglected bin somewhere around.

Worth investigating, at any rate: The vehicle, if he headed straight on in his southbound direction, wouldn't be more than a couple of paces out of his way. So he'd limped across the lot on a minimal diagonal, keeping mostly to the shadows, moving deftly (notwithstanding the blisters on his heels), as was his athletically coordinated wont. Past the boarded-up facades he stepped along, over the stunted weeds striving upward through the pavement, stealthily approaching clear up to the driver's side of the derelict vehicle—an ancient Buick, probably thirty or more years old—and took an inquisitive look inside.

He hadn't expected to find it open. When he pulled the rear door handle out, he hadn't the slightest premonition that his fingertips might actually make the pitted metal move. If there'd been a gambler around to bet him, he wouldn't have taken the bet at thousand-to-one odds against, that the lever would actually slide forth under his fingers, letting the latch pop free and freeing up the hinges so that the door could swing and creek. He wouldn't have taken that idiotic bet—But if he had, he would have won the lotto jackpot of all time. For more than anything else just there, just then, weary as he was, he would have given every last penny in his little stash for a comfortable place to sleep. And now he had one, and he was truly overjoyed!

So the back door opened wide—amazingly—And in he climbed, flat down onto the musty fabric, regardless of the rigid armrest pressed against his skull, compacting his six-two frame into five-three accommodations gladly, joyfully. And within an instant he was curled up limp and dead to all the world.

A long, ameliorative sleep, then; therapeutic—So that now, with the morning sunlight in his eyes, as he peeped out through the windows of the big, old car at the empty lot around him and at the periodic vehicles moving up and down the road, his mind felt rested and his body sound. And out he went, into the morning and the sunshine. The sleep had done whatever kindly good a deep sleep does, and he had the sort of gleam in his eyes and the sort of spring in his step this sunny Monday, that would pull him through this trial. He'd been in worse situations before—shot, stabbed, robbed or swindled till he was flat broke—and had always muddled through somehow. And he was confident now that he'd make it past this new distressing situation too.

All right, then: Time to get a move on. First back to the BP station, a ten-minute saunter north, to use the facilities once more and get another bargain bite to eat. A different clerk was perched on Phil's stool this morning: a woman, late thirties or so—though it would be hard to pinpoint her age with any sort of accuracy. Her skin looked a good bit older than mid-to late-thirty-year-old skin, her features seemed a little younger. She might have been a twenty-something high-school dropout with more hours in the sun than light-complexioned skin could tolerate, more cigarettes consumed than tautened lips could suck the tartar from and still stay smooth, more sorrow in her life than youthful features could survive. The bright blue eyes that were her attribute of note followed him narrowly as he entered the place, and her gravelly voice—those cigarettes again, he figured—piped up before the door swung fully shut, to ask:

"Can I help ya there, mister? You gettin' gas? I don't see no car."

"No. No gas today, ma'am—no car either. So—Phil not here this morning?"

"Phil? *Hell* no. You know Phil? He a special pal of yours or somep'm?"

"No, not exactly. He made me a couple of hot dogs late last night and I thought I'd get some more. So—have you got any ready? Do you put them on that roller grill this early in the day?"

The crusty woman's name was Pat—'BP Pat'; so said the nametag on her shirt. She was seated at the counter with a magazine—not exactly Phil's idea of a magazine, but a gossip sort of rag, devoid of the cheesecake pictures that kept Phil so entertained. As he came a little closer to the counter where she sat, BP Pat leaned forward in an inquisitional manner and propped her elbows on the wood, peering upward in a most suspicious way, and asking:

"So, uh ... ain't it kinda early for hot dogs there, mister—don'tcha think?"

"Well, I suppose you'd have an alternate recommendation that's more in keeping with the hour then?"

"Oh, *listen* to the man, will ya!? A reg'lar scholar, no less! 'Alternate recommendation,' the guy is askin' for ... Alternate ... alternate, let's see.... Ya mean like the chef's special kinda thing, do ya? Hmmm—I don't know; the breakfast burrito ain't too bad, I guess—leastways I think so. It's ninety-nine cents is all— ya got ninety-nine cents there, mister scholar? Way you're dressed is why I'm askin'. If I don't collect the money, it comes outta my personal dough, ya know. I ain't buyin' no breakfasts for the homeless today, and...."

He reached into his pocket and displayed the little wad of cash for her to see. Meager as it was, it would pay for a burrito and a drink. Roughly forty dollars left; and when the woman saw it, she nodded—less skeptically than before, perhaps—though some degree of caution still remained.

"So? Do I qualify as a credit risk then, Pat?—It *is* 'Pat', right?—But anyway, before we peer any further into my financial solvency and the nutritional value of your food, I'd like to run back and use the little boy's room for a minute or two—If that's all right with you, I mean."

"Whoa!—Hold on there, Professor Hot Dog: The little boy's room's outa commission right now. I got it locked up tighter'n a drum. Your buddy Phil—the hot dog master chef, I mean—he's asposed to clean it at the enda his shift, see? And he went ahead an' left it—Well, you don't wanna even *see* the disgustin' way he left it; trust me on that. And it ain't my job to clean up what yer buddy Phil don't do, so it's outta commission till the boss comes in at three, so's he can see what yer good pal Phil done left his co-league Patty to do. The little girl's room ain't much better neither—He's asposed ta clean that up too. And it's acause-a him that I been runnin' over to the Wendy's 'cross the street to use theirs."

How inconsiderate of Phil to do such a thing! That's what he commiserated to BP Pat, with authenticated sympathy. But, anyway—as for the awful mess in there—well, he didn't really mind a little mess himself, and he'd really like to have a morning wash. So if he could just use the restroom—*please*—even as filthy as it was; if she would just unlock the door and let him in there for a couple of minutes, not much more, well that would be....

"No sir, Mr. Scholar, you just trust me on this; you don't wanna even open that door, you sure as heck don't. That's why I got it locked up tight like 'at. Made me sick just ta stick my head in there this mornin' when some guy come out here t' the front and screamed bloody murder 'bout what he seen in there. Hey; why'nt ya run on over to the Wendy's like I done, then come back 'cross here and I'll have that burrito for ya nice and hot and...."

And on she went, adamant from the get-go and growing less and less persuadable the longer she babbled on—Which rigid mindset wouldn't do at all; this would clearly require an alternate approach. And so he thought a bit as she griped and moaned and finally wound to her conclusion; and when she'd finally finished up he came up with—rather cleverly, he thought—the pretty darn unarguable proposal of this:

"OK, look, Miss Pat; let's try a different solution to the problem, shall we? How's this?—What if I were to run in and clean up both the restrooms *for* you? *You* obviously don't want to do it, and Phil's not here to make things right, and it would be a shame to have the facilities shut up all day and you having to run across the street every time you need to use the john; so—You've got some cleaning supplies in the place, haven't you?"

Pat's frown relaxed a bit—just a bit at first—But then it brightened gradually into a look of labored thoughtfulness. Then she gave a little nod, and ventured:

"You mean like a bucket and a mop, you're askin'? Sure we got a bucket and a mop. In that closet there—See? The skinny door between the pair of johns?"

"Well? Is it open?"

"Naw, but I got a key."

"OK then: give me the key, and I'll clean up both the restrooms for you. All I ask in return is that you let me use the men's room when I'm done. Give me—oh, say, fifteen minutes in there to get myself cleaned up properly—fifteen minutes of privacy, I mean, so I can lock the door and wash up undisturbed. And if you agree to that I'll leave you with a couple of restrooms that are as neat and tidy as a hospital operating suite, I promise you that—Is it a deal?"

Pat screwed up her face, squinting at him most dubiously, then fetched the master key out of a little drawer beneath the register, handing it over with a nod and the wariest of smiles. And he opened the skinny door between the johns, and found inside the closet door everything the most demanding sanitary engineer would jot down on his working list: gloves, mop, bucket, sterilizing solutions, and all the rest.

Whereupon the work commenced forthwith. It took a good, long nauseating while—twenty minutes each for the two abominable rooms—Pat was absolutely right: the ladies' toilet wasn't a whole lot better than the men's room was. But they were spick and span when he was done: unclogged toilets, floor mopped clean, sparkling porcelain; superficial graffiti that were removable, pretty well removed; sanitary pine scent deodorization throughout—the whole salubrious ball of wax. Pat, when she was ushered over for her follow-up inspection, was manifestly thrilled!

"Wow! Them toilets never looked so good before, professor. Cripes! you don't even gotta pay me fer yer hot burrito. Fact is, I'd like to pay *you* somep'm for the work you done if I could, but…. Well, I'm just plain ol' hired help here at the place, and the boss is pretty finicky about the petty cash and all like that. But I can write off a coupla burritos as spoilt or somep'm: So here: I'll heat 'em up fer ya. Two enough? Or I could nuke the hot dogs in the micro pretty quick if you like, or...."

"Well, what I really wanted was to use the restroom for that fifteen minutes we talked about—to try and get cleaned up, that is. So...."

Sure thing, said BP Pat. Go right ahead!—Anything she could do for him—anything at all!—Oh, and by the way: Could he use a razor and a bar of soap to do his tidying up? She had a box back there *be-hint* the counter where her and Phil and the other clerks dumped the remnants of the station's damaged merchandise and such. There was a brand new bar of Dial she'd found th' other day as well, with its wrapper tore—it was right on top when she rifled through—and a three-pack of disposable Bic razors from which one had been shoplifted out—Go ahead an' take what he needed from the box—she laid it out atop the counter—Oh yeah, and grab a coupla fresh towels from the cleanin' closet there too, by the way; help yerse'f.

He thanked her, and shook her hand, and headed to the restroom with not an instant's more delay. Fifteen minutes later, the result was little short of astonishing, even to his own two jaded eyes. Scrubbed squeaky clean from top of head to toe jambs, the mud on the bottoms of his baggy jeans scraped off, the oppressive shoes rubbed to practically a patent-leather sheen again—why, even the sweatshirt and gym shorts washed out and wrung as dry as a vise-like pair of fists could wring such saturated habiliments in headlong haste: He and his clothes and his sculpted light brown hair were a trifle damp when he was done, of course. But he was neat and clean and presentable, his skin pinked up, his hair slicked neatly on the sides, his face clean-shaven once again. A trifle haggard still and rumpled as to clothes; not quite the elegant fashion plate he was accustomed to seeing in the mirror, perhaps; but thoroughly presentable. The shabby parka and clown-suit jeans made him look a little like a low-wage laborer, no doubt. But he had the aura of a *clean, neat* low-wage laborer after his intensive sprucing up. A patrol car prowling through Paxton for vagabonds to collar wouldn't swerve across a busy road to throw him in some holding cell today—not this morning, at any rate—He'd make it in and out of town OK.

That pair of breakfast burritos, which Pat doled out complimentary with another thankful smile—they got him going for the day. The enthusiastic 'Wow!' from Pat's admiring lips, the trusting glimmer in her eye, and—more objectively—the mirror's image in the BP restroom: Every visual input showed him so enormously improved, so thoroughly transformed from his prior state of grunginess, that he had the confidence to stroll right down the sidewalk of the main road into Paxton, nodding at the small-town passers-by who nodded first, and waving back cordially when a nice, old lady in a shiny green Chevy tossed a friendly wave.

It was a little over a mile to the business zone of Paxton. He could sense its proximity as the residential blocks gave way to commercial properties along the way: small factories and workshops at the periphery, then a block or two of offices for trades. A run of shops and restaurants came next as the epicenter of the city loomed: a toy store here, a Chinese take-out opposite. There was a gun shop next to an out-of-business cinema. Its display window bristled with ammo and camouflage, and some truly admirable boots—But boots like that cost way, way more than he could, in his present straitened circumstances, possibly afford.

Just a mile and a half of walking, and the shoes were beginning to chafe again. Tissue paper, no matter how soft or artfully applied, couldn't begin to substitute for socks—or for the appropriate kind of shoes. The blisters were beginning to open again, and he wouldn't make it very far today unless he found a better pair of shoes. That was the number one priority on the day's agenda, the single thing he absolutely had to do before he headed out of Paxton on his mandatory journey south.

And so he kept on plodding down the street. He passed a hardware store, a gift shop, a solemn window featuring religious books: next, a card store, a liquor store, a showroom of appliances and digital TV's. Then a random right at the first main traffic light onto another intersecting center-city street, a somewhat quieter thoroughfare with one small antique dealer on the right, another larger one across the blacktop on the left, a newsstand beside the larger shop, a children's clothing store next space down....

And then he spotted it: There, maybe a hundred feet away, straight on, with a placard jutting crosswise from the brick, beckoning promisingly:

Marjorie's Thrift Shop
Discount Manufacturer's Specials
and
Gently Used Second-Hand Goods

All right, terrific, he thought; worth a try at least. His feet throbbed; his knee pinched just a bit: Not quite the jaunty spring in his steps he'd been accustomed to, as he hobbled painfully along. But he got there all right, after some pain and time. Once there, he gave the hopefullest of glances through the window, smoothed his borrowed coat and jeans, ran some fingers through his fresh-scrubbed hair … then slipped into the shop.

"Can I help you, young man?" It was a sweet-faced lady with a singsong voice, pudgy and rosy and with a manifest smile of kindness in her eyes: A woman of unquestionable good vibes. She gave the very air within the shop a fragrant attar of benevolence.

"Well yes, ma'am, I'm hoping that you can—You don't happen to sell shoes here, do you?"

"We *do* have *some* shoes, yes—What sort of shoes do you need?"

"I don't know; something soft and comfortable; easy to walk in. Possibly an athletic shoe of some kind. The problem is, ma'am, I don't have an awful lot of cash."

"Well, our merchandise is pretty reasonable, young fellow. The shoes we sell are manufacturer's seconds. Do you have twelve dollars to spend? You won't find a pair for less than that in town; I'll promise you that. These are the same exact make they sell out at the Superstore for over twenty, and…."

"Twelve! Twelve dollars for a pair of shoes? Honestly? I was figuring on…. But if you're serious, you wouldn't happen to have a pair of *soft*-soled shoes for that price—would you? Athletic shoes, I mean? I honestly never expected to find a pair of *anything* for as little as twelve dollars; but—do you think you might have any soft-soled shoes in that price range in my size?"

"And what size would that be, young fellow? *All* of our shoes are soft-soled, so if we have your size, I'm sure I can help you out. They've got some minor blemishes, you understand, but they wear real well, from what the customers say—So what size are you looking for then, may I ask?"

She had them. Luckily, thankfully—the sweet-faced lady had them. He went for the ten-and-a-half's in an old-style Ked-type gym shoe—nothing fancy, but eminently suitable for the purpose—with a pair of runner's socks thrown in: The socks were two pairs for a dollar, but she threw them in for free to clinch the deal. Twelve bucks all told, meaning roughly thirty left: maybe enough for a humble room and another couple of hot dogs from Phil or Pat or whomever at the newly sanitized BP— He'd stick around another day to let the blisters heal—Yes, one more good night's sleep tonight, maybe in the rusty car if he couldn't swing a room; another bargain snack with Phil or Pat tomorrow morning; and he could hit the road and head on south by ten o'clock or so. Figuring twenty-five miles a day in those nicer softer shoes—maybe even thirty if the weather held—by the following weekend he'd be there. Food would be a challenge on the route, for sure; but he'd scrounge up something: Wash dishes at a roadside diner, maybe; sift through the garbage at a fast-food joint—Possibly even....

"So are you staying here in town, young man? You're not a local, I assume. What do you plan to do with your nice new shoes?"

"I'm not sure, ma'am. I haven't got a lot of money left; maybe just enough for an inexpensive room. Do you know of someplace that...?"

"How much do you have?"

"Cash, you mean? Oh, enough for a little while, I suppose."

"Well, where are you going? How far are you from home?"

"Not far. Close enough that I can walk there if I have to. That's why I had to get the shoes."

"You know—If you like, you can pay me later for the shoes. Or mail it when you get home if that seems more convenient. I'll give you the address."

"No, ma'am, no need for that. I'll pay you now. That's twelve? Twelve even? Isn't it any extra for the tax?"

"Is that all you've got, young fellow?—That money that you have there in your hand?"

"It's more than it looks like, though...."

"Let me see it. No, don't pull away, don't you *dare* pull away, or you'll pull old Marjie over and break her hip, I swear. I want to see; let go.... Twenty ... thirty ... five ... six—what's this? Is this all you've got, to get where you need to go? If you pay me twelve dollars for the shoes, you won't have enough for more than a decent meal, you foolish fellow you. No. Absolutely no. I'm not taking your money; you haven't got enough there even for a room to sleep tonight, and I'm not leaving you with less than thirty dollars in your pockets to get to your destination, wherever it is—walking or otherwise. You take those shoes and pay me when you can. Here's a card with the address of the store. My name is Marjorie—Marjorie Anthony. Mail the money later when you get back home."

"You're very kind, ma'am, but...."

"Nonsense! I'm only doing what any decent Paxton citizen would do for a nice young fellow passing through. You take those shoes, young man, and be on your way, and.... But even that measly forty dollars you've got won't get you very far. Look, we have—Since you seem to be strapped a bit for funds right now, would you ... well, would you care to work a bit to earn some extra cash?"

"To work? ... Well yes, I suppose so. I hadn't thought of that, but—Sure—What exactly would I have to do?"

"You look like a fit enough fellow to me—you look like one of those professional football men, in fact, so.... Do you think you might be able to rake some leaves?"

"I.... I suppose so. I haven't raked leaves before, but I suppose I'm smart enough to learn."

"Fine, then. I'll give you the address of my house—it's only half a mile from here—and I'll tell my husband that you're on your way. We need our lawn raked something *awful*, and the boy who usually does the gardening and stuff.... Well, never mind about him, he hasn't been very reliable these past few months—All the neighbors have been complaining to no end. But if you want to rake the leaves and bag them and set them on the curb—the city truck comes by on Friday—I'll give you what I normally pay him."

"And how much would that be, ma'am—Mrs. Anthony—if I might presume to ask?"

"Well, from the way you talk and present yourself, I'm sure you normally earn a whole lot more, but ... would fifty dollars be OK?"

*

He hadn't raked before, but he sure enough raked today! Mrs. Anthony called her husband, as she told him she would do; and *Mr.* Anthony, when the 'nice young fellow' made it to the house fifteen minutes later, presented him with a brand new rake fresh from the hardware store and a box of trash bags fresh from the Superstore, and told him in a general sort of way what a practitioner of raking autumn foliage was supposed to do.

So he set to work and got to working hard, for he had stamina to spare and dexterity and strength to compete with the very best. The job required upper-body strength and skill, and he had enormous reserves of upper-body strength and skill. It took about an hour to finish up the lawn, working at his utmost speed, and it was neat as an English flower garden when he was done.

Well, Mr. Anthony was tremendously impressed with the top-notch work, and phoned a neighbor down the street. And that neighbor—once his own front yard of leaves got raked and bagged and on the curb, and he'd been *equally* impressed—that neighbor down the street paid up in full, in cash, and phoned *another* neighbor *farther* down the street. And then that other neighbor farther down the street phoned *another* neighbor on a *neighboring* street....

And, in short, by seven that night, when the daylight was ebbing and the air commenced to grow chill—Why, he was practically a wealthy man again, relatively speaking. Grand total of five hundred dollars in his pocket, in cash—five hundred and twenty-seven, in sum, once he'd insisted on paying Mrs. Anthony twelve of his prior thirty-nine for the invaluable pair of shoes.

The Anthonys let him use their place to tidy up, and fed him roast beef and carrots and apple pie, for which they wouldn't take a cent, despite his vehement attempts to pay. And nice *Mister* Anthony—just as obliging as the missus had been— gave him a disposable razor to get himself shaved smooth for dinner and spiffed up even more. When he was done, he looked in the bathroom mirror, and—well, but for the grungy sweatshirt and the baggy jeans—he was pretty nearly back to his old rather respectable-looking self again.

He raked lawns the next day too, dawn to dusk unceasingly; and the following day after that as well. And he slept in a motel room those three snug nights, beneath soft blankets at the Motel 6 just north of town, not far from his beat-up Buick sedan on the two-lane road toward Stanleyville.

And he went to the local Superstore—the Anthonys drove him the very next night after a supper of pork chops and string beans and kraut—and bought himself some presentable clothes at last: a pair of better fitting jeans, dark slacks, a couple of stylish shirts, another pair of shoes—black casual soft-soled lace-ups to go with the nicer slacks. And he tossed into the cart some socks and underclothing too, and a fine new shoulder bag to stuff the brand new wardrobe in.

One more little cleanup task for the sake of the Anthony's—a dastardly devil named Anderson with a skinny little neck: That little bit of business he finished very late on Wednesday night.

Then bright and early Thursday morning, three days after he'd arrived—before the bus rolled out at ten a.m.—Before that half-filled Tramways bus departed to take him to a place where the two most beloved of all his friends had lived, and the one most dread of all his foes....

He dropped by the Paxton post office out on Front Street and sent off, registered, a wad of cash to an address in Pittsburgh, copied from a tattered envelope, directed to a fellow named Graeber who owned an isolated hunting camp up north, close by the local creek: Payment in full for groceries and Levis and a ratty parka, plus forty-seven dollars borrowed from a sugar bowl, with compound interest on the cumulative sum of it to spare.

And he stopped by the BP station and saw blue-eyed, deep-voiced Pat again, and gave her a friendly hug and a kiss on the cheek, and a promise that if he was ever back in Paxton (though doubtful, he thought it, at best), he wouldn't fail to look her up.

And he hiked on out to that rusty Buick one last grateful time, lone and untended, and left a crisp new fifty on the dash. Comfy accommodations, he figured, worth ten times and more the price: Maybe the owner would find it there someday and the crisp new fifty would help to get the poor, old tired vehicle back on the highway and gussied up like new again. If he'd had the cash right there and then, he'd have paid for the restoration himself, new tires, fresh paint, rebuilt engine, and nice fresh comfy fabric on the seats—the works.

And finally he went, last but certainly not least essential of all, to the local flower shop just before the bus left Paxton for its journey south, and paid a hundred dollars cash up front to send nice Mrs. Anthony some blossoms: An enormous assemblage of roses—the very most in number and the very best in quality the little florist could provide....

A gift the likes of which—as she was wont to tell every single wayfarer who set foot in that thrift shop for years and years to come—she'd never, ever, so much as imagined anything half as lovely, and elegant, and thoughtful, before.

6

Un-be-LIEVE-able! thought Special Agent Braman, once he was out of the sheriff's vehicle and down those concrete steps to get a look-see for himself.

Un-i-MAG-inable!—For the place, once you wrapped your mind around the craziness your eyes were taking in, wasn't even *remotely* like the static shots the crime-scene pictures showed. You couldn't convey it in plain old, ordinary pictures—although they'd taken quite enough of the silly things, God knows: that funny sheriff and his dog-faced deputy who scarcely said a word, with their donut-frosted smackers and big, round bulldog guts.

But the—Holy Moses—the enormity of it alone. The detail. The sheer perfection! No, a plain old set of crime-scene photos couldn't capture that at all, though the shots they'd taken of the body had conveyed the gist of *that* amazing bit of weirdness well enough. No matter how many of these grisly scenes you had to look at in the sickly line of duty, they always had the same unpalatable effect.

"So—let me ask you then: Is this the way you found it, Sheriff? Nothing in the room has been disturbed? Nothing opened? Nothing removed?"

The sheriff pulled a salivate cigar from out between his lips and answered with a labored drawl: "No, sir—nothin' but that there body Dep'ty Will and me hauled out—the both of 'em, is what I mean."

"And the body—the hanging one you found down here—It was—*where* exactly? On that hook, correct?" He moved the amber search beam of the flashlight over to the hook suspended from the ceiling like a meat hook in a butcher's walk-in fridge: "There? Over by the counter there? Is that where you found the unburned body before you fellows took it down?"

"Yepp'ir, jus' the way I showed ya in them pitchers we took. I got 'em with me, Agent Braman, if you wanna have a look at 'em again."

He shook his head to indicate that, no: He didn't need that nauseating look a second time. He'd seen entirely enough back in the sheriff's office when he'd first arrived. Those snapshots weren't what a normal, well-adjusted person would consider pretty things to stare at; not the kind of naked poses you'd want to gaze at all that often or all that long.

And besides, even if a fellow *hadn't* seen his proper fill of horrifying details on that first glance through; even if he actually *liked* eyeballing snapshots of some unclad dead guy dangling upside down with his chest sliced clear through to the bone— Even if some twisted pervert-of-a-sadist were somehow *into* that demented kind of thing: Down here in the basement, down in the dark and out of the daylight, there wouldn't be a helluva lot of detail even the eagerest sort of twisted pervert might actually get to *see*.

So then—having rejected the sheriff's offer in as nonjudgmental a manner as he could, he stood there, the puzzled Special Agent did; fingers on his cheeks, furrows in his forehead, and inspected the room again, shining the flashlight now here, now there, to try and get a general sort of handle on the place, trying hard to figure out the how and why of this inscrutable mystery—which might eventually lead him to the eventual bottom line of—*who*?

And to eventually find that inevitable 'who,' the primary factor of all would have to be: This extraordinary room!

Extraordinary?—Hell, 'extraordinary' was putting it mildly: The place was flat-out nutsy cuckoo if any crime scene ever was! Way off the charts; incredibly, pathologically ... *Looney Tunes*!

It was the ill-lit basement of a mid-twentieth-century century country house. But it looked nothing like the basement of any country house *he'd* ever seen before—or of any house *anywhere* that *anyone* had ever been in before, or even so much as *imagined*, so far as he had heard or read, or even visualized in one of his weirdest, craziest, vividest, criminologic dreams.

The room—for it was a single, wide, long, unpartitioned room, twelve feet high, fifty-five in length, thirty-eight in width (according to deputy Will's paced-out estimates jotted on the detail sheet)—was pretty much a miniature hospital in its layout and decor, to judge things by appearances. The floor was a lot like linoleum; but if it *was* linoleum, it was a super-high-tech, high-quality variety of linoleum: the kind of rubbery yet rock-hard surface that can be scrubbed and sterilized a million times without pitting it or dulling it down. And the walls were of a similar but slightly different composition, as imperviously scrubbable, as immaculately polished, and as structurally adamantine as the floor.

The whole place had a Mayo Clinic look to it; state of the art, as to the flooring and the walls. And the ceiling too, when he shone the feeble hand light up to it just now, from left to right, and fore to aft: plaster boarded, painted high-gloss white, semi-reflective, smooth as polished metal without a noticeable seam. It had close-spaced, glassed-in fluorescents and periodic recessed spots farther down toward the far wall of the room, above the stainless countertop that ran across its fifty-odd-foot length. Enough lighting, if every bulb of it were lit, to illuminate, not just a basement room like this, but the whole damn innards of the Mammoth Cave: Clear enough, sharp enough, bright enough illumination for some old half-blind biddy to do her finest decorative stitching in.

The overheads were dead, of course. The electrical outage had seen to that. So the dimness of the place was relieved from utter obscurity only by a wisp of daylight filtering down the stairwell from the kitchen door above—that and by a ten-buck cord of feeble light bulbs strung up hastily that morning by silent Will the Deputy (whose only spoken words thus far had been a gurgly grumbling about the pre-dawn work he'd had to do). Will had grumbled about having to run out for a generator too, to feed the bulbs, and gas to feed the grumbling generator in its turn; and it sat there chuck-chuck-chucking through the intervening concrete from the lawn out front where Will stood glowering silently above it, lamenting, one could only postulate, the mandatory rigors of his early morning work.

But despite Will's best, most begrudging efforts, it was dim enough down there, and close enough, and confined enough in that airtight, breathless space with its string of low-watt bulbs and stagnant atmosphere, to feel a bit unnerving—And Sidney Braman might have felt as claustrophobic as the wheezing sheriff evidently did, were he not diverted totally by the gape-mouthed fascination of the place.

For the room *was* fascinating, dammit all!—fascinating tottering on the margins of *incredible*—that was for sure. What was one to make of it? Oh, he'd seen what he'd thought was pretty nearly *everything* these past ten years at the Pittsburgh Branch—

but never anything quite as all-out otherworldly as *this*. No, nothing in his ten-year experience, nothing he had read about or heard about or even sat there watching in one of those far-fetched sci-fi flicks—none of it compared to *this*—Sheer lunacy paled woefully in comparison to *this*!

And it was thus in a state of utter stupefaction that he finally turned toward the pudgy lawman at his elbow and asked:

"So what have you come up with so far, Sheriff? Do you have the foggiest idea what might have been going on down here?"

"Nope," said Sheriff Stoner, stepping around to face him with that big round backside a foot or less away from the operating table—Yes, operating table; that's right!—And not just *any* chintzy operating table, either, mind you. No sirree; it was state-of-the-art, top-of-the-line, power everything, with all the bells and whistles alongside: stainless steel tray, and cart, and precision instruments, all standing at the ready for the most proficient surgeon out of Boston to do his finest work. Lights too; two great big surgical lamps on articulated arms poised for action, one at head, one at foot, ready and eager to light the top-notch surgeon's way. A super-specialist could step right in, right now, and unclog a clogged-up heart or transplant a failing liver with the equipment sitting here.

"Was the guy a doctor who owned the place?—the burned man, I mean?"

"Not as we know of, Agent. Deed's in the name of some feller named Finotti, Anthony Finotti. That must be the ID fer the burnt guy, best as we can tell."

"And he wasn't a doctor? You check the local hospitals to see if they had anybody on staff by that name?"

"Yep, sure did; nobody rount here knows a thing."

"Well, *somebody* must have known him. When did he buy the house?"

"A good twenny year now, 'cordin' to the deed. Nobody rount here seems to know nothin' 'bout him, though. Whole town scarcely knowed he was here."

"Hey! Don't touch that, man! Holy Moses! Don't touch anything until forensics gets here and dusts the place." Sidney practically screamed this admonition, as he grabbed the sheriff's forearm and dragged him bodily away from the surgical table, which he seemed just about ready to take a catnap on. One buttock was pretty nearly on the cushion itself when Sidney managed to yank him off.

"Holy Moses, Sheriff! Get *with* it, will you! Are you sure you didn't disturb anything down here before I arrived?"

"Yepp'ir, Agent, real sure. Just kinda fergot myself there for a sec. Sorry. Kinda close in here, you know, and…."

"You sure you didn't touch anything, though?—What about the blood? Did you or your deputy clean up any blood?"

"Nope; warn't no blood ta clean up."

"You mean to tell me there was a body hanging upside down on that hook with a twelve-inch gash in its chest and there wasn't any blood around?"

"Nope; jes what them pitchers showed. Jes them two teensy-weensy little drops."

Sidney stepped over to the place where the photos showed the body to have been. Above him, that vicious-looking hook hung down from the ceiling, with its lowest point roughly two feet above his head. Below him, as he crouched to examine them, he saw the pair of purple droplets he had noticed in a photo, now coagulated into a couple of viscid lens-like gobs.

"That's it? Nothing more? You're sure?"

"Nossir, Agent, nothin'. That's all the blood was in here. Honest to Pete, it is."

"Well, how is that possible, then, Sheriff? You think someone *else* cleaned the place? You think your man Finotti did? A body like that with a wound like the one in the picture—there should be blood all over the place: floor, walls, even the ceiling. Blood is messy stuff. Persistent. It gets around and it takes a lot of time and effort to clean it up."

"Warn't none, though. Jus' them couple little drops is all. We didn't clean none up oursel'n."

"OK, OK, let's forget about the blood for now. What have you learned so far about the burned guy up the stairs—this man Finotti—the one whose name was on the deed?"

"That's jes it, Agent. We ain't learnt nothin'. Don't seem to be nothin' to learn. Like I tolt you, nobody round here knows a blasted thing."

"Come on now, Sheriff! Are you sure? Are you positive? No records at all? No arrests? No priors? You know, from the looks of things, this isn't the first time something very sinister has happened in this room. I doubt Mr. Finotti spent all these hundreds of thousands of dollars just for the one unlucky corpse you happened to find."

"Hunnerds of *thousands*? You think these here gizmos costed that much?"

"They sure as hell did. Come here; step over here with me and take a look."

Sidney led the sheriff over to the wall beyond the ceiling hook, fifteen feet past the operating table and its adjuncts, and shone the flashlight across a stainless counter that ran from far left to far right of the room, a good fifty-odd feet in length. On it, spotlighted sequentially by the glimmering beam, sat a vast array of scientific implements of every imaginable kind: a video microscope, a couple of diagnostic ultrasound units, various devices for blood analysis and typing, some high-speed centrifuges, a microtome—even (and this the most astounding of all!) a compact DNA analyzer, something far beyond the scope of even the best-equipped university hospital lab, and a handy little convenience that forensics at Quantico would be pleased as punch to own.

"*More* than a few hundred thousand, I'd bet," said Sidney. "Likely a whole lot more than a *million* would be my guess."

"So what was he doin' with the stuff? What was he doin' with that there body me and Will done found?"

"That's question A, Sheriff Stoner. Question B is: How many dozens of times did he do it with a bunch of *other* bodies you and your deputy *didn't* find?"

That second question got a whole lot more pertinent when Sidney left the sheriff there staring into nothingness and wandered over to the far end of the room.

Over against the wall adjacent to the staircase, a couple of paces forward of the bottom step: Doing a bit of snooping there he found a freezer—one of those great big, institutional-sized things—which, when he opened it, was found to be, not only stuffy-warm inside—not currently plugged-in and working was what that meant—but entirely empty, devoid of everything—missing even its shelves. No stains in there, blood or otherwise, when he crouched down low to have a look with the handheld light, so unlikely that the body dangling from the hook had been....

So he shrugged and shook his head and shut the freezer door again, puzzled to no coherent end—For here was a high-tech medical facility that some wealthy nutcase had spent a ton of time and money on; and in it this empty freezer of no apparent use—Strange, like all the rest, bordering on the lunatic.

At any rate, he shut the freezer up again and moved a little farther down the side wall to another massive thing, the very largest object in the room in fact, fully twice the size of the operating table and surgical lights combined.

It was shoved up tight against the wall, bolted there five feet farther onward from where the empty freezer stood: A huge, boxy, metallic cabinet-of-a-thing, big as a commercial dumpster, with finished surface panels done up in a high-tech bronze-ish brown, and opening at its leading end with a massive stainless door. It didn't look particularly familiar at first ... but then a little bulb snapped on in Sidney's noggin, and it maybe, kind of *did*: He reached for the handle of the door and pulled it open, flashed the light inside, then motioned across the room to the sheriff with a waggle of his fingers, beckoning:

"So—Sheriff—here's a partial answer to our puzzling question B. Have you guys noticed this nifty little gadget yet? Do you have any idea what it does?"

Sheriff Stoner stepped across the room—he and that protuberating gut of his, and the relict of that salivate cigar. He'd been loitering over by the blood spots, daydreaming perhaps, perhaps pondering that box of donuts still residing on his County Courthouse desk. Sidney's wiggling fingers probably caught the man's attention before the spoken question did. For he set himself in motion before the sound had reached that far, and made it pretty close to the place where Sidney was standing before the next few words came out. Not all that *much* before, though: His sluggish transit of the room, replete with heavy wheezing, took a good, long eon-of-a-while.

But Agent Braman waited patiently till the lumbering lawman got near; and then advised the sheriff with a finger point:

"Look here, Sheriff Stoner: You see this boxy sort of thing I'm looking at? You see the pipes running in and that vent stack coming out up above?"

"Yeah, we was wonderin' 'bout that oursel'n there, Agent. Dep'ty Will there—he thought maybe kinda like some sorta sterilizin' thingamajigey fer medical stuff 'n 'at. Like a—whaddya call it?—like one-a them there autyclaves er somepin'?"

"Uh-huh, that's kind of in the ballpark, I guess—But it's got a pretty big capacity just for medical stuff, don't you think?"

"Yeah, I kinda thought so too myseln there, but...."

"See inside?" Sidney opened the door and lit the innards with his flashlight. The stainless steel was two full inches thick. "Here: Take a look. You see this?"

"Yeah, it kinda looks like...."

"*What? What* does it look like?"

"I dunno—a oven, maybe? Some kinda oven prob'ly. You say it's way too big fer a autyclave, so maybe they used it fer … fer maybe—burnin' trash or somepin' like 'at—Ya think?"

"Right, you got the concept down, in a general way. You see the double-chamber configuration?"

"Huh?"

"Double-chamber. It'll get a body up to two thousand degrees. See the baked ceramic walls?"

"Walls?—*Body*, did you say?"

"Right. You see the ceramic walls? They reflect the heat back and don't get melted by the temperature. Two thousand degrees, that's what it takes to do its business. It's a crematory oven, Sheriff. Looks like it's been used a whole lot of times before."

"A—a *what*?! A—you mean fer…?"

"That's where your body would have gone if not for the fire. My guess is, there were a whole lot of other bodies down in this basement before your ATV-ing lumberman friend happened onto this most recent one."

"You mean…. Are you tryin' ta tell me…?"

"Twenty years, you said? Is that how long that Finotti fellow lived here?"

"Yepp'ir; twenny, maybe twenny-one; I gotta check the date."

"That's a heck of a lot of time to cremate bodies…. OK, Let's do this then, Sheriff: Let's get the records from the local gas company and see how often a surge in usage occurred—that'll give us some idea of the frequency and maybe an estimate of the victim count if they can go back the whole twenty years. And check the police records for missing persons too—anywhere within driving distance of Stanleyville for starters, also for the past twenty years—can your department do that right away?"

"Sure can, Agent—I guess."

"And—do we know what this Finotti character looked like? Have you got a decent description?"

"I got his license records sent over f'om the DMV. Latest pitcher an' all. Sixty-two, it says, five-nine tall, one-sixty-five fer weight, brown eyes. That's all we got so far."

"Well, do we know if the burned guy matches those parameters?"

"Matches what?"

"What's on the license."

"Nossir, we don't know that yet; not till the cor'ner's report gets done."

"And when will that be, pray tell?"

"Ol' Doc Campbell, last I heard, said sometime today, he thinks."

"OK, well, when you hear something, let me know right away. Holy Moses, Sheriff!—If this guy Finotti did all the awful stuff he seems to have done, and if that crematory oven got used as much as it looks like it's been used—For everybody's welfare, I want to make damn sure this murdering son-of-a-bitch is dead!"

So the sheriff waddled up the steps and out to his car to make the necessary calls. And Sidney plodded up the staircase shortly afterward to have himself a sort of general look around.

A good bit of the first floor had been relatively spared— Not spared a hell of a lot of damage, no indeed; for it was a damp and sooty mess in there to try and rummage through in hopes of finding clues. But at least the ceiling joists were stable, and the floorboards sound, from the look and feel of them. And the walls seemed reasonably secure: not about to topple over on a fellow, anyway, if he leaned a bit too hard or stumbled up too close. Part of the plastered ceiling had fallen in, of course, and there was endless rubble everywhere; but Sidney found a metal-tipped umbrella lying in the entryway and used it like a probe to shuffle through the ashes and gently poke around.

The fellow who'd called the fire in—that VFD alum named Roger Whatever-it-was—he'd gone on and on *ad nauseam* about the elegance of the place before it got consumed. Sidney had read the fellow's statement in the sheriff's SUV on the journey out from Stanleyville, and he'd been reasonably impressed. And keeping that impression in mind as he was rooting in the remnants, he could see the signs of what Good Samaritan Roger described as elegance pretty nearly everyplace he looked: Silver-plated table lamps lying about the front room; marble and granite countertops and moldings in the living area and kitchen with their wooden bottoms mostly burnt away; a gorgeous oriental rug beneath the fallen ceiling—a room-sized Persian carpet that looked, below the ashes and the plaster, prodigiously expensive and selected by a pro. Elegance galore throughout, in short; expense account unlimited. The finest china, the weightiest silver serving bowls, gorgeous remnants of designer custom furniture that looked top notch, first-rate— Impressive stuff, even to a multi-millionaire like Sidney who'd never in his super-affluent lifetime been all that easily impressed.

So there was one *more* fascinating fact he knew about the perpetrator, this mysterious fellow Finotti, supposedly: A murderous monster, granted; but at least a murderous monster with exquisite taste: Rich, smart, medically astute: A serial killer of who-knew-how-many victims in the past. If the killer was Finotti, and if the coroner could match the burnt remains of the upstairs corpse they found with what Finotti must have looked like—well then, the case was pretty nearly done. So, terrific!—All well and good, all cut and dried. But there still remained the vexingly unanswered question as to … *why?*

For there didn't seem to be a single other clue as to the culprit's motivation, or method, or—since they really knew nothing of Finotti himself—the murderer's actual identity. No address book; no notepad—not even a *telephone*, for heaven's sake! Nothing whatever here in the living room, back there in the dining room, or behind the dining room, over to the right, amid the kitchen's flagrant mess. Nothing at all anywhere so far. Zero. Zilch. Garbage!

Oh, there was more to be examined, sure. He'd seen the floor plan of the house in the sheriff's skinny file and could visualize the pre-disaster layout fairly well: Two more rooms down that hallway behind the stairs; and then of course the garage itself where a couple of costly vehicles sat reportedly torched. He'd check the downstairs out, obligatorily, then have maybe the faintest, farthest, remotest chance of finding something useful amongst the ash and cinders that were left upstairs. He could spend another several hours here, snoop

60

around till midnight if he chose. But, gauging from experience, if there's nothing useful in the primary living area of a house....

Oh well.... He shook his head, tiptoed back across the rubble of the front room to the vestibule again, and stuck his head out the open door. The sheriff was standing just where he'd been standing fifteen minutes earlier, mouthing that cigar and staring vacantly at the ground to no productive end. The big man seemed to start a little when he heard his name and title called:

"Hey, Sheriff. Sheriff Stoner!"

Up went the sheriff's hand, out came the saturate cigar, a quick expectoration, a clearing of the throat, and after a hiatus of a dozen seconds (though it seemed like many more):

"Yup?"

"Anything from the coroner yet?"

"Jes' now give him a call. He's asposta call me back."

"Soon?"

"Yup."

"OK, I'll poke around a little more. Let me know when you hear something, will you? Once I'm done in here, I'll probably take a look around the property, so if I'm not inside, check around out back."

So back around the stairwell to those other couple of downstairs rooms, which would be pretty much in shambles, from what the sheriff's photos seemed to show. Not much chance of pay dirt there, he figured, but still worthy of at least a fleeting look.

The first one was a high-tech, high-cost home theater sort of place, judging from the hardware that the fire had mercifully spared: Big-screen TV, full range of audio and video equipment—most of it singed or melted into gooey plastic globs—a lot of DVD's littering the floor, some with legible titles left: Not of consuming interest, though: Documentaries mostly, with a scattering of horror-type fantasies thrown in—Bela Lugosi and vampires and such. Finotti's taste in cinema ill-accorded with the general excellence of his aesthetic sense.

So out of that first room, not much the wiser from the experience, and ten steps farther onward to the second and last room down the hall. This one was a well-equipped home gym, replete with every sort of weight and workout station the finest health club might boast in an equivalent amount of space: Multi-task universal, barbells, pulleys, elliptical: Not as badly damaged as the rest of the stuff in the home—fire isn't as hard on lead and iron as it is on paper and fabric and wood.

Still, not a whole lot useful in the home gym either. No notes, no memos, no names. Not anything at all, really, besides one frightening, salient thing: That sixty-two-year-old, five-foot-nine Finotti?—A damn good thing the guy was dead: The bench press lever and added weight bar came to nearly four hundred pounds—And you could see from a series of scratches in the slots, that the weights had on occasion been notched a good bit higher still. Finotti didn't need an accomplice in his work. He could have hung that body on the hook, and tossed it casually into the crematory oven when he was finished, all by his powerful self. Without so much as breaking a sweat!

Whew!—Well, after that disheartening bit of revelation, there was the garage still to be looked at, and, for completeness' sake, Sidney pushed away the remnant of a door leading outward from the hallway and took the two required steps down to the ashy concrete floor. The interior of the garage had been cooked so completely by the fire that the tires on the vehicles had melted down to a blackish ooze a little bit like tar. Above the tar and ash and cinders, he found a big-bed Chevy truck, and next to it a late-model, top-of-the-line Cadillac sedan, both scorched almost beyond recognition: so profoundly altered from the nice smooth rides they once had likely been that you could scarcely tell the colors or identify the makes. Not exactly a mine of information, true, but not a total zero either; for the serial numbers could still be traced, the license plates, the service records; when the vehicles were bought; where; by whom. They'd lead back in a maddening loop to this character Finotti, no doubt, whoever he was, whatever undiscoverable things he might have done, past and present; so the search would probably wind up there.

All right; well, anyway—so out of the garage again, little the wiser for his pains, and back down the hallway into the living room; where, curiosity getting the best of trepidation, he found enough solidity in the rickety steps to make it safely to the second floor. The path was tenuous, true, those shaky treads and risers; but he discovered that by keeping near the wall and tripping lightly where the wood looked firm, the steps could adequately support his weight.

Not much up there, though, either—not at first. Four bedrooms, from the look of the general layout—as far as one could make the general layout out. The one where Finotti had been—that's assuming the upstairs victim had actually *been* this guy Finotti—showed obvious signs of use. There were shards of clothing in the closet: not much left of them, naturally, but one could tell that there'd been fabric there: a collar of a jacket, a blackened fragment of a tie.

Near the remnants of the bed, among the cinders on the floor, Sidney found a couple of solid objects as well, as he poked through the rubble with his umbrella-of-a-stick: metallic objects that used to be a watch, a ring, a spoon. He found a bowl there too, preserved ceramic, beside the spoon—four-hundred-bench-press Finotti had probably treated himself to that one final meal before the fire—something very, very flavorful, a kindly friend of his might hope—then burnt to cinders in his sleep…. Well, *if* he was lucky enough to stay asleep. If he turned out to be the guy who ran that crematory oven down in the basement—who knew? Maybe he'd had a justly fitting end.

All right, then; no more speculation, let's get back to work: Out of the sickly-pungent dead man's room—for the walls *did* stink offensively of molten human flesh—and into another bedroom, straight across the hall.

It was a whole lot larger room, this second one: a master bedroom sort of space, with its own connected bath—And it was pretty well incinerated too: the bed, the nightstand, the clothing in the closet—rendered into ash and cinders just as absolutely as the objects in the burned man's room had been; just as barren of useful information and just as maddening in their tantalizing blankness as Finotti's bowl and spoon.

Sidney poked through the fire's refuse with his makeshift umbrella-of-a-stick: now in this little ash heap, now in that. The cinders scattered, the ash took flight and drifted in the breeze, escaping through the open window. There were some charred relics of bedside furniture over by the upright remnants of the bed, and he fished through the flakes and powder, idly, with little enthusiasm and not a jot of hope, until …

Click!

There—What was *that*? A sound of metal against the umbrella's shiny tip, a hasty shuffle through the cinders, and— There!—down there! A glint of something buried in the pile of soot. He spread the ashes out around and fished the metal something out and held it up to catch the misty swath of daylight filtering through the open window…. Hmmm: It was….

A watch. Dusty, blackened, the leather strap pretty badly singed away—But the face, the dial—what did that lettering say?

It was … it was…. Did that say…? P-a- t … Patik? Was it a … Patik Philippe? Was it *really*? Actually? The sort of watch appropriate for a person—not just of wealth, no—but of *egregious* wealth, *ostentatious* wealth: the kind of wealth that gets tossed around—not just casually, not just liberally—but *unconcernedly*, *flagrantly*. Some of the big shots in his father's country club wore Patik Philippes: the self-appointed trendsetters on one end of the spectrum, the guys who loved to shove their fortunes in your face on the other. And then the occasional decent guys at heart who just preferred the finest things available—and could afford to indulge their tastes: They were in there too, the rich but nice guys. All those folks, both good and bad, had one decided thing in common though—the prodigious kind of money they could toss around and burn.

Great wealth to burn, assuredly—But none of them actually got to the point of burning it. Rich men were invariably cautious men. Ninety-nine percent of them were. They didn't buy bad stocks, they didn't back bad companies. And they didn't leave fifty-thousand-dollar watches lying on a bed stand in an empty room. None of them did, none of them *could*, none of them would *dream* of such a thing—

Which meant….

Hmmm…. The outside wall of this larger, nicer bedroom with its own connected bath was burned clear out to the masonry, the window sash pulled open, and singed in that fully opened state—Which meant it clearly had been opened before the fire had begun—or … or *while it was going*.

Sidney stepped quickly to the window and stuck his head out through, examining the ground below. Twelve or so feet up, by his offhand estimate, from window sill to ground: Not that terribly hazardous a leap; although the guy who would have done the leaping would drop smack down onto that flagstone deck out back—which might prove to the twelve-foot leaper's legs and feet a little hard. And there was a chair there, too, close below—that metal chair just slightly left of the putative site of impact. A sturdy chair, angular and rigid, which seemed a bit more problematic a landing place to hit. And the chair looked … was it bent a little? The arm on the right-hand side? The subjacent leg? At least from twelve feet up it looked that way. So might that mean…?

Holy Moses!

He scrambled out the bedroom door and down the fragile stairway, clinging to the wall in haste, leaning forward all the while, so that if a stair step *did* give way he'd fall forward, away from the splintered shards of wood below—no point in getting skewered like a chunk of shish-kabob if one can help it— But anyway, thankfully, he made it to the front room safe and sound, and scooted out the back door near the kitchen sink, then right ten feet or so to where the patio pavement commenced and the metal chair resided beside a soggy, metal lounge and.... .

Yes—YES. OF COURSE. He knelt beside the twisted chair: Something had hit it certainly—He could *tell* it had; he could *see*. The arm—bent just here at the proper angle. The leg—twisted in at just the proper place: Angled here, torted there; so that an object or a person falling onto it from precisely where that window stood above would have.... Of course—It was obvious—No doubt or question at ALL.

He stood and peered around him on the grass; stooping low out beyond the patio, dropping to his knees, feeling the lawn and soil with his rubber-fingered hand, prodding, smoothing: Were those footprints? They were faint, equivocal, but ...yes— undoubtedly YES.

He got himself upright and followed the dubious steps out toward the woods behind the home. Very faint, very minimal at first, for the ground was dry here. But over there—There. A low spot, where the runoff from that storm the other day would be generally prone to pool: Down there in the mud—Yes— Those were legible footprints for *sure* where a bit of standing water lay. A hard-soled shoe—almost like a dress shoe, an expensive shoe, leather sole and heel, with a whole lot more weighty footprint for the right foot, a whole less weighty imprint for the left.

So that was it—OF COURSE. A guy (for it was a fellow's shoe—no doubt) had jumped down from that twelve-foot window and jammed his left leg on the chair, then stumbled this way—over toward the woods....

Astounding—a second culprit in the house—Incredible! He'd get the sheriff's men to do a search, follow where the footsteps led, cast the prints in plastic for ID regarding type of shoe and brand, scour the woods for any other useful clues— Amazing!—A second potential villain in the piece.

He turned and stared back at the house, trying to gauge the trajectory of the jump, the impact on landing, the force, the velocity, what sort of damage the secondary suspect's leg had probably sustained....

And then....

Something *else* occurred to him: It suddenly dawned on him. The house: Standing where he stood, fifty yards away from it, putting things in perspective, looking at the length of it in a distant broadside view.... The horizontal scale was very large. *Very* large! Very long from right to left, eighty feet at least, maybe close to ninety. Similar-era homes had basements end to end— But the dimensions of *this* basement, when silent Will the Deputy had paced it out, had come to only fifty something—fifty-five or -six or -seven.... Which meant....

Eureka!

He ran back in through the door beside the kitchen sink and scrambled down the basement steps. The flashlight was sitting on the bottom tread where he'd set it idly half an hour before; and he picked it up excitedly and clicked it on.

He went behind the steps and started there, feeling, knocking, listening for the faintest resonance as he tapped: But there was masonry and concrete all across, no hollowness, no hint of a portal; nothing but solid, impenetrable wall.

So out from beneath the staircase and moving five feet farther down from the bottom step, he tapped again and felt and listened:

Still nothing.

Then five feet more, just to the staircase-side of the freezer:

Nothing still.

And five feet farther after that, on the *opposite* side of the freezer:

But again, nothing: solid, sturdy masonry all the way across, right up to the crematory oven. If there was an opening in the wall—*any*place—well, it couldn't *possibly* be *behind* that crematory oven—could it? No, that enormous thing was immovably fixed in place; it'd take a dozen workmen a couple of dozen hours to disassemble the prodigious bulk of it and disconnect the gas line in and the vent pipe out—And then to try and *move* the maybe five-ton weight of it.... No, no way; not a practicable doorway for any form of access, no chance of a functional opening being there.

Which left....

The freezer?

But—was it *possible?* Could there possibly be...?

He stepped across and pulled the big door wide again. Vast, empty, unaccountably devoid of shelves. The back panel, when he prodded firmly, felt very slightly loose and minimally movable when he gave a little harder push. And when he looked—looked very closely and very carefully this time, first up high, and then down low, using the handheld light, and getting his face right up to the sheet of plastic all along the seam....

There! Midway down the left-hand side: Wasn't that a sort of lever beside the temperature adjustment dial? He pulled it till it made a tiny clicking sound and then....

The whole rear panel sprang backward like a spring-topped box, opening widely into a totally dark, stuffily temperate, but rather cozy-smelling room.

7

"Hey, Stoner! Sheriff Stoner!—You mind coming over for a sec? You too, Deputy Will, I'm gonna need a little help."

The sheriff waddled over with his deputy in tow. It took a while for him to get there; and then, once he finally arrived, it took a little longer for him to pull that saturate cigar from his mouth and query:

"Yep, whaddya need there, Agent? Jes' say the word there, and me'n the dep'ties'll do whatever it takes ta get the som'bitch done." And in went the cigar again, stuffed amidst the donut frosting and tobacco spittle on his lips.

"Light. I need a whole helluva lot more light, Sheriff! Downstairs. In the basement—Not where we just were, I mean, but in another room. There's a whole other room down there, fellas—Holy Moses!—which you're gonna have to see to believe—But it's black as ink in there, Sheriff, and I'm gonna need a lot more illumination than this useless little flashlight puts out—I need it *now*, though, fellas—I need it—Holy Moses, man—I need it, like—*yesterday!*"

This message uttered, and presumably assimilated, the sheriff raised his shaggy brows, nodded once definitively, then waddled off tortoise-like in the direction of his shiny SUV. And while he was waddling, and Deputy Will was waddling in his wake, Sidney scurried in, as impatient as a bridegroom once the wedding guests have left, and started looking for….

Well, he wasn't a hundred percent positive just *what* he ought to be looking for—though maybe a fuse box might get things done a little quicker than Silent Will and the lugubrious sheriff might do. It wouldn't hurt, at any rate, to have a try.

Fuse box … fuse box—Sidney didn't know all that much about fuse boxes and wiring and such; but if such a thing as a fuse box could be found, and if it happened to be salvageable, or remediable, and therefore maybe functional, a guy should probably look for it. … Hmmm, where *would* something like a fuse box be most likely to be found?

Maybe best to try back down in the basement for a start. For, after all, that was where the medical toys and goodies had been kept—and they obviously required an enormous amount of juice. That was where *he'd* be, thought Sidney logically, if *he* were such a box for such an inordinately large amount of use.

So down those concrete steps again was where he headed first, with the fading flashlight in his hand. And once he'd made it down, he commenced to fumble and fiddle around, now fiddling here, now fumbling there; shining the light first up, then down, then swinging it from side to side. Here, there, hither and yon....

Until he ... yes! He found it!—*Eureka!* There, under the stairwell behind an access panel that he'd passed right by on his first time through, but not paid the slightest attention to before.

The main breaker had been thrown—at least he *assumed* that larger bottom thingamajigey was the main breaker, and that it had been thrown, not knowing much more about breakers, thrown or otherwise, than he did about the boxes or the fuses themselves. But it looked as though it likely was the primary breaker and as though it likely had been thrown—whether by the firemen, just to be on the safe side, or whether the circuit had just spontaneously clicked off by some preset safety switch—One or the other; he didn't have a clue.

But what the hell, he thought: What downside could there possibly be if he sort of potchkeyed around with it a little bit (as his father Jacob and granddad Samuel Chaim Bramanovich were often heard to say)? So he potchkeyed around and potchkeyed around some more, turning all the lesser breakers to OFF (or what he *thought* would likely be OFF), then clicking the main one to ON, then flipping the others ON again for an instant each, one at a time in sequence, until....

Until—There!—Wow! Finally a little light flashed on behind him—which was....

An emergency light in the proximal part of the room, a single conoid bulb that lit the stairwell and filtered back around the edge of the staircase to the impenetrable dimness where he worked. He left that biggest breaker ON, with all the others set to OFF, then went back to the freezer door again, and opened it, and passed a foot or two beyond the secret panel of the freezer to the hidden room, and used his flashlight's waning output to find a bank of switches—there beside the freezer's secret doorway—

there they were—which he flipped (each one of them) to the position UP that he was pretty sure would likely be ON.

It took only a try or two back at the breaker box to get the proper circuit opened up; and when he flipped the one appropriate switch *this* time (fifth down on the left, green handle), a sudden—and rather friendly—beam of illumination came peeping lamely past the open freezer door into the dimness of the basement, casting a cheerful sort of glow into the otherwise dank, medicinal room.

OK, he thought: Terrific! Now he probably could see. And he'd taken a very eager step or two away from the fuse box, moving out from beneath the staircase in the direction of that fascinating secret room again—and would have made it there in no time at all….

If he hadn't heard the sheriff's sluggish voice again, hollering from the kitchen opening down the steps:

"Hey, Agent! Ya down there right now?"

"I am, Sheriff. Make it quick, though: What is it you need?"

"Need? Nothin'. I got some news fer ya there, though. The Doc jus' fin'ly callt back. Doc Campbell, that is."

"Doc Campbell?"

"Yeah, the autipsy guy up at the hospital there, like I tolt you—The cor'ner is what I mean."

Sidney moved to the foot of the steps. The sheriff was standing twelve feet above, backlit in the doorway from the kitchen, looking eagerly, and a little urgently, down.

"OK, well—can it wait a bit? I'm kind of antsy to get a look inside that room, and…."

"Where's the room you mean there, Agent? Where that there light's a-comin' from?"

"Uh-huh. I found a fuse box and got the lights in there to work. Come on down and take a look with me if you like. But … can we go over the coroner's findings a little later? Give me— oh—maybe fifteen minutes or so to look around that room. Hang tight for fifteen minutes, Sheriff, and then I'll…."

"No, sir—NO-O-O-O, S-I-R! you ain't a-gonna wanna wait fer THIS, Agent Braman—You're gonna wanna hear *this* li'l piece-a info right straight off."

The sheriff was ploddingly descending as he talked; wheezing and waddling at his customary pace. And once he finally made it to the basement floor, breathless, he put one hand out and raised it up to grasp Sidney's shoulder: a firm grasp, yet a gentle grasp, as if in preparation.... But in preparation for *what*?

For the gesture seemed exceptionally odd. The two men hadn't physically touched before—well, except for that soggy hand clasp back in the courthouse offices by way of introduction, when the paunchy sheriff had said hello and risen from his desk. Thus the shoulder clasp seemed sort of strange and out of place. It seemed considerate, though, in a weirdly curious way; and oddly familiar in a different and very wrenching way. A detective had grasped him in just that selfsame manner ten long years ago—in *his* office, at *his* desk up in Bramancorp's private administrative floor—though he didn't like to think of that these ten years past, and very rarely allowed himself to do so. But he shook the bad thoughts off abruptly with a shrug, and asked at last, feeling a growing sense of urgency:

"Well what is it, Sheriff? What's the problem? Holy Moses, man—Tell me in a word or two so I can get on with...."

"No sir; NO-O, SIR!—You're a-gonna wanna sitcherself down fer this one, Agent. Jes sitcherself right down there on them there steps, so's I can tell ya what Doc Campbell jes got through a-tellin' me on that there cel'lar phone outside when he callt me back."

OK; I give, thought Sidney, and sat compliantly. Something was up for sure, something pretty momentous—so there was no clear benefit in arguing just now. The mysterious room would wait; it wasn't going anywhere today. He looked up at the sheriff from his stair-tread seat and promptly heard the big man say:

"That body? The one me 'n Will took down f'om off that there hook?"

"The one from the basement?—Yes?"

"Doc Campbell there, he said.... You ready fer this one, Agent?—He said that there body ditten have no blood in it."

"Did he? Well, I kind of thought it looked pretty pasty in the photos. The guy bled out from that wound in his chest, that's all. That isn't so unusual, Sheriff. He probably bled out and they cleaned up all the blood—all but those couple of tiny drops we found on the floor."

"No sirree! It IS unushal, though, Agent Braman, it IS! Doc Campbell said he ditten fint even a *little* bit-a blood in there.

Not *none*. There warn't a single droppa blood in 'at 'ere hangin' guy at *all*."

"None?"

"Nope."

"You mean … you're telling me—in the organs *too*?"

"Yep, organs, brain, eyeballs, ever'place. He said it looked like somep'm went and sucked the whole of whatever was in him there a hunnert percent out."

"He said *that*? The doctor said those actual words? That the blood had been evacuated completely?"

"He ditten say 'evacyated'. He said sucked out. F'om the neck. From here." The sheriff pointed at his larynx, but he probably meant the carotid, or the jugular, though it was impossible to determine which. "He found a sorta pun'ture in the neck—he's the one callt it a 'pun'ture'—the place all 'at blood got sucked out through. All of it, he said. The som'bitch was bone dry."

"Wait a minute; hold on a minute. So what you're saying is…. Well, what did the doctor think had happened then?"

"You b'lieve in vampires, Agent Braman?"

"Sure. Same as I believe in werewolves and little green creatures from outer space. And tooth fairies too—don't leave them out. And … what else? Angels, demons, Santa and his reindeer and elves, green cheese in the moon?—Hey, come on now, Sheriff! Don't tell me that you—you and your coroner friend, I mean—don't tell me that you guys actually believe…."

"How else you gonna try an' explain a crazy thing like 'at?"

"I *can't* explain it—not just yet, anyway. That's why I'm chomping at the bit to get inside that room…. I'll tell you one thing, though, Sheriff Stoner: Somebody jumped out an upstairs window the morning of the fire—I'll show you the tracks that I'll need your guys to follow to see where the hell the person went….

"But, bottom line, another guy was here that morning— that's for sure; no myths or legends or fairy tales. Another *guy*, I'm saying because he had a man's watch that I came across, and a man's shoes, that I discovered the tracks of—And he made it out through a bedroom window across the hall from the burned man's room.

"And if that other guy was the kind of vampire you and your doctor buddy have been expecting from the B-grade movies and the two-buck novels all those writers of purple prose turn out, you're gonna be seriously chagrined: All that blood you think the guy sucked out didn't help him the least little bit getting down from that upstairs window—Your vampire couldn't sprout a pair of wings and fly worth a hunk of shit!"

The sheriff looked considerably abashed at that particular juncture, and seemed not a little desperate to get his bulky butt upstairs. So Sidney tapped him on the shoulder for encouragement, and watched his trembling back for him as he plodded up the steps.... After which, with an impatient smile and an inevitable muttering of his trademark 'Holy Moses!' he—finally—*finally!*—shook his head and pursed his lips and headed for the freezer door.

So into the freezer and past its double openings into the cool mysterious room, he beat a hasty path. He had light now aplenty inside the hidden room—overheads, spots: the lot glowing bright as noonday sunshine—And all those secret little nooks and crevices that the flashlight had failed to expose in sufficient detail would be revealed now, in full illumination as plain as brilliant day. Here was a world-class mystery the likes of which even Sidney Braman had never, ever seen before, until today. And he was probably about to take a giant leap forward in solving the most perplexing criminologic riddle he'd encountered these ten years past. He truly couldn't wait!

What he'd tenuously glimpsed with that expiring flashlight bulb, had been a large-ish room with lots and lots of books. But now that he had actually stepped into the place with the overhead lights ablazing bright; now that he had crouched a bit to get his six-three frame in safely through the secret door—The capacious *size* of the room; the enormous *quantity* of books! Uncounted *thousands* of them! Volumes by the shelf-full, by the wall-full, by the *room*-full. As much material as many an academic library might hold; and all in meticulous, orderly array.

It was a snug room, despite its size, its dimensions commensurate with the remainder of the basement, thirty-some by thirty-some by a generous twelve feet high; and the books festooning the bookshelves gave it an atmosphere of comfy elegance and warmth. The walls were literally stuffed with books, three of the four walls covered with shelving from floor to ceiling, practically groaning under the burden of the volumes' ponderous weight: cloth-bound, leather-bound, ancient folios, brand new shiny-jacketed releases; then the occasional paperback here and there: The effect of it gave the room a snug and homey feel, a discernible warmth, and a pleasant wood-and-leathery sort of smell.

There was a dark red chesterfield sofa at one end of what was probably a fifteen-by-twenty Persian rug, and a couple of wing chairs straight across covered in the same red leather to complement the red and navy carpet on the floor. Then recessed cherry paneling on the single wall devoid of shelves; and against the paneled wall, with a tufted leather swivel chair pulled up to it, was an enormous cherry desk....

Oh, and a computer on the desk, by the way—which Sidney noticed with a quickening pulse and a right-out-loud "Aha!"—And which he started over to instinctively ... until he stopped and reconsidered: Systematic investigation always—everything in its proper time and place: First the obvious evidence sitting smack-dab in your face, then the secondary data—electronic and otherwise. He'd get to the computer when the other, simpler investigational inspection was done.

So first the books: He walked along the shelves, scanning them from top to bottom, side to side: Every academic subject in the world—and out of it, as well. History, art, literature, music, biologic science, physical science, geology, astronomy, loads of texts of medicine; old books, new books, leather, cloth, and paper. There were math books, compendia on architecture, texts of chemistry, economics, and law. Every branch of human knowledge, a library of the most essential readings of all time; all organized by subject, then alphabetically by author or chronologically by historic time.

The books had been read too, the lion's share of them. Sidney plucked a few off the shelves at random. All the ones he opened had been opened before, repeatedly, thumbed visibly, many of their pages folded over or otherwise marked indelibly as often used and read. Holy Moses! Finotti—if this fellow Finotti was the true proprietor of such a house and such a room—or the man who'd leapt from the window, if the place was really his—whatever person it had been who'd used this room—had been so broadly lettered as to have been a sort of polymath, a renaissance scholar right up there with the smartest of the smart, the most highly educated of the Harvard elite. A mental colossus who, with all those mammoth brains, had been fit enough to press four hundred pounds as well! Intellect and might combined: If Finotti was the homicidal villain he showed evidence of having been, it was lucky as hell the guy was dead. If he *wasn't* really dead—if the burned corpse wasn't his—or if that other unknown leaper-from-the-window had been the actual owner of the place—If the user of that basement and that oven remained alive—at large— Holy Moses!—The FBI had a full-scale homicidal nightmare on its hands!

Sidney's neck was sopping wet, and his hands felt moist within their rubber gloves. And it was with soggy collar and saturated palms that he finally set himself down at the enormous desk before the computer screen to finish up the long day's fascinating work. He checked the drawers out first, briefly, cursorily, once more to be complete: Pens, paper, a magnifying glass—those nondescript, anonymous sorts of desk-borne things. But nothing more: No address book, no notepad. And still— incredibly—no evidence of a phone.

So on to the computer then, at last. He raised a finger to the console, and pushed the power button in:

Whir! Brrrp! A little light flashed on, and the monitor came alive, the images coalescing into the customary assortment of generic icons in their orderly vertical rows. Internet, Word, Security: None of them were in the least distinctive or otherwise than plain-old run-of-the-mill stuff. He tried to click on the Internet to see what the proprietor of the place had most recently perused, but there wasn't a remembered password, so that line of investigation was out— at least for now it was—until the digital wizards at the Pittsburgh Bureau Office had a try.

That left the files for him to check—if there were any stored in the hard-drive's memory, and if they could be accessed without some other cryptic password he didn't know. He clicked MY COMPUTER, and up flashed the standard road map. He clicked DRIVE C, hoping against hope for something—*anything*— and....

Whoa—Files! The hard drive was thoroughly awash in files. Five hundred gigs of memory in the super-capacious storage, and nearly sixty percent of it was filled! Holy Moses! Practically a Library of Congress of information in the overburdened thing: more than a hundred individuals could assimilate in a hundred lifetimes; *way* more than their Pittsburgh office kept on file....

But what was *in* there?—*What*?

MY DOCUMENTS: That was the logical place to start, and that was the option he selected next—CLICK!—And he knew in a fraction of a second that he'd just struck data gold!

Zip! Whirr! Brrrp! There sprang up a lengthy shopping list: Countries of the world, top to bottom on the page, and, under USA, all fifty states, plus Guam, Puerto Rico, and DC. He clicked on Pennsylvania: a natural choice: Why not start with the most familiar first?

Zip! Whirr! Brrrp! Another lengthy list: The statewide file divided into counties alphabetically. He clicked on Allegheny, right there poised and waiting at the top: That was Pittsburgh and environs—starting with the most familiar, as before—Obvious choice again; why not?

A list of names came up—personal last names, alphabetically displayed, just like the county list. 'Aaron' was the first, two of them, denoted D. and K.; then 'Abarth,' and on and on from there. The file scrolled down forever, it seemed. By the time he had made it to the end of 'A's and beginning with the initial 'B's, the little indicator bar at the side of the column had scarcely moved. A thousand names, perhaps, possibly more, judging from the diminutive movement of the side bar. Idly, randomly he scrolled.

'Behrens' ... 'Bhagavan' ... 'Bittern' ... 'Bjornson' ... a litany of names. Likely many *more* than a thousand in the file, just for Allegheny County alone—whoever they were, whatever they represented —'Black' ... 'Bohm' ... 'Brackens' ... 'Braden' ... 'Braman'....

Braman?!

Was that ... *Braman*?

BRAMAN?!!

What was the name 'Braman' doing here? Holy Moses! This wasn't the Pittsburgh Area Telephone Directory; it wasn't the county tax rolls; it wasn't the voter registration files for Allegheny County residents—No: Here was no all-inclusive group of names of little meaning or portent: It was a selective, deliberative list—a thousand or so names purposefully collated from a populace of well over a million. Collated for what specific purpose, he didn't have a clue. But it was certainly a list of *something*—of something meaningful to ... well, to a putative murderer; that was pretty clear. And pretty certainly a *mass* murderer, too, with considerable intellect and enormous physical strength.... And there was a *Braman* tucked inside the fellow's lengthy file?! But ... *how*? *Why*?

Holy Moses! It wasn't as if Braman was that commonplace a name. It wasn't Smith or Jones or Thompson—Hell, it wasn't exactly Goldberg either, or Levy or Cohen. No, indeed, Sidney didn't know too many other Bramans outside his own exclusive clan—So if there was a Braman on this demonically selected list—well, what in heaven was it *doing* there? Was this one of *their* Bramans?—A relative maybe? Uncle Harvey, possibly? He'd been cozy with a couple of union bosses back in the day, so what if he...? But Uncle Harvey was.... And what if it *wasn't* Uncle Harvey? What if it was ... his dad!

Oh my GOD!

He clicked on the name:

Zip! Whirr!

"Braman, J" said the top of the cover page. J. *Braman!*—But ... but that *was* his dad, for heaven's sake!—Well, but why in blazes should his *father* be on a list like this? Was it a hit list? Could it be? Yes, but Jacob Braman had never hurt a single soul; everybody loved him; even his competitors in business considered him a saint, fair as he'd always been with every individual he'd ever dealt with—always. He'd never cheated, never lied, always on the up and up.... But had he gotten on some murderer's hit list anyway?—Some long-forgotten grievance from his youth? An inept worker dismissed with reason, for reasonable cause, but still disgruntled? Was Jacob's name in this frightening catalogue a credible threat? WAS it?

He scrolled down farther, anxiously, on past the cover page into the introductory body of text: "Braman," said the topmost line ...

"Jodi Braman."

Sidney froze. Every single function in his body shut down; his brain went blank completely—Well, not 'all' the functions, not a particular reflex one: That finger kept on going, scrolling downward on the mouse, as if on cruise control, preset. And as it slowly scrolled he told himself: Oh good God! This had to be the file from ... this had to be the records from....

A picture slid up next when that involuntary finger took the imagery down a little more. The finger moved robotically, automatically, an uncontrollable finger scrolling toward what no adoring husband should ever have to see—These were things that Sidney had never, ever glimpsed before; this text, these ghastly images. *Horrific* images! His dad had told him, with tearful eyes and protective hands upon his shoulders: "Better not, Sidney. It won't serve any purpose for you to look."

And he *hadn't* looked. All these years he hadn't looked, though the file had rested back there in the Bureau Archives all the while, residing in the UNSOLVED cabinets with several hundred more.

And here it was in all its graphic detail—the FBI file on Jodi, digitized and unexpurgated and complete, graphic and unsparing. He had seen on this strange computer in a strange house deeded to a strange, dead man found roasted in a fire, what he had never before allowed himself to see.

And now that he had seen it, now that those long-neglected images were etched into his mind, inexpugnable forever, he put his head down in his hands, rested his elbows on the elegant cherry desk, and for the first time in ten long years, gave vent to an interminable plenitude of sobs.

8

The boy stopped and turned and glared in his direction, then started across the street.

A sort of run-of-the-mill, penny-ante tough kid, small but muscular enough in a juvenile sort of sense, with a chip on his shoulder that you could spot a mile away: A young boy, mid- to late-teens, but with the face of a full-grown man with a full-blown grievance graven there: A raging adolescent with tautened lips, predatory eyes, flaring nostrils: the whole incendiary ball of wax—bad vibes by the cartload. The kid looked baby-faced enough that he should have been in school at quarter-to-ten on an autumn Thursday morning, but wasn't. There was bound to be a reason for that.

Nothing about the fellow looked familiar; no question that he'd never seen the boy before. But on he came, for whatever unknown reason; charging like a maddened bull, with that boxer's baby face and hostile stance, dodging his angry way among the traffic passing by. There was trouble in the making, certainly. Whatever the cause, whatever unknown issue had fluffed the little fellow's feathers, it would be appropriate to be prepared.

Oh, not that the kid posed all that terrible a threat: Even if he had a weapon—well, short of a firearm, at any rate—he wouldn't be that big a challenge to disarm. And weaponless, as he clearly appeared to be there in the middle of the blacktop, chomping at the bit, waiting for a dawdling moving van to pass—without a gun, without a hatchet or machete—hell, once he made it past the vehicles and got up close, you could probably knock him over with a finger to the larynx or a fist below the xiphoid. That would floor him fast enough, put him down for the duration. But still, any confrontation out here in the open would cause a devil of a scene—and *if* it caused a scene....

No, it wouldn't do at all to have a scene. That would ruin everything. There had to be a peaceful way to settle whatever needed to be settled. And as he tried to think of one, and wondered what the hell had set the fellow off, and set himself to neutralize the onslaught if the peaceful gesture failed.... As he prepared himself for—whatever—

He felt the girl's fragile little body tensing up.

She was mid- to late-teens too, same age—give or take a year or so—as the roughhouse boy. Not particularly noticeable until now, poor thing, though she'd stood an inch or two away these several minutes past. Standing there beside him at the bus stop, with her floppy mouse-brown hair and schoolyard nest of freckles on her cheeks, the girl had scarcely drawn a glance from anyone around. But now that he turned to take a look at her, it struck him that she was, more than anything, emphatically and assertively ... plain.

Plain as anonymity itself, plain as an off-white placard on a whitewashed wall; Not particularly ugly, not especially attractive, bland as saltless soup or soggy bread: not the type of girl a vengeful juvenile delinquent would pay the least attention to. Yes, clearly the case—But she knew the fellow well enough— it was obvious that she did. She made a sort of whimper as the moving van passed on and the boy inched closer; then the girl reached up to grasp the nearest point of human contact within range—this being the neighboring elbow to her right—*his* elbow—clutching it impersonally, in desperation, like a drowning swimmer reaching for a lifeline tossed out from a passing ship.

And as the boy came fully halfway across the street toward her, then onward farther, five or six quick steps away, she uttered in a tiny voice, practically inaudible:

"Oh God! Oh God, not now!"

OK; all right, then—so it was *this* pathetic little thing the boy was after, and not the big strong grownup at her side—Fine, then, that made a whole lot better sense; that at least cleared the issue up, made the situation comprehensible—

But it didn't help the problem out one bit. Whatever unknown vengeance the angry little bruiser had set his bad vibes on, there was *still* inevitably bound to be a scene—And the one thing impermissible right now would be a scene. Not now, not here, not today, this Thursday, of all the least auspicious sites and days....

And so he asked the girl, quite quickly, while the boy stood furiously waiting for the last of the intervening vehicles to pass:

"Is there a problem, miss?"

80

"Huh?"

"Are you OK? Is anything wrong?"

She grasped the elbow tighter, leaning into the elbow's owner at her side. But that final passing driver honked his horn and hit the gas and drove on past; and the boy came charging through the empty lane and right straight up to her before she had a chance to answer what her elbow-mate had asked: Right in her face he stuck his own pug face, the kid six inches below her on the blacktop, she atop the curb, so that his height advantage was negated by the difference; and they were nearly nose to nose and raptor's eye to prey: And in that taut geography of confrontation the rabid, foam-mouthed youngster screamed at her in furious treble pitch:

"Bitch! You dirty BITCH!"

The fellow grabbed her by an arm, pulling her violently toward him off the curb, she pulling the lifeline-of-an-elbow along with her. "BITCH!" the young man hollered once again, even louder, and went to raise a hand. Behind them, several of the men and women in the line backed off or turned away. Not their business, obviously; just what you'd expect. Vibeless to the last, as usual, the lot of them. No one intervened....

Until *he* did. *He* got involved; his *elbow* got involved. And even if the elbow hadn't, it wouldn't do at all to have a battle in the street like this: not here, not now, not today. A battle in the street would beg attention, lead to inconvenient questions being asked, personal documentation of each eyewitness being required—particularly in light of the elbow's intimate involvement here—documentation of which he had not the faintest, slightest shred.

So no scene now, today, in this specific set of circumstances; that was impossible; it simply wouldn't do. And so around in front of the girl he stepped, a long pace forward, and grabbed the boy by the upraised forearm with his right hand while he ushered the girl back up safely on the curb with his left. And as he did this, he turned and told her in a calm and quiet voice as he held the boy at bay, struggling vainly:

"Keep my place in line, OK?"

"Yeah ... OK ... sure, mister—Thanks! Sure."

He held the boy with his fist around that upraised sweatshirted forearm, holding very tight, and the other hand ascending to the fellow's neck. The neck grasp did the job effectively enough. Right above the trapezius, pinching hard into the spinal muscles. Enough pain to quiet him down, give him something other than the girl to fix his angry focus on. Back toward the doorway of the drugstore they went conjoined, twenty feet or so from the girl standing at the Trailways bus stop placard on the corner. And what he told the boy once they got to the drugstore doorway; told the struggling youngster so quietly that no one else could possibly have heard the words he spoke, was:

"I don't know what your problem is, my friend; but right now, and for the next ten minutes till the bus takes off, you're going to leave that girl alone."

"I *ain't*! She's nothin' but a goddam...."

He tightened his fingers' pressure on the neck. Not enough to snap it like that cleanup job he'd finished off last night—not quite—That would take both hands to do things properly—but plenty tight enough to get the kid's attention to an awful lot of pain.

"Listen to me, fellow—You listening?"

The boy gave a questionable nod. A more conspicuous nod would have been pretty nigh undoable for him, with his neck compressed and bound the way it was.

"Now I'm going to let you go—you listening?—and when I do, you're going to walk away. Quietly and calmly—you understand? Not another word, not another gesture; don't even turn around. If you run, no matter how fast you run, I'm going to catch you, and you don't want to be caught—I can assure you of that. But I'm going to let you go now, and you're going to walk away down the street, calmly and quietly, and not come back until the bus leaves with the girl and me on board. If you don't do what I say—precisely to the letter—the discomfort that you're feeling in your neck is going to seem like the greatest pleasure you've ever known compared to what I do to you next. Now walk; don't run; straight down the street and around the corner till I can't see you anymore. And don't let me *ever* see you again—*Ever*—you hear me?—Not here, not *anywhere*. Now go!"

He relaxed his grip and the boy left, quietly and calmly, as ordered. He didn't look back, he didn't hesitate; but walked slowly halfway down toward the next corner, then sped up a bit, then pretty nearly ran. He turned the corner at a frenzied sprint, and didn't reappear.

Back in line behind the girl he went; the tall man beside her stepped aside to clear the way. No one looked at him; no one spoke. *No* one—well, other than the girl, that is, who stared up at his face with a grateful little smile and told him shyly:

"Thanks, mister. The thing that happened with that kid is...."

"Never mind, young lady; no reason to explain. Whatever grievance he's got is between you and him, and I'm sure you'll settle it yourselves in time. Thanks for keeping my place in line, though.... So—The bus'll probably be here soon, shouldn't it? Doesn't it leave at ten?"

"It's supposed to. They told me ten when I bought the ticket. But look, mister, about that kid: It's not what you probably think. What happened was...."

"No, no. No explanation required. Really." He waved her off, and she offered nothing more before they finally climbed on board.

At 9:55, right on the nose as promised, the Trailways Coach pulled up and the driver pushed the button to release the door. He stood behind the girl, second in the little line, and boarded immediately after her. She dropped her backpack on a seat in the second row, then slid in next to it, smiling up at him as he passed her by to take a seat down toward the back. After two or three more passengers had boarded, there was a delay: An elderly, grotesquely heavy woman with a Samsonite suitcase and a cane struggled up the steps, assisted by a younger man behind. While she was struggling, the girl got up, grabbed the backpack, and moved eight or nine rows rearward to the seat in front of his. The immense old woman got seated just behind the driver, the rest of the few remaining riders climbed aboard within a minute more, and the driver was just about set to shut the door and head off down the street toward blessed safety when....

The Paxton Police car drove up.

He didn't remember uttering as much as a single sound; he wasn't certain if he'd moved an inch. But there must have been *something* that he did or said or gave off in a vibration to let the girl know. A cough, perhaps; a clearing of the throat, a quickening of the breath—He couldn't say precisely *what*, either then or later. But there had to have been some unconscious clue....

For she turned around and looked at him, looked him up and down, knowingly, purposefully; then turned back toward the window, watching the police car as it stopped and parked across the road and the two young cops got out and crossed the halted traffic toward the bus.

There was scarcely time to think; instinct for survival would somehow have to get him through—as it had done innumerable times before. He looked about him, scanning the various options to the sides, up front, and to the rear. The back door of the bus was closed—it hadn't opened during boarding— But twenty-odd feet forward stood the front door that was standing open wide. If he moved right now, this instant, he could make it out, just barely, before the dawdling pair of officers came close and made it in. If he made it to the door—say he made it to the door—once he hit the street, he was absolutely positive he could outrun them both—for a while—maybe dodge into a hiding place somewhere; shimmy up a drainpipe to a rooftop, perhaps—for his knee was a hundred percent healed by now— On the roof, or hidden in an alley somewhere, he might wait it out till nighttime came and the darkness obscured things, when it would be safe for him to move again.

Ah yes, but there would be more police called in, of course: the state boys, the experts, maybe a relentless pack of dogs. They would have a description by then; thirty pairs of eyes had clearly seen him round about the town. No good options under such a set of circumstances; not a one—Still, if he made it to the door and outside to the street, made it to the corner where the boy had turned—There was still a little time, and if he moved right now, this instant, at least he'd have a chance.

He clambered up out of his seat and grabbed his little bag from the overhead bin and took one step up the aisle—one hesitant but thoroughly determined step ... when the freckled, brown-haired, not-all-that-pretty teenaged girl grabbed his arm and pulled him toward her forcefully, so that he stumbled onto the seat atop her backpack: which she pulled away from under him, set atop her lap, and in the quietest of voices told him:

"It's OK. I know them. Don't be afraid."

"Know *who?*"

"Just sit still and let me talk, and go along with everything I say. Don't say anything yourself, though—not a word."

Her face was stoically immobile, rigidly controlled, and her hands, resting on her lap, stayed calm and still throughout. He glanced aside at her through the corner of his eye. Undistinguished in her looks, but the kid was bright—or *more* than that, the kid was brilliantly intuitive, a brilliant intuition he had experienced once before and one time only in darling little Jennifer. Like Meredith and Jennifer, this clever girl would do her all to help him if she could, but whether it was in her power to help or beyond her utmost ability, that he didn't know.

Fifteen seconds had elapsed by now; escape was over with and done. The first officer had just reached the bottom step: he wasn't in a rush. The other stood outside the bus, along the curb, his hand resting on his pistol case, anticipating something sudden and significant, one might naturally assume. The officer at the entry door said a word or two to the driver, something not quite discernible from this far back in the bus, then climbed the metal steps. The driver turned the ignition off and shut the door, making it eerily silent on the bus, all but for the hiss of chilly air coming out the vents above. And in this hushed, expectant atmosphere, the policeman faced about and addressed the passengers with:

"Hey, folks: Sorry for the delay. This stuff'll only take a minute or two, though. Me and Officer Torenson are gonna need your cooperation for a bit. We just got a call from headquarters instructing us to check the passengers on every bus leaving Paxton both ways. There's an all-points bulletin out for...."

The rest of the speech was rendered indecipherable by the pulse-beat in his ears: 'Whoosh!' it went, 'Whoosh-whoosh!'—*Think*, he told himself—*think*—*THINK!* ... He glanced back over his shoulder. There was an exit behind the hindmost seat: it could be forced, not all that hard to do most likely—but getting back and opening it would take a lot of time: No chance there; that would be impossible to manage this late in the game—So how about the windows then? They could be pushed out in the event of an accident; all public conveyances were designed that way. If he moved right now, leapt over to the vacant seat behind and got the window opened up, then chanced to make it through; there would be the fellow with the pistol to contend with, but....

"Relax," said the girl. "Just chill, OK?" She spoke in a guarded voice, inaudible a foot or more away, and kept that death grip on his arm. "Just trust me, sir—OK? It's gonna be all right—I promise you it will. But if you don't calm down, though, Ronnie there is gonna notice you, and that'll be the end of it; he'll come back here for sure. So just sit tight like I told you to, and do what I said to do. Keep still and don't say anything and it'll be OK. Just sit there and let me talk."

Too late now; no other option left to him. Well, he could grab the fellow's gun, no problem there—but if something went wrong—if some innocent passenger was shot and killed; No, that couldn't be an option. But what other option was left to him? What—WHAT?

The heartbeat in his ears rose to a crescendo: Whoosh! Whoosh! Twice a second the strident whooshing came. The officer up the aisle was checking every passenger, though casually, asking for a photo ID, being unusually polite—He knew these small-town folks, most likely—The huge old lady in the front who'd stumbled in and caused the regrettable delay opened her purse and gave the officer a sort of card—a driver's license or whatever—which he glanced at for a fraction of an instant before he passed it back and paid her with a hesitating smile. Then he proceeded to the man in the seat immediately behind, the middle-aged fellow who had helped the plump old lady board.

Down the narrow aisle the policeman came, one passenger at a time: Six rows away: "Thank you, ma'am." Then four: "Thank you, sir." Then two: "Thank you, ladies." Then:

"*Hey*, Ronnie, how ya *doin'*?"

"Oh, hi, Linnie. I didn't notice you before. How's things? What did the doctors say about your mom?"

"That's just it. I'm on my way to see her now. Down in Pittsburgh. She got admitted there. We're—oh, this is my cousin Vaclav who flew in last week from Slovakia to see my mom and me and help out with a bunch of stuff. He's Mom's uncle's kid; he doesn't know a lot of English, just a couple of words here and there—But Mom's bad, Ronnie, really bad. I don't know what we're gonna do; honestly I don't. I don't know how to handle any of this, you know? Nothing prepares you for a shock like this."

"Yeah, I know, I know. Look, I...."

"You need to see our ID? I'll get my wallet out of the backpack."

"Are you kiddin'? Don't you think I know you well enough, Linnie? Chrissakes! It's just for strangers and stuff—Hey, tell your mom I said hello, OK? And Carol too; I think of her a lot. And good luck with everything—Hey, give your mom my love. And tell your uncle it was nice of him to help you guys out—You speak Sylvakian?"

"*Slo*vakian—I know a few words; that's all. But I'll try and tell him, Ronnie. Thanks."

Three more passengers in the rows behind: "Thank you, sir." "Thank you, ladies." And the officers drove off, letting the bus get under way.

Whew! Incredible! His brow was literally dripping; his shirt was sopping wet. "I ... Linnie, is it?"

"Lynette, actually. It's an awful name, I know. Sounds like a country music star."

"OK, Lynette; well, I don't know.... I'm not sure...."

"Look, mister—sir—You don't need to thank me, if that's what you're trying to do. I really owed you one, a really, really big one, and it was great to have a chance to pay you back."

"But how did you figure out that I...? How could you possibly sense that...?"

"Hey, I'm not a total idiot, you know—And even a total idiot can sometimes read between the lines. Actually, the teachers think I'm pretty smart, if you want to know the truth, sir—All A's in school and—I even won a science prize last year."

"All right, well, anyway: I could have said a few things in Slovak if you'd given me a chance—And, by the way, you need to understand that I'm not a threat to you. Whatever the officers are looking for, whatever they think I might have done, you need to know I'd never hurt you or any of the other people here in any way."

"Hey, I know that. I can tell—But ... you mean you speak Slovakian? You actually do?"

"I speak a lot of languages, sure; Slovak happens to be one of them—So ... anyway—that stuff about your mother: Is she really ill?"

"Yeah, 'fraid so. I'd never make something like that up. The other stuff was pretty easy to come up with, though. My grandpa—Mom's dad, that is—he's from Slovakia, and his brother's name was Vaclav, so I didn't have to think too hard about *that* part of the story."

"You did great, young lady. There's a decent likelihood you saved my life—honestly—So let me ask you: Is there something *else* that I can do for you? Some other little favor that you need?"

"Hey, you've done a ton already. That awful kid—What happened was—let me explain it so you know—What happened was, I saw him break into one of the neighbors' places down the block. He's kinda known for that sorta thing, but I happened to see him do it late one night. So I called 9-1-1 and Ronnie came—the cop back there who asked about my mom and stuff—Ronnie used to date my sister—She's married now and lives in North Dakota, but he still asks about her all the time. I guess he still likes her after all these years—So anyway...."

"Anyway," he offered, interrupting, "I had an inkling that kid was a public threat. I guess I get the picture well enough. But tell me about your mother, though. What kind of illness does she have?"

The girl declined to answer. She teared up and turned her face away, staring out the left-hand window toward the passing scenery as it flitted by, leaving nothing but the mouse-brown hair in view. He didn't press her. A couple of minutes passed in unremitting silence as the bus veered onto the Interstate and accelerated up to speed. And once they were going sixty and merged comfortably into the company of vehicles in the right-hand lane, she turned her face to him again, wiped her eyes with a pair of tomboy knuckles, and tremulously told him:

"She's—my mom, I mean—she's scheduled to have some operation tomorrow, and...." At which point the poor kid's verbiage stalled; and she began to quake and sob—not audibly, so anyone could hear it, but in agonizing silence, the pathetic silence of her weeping making the sadness she exhibited that much harder to be borne. She sobbed like that in silence a good long poignant while; but eventually the muted sobs let up and the quaking got controlled—enough for her to be receptive, at any rate—And once she seemed receptive to a manageable degree, he told her:

"Look, Lynette—Linnie—If it's too hard for you to talk about, that's OK. I don't want to intrude. Don't say anything more if it upsets you; but I just thought that—well, I know a good bit about medical things, and I thought that maybe...."

"You *do*?" Her face brightened visibly, though the tears flowed on. "Are you a doctor or something?—You sure don't *look* like a doctor."

"No? Well I'm not—technically speaking, that is—not *now*, I mean, not anymore; but I've got a decent working knowledge when it comes to the mechanics of disease. So I thought that—well, maybe I can help you and your mother with some advice. A lot of people don't get handled properly by the medical community these days, and I might be able to tell you what kinds of questions you and your mother need to ask. Patients and their families usually don't ask the right questions, and they suffer for it in the end."

She wiped her eyes again, the tear production lessened now, and queried:

"OK, so—like what?"

"What kinds of questions, do you mean? Well, first you'll need to tell me something about your mother's condition. What kind of operation is she having done?"

The tears again, fresh and copious, and the attendant delay. This time the episode was brief, however, and when it passed:

"Mom's got ... she's got ... cancer."

"She does, does she? Well, I'm sorry to hear that; I genuinely am. Maybe I can help you, though. I'd really like to help in some way if I can—So—All right then; can you tell me any more? Do you know what type of cancer it is? Where it started?—What organs are involved, I mean."

"It's ... in her liver, they said. I remember one of the doctors saying that."

"OK; that's not the cheeriest news I'd want to hear; but—do you know whether the tumor *started* in the liver?—Or did it spread there from someplace else?"

"Spread, I think. I think the doctor told us that it spread."

"All right, that's not great either—But ... do you happen to know where it started?—the primary site?"

"You mean before it got to her liver? Umm, well she had a lot of bleeding—when she went to the bathroom to move her bowels, I mean. So maybe that was where the cancer started up."

"Uh-huh, that's probably right; so then—from what you've said so far—it sounds like a colon tumor, I'd guess. If it was bright red blood, it probably came from the colon—Which is good, relatively speaking: Colon tumors are less aggressive than some of the other primaries—more responsive to treatment, that means—But the liver involvement isn't all that good—I'll be honest with you there, young lady—Do you happen to know what the doctors intend to *do* tomorrow?—the kind of surgery they've got planned?"

"No; just that she's having the operation done tomorrow; I don't really know what kind."

"All right, it's not a major problem if you don't exactly know; we'll figure things out from what you *do* know. So, first of all, do you know if she's had any prior treatment up to now? Any chemotherapy or radiation or other interventional procedures like that?"

"No, I'm pretty sure she hasn't. They were gonna do that after the operation tomorrow, I think. In the next few weeks, I mean."

"Good. That's definitely a major plus. OK, look: I'm going to write down a list of things for you to ask the doctors—that you and your mother should ask, I mean—and if the treatment doesn't correspond to what I write—if it deviates in any even minimal way from what I specify—you may want to have your mother hold off on the operation tomorrow and get a second opinion. I'm pretty sure, from what you've told me, that there's no need for either of you to rush. A week or two's delay won't make a lot of difference, so you've got a bit of time."

"OK, but … well do you think she'll be all right then? Is there anything we can do that'll make sure she's all right?"

"Yes, as a matter of fact, there *are* things. Lots of things. It's a little complex, and a little difficult to explain, but I'll tell you this: Most doctors have a faulty understanding of the principles of cancer. More often than not, the treatment they recommend only makes things worse. If I only had…. If it were only a week ago and I had my equipment and my place—If I could have taken your mother to where I had my things, I'm pretty sure I could have…. "

She poured over his face with those big wide wet imploring eyes of hers, pathetically beckoning, and he turned away and stopped a while and thought. Then he nodded to himself in making up his mind—there wasn't any other option, after all; what else could he do?—and looked back at the sad young girl, and gave a nod, and tapped her on the forearm definitively, offering:

"But all right; never mind all that; never mind the troubles that I've had. Look, young lady, you absolutely saved my life today, and I really owe you something special in return, so—What I'm going to do for you—for you and your mother, I mean—is this: I'm going to…. I suppose I can catch the bus tomorrow just as easily as today; one more day in Pittsburgh won't be a problem in the end.

"So what I'm going to do for you is this: I'm going to go with you to the hospital to meet your mom. Maybe I can help her—actually, I'm really pretty certain I can help her if we get a little luck and find the things we're going to need. If you trust me and go along with what I try to do—though it'll be a major challenge for us to put things together at such short notice....

"But OK, anyway: If you go along with what I recommend, and don't ask any questions, and don't tell anyone afterward what we did—you'll have to swear to me right now that you won't—

"But if you promise to keep things quiet and if I can manage to scrounge together what we need, I'm pretty sure that you and I together, if you're willing to help out a little bit, can give your mother the treatment that she needs to truly make her well."

9

Madam was as cranky as a rattlesnake this morning, and in her nasty fit of crankiness, she cut up Wilson's arm.

Those nails of hers!—Far better than the knife of course: At least she never tried to use the knife on *him*—not yet, at any rate—But then again, she needed him. Without him, she'd have to do things on her own, to fend for herself, go out in the world, get noticed and remarked and commented on—which was unthinkable for Madam, for sure.

So no, she needed him and would never think to use the knife to do him harm. She hadn't needed Brother when she'd stabbed *him* in the chest—What use was he to her by then?—what with another Helper on the hook to do her will?—So as for Brother, usefulness was not an issue when she'd stabbed him with the knife. But as for Wilson himself, all lobotomized and fit to suit her needs: Yes, he was relatively safe: that was what he thought.

Those nail marks, though: quite unsightly—And so he taped some gauze across his forearm skin, lest the doctor pay it heed, and headed out. And *as* he headed out, and idled slowly through the gate, and pushed on the remote to swing it closed … he saw a man.

Same man as the other day, tall and rangy, incipiently gray, mid-fortyish, dressed for playing golf, standing in the exact same spot he stood the time before, nearly to the inch. A spot where someone standing in that specific place, peering from that specific angle, could look in through the iron railings of the gate and see the frontal windows of the house, upstairs and down. Madam had seen him looking at the house a week ago and asked who he might be, and where his house might be, assuming it was near. A neighbor, she assumed; and that was logical, so far as Wilson had concluded for himself; for Wilson had observed him down the road a couple of times before, supervising the yard work on his home or merely going for a walk with that big brown dog of his that Madam had caught a couple of weeks ago and done her bloody will with out on the lawn.

A neighbor, then; probably wondering about that handsome missing dog of his, thinking maybe that it might have wandered onto the property and disappeared—as the local animals quite often *did* disappear, what with Madam on the lookout and way too ready with her knife on the feisty days when her blood ran full and Wilson on an errand, say; and no one therefore home to intervene.

And that damaged section of the wall out to the side that the occasional domestic pet strayed through, to its inevitable demise. And now and then a child—less often though, thank heavens!—never to emerge again but as a gritty residue of liquid run out viscid through the shredding mill. Like that little girl a month or two ago with the frilly dress and pretty round-toed shoes—She too—which had been a close run thing, all right, what with the law and all their snooping round the neighborhood the first week afterward, until he (Wilson himself, thinking on his feet before the warrant got agreed to by a judge)—yes, until he came up with that clever little ruse to put them off the scent.

Oh, and then that other little girl a couple of years ago, poor thing; and the two religious canvassers going door to door—though no one had ever come snooping after *them*, thank goodness!—*That* had really been a plus!—Madam always got her way, however, as far as those things went; though it usually took a bit of work on Wilson's part to get her willful way safely straightened out.

Prevention, as he knew quite well, was a whole lot better than trying to fix a problem after the fact. So Wilson stopped there as the heavy gate swung closed behind the Lincoln's trunk; he put the car in park; he rolled the power window down; and with a studied effort at politeness asked the man:

"Yes. Hello there. May I help you, sir?"

"Perhaps you might. I'm looking for a dog." The man pretty nearly growled that final syllable-of-a-word, in the tone and nature of his big brown lately butchered dog.

"I haven't any dogs, though, and haven't noticed any around. They can't very easily get onto my property, as you can clearly see."

"Oh, but they *can*, though. Don't you know about the break in the wall out around the side?"

"Yes—Yes, I *do*; you're *right*! And I've been meaning to get that fixed quite soon."

"A lot of pets might have wandered through that break, you know. A lot of pets go missing around here."

"Yes, well, I wouldn't know. If they *have* gone missing, I never saw them. Not a one."

"And a little girl too. Did you know about the missing little girl?"

"That was a tragic thing, wasn't it? I read about it in the papers."

"Just *read*? Didn't the police stop by to ask? They sure stopped by *my* place and asked."

"Yes, you're right; right again. They did stop by and ask; but then they found some evidence away from here, I thought. Someplace out on—where was it again?—Several miles away, I thought—A dress or...."

"A lot of people are wondering about that girl and asking about their missing pets, Mr....."

"It's Wilson. Alexander Wilson. Pleased to meet you. And *your* name is?"

"Who lives there with you in that great big shuttered house?"

"With *me*? No one at all; I live alone."

"*Do* you! And who is that person I see in the window from time to time? And on the roof too. One day I thought I saw a tiny little person on the roof."

"Person? Roof? There isn't any person on the roof. Not that I can think of."

"A woman, I think it was, though it's pretty hard to tell. A little, tiny woman with a long black dress. Very short and pale, I'd say."

"I can't think of who you mean, Mr...."

"*Can't* you now. Well maybe we'll have to look into finding out, then. Maybe you've got a bunch of ghosts in there who are killing dogs and making little children disappear. Maybe we'll have to check that problem out for you."

"No, no—A small woman, did you say? That must be the cleaning lady then. I'll ask her if she's seen your dog. What was your name again, sir?"

"A cleaning lady, is it?—One who cleans the roof? That's good to know, Mr. Wilson; interesting to know. Well then, fascinating: A lot of pets seem to disappear around this place;

vanish into thin air, I guess. And little kids as well—that Carson girl and the Jenkins eight-year-old a couple of years ago—cute little thing; you might remember her. It all seems really strange, doesn't it? ... Well, keep an eye out, Mr. Wilson—And I'll keep my eye out too."

Whew! Twenty years, Brother had told him—and that was twenty years ago. Brother had said that twenty years was about as long as it was safe to stay in the same location with no one catching on; and this was—what? Thirty-some at least—closer to forty—that Madam had lived in this big old cloistered home.

They couldn't relocate very far away; not with their dependence on Gonzalez being what it was. But somewhere just out of the city might do, if only for a while: A fresh new start with unsuspicious neighbors, undecimated pets, the little kids all cozy in their comfy homes.

And, too, with Madam growing ever feebler close to her infusion times: So maybe less likely to wander out and make a bloody mess, what with the lawn needing to be hosed and cleaned, and the occasional knocker-at-the-door needing to be put into the shredder, and the authorities' attention needing to be diverted by some impromptu clever ruse.

Yes, someplace close enough to get the drop-offs from Gonzalez every month, yet far enough away to make a brand new start. That's what Wilson thought, robotically and emotionlessly, as he navigated the streets of central Charleston. Today was the doctor day, serving a double purpose: Two tasks in one, thus less time required to be away: Which was far, far better—what with Madam so unpredictable of late—Not herself these past few years, as Brother had predicted long ago.

So over to the doctor, both for his troubled kidneys and to check up on the girl. He had seen it in the papers when she came back to the area last year: Just out of training, said the blurb, setting up her practice here in Charleston—That was last July; and he had shown it to Madam right away, knowing she would want to know. "It's her, Madam, the daughter. It has to be."—"Let me see it, Wilson. Hand it here so I can see."

Keep an eye on her, just in case, Madam had instructed him: "He isn't dead; I know it. And if the girl is here in

Charleston, then he will come here too, sooner or later, mark my words. Be sure and keep her close."

And so he'd called and asked if the brand new doctor would take a patient with problem kidneys, and had been told that, yes, she would; that problem kidneys were, actually, a specialty of hers. So the appointment was made accordingly, and kept thereafter every three months or so, today being the fourth time he would go in for his visit, with his kidneys doing pretty well on the regimen she'd prescribed: a change in diet, saltless food—Which was all right; he didn't much mind what he ate—A nice, smart, caring doctor: Pity if she ultimately came to any harm. But that was up to Madam in the end, of course. One always did as Madam ordered one to do.

"Mr. Wilson?" The young woman at the check-in desk was new and didn't know him to look at, so she had to ask. Have a seat, she said. Please, she said; the doctor is a little bit behind— She always was, it seemed; she being a nice, thorough doctor who took lots of time with him, and probably with the other patients too, and so ran late. She couldn't help but run a little late, sitting so long with her patients, friendly as she was.

He sat beside an old, decrepit man with hollow cheeks and diminishing gray hair. Wilson, of course, rarely talked to anyone if he could help it—but with *this* man, well:

"Say there, feller: Ya here ta see the doc?"

"I am," said Wilson, curtly, though not dismissively; no point in being rude. "And you must be too, I'd assume."

"Naw, not me. Brang me baby brovver in is why I come. Lester got some probbums wiv his kidleys. You here fer kidleys too?"

"Yes, I am. An old condition. I've had it the better part of my life."

"Yer from arount here? I ain't seed ya afore."

"I *am* from around here, actually. I was *born* in Charleston. And you?"

"Not original. Me'n Lester; we come f'om out easta the state. Worked in the mines until we gets retirement checks. Lester—he gets two retirement checks f'om two differn jobs. Lester: He's in the chips, I tell ye. Pays me fer me gas."

Wilson nodded conclusively and picked up a magazine to turn the conversation off. Which worked. The man said nothing else; and ten minutes later the receptionist who didn't know him to look at, took him back into a room.

"Well! Mr. Wilson—Hello there!—How have you been feeling?"

"Just fine, Doctor. No swelling anymore." She was a beautiful woman now, this little girl that he had briefly glimpsed when she was just a skinny kid in school. Beautiful, smart—and pleasant too. She had it all. He smiled at her and thought how nice it would be if Madam never chose to kill her, and he never had to cut apart her joints and toss her in the hopper to chop the remnants up.

"Good, terrific. Any problems with the diet then?"

No, he told her, no problems at all; and she asked him more about his general well-being and his attitude. She always did this sort of thing, however long it took, and did it by herself with no uncaring intermediaries, the way the other doctors used to do things in the past. Hard to find a doctor like that these days.

A nice, considerate doctor; hard to believe it was the selfsame skinny girl he'd seen so long ago. Madam would have killed her back then if she'd had the chance—killed her and her mother too if they hadn't run away—And it seemed strange that this nice girl that Brother had called his little Jenny back in the day—strange that she had come back here of all the thousand practice sites she might have picked to go.

But Madam wasn't that much of a threat to her these days, as hard as it was for her to leave her big old home. Jennifer the doctor was safe now, relatively speaking.

And that was good, since she was a nice, smart, caring doctor, and his kidneys were doing just splendidly under her expert and interested care.

10

Up the steps to Four, out the exit from the stairwell, and over to Forensics' entry door, where Lederer stood waiting, hands in the pockets of that raunchy lab coat, stained around its middle with pathologic stuff you didn't even want to *think* about, let alone agree to touch.

Lederer looked as snooty as he always did, always the know-it-all; that was a given. But there was something somehow different in his face today: A half-begrudging look of softness—one might almost call it sympathy: A decent bet that word was out about a certain agent having seen a certain file on a certain strange computer up in the boonies north and west—Gordon must have heard.

"So what've you got for me, Gordon?" Sidney asked him right off the bat. "I would assume you dug up something helpful by now, huh? We've shipped you three nice fresh corpses these last few days; and I'm dying to learn if you found any connection between them and...."

Lederer cut him off with a proffered handshake and a sympathetic grasp around the arm. Sidney declined the handshake—who knew what that pathologic palm had touched today?—But the arm grasp he accepted with a nod. And Lederer obligingly answered:

"I know, Sidney. Look—everybody in the place knows about that file by now. I'm sorry you had to see it the way you did. I know you never had the heart to look through all that awful stuff before, and so...."

"I didn't. You're right about that, my friend. But now that I *have* looked through it.... OK—well, anyway—you were around back then, Gordon; weren't you? I'm sure you're familiar with the disgusting stuff that's *in* that awful file."

"I *was* here, Sid. My name's on a lot of the reports in there, truthfully; and I remember the findings as though I wrote them yesterday. Better if we don't go there right now, I guess, but—But, anyway—you asked about a correlation—I mean, between the current victims and ... well, and that terrible business ten years ago—So—you really think there actually might *be* one?"

"Hey you tell *me*, buddy boy! I got a killer of who-knows-how-many unaccounted-for dead folks, and he's got a file in his computer on my *wife?*—On my murdered *wife*, I'm saying!—And not just her, Gordon—Not just on Jodi—A whole lot of those other files too: There's a ton of 'em like that in the suspect's hard drive: Unsolved cases, I mean—but not *just* unsolved cases: They're pretty near a hundred percent unsolved *murder* cases; and the ones we've looked through so far are just as goddam grisly as that horror show I wound up getting into—So *yeah*, I *do* think there's likely to be a correlation. And if there *is*, Gordon—If there *is*, my friend—This is what I've been waiting ten long years to find. If I can link these murders to what happened to Jodi...."

Sidney paused and took a long deep breath to get his heart rate slowed to normal once again, then, marginally calmer, went on in a somewhat quieter voice:

"So anyway, Gordon—Let's skip the empathetic bullshit for a while and cut right to the chase—I'm gonna ask you again, my friend: I've sent you three nice corpses so far, the two from Stanleyville a couple of days ago, and then this last kid in the Paxton dumpster from last night. So? What have you got for me on our recent crop of dead guys? I hope to hell it's something extra special good."

Lederer nodded resignedly: "Fine then, Sidney; whatever you say; whatever I can do to help—OK then, skipping the empathy like you said—what I've got is basically a mystery. You sent me one corpse burned to a crisp—OK? And then those two other dead guys where the only thing in common is the identical way they died—All right Sid, look: Let's run back to my office. I want you to take a gander at the films."

So Sidney harrumphed and shrugged and followed sly old Lederer back to the pathologist's inner sanctum in the place. And once they got there, the venerable Gordon Lederer took a seat in the tiny room, and Sidney slipped into a neighboring seat with its arm a foot away; and Gordon clicked a couple of keys, scrolled down a little with the mouse....

And voila! up the rival images came, side by side on the pair of ultra-high-def monitors along the wall: two corresponding lateral X-ray images of the head and upper spine of two entirely different subjects, both of them similarly dead, though having died at significantly different times.

"OK, Sid; the film on the left is your hanging guy from Stanleyville—OK? And the one on the right is the guy they sent down yesterday from Paxton. You see the cleft here?"

Gordon pointed with a pen to the image on the right.

"Just below the skull?" asked Sidney. "Yeah, I see it, sure."

"How 'bout the monitor on the left—You see it there?"

"Yeah, same place, isn't it?"

"It is. Exactly. Neat as a pin, right at C-3. Snapped the fascia of the vertebrae and ripped the cervical cord in two. Both of them must have died right on the spot."

"So it had to be the same perpetrator then, right? Both snapped like that by the exact same pair of hands?"

"Right, Sidney, absolutely right."

"A pretty *strong* pair of hands, wouldn't you say?"

"Yep, damn straight—a regular muscle man. Knew what he was doing too. Textbook, classic style."

"Why classic, Gordon? You ever seen this kind of thing before?"

"Sure. In the military I did. A couple of times overseas. Snapped clean as a whistle at C-3."

Sidney raised those dark Semitic brows of his in puzzled inquisition:

"You mean the *soldiers* killed like this, Gordon? *Our* guys? With their *hands*?"

"No, Sidney; not the soldiers; not the lowly grunts. The soldiers don't get taught this kind of thing."

"Then who?"

"Who?—Special forces is who. CIA operatives learn it too, though not too many of them get as downright proficient as this. Right clean at C-3. The fellow's got it down to an art—So— these two the only ones you got so far?"

"Yeah, well that's what I ran up here to ask you, Gordon. What about...?" He paused to get his diminishing composure back. "What about that case ten years ago—my Jodi: About the spine thing—C-3 and all: Was there...? I mean: Did you find ... or did the lab techs find ...?"

"I don't know, Sid. Better if we don't get too far into the intimate details of the case back then; but suffice to say that there was insufficient evidence at the time for any closer correlation than we've got right now. No definite similarities that I can document, no—But the jury'll have to be out on that stuff for the time."

"OK, Doc. I was hoping for something clearer cut, truthfully; but I've got enough of a link in that file to keep me going anyway. And besides, with all the other victims likely to be out there.... Hey, they told you about the crematory oven, didn't they?"

"I heard about it, but I didn't hear how many times the goddam thing got used."

"We don't know that yet—not for sure, I mean. But I had our techs compute the amount of gas use—they took all the cubic feet supplied and subtracted the consumption necessary to heat the home and heat the water to pretty much average values. The gas company went back and got the figures for the last twenty-some-odd years."

"And?" Lederer's eyes got inordinately wide.

"Twice a month, they figured. Twice a month for roughly twenty years. That's how long the present owner had the place."

"Twenty-four a year for twenty years!? That's—Damn, Sidney! Nearly five hundred people total? Are there that many people *living* up in the boonies there, for Chrissakes?"

"Not anymore, apparently. We're in the process of checking all the local missing persons out for the last two dozen years; when we get some firm statistics I'll let you know. So—you got anything else for me, Gordon? We know the guy that died in the fire wasn't the murderer now; that's abundantly clear. He got cooked to cinders a couple of days before this second kid turned up—right? What do you figure for a time of death for the second guy?"

"The dumpster dude, you mean? The one from Paxton? Oh, I'd say Wednesday late; maybe early Thursday morning. My bet is Wednesday, though." Which was gospel, pretty much; Lederer's estimates were always on the nose.

"But this one—the dumpster guy from Paxton:" Sidney shrugged his shoulders. "He wasn't hanging upside down, the locals told me. Nobody drained the blood out of *this* one—right, Gordon?—this one had a normal fill of blood?"

"Right. This Paxton character just had his neck snapped. Body was full of blood. The other one was killed to use for a donor, Sid; that's iron-clad guaranteed."

"Because of the missing blood, you mean?"

"Yeah, the blood for sure," said Lederer. "You know? We didn't find even the slightest *trace* of blood in that Stanleyville body. Like zero. Looks like it got drained out through the carotid first, then the jugular once the carotid ran dry. There's a couple of neat little puncture wounds in both. Used a fourteen-gauge catheter to drain the blood; that's the size of the holes…. But it's not *just* the blood, Sidney. The blood's only part of what they took. Whoever harvested the blood, harvested a whole lot more besides."

"More? You sure?—Well—like what? The coroner in Stanleyville didn't find anything but the blood that seemed to be removed."

"He didn't notice the goddam *chest wound?*"

"Come on, Gordon! Sheesh! Even a *blind* man could tell the victim had a chest wound. Far as I've been told, though, there wasn't anything that got *removed* from it. The coroner up in Stanleyville didn't mention any other bits and pieces missing from the corpse."

"He didn't look too awful hard, then, my genius agent friend. You know, Sid?—it's damn lucky you had your evidence shipped down here. We found a *lot* of stuff that nitwit up there didn't find. He screwed things up pretty good doing his autopsy too, really made a mess—I'd lay you even odds they use a goddam *chain* saw up in the boonies when they do their posts— But anyway, my team down here—we went over everything again, and there's a helluva lot of other stuff we came across."

"Yeah? Well, like what?"

"Well—the rest of the stuff that got taken out, like I said before. And the medicine the murderer put in."

"Put *in?*—*Medicine?* OK, so—*what?* What else got taken out?—And what did you find that you think the murderer put in."

"That slit in the chest was where the thymus got taken out—nice, neat incision underneath the rib cage and up through the diaphragm. And a big dose of propofol was the stuff your murderer put in."

"Thymus? I guess I've heard of a thymus someplace, but why would anybody take it out?—What the hell does a thymus *do?*"

"It makes T-cells, is what it does—the ones that get chewed up in folks with AIDS, you know? And it's got a pretty good stock of stem cells stored up in it as well. The long bones do too, and when we checked your Stanleyville dead guy—your human tissue donor, I mean—we found a bunch of holes in *them*."

"*Stem* cells—Holy Moses!—On top of the blood?—Why the hell stem cells?—And ... and what about the *other* stuff you found? Some kind of drug, you said? propo-something, was it?"

"Propofol, right. Somebody sedated your Stanleyville dead guy with propofol before they snapped his neck. It's a powerful amnesic sedative; they use it in pre-op to allay anxiety before they start sticking needles in a guy. There wasn't any blood to test, like I said before; so we had to grind up a hundred grams of liver to ferret the damn stuff out. But it was there all right. You got a gentleman of a killer who doesn't like to hurt the guys he kills. A nice murderer, Sid old pal. Considerate. All our murderers should operate that way."

"The whole thing's pretty crazy, Doc—You know?—the sheriff up in Stanleyville asked me if we maybe stumbled onto some kind of modern-day vampire at work."

"You mean your guy that jumped out of the window was a vampire, eh? Is that what you're asking?" Lederer gave a muffled little laugh. "Well, honestly, it sure would've been nice if we had some of that nifty vampire DNA to examine; but all our techs came up with from the place in Stanleyville was a couple of hair bulbs that match the tissues from the guy who got cooked—that Finotti guy, I mean—him we could ID from the driver's license photo and what was left of his head—So the cooked guy's definitely Finotti, and he's kind of off the hook now as a suspect, like we said—I mean, he'd been dead for a good three days before this dumpster dude turned up—right?"

"Yep, three days, nearly four—So ... there wasn't any other DNA anywhere in the place?—Nothing that might have come from our missing guy who jumped out the window?"

"Nope, nothing we could get a decent reading on. I don't know whether the fire burned the good stuff up, or some crazy-clean fanatic really scrubbed the place, or.... But anyway, bottom line: usable DNA from your neck-snapping window jumper woulda been a nice diagnostic detail if we'd've found some, but we haven't got a trace."

"Yeah, 'woulda been nice' is right—But OK—well, we'll just have to make do with what we've got, I guess. There wasn't any foreign DNA on Jodi's evidence either, was there?"

"Nope, Sid. There wasn't; not a shred."

"And I don't suppose you've got any DNA samples of vampires to compare our jumping guy's with anyway—even if you'd found some up in Stanleyville—even if he'd left a nice fresh liver or pair of kidneys on the table for us to test—huh, Gordon?"

"No, we *don't* keep vampire samples here in our modest little FBI collection, Sidney—But you know what?"—Gordon laughed out loud and got a wryly mischievous expression on his face—"Maybe nice old Doc Sniderman does—You ever have occasion to deal with the legendary Professor Sniderman down at Pitt?"

"With…. *Philip* Sniderman, you're asking me? The chief of Path at the University?—Yeah. *Hell* yeah—Matter of fact, I've known him a helluva lot longer than I've known you, when it comes to duration—but mostly in a social kind of way. He used to play golf with my dad—Uncle Phil, I used to call him back when I was a kid; and I still do now sometimes when we get together. His wife cooks the toughest goddam brisket I ever had to eat—And her kreplach!—Holy Moses! A dinner at the Snidermans' is a dinner straight from hell."

"Well, leathery brisket or not, my friend, as for your good pal Uncle Phil, you might want to get to get acquainted in a professional kind of way this time; that's what I'd suggest. Sniderman's the best forensic pathologist anywhere around—yours truly included—And this vampire-type business is just the kind of stuff he loves—Are you familiar with his book?"

"He wrote a book?—My Uncle *Phil*?!—Hey, if he did, it's front-page news to me, Gordon. What kind of book did Uncle Phil stop kidding around long enough to write?"

"You actually don't know it, huh? You're not just pulling my leg?—Hell, Sid, it's a med school classic by now. Us warped pathologists absolutely *love* that kind of shit—Look, give old Sniderman a call—Bring all the weirdo garbage you've dug up and talk to him—That's my professional recommendation of the day. And be sure to ask him about vampires right off the bat—OK?" Gordon chuckled devilishly. "You're in for a metaphysically academic treat!"

*

Well Sidney shrugged and gave a nod, and agreed to track down nice old Philip Sniderman that very afternoon, without delay. Then out along the Fourth Floor hallway, and down the single flight of steps, and through the stairwell exit door into his own familiar corridor; and plodding along it pensively toward where the action was, the bustling office on the Bureau building's illustrious Level Three ....

And he'd barely made it to his desk and got himself reclined down snugly into the proper sort of slump, so that those legendary brain cells could start their herculean labors on the arcane mystery of absent blood and missing stem cells, and an AWOL thymus and those curious little holes drilled in the dead man's bones, and some possible relationship between all those arcane findings and the tragedy that got him working for the Bureau in the first place ... Those Braman brain cells had just got scrambled up to warp speed and started problem-solving....

When wouldn't you know it—but diffident Audrey Hamblin reappeared just left of him—AGAIN—and tapped him on the shoulder with her sympathetic touch, tapped almost reluctantly; at which the eminent agent turned and growled:

"What is it *now*, Miss Hamblin? Ho-ly Moses! If the Bureau expects me to get anywhere with this cockamamie case, I'm gonna have to think; and if I'm gonna think, I'm gonna need some cockamamie *time* to think—some *quiet* time, undisturbed—and if you people keep coming over here every couple minutes or so and...."

"I'm sorry, Agent Braman, but it's the Chief again. They want you down in Interview. The lady they brought in from Paxton won't talk to the other men, and the Chief asked if you wouldn't mind...."

"*Which* lady? The woman from the BP station? But I thought she *did* talk, Audrey. She's been down there since early this morning, hasn't she? Didn't she get here a little after nine?"

"No, no; the BP attendant finished her statement a couple of hours ago and left. You've got the summary; I set it on your desk; and the whole of her statement has been entered into the file for you to read—just click on the Finotti case and it'll come up on your screen—But the woman downstairs right *now* is...."

"Wait a minute; hold on a minute, Audrey—Before you get me involved with any *more* women, any *other* women—while we're on the subject of the Finotti case: What have you got for me on Finotti himself?—Any other pertinent info come in?"

"I'm just starting to get the emails now, sir; tomorrow I'll have a whole lot more. But what we know so far is that he had a record, but it was over twenty years old; and mostly for little things—minors, misdemeanors, spousal abuse—that kind of stuff—All of it in West Virginia too; he seems to have lived there till twenty years ago. There were a couple of assaults involving minors, but no convictions on that; a couple of bar fights; one arrest for petty theft—But nothing on him at *all*—not even a parking ticket—for the past twenty years—Not a single solitary thing."

"And the file on that computer up in Stanleyville—You get anywhere with *it*?"

"Uh-huh—Just getting going on it though. The Allegheny County file has 1278 names in total—I haven't started on the other counties or the other states—But as for the Allegheny entries, the ones we've checked so far are either unsolved murders of ours here at the Bureau—they're actually copies of our files—or similar cases of the locals or the State Police. Probably half of them are files like that, and then the other half are files on suspects who haven't yet been charged—really awful people but with insufficient evidence for an indictment. That seems to be the general trend; but there's no definite pattern except...."

"Well? Except *what*?"

"Well, like I said, they're only what you might call the worst of the worst. Only the really scariest suspects or the victims of the most horrific crimes are in there—What I mean to say is, there aren't any embezzlers or counterfeiters or white-collar criminals—none of the little minor things, that is. Just the really heinous perps are in there—murderers, child abusers, psychopaths, violent criminals who haven't yet been convicted by the authorities—All horrible cases; either the offenders are horrible themselves or the victims are—or were...."

Audrey stopped right there and turned an unearthly shade of red.

"Were like my Jodi, right? That's the kind of case you're finding in that file?"

"Yes, sir; like that one." Audrey answered *that* particular question in a muffled voice with glistening eyes: Nice, sweet Audrey: Not yet hardened by this place the way the other folks around here had been. Not Audrey; her voice choked up at the most revealing, least convenient times.

"All right, then, Miss Hamblin; enough of that for now; it wasn't the best thing in the world for me to see that file—It didn't aid my generally sanguine disposition, is what I mean to say. But anyway—getting back to the woman you were telling me about; the one who isn't talking; the one who isn't from the BP."

"OK then, sir." Audrey cleared her throat. "Well, the lady downstairs is the *other* one—not the BP attendant, but the older lady with the resale shop—a Mrs. Anthony, I believe it is. She said she won't tell the interviewers anything they're asking unless they tell her something first. So the Chief wondered if you wouldn't mind running down and trying to talk to her yourself."

"*Me! Me* again? Holy Moses, Audrey! Can't those blithering idiots do anything at *all* without my help?"

"Apparently not, sir. That's why the Chief sent me over to ask, so...."

"So *what*? Why doesn't *he* do these goddamn interviews, huh? Why always *me*?"

"I don't know, sir, but ... you realize that *I'm* the one who's got to go and tell him you won't do it if you don't—which means...."

"It means that you'll be the one who has to get the crap—right? Damn!" Sidney paused a bit and thought. "All right, OK, they've got me for ten minutes, not a second more. Let me just look at this BP woman's statement first and.... Who's with the other lady now, by the way—Kellerman?"

"I think so, sir."

"*That* figures; first get the idiot to do things wrong; then send for Braman to set it right—huh?—Ho-ly Moses!—So—he's got the picture of that dumpster dude to show her, I assume—the kid from Paxton?—Oh the hell with it—Which room is she in, Audrey?—One?"

"Two, I think. I believe they said Interview Two."

"All right, I'm on my way. Tell the Chief you talked me into it; at least *one* of us'll be on his grateful list."

So a minute more to scan the monitor, and out went Sidney to the stairwell at the end of the corridor. He had no time to wait for elevators, and no breath to waste in talking to the lazy imbeciles who rode them up and down, coffee cups in hand, wandering aimlessly to no constructive end. Down the steps and out the stairwell door on Level Two, then up the hall, and across it ten steps farther on to Interrogation. Kellerman was standing at the door to Room Two, longing for replacement, with downcast eyes and a frowning mouth and the yellow folder in his hand.

"You get anything at *all* from her, Kellerman?'

"Nope. Name, rank, and serial number—that's about it. The broad is stubborn as hell."

"Not 'broad', Kellerman. You like it if I called your *mother* a 'broad'?"

"No, but…."

"'No, but' … 'No, but'—Or maybe your *wife*—eh, Kellerman? Is your *wife* a 'broad'? *My* wife wasn't a broad, and the guy who did those sicko things to her may be at the distant end of this questioning—understand?—so we do whatever it takes to learn the stuff we need to learn. It's your smart-ass kind of attitude that bollixes all these interviews up, you know? Now get the hell out of the way, my useless friend. I'm going in there, and I'm gonna find out everything I need to know from nice Mrs. Anthony here. Go crawl back behind the glass and have a look so a competent agent can show you how it's done."

Click! He shut the door behind him gently. He would have slammed it in lame-brained Kellerman's face—But as for Mrs. Anthony there in the rigid plastic seat: with due regard for *her*, he closed it quietly, respectfully—whoosh … click—and addressed her in the same respectful, quiet way:

"Mrs. Anthony?"

"Yes?—And who are *you*?"

"I'm Special Agent Braman. Pleased to meet you, ma'am." He put his hand out and she took it coolly, then dropped it right away, as Sidney asked her: "May I sit down to talk a little bit?"

"Yes, sir. You fellas can talk till you're blue in the face. But I'm not saying a single solitary word to you or anyone else unless you tell me what the heck is up."

He sat across the table from her, put his hands up onto the well-worn surface of the wood, and smiled as affably as he had ever smiled at anyone in his life—Well, all but Jodi; she'd had the most affable of all his all-too-grudging smiles—Not for long, the sweet, angelic thing; but she'd had them for their joyous couple of years together anyway. But he put that out of his mind, resolvedly, and queried wary Mrs. Anthony with:

"Well, ma'am, what exactly do you *think* is up?"

She pursed her lips and glared at him unmercifully: "What I *think* is: I think you fellas are chasing after a nice young man who hasn't got a mean bone in his whole sweet handsome body; and I'm not gonna help you out one teensy weensy bit unless you tell me why you're after him."

"I can't say for sure that we *are* after him the way you probably think we are. We just want to question him about a … well, about an incident up north near Stanleyville—do you happen to be familiar with Stanleyville, ma'am?"

"Sure, George and I used to take our two kids camping up there when they were young. Up in the State park, I mean— That's just *above* Stanleyville, you know."

"George is your husband, then?"

"Forty-seven happy *ye*-ars." The '*ye*-ars' was bifurcate and musical; and as she said it, her frown dissolved to nothingness like the early morning dew.

"Wow! Congratulations! People don't even make it *five* years nowadays in these modern-day marriages—you know?"

"You're right, young man. Standards aren't nearly what they used to be."

"They sure *aren't*; you can say *that* again! That's why the country needs guys like *us*."

"You mean the FBI? I guess you're right about that—sometimes. I guess you fellas do the occasional good thing now and then."

"We do; we definitely do. One thing about the Bureau, though, ma'am—we treat everybody fairly according to the law, and never intentionally do anything harmful to the innocent."

"Well, you're supposed to anyway."

"No, we do; we absolutely do. I've been here ten years now, Mrs. Anthony, and I can tell you in no uncertain terms that we definitely do."

"So what about nice Mr...?—You know?—he never actually told us his name. Who *is* the man you're looking for?"

"We don't know that either," shrugged Sidney. "All we know is that he was in a house that got burned—accidentally, as far as we're aware—and that he managed to jump out a window and run away. I had the sheriff up in Stanleyville get his deputies to follow up the tracks; and they followed them all the way to Paxton. It took three days of twenty-four-hour tracking, but they finally led us there. So we asked around a bit, and that asking led us to you and another nice lady who works out at the BP north of town. She gave a good description, and we were hoping that you could add in some of the details of what he might have talked about, and maybe some clues as to where he might have headed once he left town. We aren't charging him with anything, mind you—not yet—All we want to do is question him about another man who owned the burned-up house—It's the other fellow we've been investigating up till now, a fellow who got killed in the fire. But your handsome friend hasn't really been a suspect until just recently—We regarded him more as a witness primarily—At least up to the present time, that's where the case has stood."

"He's a wonderful young man, I'll tell you that, sir. You know? He was considerate enough to send me flowers."

"Yes, the BP lady said the same general thing—about him being a decent sort of guy, I mean. I haven't read the whole of her statement yet, just a one-page summary, but I've got a general concept of what she said: A very nice, very handsome man who was willing to do even the most unpleasant work for hardly any pay."

"Well, I wouldn't call raking leaves all that unpleasant—Hard work maybe—And the pay wasn't all that bad."

"Yes, we interviewed a lot of people he raked leaves for. A couple of dozen, I believe—weren't there?"

"Oh, at least; probably more."

"He must have done a pretty good job then—with his raking."

"Good! I never even *heard* of a fellow working that hard. George said he finished the whole front lawn in an hour. An *hour*! It usually takes the boy who does it the greater part of the day."

"Must be in pretty good shape, then, your handsome stranger-friend."

"Hah! Like one of those football men you see Sunday on TV. Big, broad shoulders, skinny waist—Like an athlete; a movie star."

"Did you ask him how he stays that way? If he works out? I wonder if he can bench-press four hundred pounds."

"I don't know what you mean by that, young man; but George *did* ask him—about sports and things, I mean—what games he plays. I don't think he ever answered."

"You mean he evaded the question?"

"No, not so much *evaded* as he asked *us* a lot of things instead. He would always ask about *us*—over dinner, I mean; I made him dinner a couple of times—but he'd ask about our boys and George and me; and then he asked George about the war—George was in Viet Nam, you know; he won a couple of medals there. And once they got to talking, that fellow knew an awful lot about the war."

"Did he? Did he give you the impression that he'd read a lot of books?"

"No, he didn't really talk that much about himself—he didn't volunteer too much, I mean—just asked *us* a lot of questions. But you know? Now that I think of it—hmm, that's strange—the questions that he asked were really very knowledgeable ones. They were—this may sound funny, Agent Berman—It *is* 'Berman', isn't it?"

"Yes, close enough. 'Berman' will do just fine."

"All right, Agent Berman; well, the questions that he asked were—how can I explain it?—I guess they were the kinds of questions that a fellow *our* age would probably ask—George's and my age, I mean—He asked things as if he'd been around to live through the same things *we* lived through—the Viet-Nam War and all, and the TV shows that were on then, and the political things. Which seems kind of funny now that I think of it—He can't be more than thirty-five or so, if that; but he seemed to know things that happened back in the Sixties the way a seventy-year-old fellow would know them—Doesn't that seem strange? ...

"And you know something else, Agent Berman?—This is *really* funny, now that it comes to mind; but when George mentioned that his family came out to Paxton back in 1857—that's when they bought the family farm, from what the records say—that handsome fellow shook his head and said that people moved around a lot that year because of the depression—there was a bad depression in 1857, he said—and that nobody thought there'd be a war just a few years later. And how miserable it'd been for everyone when there *was* one."

"Not all that strange, Mrs. Anthony; not to us. We had a fellow in here about five years ago who was convinced he was a rebel soldier, which made him kill about a dozen Yanks—Anyone dressed in blue seemed to qualify, so he had plenty of targets—So it's not that unusual by *our* standards. But let me ask you one thing more; one final subject before I let you go. I'm gonna run out and get a photo for you to look at, OK?"

"All right, Agent Berman. Is it a photo of the handsome man?"

"No, ma'am. It's someone else you may have seen around. Someone from Paxton; I'll get the photo in a sec; hold on."

Sidney shuffled to the door and took the folder with the photo from Kellerman's waiting hands. Kellerman handed it over without a word. He was still pouting. And frowning. Not a happy camper today.

"Here. This fellow—There; take it, hold it wherever you like—Is the light OK?—So? Do you recognize him? Does the picture look familiar?"

"*Him*! *Sure*, I know him. Don't *you* fellows know who he is?"

"Not exactly. We've got his high school yearbook photo here—an enlargement, of course; that's what you're looking at— And we know his name and height and date of birth. But the complete file from Paxton hasn't yet arrived."

"Well, when it does, you'll get quite an earful, all right. This is that young Anderson fellow who broke into my store when I was doing inventory one Sunday night and held me at knifepoint for almost an hour until George drove by and saw him through the window and called the police to come. His lawyer got him off—you know: that sort of legal mumbo-jumbo—But every time I see him walking around the town terrorizing other decent folks—Whooh!—I always kind of cringe."

"And did you happen to tell that story to your handsome friend the stranger?"

"I don't remem—.... Oh, but yes, I did! I *did*! George brought it up. We were saying how safe it used to be living in a small community—like Paxton used to be, you know. And then George told him what had happened, and that that Anderson fellow had gotten off scot free and done the same darn thing to another lady from the town, and then just got a wrist-slap sentence like with me and was out in a month or so. And he molested a little girl too, they said, but the family didn't want to make her testify; and then there was another girl as well, an even younger one, I think...."

"And did your handsome friend say anything when you told him all that stuff?"

"Yes, I think he did. Now that you mention it: I think he asked the fellow's name and where he lived."

"And you told him?"

"The name, anyway. I don't know or care where that terrible Anderson boy lives, just as long as he stays away from me!"

"Oh, he *will*. You can bet on that. That handsome friend of yours may have done more than just send you flowers, Mrs. Anthony. We found young Mr. Anderson early this morning in a dumpster. Somebody picked him up and snapped his neck and tossed him in with the garbage like a little plastic doll. It must have been a person who had a darn good reason for doing it and could bench-press four hundred pounds. Or more."

Mrs. Anthony got a peculiar look on her face, a strangely contemplative look. He left her there that way. If she had anything more to tell the Bureau, she'd tell it now. Even to Kellerman, idiot and sluggard though he was.

So back upstairs to his floor and his unit and his desk. And he was slumped there no more than a minute or two in deepest meditation before nice Miss Hamblin interrupted him— AGAIN!

"Agent? Sorry, sir—sorry—but—you'll be interested in *this* one. *This* time you won't be upset about my interrupting your important train of thought."

"All right, Audrey; you've succeeded in getting my attention—So—let's hear it: What's the problem now?"

"That body they found in Stanleyville hanging upside down?"

"Yes? What about it?"

"They found another one exactly like it. Not upside down this time—they found it spread out on a counter; but the blood was drained and the chest was cut just like the man from Stanleyville—like the pictures that sheriff sent, the first responders said. The Police are emailing the images now. A lab technician found it this morning when she first came in to work."

"A *lab* technician, you said?—It was ... you're telling me that somebody found this latest body in a *lab*?"

"Yes sir, the research lab of the University Hospital here in Pittsburgh. I told them not to touch a thing before you get there—*If* you want to stop on by yourself and have a look, that is."

11

They volunteered to drive him to the terminal, and he saw no cogent reason to decline.

There was a good half-hour delay before the three of them finally made it to the car, of course: All that fuss and rigmarole in the pre-op unit when the scheduled nine o'clock cancelled her surgery, and got herself washed and dressed and packed and set to leave.

Adrienne Hartman was the nine o'clock patient's name; Lynette, her plain but clever daughter, sitting up all night beside the bed with the handsome stranger at her side, a hunky fellow, strong and agile as a football star. And once that sleepless Mrs. Hartman had repossessed her clothes, and rinsed her face, and pulled on that baggy pair of jeans and saffron V-neck sweater— Well, of course there were the obligatory forms to sign, absolving the Medical Center of any actionable accusations of neglect; there were the grim-faced doctors to contend with; the officious nurses; the Assistant Administrator named Kaminski, who trotted all the way from Patient Services in Building D to go over the medical liability issues of the case.

The handsome stranger who had sat all night beside her bed, alongside her clever daughter: He told the sleepy patient what to say; and she was cooperative enough to follow his instructions to the letter. Cooperative?—Oh yes, without a doubt—But more than that—*way* more than that, indeed—the kind-faced Adrienne Hartman had found the faith to *trust* him.

Oh, not that she had a ton of whole lot better options, truth be told: Stage 4 carcinoma of the colon metastatic to the liver and the lungs—under the very best of circumstances, that dread diagnosis has a pretty dismal outcome in the end: One-in-fifty survival rate, at most, even with the torturous treatment she'd so trustingly declined.

So they got her primped and dressed and down the elevator in a wheelchair by quarter-to-nine that cloudy Friday morning—the hospital insisting on a wheelchair, though she could walk just as easily on her own. A reasonably vigorous forty-two-year-old woman, even *without* a wink of sleep—the cancer hadn't made it to a debilitating stage as yet. She felt OK just now, and would be feeling pretty much back to normal in a month or so—Thanks to those T-cells and stem cells and some other select components of the blood stream centrifuged out late last night in an upstairs lab. Healthy, vigorous, multipurpose cells too. Lucky that he'd stumbled on the ideal pair of donors just in time.

The sleepy patient's rusty car was sitting in a parking structure right adjacent to the building she never really got to sleep in; and she climbed behind the steering wheel, with her bright, affectionate daughter beside her on the seat, and their helpmate-of-a-stranger scrunched painfully into the back. Then they all strapped in, and she fired up the little engine, and headed for the terminal downtown. And as they started off, rolling down the ramp toward the exit, the stranger in the back seat cautioned her, preemptively:

"Now it'll be a month or two before the symptoms of the tumor are completely gone, Mrs. Hartman. Don't be too concerned if you're not back to normal right away."

She stopped the car and pulled aside and turned around to look at him.

"But I *will* get better? You're a hundred percent certain that I will?"

"Yes, of *course* I'm certain. I wouldn't have gone through all that risk and trouble—trouble for the *both* of us, that is—or I really should say for all *three* of us...." He gave a wink to darling little Linnie, who smiled from the passenger seat amiably back. "I wouldn't have put the three of us through all that risk and bother if I hadn't been absolutely positive you'd get a hundred percent better in the end. I promised your daughter that I'd fix the cancer; and that's exactly what I've done."

"But.... I'm not too sure what you actually *did* do, though—That stuff you gave me in my vein: A special kind of blood, you said?—But—umm, where did you get the blood *from*? And how does giving someone a special kind of blood cure a person's cancer? And if it works as well as you say it's going to work, why don't they use that kind of treatment on everyone? And ... and besides all that...."

"All right, all right, hold on there for a minute, ma'am. Look ... I really need to make that bus this morning. I'm a day late already, and I can't afford to lose *another* day. So—let's head out, if you don't mind, and I'll tell you a little more along the way."

So she smiled at him in the rearview mirror, drove on downward to the exit, paid the attendant the several dollars due, and rolled out of the lot; then headed straight on toward their subsequent destination downtown.

Fifth Avenue, once they hit it, was intolerably slow: A red light here, a traffic tie-up there, pedestrians inching through the vehicles, then a couple of blocks of road construction near the park: They moved a bit, but at a lamely plodding pace. And with the plodding stop-and-go, wherein both weary mom and clever kid up front could listen through their sleeplessly debilitated eardrums enough to understand—at least he hopefully *assumed* they'd understand—he proceeded to explain things as comprehensibly and yet concisely as he could.

He laid things out in plain old laymen's terms, he thought; that's true. But less than a minute into the explanation, young Linnie interrupted with an upraised hand:

"OK, hold on a sec—OK? You're saying that cancer is caused by poor immunity, right?"

"Well yes and no. It's caused by a specific lack of immunity to the specific type of cell that's causing the cancer—Let's take lung cancer for example: Say a group of cancer cells pop up in a fellow's lung. If the man is perfectly healthy and his immune system is sound, some specific immune cells in the bloodstream will recognize the cancer cells as undesirable and kill them off—But if that specific kind of cancer-killer cell is missing for some reason, then the cancer starts to grow and eventually makes the person sick—Do you understand?"

"Uh-huh, I guess.... So then you're saying that Mom didn't have the right immune cells for the kind of tumor that she got?"

"That's right, more or less. Something made that particular group of immune cells to that particular type of tumor die out. And what we did last night was give her new ones."

"So then—won't the new ones you gave her die out too?"

"Maybe so; maybe for the same reason the old ones did. But we also gave her a tremendous dose of stem cells that'll develop into the protective cells she'll need later on. That way she won't get the old cancer back, and, more importantly, she won't develop a *different* type of cancer later on once the current one is cured."

"So—I'm not exactly sure about what kind of treatment you did, though: Where did you *get* the healthy cells you gave my mom? I mean—do they keep them in the hospital for a cancer patient's use?"

"Look, Linnie, let's not worry about that right now. You'll figure it out in time, I'm pretty sure—you're very clever in that way. Just remember this no matter what: Everything in life is a trade-off of one kind or another; and if you can trade something much, much worse for something much, much better, nobody will ever accuse you of making a lousy bargain in the end."

"Yes but...."

"No; no 'yesses' or 'buts' right now. Let's drop that kind of inquiry for the present. Your mom is going to be healthy; that's a fact. What we did last night is going to make her healthy, however the things we did for her were done. You need to focus on that, now and afterward. Whatever else you hear or see or read about in the papers in a day or two, don't lose sight of that."

Which admonition given, the girl seemed to comply; *both* of them seemed to comply: No further questions, even though those questions would have been perfectly appropriate to ask. They'd stopped just then at a traffic light, and when he glanced up, he saw the sleepy mother's eyes in the rear view mirror pointed once again at his. They were effectively eye to eye for the thirty-second interval that the car remained at rest. Perhaps Mrs. Hartman saw something in that thirty-second period of intersecting gaze that made her change the subject right away— Maybe yes, maybe no—But whether or not she *had* seen something that warned her off, she *did* change the subject completely, and with startling abruptness. When the car set off again and her eyes got diverted from the mirror to the road once more, she divertingly interjected:

"You two and your scientific gobbledygook! You know?—Maybe Linnie can understand this complicated medical stuff you're telling us, but *I* sure can't. She's our regular little genius in the family. Did you tell him all about your awards, honey?—Did she tell you she's gonna graduate next year?—And she'll barely be six*teen*."

The girl *hadn't* bothered to tell him that, but he'd sensed right from the very get-go that she was a bright enough, alert enough kid. The way she'd handled that dicey situation on the bus: That alone showed him she could think under pressure, and direct her pressured thinking to a beneficial end. And, too, she seemed to be following his detailed explanations reasonably well: yes, a truly clever kid, a truly *decent* kid. The kind of mind worth teaching something vital to: Like Jennifer so long ago, this girl was like a diamond-in-the-rough just waiting to be polished. A mind like hers: if he only had the time to spend with her that he'd spent with his youthful soul-mate Jen; those incredible three months in Charleston—the joy and climax of his life!

But just like Jen, just like Meredith, brilliant little Linnie here and kindly trusting Adrienne would be torn out of his life like all the others who had wandered through it for a fleeting bit of time. Would he see any of them ever again?—Meredith? Jennifer? This perky, brilliant Linnie he'd just met and joined with in a bond? One more glance, one more hug, once more to merely touch the hands of those paltry few that he had known and loved: It was the fondest of his hopes, but as for any likelihood of such things ever happening, that held the slimmest, faintest chance at best.

Well, at any rate, even a fraction of an hour interacting with this brilliant little brain—yes, even that briefest momentary contact might just do some good, an invaluable lesson for her and a conduit of beneficial knowledge for the rest. And so he thought about it for a little, and then started up again:

"So I think you get what I'm saying—don't you, Linnie? About the immune cells and stem cells, and all?"

"Sure. That's a pretty basic concept once it gets explained that way. Besides, I know a lot of it already: I've been thinking of maybe studying to be a doctor after college. That or maybe a research biologist—depending on whether I get a scholarship or get accepted to a cheap-enough school."

"Good. Terrific! You'll do well in either field, I'd bet. And—who knows?—maybe you'll get that scholarship you need; I know you're smart enough to earn one. So—since you're kind of medically oriented and bright enough to understand, can I answer any other questions for you?—other than the specifics we needn't talk about, that is. Do you have the concept of the cancer problem down well enough?"

The girl had slipped her shoulder through the seat strap and turned halfway backward in her seat. Arm over the backrest; chin against the headrest; big, wide sleepy eyes shining contemplatively in his face, she crinkled up her brow and asked him:

"Uh-huh: I was wondering, umm: If the immune cells and stem cells are the best treatments for a person's cancer, then … why was my mom going in for surgery and all that other stuff?"

"Good question; *great* question, in fact—Those methods are the standard treatments now; but they're based on a faulty understanding of the disease. You understand now that cancer is an immune disorder, right? I've convinced you sufficiently of that?"

"Uh-huh; I get that, the way you've explained it so far."

"OK, so if it's an immune disorder, the last thing in the world we'd want to do is damage the immune system anymore; right?—But that's what chemotherapy does, basically; it poisons the immune cells throughout the body when it tries to kill the cancer cells off. And radiation does pretty much the same thing too, to a lesser degree. And as for surgery, manipulating the tumor during an operation only squeezes more cancer cells out into the bloodstream, helping it to spread—So can you see why we treated it in an entirely different way?"

"Sure I can; of *course* I can. So then—I don't get it—why don't the other doctors know about the stuff *you* know? The immune system and all, I mean."

"Well, best way I can explain it is: Have you ever read about Joseph Lister and Alexander Fleming in your studies, Linnie?"

"Umm, they were doctors, weren't they? I think Fleming was the guy who discovered penicillin—wasn't that who Dr. Fleming was?"

"Good. Terrific. Fleming was working with bacteria and noticed that they weren't growing in a culture dish that had some bread mold in it—Do you remember reading that?"

"I do. Now that you mention it, I do."

"He made that observation all the way back in 1928, but it took until 1940 before a group of other researchers could isolate the penicillin from the mold and produce it in large enough quantities that it could be used. A pretty long time in coming, right?"

"Uh-huh."

"Lister was a surgeon long before Fleming's time who tried to do something about the infections that were killing patients after operations. Back in Lister's early days almost half the people died after any major surgery was done."

"Uh-huh; I remember reading about that too; somewhere, I think."

"He noticed—Lister, I mean—he noticed that when farmers sprayed carbolic acid on their fields when fertilizer had been used, it reduced the odors of the manure, but didn't seem to taint the food. He didn't know how or why it worked, but he decided to try the carbolic acid in surgery to clean wounds and instruments—And, lo and behold, it did the trick; the infection rate dropped dramatically, and all those people who might ordinarily have died, *did*n't. But that took a lot of time too; a couple of decades before carbolic acid made it to the operating room from the farmers' fields—So do you see where I'm going with all this?"

"I think so. The world isn't ready for the new cancer treatment yet?"

"Right. Not until the stem cells and T-cells can be produced in sufficient quantity the way the penicillin ultimately was. Till then, it'll remain an idea without much practical use. Maybe *you'll* be the one to introduce it to the world."

"*Me?*"

"Sure, why not? Don't you think something like that happened with Fleming and Lister?"

"Did it? You really think it did?"

"Of *course* I think it did. It *had* to, didn't it? Look—Fleming didn't drop the moldy bread into that culture dish all by himself—Why *would* he?"

"S-o-o—somebody *else* did?"

"Somebody else *had* to, don't you think?"

"You mean somebody like *you?*"

"Maybe. Maybe a *lot* like me. Lister wouldn't have known about the farmers' fields either, unless somebody pointed it out to him. He wasn't the kind of fellow who would go anywhere *near* farmers' fields. He was a busy surgeon. A little pompous too; not too friendly to his nurses or assistants; not that nice a guy, to tell the truth. And he was sloppy in his surgery too, with dirty gowns and filthy fingernails—until that carbolic acid business was pointed out to him, he was. He was smart enough to run with the ball that got tossed to him, but that doesn't mean it didn't get tossed—you follow what I'm saying, Linnie? You starting to understand?"

"Yeah, I think so. I think I do. So … but it sounds almost like you actually *knew* Lister. And that stuff with Fleming—how could you actually know that…?"

"No matter. Forget my little fables. But as for you, young lady, study hard, and go to med school—some passing stranger you know might just foot the bill someday when he gets back on his feet—'Cause you've been tossed a pretty useful football—understand?—and I expect to see a pretty darn impressive touchdown run."

At which pregnant juncture—with a few questions answered and a thousand left unasked—the downtown Greyhound Terminal happened into view:

"I'm gonna run in with him, Mom, OK?—To make sure he gets the bus OK and so I can say goodbye?"

Obliging Adrienne nodded her sleepy head and glanced up in the mirror one last time. Her eyes were crinkled in a truly grateful smile.

"OK; there's no place for me to park, sweetheart, so I'll drive around a while and come back for you—What would you say, Mr … um….? Fifteen minutes?"

No name; they never asked his name, no one ever did. As though everyone he'd ever talked to concluded that a name for such a thing as he, was inappropriate. Finotti had called him—what? 'Sir,' or 'Boss,' or 'Say there'; sometimes he'd only cleared his throat to get attention when he stepped into a room.

The girl had called him 'sir' or 'mister' without a proper name appended, and intuited enough never once to ask. And now, at the end, even the mother had caught the 'mister' designation from her daughter's friendly prompt. A pair of sleepy, clever, eminently decent folks: Whatever kindnesses he'd done them, as with Jen and Meredith, he owed them a whole lot more than they had given in return.

So out of the car and in through the door of the terminal the pair of them proceeded arm in arm—the girl grabbing for that elbow again, just as she'd done at the bus stop a scanty day before. And once they were inside, surrounded by a vast amount of footage containing a minimal group of folks, she disengaged the elbow, looked up in his eyes, and took his hand:

"So—can you tell me where you're going then?"

"It's not important. The bus I'm getting on is heading south. That's all you need to know for now. If I give you too much information, and someone someday asks you what I said, you'll eventually have to tell him what you know. You won't want to do that, I know you won't; but you won't really have a choice. So it's much, much better if you don't have anything to tell. If you hear any more about me, or read it, or see it on TV: just don't ever think that what I did and what I've done in my life before you met me is evil in any way. Everything is ultimately for the good; that's the way the program's been designed."

She gave a deeply questioning look, but held the pent-up question back, and he concluded: "OK, so give me a hug and go back to your mother. She'll be perfectly fine now; that I guarantee. As I told you in the car, the thing I did is less a treatment than a cure—And as for you, my darling Linnie— You're a really clever kid; study hard and remember what I taught you—Not just the cancer treatment, but the idea of looking outside the box for answers to the things you don't completely understand."

Her eyes were tearing up, but that was only natural. They'd known each other for—what?—twenty-four fleeting hours now? Hardly any more. But in that compact day, the two of them had shared more trust and generosity, more confidence and risk, more life and love and sacrifice, than most best-friends share in a lifetime at one another's sides. Whatever little he had done for her in curing her mom's disease, his debt to little Linnie was a whole lot more. And thus, before he said goodbye and sent her on her way, he asked her:

"That boy in Paxton—Do you think you'll have any more trouble with him later on?"

"I don't know. Maybe. But don't worry; I can take care of myself."

"Do you have anyone else there? Anyone to help you with a problem? A big brother or big sister maybe? Someone to look after you?"

"No, nobody like that. I'm an only child."

"How about your dad then? You haven't told me anything about your dad?"

"No, no dad either. My dad left when I was three. He lives in Georgia now—or maybe it's Kentucky. I've never met him really—not that I can remember. Mom says it's better that way."

"Better for *you*, maybe. He's the one who's missing out—Look, Linnie, I'm a little concerned about that boy. I didn't like the looks of him. I didn't—I guess I just didn't like his vibes. Tell me your phone number and I'll call you in a few days. And if that kid is bothering you—if he threatens you or touches you, or even *looks* at you in a confrontational way, I'll be back there to fix things, I promise. You won't see me if I come back, but you'll know."

"*How? How* will I know?"

"You'll know."

"Will I ever see you again?"

"I can't say for sure. Maybe if you knew me better, you wouldn't really want to."

"I would! Of *course* I would! How can you even *say* that?"

"If you knew a little more…."

He stopped a while and thought. The girl had saved his life, no doubt; a precocious little adolescent kid who'd put herself way out on a limb for him solely out of trust. And that business with her mother too: The only person in the world the kid had in her corner was her mother, and she'd entrusted that divinely precious mother to his care.

She deserved an explanation—at least enough to understand. If anyone deserved it—anyone since Meredith and Jennifer, at least—it was she.

And so he took her by the arm and led her to the far side of the terminal, over to a pair of isolated seats where they could sit in quiet and alone. And when they got there and sat down side by side, he turned to face her, and took her hand in his, and said:

"Linnie, let's let your mother drive around a little more. Stay here with me for a while. I'm going to tell you some amazing things about myself that I've only told to two other people in all the many centuries I've been alive."

12

"Sidney! Boychik! Come on in. Grab a seat—What's cookin' with the FBI?"

Philip Sniderman was his dad's age—sixty-eight or so—but looked to be at least a hundred and ninety-five. That heart of his—There's the culprit that had really aged him fast: First bypass when he was in his early fifties, then something similar every couple of years ever since—angioplasties, ablations, infusions, and all the rest. His hair went—first gray, then pink where the scalp peeked through—His face got mottled and round. His skin puckered up like a dried-out orange in the sun. He stooped; he limped, he trembled. Not much left of him these days other than his brilliant mind and his twinkle-eyed wit. That wry sense of humor was the thing that always got him through.

"Jacob OK? He hasn't called me in a while."

"He's fine, Phil. He doesn't make it to the club much anymore. That's probably my fault though, I guess."

"Sidney?—a man's gotta do what a man's gotta do. With what you went through, the stuff you're doing now is therapy, believe me. And Jacob loves the business anyway. I'm not so sure he'd be all that happy giving up his money-making work and sitting home. But honestly, I kinda miss the golf games though."

"Yeah, Dad never plays anymore—You know? You're the only guy he ever used to play with. When he stopped playing with you, he stopped playing with everyone."

"Sure; figures: 'cause I was so miserable a golfer. I was the only fella he could always beat. It was worth paying the membership in the club for him so he could go out every week and make me look pathetic."

"You never were pathetic in anything, Uncle Phil—But *membership?—What* membership?—*Your* membership?"

"Sure mine. Naturally. What? You didn't know? Jacob paid my membership every year—He never mentioned it?— That figures! Thirty thousand bucks every goddam January.

Twenty years at thirty thousand bucks every goddam January. Tell you the truth, Sid, I woulda rather had the cash."

"He paid your fees? My father really did?—I mean, that sounds like Dad; he does that kind of stuff, but…."

"Yeah, well, he paid 'em all right; *I* sure couldn't. You think a humble schlep like me could afford a high-falootin' club like that? I'm an academic pathologist, Sidney; I don't own a lab. The real money's in the lab tests, buddy—You own a lab, it's like owning a goddamn Burger King: Sell a thousand Whoppers, do a thousand liver tests—same thing—a piece of the action, boychik. That's what an academic pathologist hasn't got."

"So Dad actually paid for your membership every year?"

"Sure. He'd still be paying if I didn't finally resign. Now I see him once a month for lunch at the deli on Murray Avenue. He picks up the tab: I get a tuna fish on rye; he gets pastrami— He's got a better heart than I got, I guess. I eat omega-3s and take Lipitor, he eats fatty brisket and takes Viagra with the girls; that's life!—So, anyways, enough of blissful reminiscing—That secretary of yours—Andrea, right?—She called."

"Audrey."

"Audrey, Andrea—all those gentile names sound the same to me. She cute?"

"I don't know; I guess so, in a secretary sort of way. I never think of any of the people I work with as cute. She's a good kid, though. Really. She looks after me in her way. We never really acknowledge it, me and Audrey, but she does."

"So? Let her look after you after hours too. You can't dwell on the past, Sidney. Jodi's been gone a long time now. You needn't become a monk."

"OK, Philip; we'll see about that someday. A man's gotta do what he's gotta do, remember? Anyway—the reason Audrey called and set up the appointment, though…."

"She said you had a miserable case you needed a little input on. That's what she said when she called: So? Tell me the miserable details already—shoot."

"OK, Phil, I will—You know Gordon Lederer? Our forensics guy at the Pittsburgh Branch?"

"Sure I know him. He sends me bags of organs all the time. We gave a course together maybe fifteen years ago at a conference in Philly; that's where I met him first. So? What about old Lederer? He still driving that goddam Nazi car?"

"Car? He's got a Porsche, I think."

"Same as before. Goddam Nazi. That Porsche mamzer was a special pal of Hitler's—didn't you know?—So? What does your Nazi buddy Lederer want?"

"Not him. Me. He told me you wrote a book—'Occult' something or other—and he suggested…. I don't know; we've got this screwball case I'm working on…."

"*Pathology of the Occult*, buddy, *Pathology of the Occult*—Pretty spooky title, eh?—Wo-o-o-h!"

Phil put up both hands and wiggled his fingers in an eerily sarcastic way—At which gesture Sidney broadly smiled.

"What happened with that cockamamie book I wrote was this, Sid: I gotta give these lectures to the med school kids, right? And if you don't make it interesting, you can't keep the little cockers awake—So?—What?—I made it interesting in spades. You shoulda seen 'em, Sidney; with those big eyes wide as flying saucers—Hah! I musta had 'em stayin' up nights looking for goblins in the closets, the stupid little shits—But, anyways, then that publisher—Lipincott, it was—they called and asked me for a book, so I wrote it down. Took me all of a coupla weeks, I think—half basic science, half basic crap. I just expanded a little from the lecture notes, you know, and stuck a lot of gory pictures in. I think it sold maybe a few thousand copies is all, mostly here in Pittsburgh to the students when they rotate through each year. They paid me—what?—five grand so far, I think—Big deal! Rosie goes and spends it on the grandkids."

"How *is* Rose?"

Sniderman laughed. He laughed so hard, the secretary in the little cubby-hole next to his office stuck her head in the doorway to look. In a second the head was gone, leaving them alone again, so Philip Sniderman could get on with his belly laughs, and Sidney Braman could sit back and chuckle merely at the jolly sight of Phil. Then when the joint hilarity had simmered down in weariness, and left their facial muscles aching in its wake, the venerable pathologist explained, with a mischief-maker's smile:

"You know what I was thinking just now that made me laugh so hard, Sidney? Remember the Pesach dinner when Rosie cooked that rubber brisket that you and Jacob tried to eat?"

With which vivid recollection, Sidney broke into a pretty hardy belly laughter too.

"I told her...."

That was it. That was as far as Uncle Philip got before the laughter came cavorting back in waves and torrents—a jointly shared laugh, this time, so infectious and invincible that the two of them were completely immobilized by it for a good long paralytic minute or two ... until it subsided—finally—into a sputtering speech, in which the jovial Professor Sniderman haltingly said—or at least made a reasonably good *attempt* at haltingly saying:

"I ... told ... her.... Ha-ha-ha-ha—I told Rosie she should sell her brisket to Florsheim to make their shoes. Damn stuf'll wear for years, I told her. SHOES, for God's sakes!—Oh! Oh God, Sidney, you're killing me to make me laugh like this— You're positively *killing* me!"

"*Me* killing *you!*—*Me*? C'mon, Uncle Phil, All I did was ask about Rose."

"Ha-ha-ha-ha...."

"So how *is* she? How *is* Rose?"

"Ha-ha-ha-ha...."

It took five more minutes of Phil's infectious laughter before their conversation could finally be resumed:

"OK, OK. Rosie is fine; thanks a lot for asking. I keep her out of the kitchen is all—ha-ha-ha-ha—OK, enough already—You're lucky she didn't try and make her granite matzo balls for you; you woulda broke some teeth!—Ha-Ha-Ha!—So, anyways—*anyways*, famous G-Man Sidney ... Ha-ha-ha-ha! ... tell me already about your big verkahkte case."

Whereupon Sidney shook his head and wiped his eyes and gave the salient details—horrendous enough to dampen Philip's humor for a while—these details accompanied by a diagrammatic sketch drawn crudely on some printer paper with his Bramancorp-logoed pen: the operating-room-of-a-basement up in Stanleyville—top-notch, state-of-the-art; the crematory oven—here, off to one side, bolted to the wall, just so; the dangling corpse devoid of blood and thymus and a bit of marrow too, suspended from a hook just left of the surgical paraphernalia, right about here—You get the picture, Phil?—So much for victim one.

And then the burned guy, number two, upstairs; scorched, but probably not murdered. And then that third corpse discovered only yesterday in a Paxton dumpster; the snapped spinal cords on both the unburnt dead men, clean and clinical, right at C-3... And then finally (at least for now) this fourth and final victim, discovered just today, just this morning, in fact, right next door at....

"And it was at the *Hospital*, you said? Somebody found this latest dead guy here at the *Hospital*?—Here at the *University* you're telling me?"

"Yep," said Sidney, "two buildings down, right on your Medical Center campus in the Eighth Floor Lab. A lab tech found it early this morning when she got here. I just came from the scene of the investigation half a block away."

"And this last fella? He was hanging upside down the way the first one was?—Blood drained and all?"

"No, not hanging when they found him, but it looks like he *had* been hanging a little bit before. There was tape around his ankles, just like the guy in Stanleyville, and it looked like he'd been strung up by the feet, just like the Stanleyville body, before the killer took him down—They found a belt—the *victim's* belt most likely—and a horizontal bar in some storage closet that the belt had probably been attached to, to hang him from.

"But anyway, Phil, *this* guy—this fourth one on our laundry list so far: It looks like he had his blood drained like the first one up in Stanleyville, and his chest was slit just like the first one too. But the *rest* of him: It's not easy to describe it, Phil—but this doctor guy: Hell, it looks like somebody took a battle axe to him. Arms, legs—everything: Like a regular butcher shop operation. Lederer said the man who did it went mostly after stem cells this time—all the long bones and the sternum seem to be opened up and suctioned out. We emailed him the images—Lederer, I mean—and I talked to him on the phone once he'd checked them out; and he said it had to be stem cells the murderer was after when he.... Well, anyway, we found a lot of blood and tissue samples in the centrifuges this time—in the hospital here we did. Up in Stanleyville, the place had been pretty well cleaned up, I guess. This time, nobody got a chance to clean."

"So where do *I* come in? What do you need from *me*, Sidney? You want me to look at the tissue specimens you found?"

"Not necessarily, Phil; not yet—Maybe later on, but no need to bother now. But—here's the thing, though—You wrote that book on the occult pathology stuff, from what Lederer told me, and.... Well, I know it sounds a little screwy; I realize it's pretty off the wall.... But, honestly, with the missing blood and all, and now the stem cells too—I kinda wanted you to assure me we haven't got some crazy kind of ... of ... well, of a modern-day *vampire* on the loose."

Sniderman's eyes got to twinkling impishly once again, but he didn't laugh this time. Instead he leaned back in his chair and put his legs up on the desk and pursed his lips in thought. A minute or two passed that way: Phil leaning back and thinking, moving his wrinkled lips as though he were having a question and answer gabfest with himself. Then finally: "Hmh," he muttered in a quiet voice and shook his head:

"Sidney, boychik? We don't know half the crazy kinds of mishugas that's happening in the world these days—Like what Shakespeare said in Hamlet, you know?—'More in heaven and earth than we....'—Well, however the language goes; I don't know my Elizabethan drama all that great—But anyways—look: We don't believe in witches anymore, right?—But the government spends millions every year doing research on ESP. And those spooky flying saucers they were seeing in the Fifties? They don't get reported too much nowadays; but a lot of astronomers are scanning the skies for radio transmissions from other worlds, even so. Lots of crazy stuff like that, is what I'm saying, kid—So honestly, we don't know even *half* the screwball stuff we sorta think we know....

"Those lectures that I gave and the book I wrote? I did a little research back then—and you know what I found? I found that every screwy legend in the world has got some underlying basis in reality. All of them do—seriously; no joke. Take werewolves, for example—A nutty concept, right?—Sure—But it's a really easy legend to understand if you think a little bit. Back before the world discovered viruses—and that's not so long ago, when you consider it, Sid—But back then, some poor schlemazel got bitten by a wolf with rabies—right?—and then he went right out and bit some other poor schlemazel and gave *him* the rabies too. So what happened in the end?—A wolf turned a man into another kind of wolf, and the legend took off. So that one is a breeze to understand.

"And as for your cockamamie vampires, Sidney, let's think through that craziness a little bit too—So OK, let's say you got some brilliant fella who's lost his ability to make new blood cells—radiation damage, maybe, maybe some hematologic disease like aplastic anemia, leukemia—whatever—can't make white cells, can't make red cells, can't make platelets, can't make nothing—gornisht, right?—Now he's a brilliant guy, OK? We already established that he's brilliant—right?—with all those books you found and the operating room gizmos and all. IQ off the charts, let's say—why not?—So what's he gonna do, huh? Let's say for argument's sake he's a universal recipient—AB positive, right? Or let's say he's smart enough to get new stem cells and *make* himself a universal recipient—to *make* himself AB positive—you see? He can get blood from *any*body then—not just the small percentage of the population that shares his blood type, but *any*body—you follow me so far?"

Sidney *did* follow him so far and nodded to assure the imaginative Philip Sniderman that his thought train was on the appropriate track.

"OK good; terrific; you get an 'A' just for staying awake—See? I'm an easy grader; probably that's why the little cockers all bought my book—All right, so anyways: so the guy needs blood cells to stay alive, right? White cells, red cells, platelets, the whole megilleh. Every couple weeks, I'd guess— four at the most—he'll need some more, given the lifespan of a cell—How often did that crematory oven get used? Did your people manage to figure it out?"

"Just about what you said, Phil; twice a month for twenty years."

"Great, terrific; makes perfect sense. So the guy needs blood and he's smart—right? He's not a vampire like the cockamamie Dracula vampires on late-night TV—sleeping all day in a coffin, turning into a bat to flit around at night, sprouting fangs when he needs to suck some blood—That's a bunch of crap when you think about it physiologically. If you ingest a lot of blood and it gets in your gut—Bam! you get sick as hell. Blood's a major GI irritant; it'll double you up with cramps—So? What! No self-respecting vampire's gonna walk around and shit his brains out every couple weeks, right?—So the fangs won't do it—not if they drain into the gut. The guy'll need to take the blood IV. Centrifuge it down so he can get the best cells out—you talked about some centrifuges, right? Didn't you say the place in Stanleyville had centrifuges too, just like the ones you found up in our lab?"

"A couple of them; yeah."

"And the ones in our lab here were used, right? You said they had stuff in them? So was it bloody kind of stuff?"

"Uh-huh, residue of blood and tissue in a couple of the centrifuges, just like you're saying. The guy didn't have the time to clean them up, I guess."

"Good. Terrific. A regular mitzvah that they hadn't been cleaned. So that's it then, Sid; that's the kind of vampire you got. A *genuine* vampire, a *realistic* vampire. None of that goddamn—B-grade-movie crap. An honest-to-goodness physiologic vampire—What kind of victims does he like?"

"What *kind*?"

"Yeah, what was the fella *like* from up in Stanleyville that got hung upside down and taken to the chop shop for his body parts?"

"Oh, *him*—Audrey just called me about him, just an hour ago, in fact. They finally got him ID'd right around noontime today. Guy name of Torrenson. A real despicable weasel, I guess. Beat his wife, abused his kids, swindled a bunch of old folks in a nursing home too; a real dirtbag as far as we know. Charges were pending on the fraud case when he disappeared."

"A pretty good choice in victims for your vampire, huh?—How about the guy from Paxton with his neck broke in the dumpster?"

"Oh, *that* one—Another lowlife too, Phil. Bad as they come. Tormented a bunch of people, they say. I just this morning talked to a nice sweet lady he held at knifepoint, and he might have molested a couple of young kids as well. No great loss to society there."

"And the guy today? How 'bout the one you found today? What was the ID of the chopped up guy you found up in the lab this morning?"

"That's what's got me worried *this* time, Phil, truthfully. The guy we found today was a decent man, far as I can tell; a pediatrician who was working in his office late last night up in the Fourth Floor of the Medical Center building down from the lab where the cleaning lady came across his corpse this morning. Looks like his neck got snapped just before the blood was drained and the stem cells or whatever got taken out. But he was a practicing doctor, like I said. If the killer just took out a bunch of lowlifes, maybe there'd be no reason to get bent out of shape about the guy being on the loose—But *this* one—this *latest* victim—this one presents us with a problem. If we've got a murderer who'd go after a *doctor*—some honest, decent, unoffending *doctor*—the whole community might be at risk."

"Yep, that *is* a problem, buddy boy; I see why you're concerned. So tell me, Sidney—who *was* this doctor fella I'm not gonna work with anymore? Can you break your agent's code of secrecy and maybe give old Uncle Phil a name? I handle specimens for ninety percent of the staff guys in the whole damn joint—Might as well find out now who to cross off Rosie's Christmas card list next December and save a coupla bucks."

"Hazelton's the name. Lester Hazelton. He was apparently working in his office sometime after ten p.m. when...."

"Hold it there, Agent Sidney; stop right there, my genius G-Man friend—Hazelton, huh?—So!—Big shot FBI man! Agency hotshot!—You don't know bupkes about Lester Hazelton, eh?"

"Just that he was a pediatrician on the staff here and...."

"Don't you read the goddam morning papers these days? Hey, I know you're a big deal macher in the federal investigation business—but don't you ever open up a Pittsburgh paper once in a while?"

"Sure I do, but...."

"Sure you do!—And you haven't read nothing about old Les Hazelton? It's been in the papers on and off for a good coupla months at least."

"*What's* been in the papers? What are you referring to, Phil? Did Hazelton do something wrong?"

"Wrong?—Well, let's see: See if you can find something wrong with this: His third wife died of an overdose of insulin six months ago, OK?—There were a lot of questions about that. Then before the third wife went, his second wife died from falling down a flight of stairs a coupla years ago; there was a *major* question about that—seeing as her skull got crushed and the place she landed was carpeted with nice thick padding and all. So that's question number two of the two big questions so far, right?—Got it so far, buddy boy?—Then before all that new stuff happened, his first wife died in their garage from carbon monoxide inhalation—she somehow got a head wound too, by the way; nobody figured out how she got it or where. Anyhow, he got a top-gun lawyer each time and managed to get off scot free from all three investigations—Until a couple of months ago, he got off, anyways."

"Holy Moses, Phil—The guy's sounds like a total monster, doesn't he?—So what happened a couple of months ago?"

"This is the best deal of all, Agent Sidney; this one really takes the cake: This time Hazelton's *girlfriend* died—Girlfriend!!—The goddam girlfriend happened to be a sixteen-year-old kid who'd been a patient of his since she was a neonate and somehow wound up staying in his house—He did house calls different than the traditional way of doing them, I guess—Anyways—Get this: *She* died of an overdose of insulin too, just like the third wife did."

"She did? That sounds pretty incredible, Phil...."

"Hold on there, Sidney. You haven't heard the rest of it. You think *that's* incredible? That's small potatoes to where the truly incredible part comes in. *Here's* the part that *really* gets incredible: That girl? She had prob'ly three hundred units of insulin in her system. We got the specimens here, and I'm pretty sure when I say three hundred that it's right. That's three hundred units in a sixteen-year-old kid—Got it so far?—Problem was: she wasn't a diabetic; never had been. Died convulsing; status epilepticus; fried her entire goddamn brain. That's way more than incredible, kiddo; that one's off the goddam charts...."

"So no, Agent Sidney, don't run out and alert the Pittsburgh community at large; not just yet. I can't say for sure, boychik; but far as I'd conjecture from the information at hand, I'd say this vampire you FBI fellows are looking for is one of the really, really good guys in the world—You got yourself a top notch vigilante vampire who's doing humanity a beneficial service cleaning house."

"You know, Phil?—That theory would hold a lot of water except for one important thing I haven't managed to tell you yet."

"OK? And? So what's the thing you haven't told me yet? The vampire murdered some malpractice lawyer maybe? Good. Let's clone him and put a dozen of them in every city in the country. I'll donate some of my own blood for their keep."

"No, Phil; this part isn't any joke. That house in Stanleyville?—Down in that room behind where the empty freezer was, I found a computer; and when I checked it out, I found a lot of curious files: Files of criminals, the bulk of them, bad guys who hadn't yet been prosecuted for one reason or another—A lot of the FBI's most wanted felons were in those files, true; so whoever used the files may have done some good in getting rid of *them*—I'll grant you that—But a lot of the names in the file weren't murderers at all, but *victims—innocent* victims, I mean—people who'd *gotten* murdered; and most of them pretty *brutally* murdered too—you understand?"

"OK, sure; sure I understand—So what? You think he killed the victims in that file? So maybe he did. Maybe they were bad guys too, and did bad stuff you FBI guys didn't know about—You big shot agents ever think of that?"

"We *did*, Phil; we *did* think of that. Except that one of the victims in that file was, Jodi. Jodi's file was in that guy's computer too."

"Jodi!? You're telling me your suspect had a computer file on *Jodi?*"

"Yeah, the *whole* file, the whole goddam file right from the FBI's archives—diagrams and pictures and all."

"And—but you didn't open it, did you, Sid? Tell me you didn't open it!"

"I did, though, Phil. I did."

"Oy, Sidney!—You opened it and saw that terrible stuff in there?"

"I opened it. The list said J. Braman, so I figured it was Dad, and I thought—well, maybe he got on someone's hit list, so I got alarmed and opened it. And once I'd opened it, I went ahead and looked at it; I couldn't help but look at it, Phil, not once I saw that first picture with her body segments in the trash. Oh God, Phil—You've seen it yourself, haven't you? Tell me the truth. I know you must have seen the sickening stuff in there."

"Yeah, I was one of the examiners back then. I saw it, all right, but I didn't get involved in the handling or reports. I opted out—Which is what you should do, Sidney. You're too close to the case. You need to get the hell out of it. Oy, my God in heaven!—you saw that awful file!"

"I *did* see it, and if this guy we're after was involved in it in any way, I'm gonna finish what I started ten years ago. I will, Phil; I swear to you I will."

"You're too close, Sidney. Listen to me, kiddo—Leave it alone. Let somebody else handle it. Ask your daddy Jacob; he'll tell you same as me: Sidney, listen what I tell you—please!—you're her husband; she was a wonderful girl and you're her husband—and you're way too goddam close!"

13

Amazing!—What he had told her was utterly amazing, incredible, almost *inconceivable*—

And it was in the deepest thoughts about their conversation and the revelations it contained—the otherworldly time span, the purpose, the program—that Linnie turned her dizzy head to glance back at the terminal … and noticed the two official-looking, darkly suited men.

And in that dazzled instant the significance of their standing there at the far end of the terminal watching, waiting, her clever brain made the obvious connection; and she hollered to her mother shrilly, at the frenetic top of her voice:

"Stop, Mom! STOP! Turn around! Now!"

"What? Turn? … But *why*, sweetheart? What's the matter? Why do you want…?"

"Just *turn*, OK? TURN, Mom! Here! Now! Just make a U-ie and go back!"

Adrienne turned. Against the traffic and disregardful of the law, but she turned. Right in front of honking horns and angry motorists, two feet—barely—from the bumper of one infuriated driver in a silver Kia who veered and hit his brakes and stuck his fist out of the window hollering something loud and not particularly understanding, most likely, but thankfully indistinct. A wide turn, at speed, into the far right lane, so that before she even knew what she was doing, they were back to where they'd just a minute previously left. And when her daughter hollered:

"STOP!"

She stopped, squealing the balding tires; and the door popped open, and out flew Linnie, up the curb and on the run, with the scarce-intelligible instructions hollered over her shoulder, uttered wholesale in a single frantic breath:

"Wait-here, or-if-you-can't-waithere-then-drive-around-the-block-somemore-till-I-get-back!"

And quick as anything the young kid went, into the dingy terminal out of the daylight, and peered around as hard as ever a young kid possibly could: peering back where they'd been sitting till just a bit ago—But he wasn't there anymore—Then over to the ticket booth—But he wasn't there either—Darn!—And all the way across the terminal to a file of passengers waiting for another bus to open up its doors—But, no; not there either; hmmm....

And then at last she spotted him; there—over at the newsstand buying a Coke, getting back some change. So she ran—Well, she started out to run at any rate, then thought a wee bit better of the act of running, since running might attract attention, which she didn't want to do, of course. So she walked—but fast!—Like—*Fast*!

"C'mere. C'mon with me!"

"What?—*Linnie*? But ... I thought you—what're you doing back...?"

"C'mon, damn it! This way. Mom's gonna be out where we first came in. Come ON!"

She didn't ask; she didn't say another word, but simply took him by the arm and dragged him bodily toward the exit door. If he'd resisted, there really *would* have been a scene, and *lots* of attention—which neither of them, obviously, sought. So he left the arm in her possession ... and went.

Out to where the car had been; that was where they hurried, arm in arm—Ah, but the car wasn't there right now. And as they stood there waiting for Mom to come around the corner, he began to ask her in a pretty darn unflustered voice, considering the circumstances:

"So what's the problem?" He stared into her face examining, while Linnie bit her lip. "Why did...?"

"The exit!" she blurted. "Across the terminal. Out the other side. I saw the two of them when Mom started out toward home. Two guys checking the busses as they leave. Nobody's in the station, but they pull the drivers over as soon as they drive out. Two plainclothes guys do; I could see them when we started heading toward the freeway. They stop the bus and one guy makes the driver open up, then he gets in."

"You *saw* them? You're sure?"

"Hey, you wanna take a stroll around the block and have a look?"

He didn't answer, and didn't have to answer; for at just that instant precisely, Adrienne pulled up, and Linnie shoved him, unresisting, into the back of the tiny car while she dove in the front and:

"GO, Mom! Let's go! Let's get outta here!"

So away Mom went, fast as the little engine could take them. Straight down Liberty, turning onto Seventh, straight across the bridge; and when they'd crossed the bridge over toward the mall there, and halted at a stoplight—then and not till then—Adrienne turned her head half sideways and asked her daughter:

"What's going on, Linnie? You need to tell me why we're doing this."

"There were some police back there, and...."

"*Police*! What do we have to do with the police? Is...." She looked up into the rearview mirror again, not sleepy eyed, but actually fully wide awake and pretty well stressed out, to judge her mindset from appearances, and asked him: "Are you ... are you in trouble with the *police*?"

He didn't answer. He didn't have the time to answer, since Linnie answered promptly in his place:

"It's not his fault; it's not like he's a criminal or anything. He's gotta stay alive and never hurts a single decent person—*ever*. We gotta help him, Mom. We gotta get him outta here. He saved your life, remember?"

The light turned green and she started off again, grim faced, wide eyed, puzzled, not as yet decided—that much anyone observing her could tell. One could sense her puzzled indecision from behind, just glancing at her eyes in the rearview mirror as they flitted back and forth, and glimpsing her mouth in quarter profile as it moved in doubtful rumination while she thought.

"We don't know that, do we?" Adrienne muttered, in reference to the putative saving of her life. "We don't really know that yet, sweetheart."

"We *do*, Mom. I swear to you we do; I know for *sure* we do. C'mon, let's take him, umm.... Where?" Linnie turned around to ask. "Where is it you wanna go?"

"Nowhere. Just let me off. Let me off here—Anyplace."

"And what *then*?" the girl demanded with a frown. "Where are you gonna go *then*?"

"Just let me off and I'll get where I need to go. Just let me off; please. You've done enough. Both of you have done more than anyone would expect you to do."

Adrienne stopped at a traffic light on Eighth, eyes in the mirror again, pensive, doubtful, asking:

"Something really serious must have happened if the authorities are after you. I want to help you, and my daughter wants to help you; but it isn't fair to us if we have no idea what you've done."

"*I* know," said Linnie. "He told me and I've got a pretty decent handle on what's going on. Please, Mom. Please, just let's get him out of here. Please—*p-l-e-a-s-e*! He'd never do anything to hurt anyone who doesn't deserve to be hurt. Do it for *me*, Mom, even if you don't want to do it for him. Trust me, Mom— *P-l-e-a-s-e?*"

And Adrienne blinked her weary eyes, met his gaze once more in the rearview mirror, then hit the gas hard when the light turned green … and drove.

They stopped in Waynesburg for a bite to eat at a Burger King. Then back on 79 South for another twenty-something miles till they were there.

Morgantown—the bus station in Morgantown. That was where they left him off, and where he said goodbye with a hug for each of them and the sincerest, profoundest thanks. Did he want her telephone number and address written down? Linnie asked him—she had a pen someplace and a slip of paper—But he told her no; all those little facts were etched inside his mind forever.

"You keep those grades up, young lady, and get enrolled in med school. I expect you to be the Lister of the twenty-first century. Or maybe Fleming; one of the two."

"OK, if I can afford to go, I'll try."

"You worry about the academics, my darling little Linnie; and I'll take care of the financing. Just make sure I don't get prominently featured in your memoirs," he smiled.

And they hugged again and parted—most probably forever—at that.

There was a bus out at three, and he was the first in line to board. By six he'd be back there in the place he'd left so many years ago. And at the thought of being there again—not just in West Virginia generally, but back in Charleston itself—so many piquant memories came flooding back to him, that he got consumed by them, and they brought emotions to his mind that he'd only half-repressed these twenty years.

He thought of Meredith first of all, who had done for him twenty years ago what that clever little Linnie had done just yesterday. Meredith had saved his life just as certainly as Linnie had saved his life, dragging him from the hospital after the stabbing before the authorities intervened, just as Linnie had saved him from the situation on the bus. Linnie had been a blessed savior, all right. But Meredith, selfless benefactor that she was, had done her blessed saving in a far more sacrificial way.

Yes, Meredith had put her *own* life on the line to protect him in the end; to Meredith he'd owed everything; and he'd done his best to pay her back in a compensatory way. Certainly he'd tried and maybe he'd succeeded. The money that he'd sent her, once he'd found a home and tapped back into his credit line again, had made life easy enough for her and for the girl. The checks he'd mailed and the funds he'd transferred to their account out east had given Jennifer a generous measure of security too: a decent place to live owned free and clear, a modicum of creature comforts, a quality education—or so he'd been assured.

Meredith had left Charleston only days before *he'd* left. He had put her in her little car with Jennifer beside her on the seat and watched them drive away—the hardest, saddest parting of his life. Three months they'd been together—a mere three months—but such wonderful, incandescent months, that if there'd been any way for him to stay with them, or they with him—the merest, slightest possibility—Ah, but his needs would never permit so unconscionable a thing: His life was set in stone; his requirements dictatorial, incompatible with any reasonable kind of bonds or family ties—How could he drag two decent people into the life he had to live?

No way he could—Impossible—And besides, there'd been Finotti to consider too: Meredith's husband, Jennifer's father—such as he was. A vile man, no doubt; but not quite rising to the level of villainy justifying death. The dead men who were donors were a class unto themselves, the lowest of the very low, the worst of the very worst. Finotti was bad, no doubt, but not quite *that* bad. He needed to be kept from the wife and daughter he had abused so flagrantly—but should he be put to death?

In the end, difficult as the choice had been, the verdict had been no: Death was for the irredeemable, the unreconstructable. Finotti, with a little cutting here and there, a little mental reconditioning, could be made into a Helper. And since Larkins, his prior Helper, had been done to death at Sister's hands, and the position was begging to be filled, it was an effortless decision to make. The right man in the right place at the absolutely perfect time.

But the man, even after reconditioning, would have some dregs of memories in the relict of his mind. Could he be kept in a place near where Meredith lived? Obviously no; so the separation would need to be permanent and absolute: A long day's drive between them; two days even better. And so it was.

Better that they parted anyway, for all concerned. Charleston wasn't safe—not with Sister lurking there, forever in a vengeful mood and on the watch. She couldn't follow very far, but 'very far' was an uncertain quantity. Would fifty miles be safe? Would a hundred? In the end, that week before they said goodbye, the three of them sat sadly at the kitchen table (for Finotti was recuperating from his lobotomy in a motel out of town) and came up with a final plan:

Out east someplace: Baltimore, maybe; Washington, perhaps—far enough away, plentiful enough in jobs, and rich enough in culture that Meredith could get a quality place to work and Jennifer a top-notch education guaranteed. They'd talked things over in thoughtfulness, in sorrow; then he carried out the cases one rainy Friday morning and watched them pull away. Twenty years now since that dented little car drove off, fifteen since the final letter came: A note of farewell and of gratitude, heartrending, heartfelt, sent to his post office box in Ohio—That was where Finotti fetched the letters once a month like the sheepish little robot he'd become—Ninety miles from Stanleyville over the state line to Youngstown, so they could keep their current refuge under wraps for safety's sake.

That note, that final, fatal note: He'd kept it by his bedside all these years, tucked in the drawer with the envelope it came in and that faded photo of Jennifer as a child—note, cover, picture: nothing but a scattering of ashes now—She was all right, Meredith had written in her dainty hand; making a new life for herself—away from all the threats and all the hopes and all the memories—which was all that he could ever hope for, for her and Jennifer—and for himself.

Jennifer was growing into a woman by then—she would have been seventeen just about—heading off to school. *Thanks for everything*, wrote Meredith. *I was lucky to have known you*—her final parting words, mailed in hopes of reaching him somewhere, somehow, with no return address for her and Jennifer—Which was fair enough, when you considered it dispassionately—seeing that she never had a proper, legitimate mailing address for him.

Meredith, bless her soul—if there exists so a gossamer an object as a soul—For all he knew, Meredith might actually be in her grave by now, or married to a plumber, or a president, or living in Seattle, or Peru, or—who could say?—maybe in Tibet.

And Jennifer too—no reason for her to be any more traceable than her sainted mother was these days. No purpose for her being within five hundred miles of Charleston anymore; *that* was for sure.

Why *would* she? What in the world could possibly lure her back there now, or ever again? Fear? Sad and wilted memories?—Well, that's assuming the girl had any memories at *all* of those grim and happy times the three of them had all-too-briefly shared. She'd been nothing but a kid back then, after all, so what would she remember twenty years after the fact? Even as close as they were—and he and Jennifer were as intimately close as any two people can ever be—it was a closeness that now was twenty years removed. Nine chances out of ten, sweet Jennifer, his darling little Jennifer—the clever little girl he had tutored about all the mysteries and profundities of life, tutored every bit as patiently and lovingly as his father had tutored him—she'd likely forgotten all about him by now—Which, when you considered the ramifications of remembering, would be immeasurably to her good.

Wide-eyed little Jennifer, courageous kindly Meredith, quick-witted Linnie with her impromptu tale of an uncle from Slovakia; then mother Adrienne who'd trusted him with her life and driven him to Morgantown, never venturing to ask him why. Ah yes, and then Finotti too, poor hapless, reconditioned Finotti, burning into cinders in his bed: A thousand and more not too unlike those few memorable figures from an endless life and the perennial requirement to stay alive: For two and a half hours of jostling on the side roads and gliding smoothly on the Interstate, he thought of them, and got a little moist of eye from time to time, and dabbed his periodic tears on knuckles or on sleeve. Then slipping into nothingness, perhaps he dozed a little too....

And he would have thought and wept and wiped, and maybe dozed a little more, as well, for another half-hour in that Greyhound's cushy seat amid the soothing grumble of the highway—dozed and thought and reminisced until the bus pulled into Charleston.... He would have sat there cloaked in memories and soothed by sleep the whole three hours long from Morgantown on out....

If it hadn't been for the shattering harshness of that slap.

THWACK! it went. He heard *that*, though there may have been a prior subtler *thwack*! he didn't exactly hear—not what with the memories and sleepiness and the rhythmic rumble of the road—But that latest loudest *thwack*! aroused him from his reverie, or from his fantasy, or from his dream.

Yes, that was the sudden sound that quickly brought him round: An alarming *thwack*! A depressing *thwack*! Open hand on cheek, vicious and sadistic and hard: A most definitive, unmistakable sound—nothing else remotely like it to the ear: A child being slapped; quite young, undoubtedly; for no adult would have stood for such a blatant affront and not got in a brawl. Adults fought back; they always did if they were able— But with a child—even with a relatively passive child, some poor thing victimized innumerable times before—one would have expected to hear at least a cry, a whine, a whimper in response.... There *was* none, however—only vacant silence ... and then a man's voice harshly whispering, hard, deliberate, and cold:

"You sit there quiet—you hear me?—or you're gonna get a whole lot more of what you got just now."

A deep man's voice, growling in its whisper ... but nothing more to follow in return: No whine, no whimper, not the faintest trace of sorrow or protestation....

And thinking such a set of circumstances particularly strange, he turned backward toward the rear, as though to follow something out the right-hand bank of windows, until....

There, out of the periphery of his far-right view: A little boy rigid in his seat, up tight against the cushion; and behind him the man; and beside the man a woman, pressed snug against the glass, compacted there, cowering silently the way the boy was cowering silently, but slumped as notably as the boy sat bolt upright.

A well-dressed fellow for a father who had just abused his child: Black preacher-sort-of-outfit not really in keeping with an intercity bus trip: Starched shirt, tight collar, black tie a bit too neat and tidy for a traveler on a bus; the woman with a plain, unfashionable blouse, prissy done-up hairdo, vacant face. The boy one seat in front of them: small, five or six, with unkempt tawny hair and a downcast gaze, sitting right beside the aisle, thus eminently visible when you turned your head that far: a pathetic little boy; one's heart went out to him. Neither shamefaced nor defiant, but what you might call stoical, inured to the abuse, complacent. A tearless boy, stone faced—despite that crimson handprint on his cheek.

Pathetic, yes, heartrendingly pathetic: The youngster didn't move a muscle, but rather sat stock still with the man's dark eyes fixed firmly on the back of his head, looking—those jet-black eyes—as though they wanted nothing better than the blissful opportunity to strike again. A mean, cowardly, bully-of-a-man—you could recognize the type and sense the evil vibes—lording over a boy who had suffered enough pain and humiliation in his infant life not to whimper when the pain and humiliation came again.

Not his business, though. The world's unending ills were not his business. Some of them were, it's true—twice a month they had to be; his needs required it—but not all, definitely not all. Sand grain on a beach, raindrop in the ocean—Father had said as much three hundred years ago: "Do what good you can, but never take a risk." Such heinous things as this were bothersome, true—wrenching in a way—but not his business at all: His business was to keep alive until his work was done—if there ever came a time when it *could* be done—To get to Charleston; to gather up his father's box and the items that he'd need for his future and security; to put that letter of his father's in a safe place that he could get to easily when the time was right—if it was *ever* right—and the instructions could be used.

His business right now, this minute, was to survive, to stay beneath the radar, to keep on doing what little good a man like him could do two times a month in cleansing the world of just the tiniest fraction of what it needed cleansing of. The little boy wasn't his business at all, an incidental and unnecessary risk, were he to take it. And he wouldn't have intervened at all, in any way … if he hadn't heard that slap a second time.

But he did: THWACK! it went again—louder, if anything, than the first time the THWACK! had caught his ear a minute or two before. No whimper, no cry, not so much as the faintest secondary sound. And when he turned to look *this* time—no longer bothering to follow the scenery now, but turning purposefully, right up front about it, loaded for bear or confrontation—When he got a look back there, the mark on the boy's cheek looked a deeper shade of red than it had looked a bit before, and there was a tiny stream of blood beneath his ear, running brightly from the opening.

Full round in his seat he turned this time, shoulders and all, and stared directly at the black-eyed man; who, for his own part, stared right back at him—for a full, long minute he did—that angry glower saying, in so many unspoken syllables: *Want some of this, buddy? Come and get it if you like.*

And when he thought about it *this* time—*This* time, he *did* like; he really *did*. So up he got from the cushy seat, and grabbed his little shoulder bag from the bin above his head, and moved toward the rear of the bus. He oughtn't do this—that much he realized for sure—but he really had no choice.

The highway was smooth and the sway of the bus inconsequential, so he took the dozen-odd steps effortlessly, agile, catlike, as was his coordinated wont. Back toward the boy he sidled smoothly, and slid into the seat immediately beside him, across the narrow aisle, and put his elbow up against his own seatback with a half-turn backward, so that he was looking around the headrest at the black-eyed man full-face, diagonally backward and rightward. The woman next to the man stared down at her lap throughout, slumped, silent, immobile, compacted against the glass. Immediately to the right, alone on the seat across the aisle, the little boy stared up at him with wide, unholy eyes. The hand mark on his cheek was scarlet red.

And as he himself sat rigid, and the boy sat red and rigid, and the woman sat laterally compacted, tight against the glass; as the bus rolled on, and the passengers up front did their level best to ignore the scene behind completely, so that they might read and doze in peace and never get involved—As the world froze silent around the three of them and nothing but he and the black-eyed man and the wide-eyed boy existed in this turgid time and place —the man commenced to growl in that angry threatening voice of his, no longer in a whisper, though low enough indeed, grumbling:

"Is there something I can help you with, brother?"

The stare and the growl belied the inoffensive verbiage. And to the cumulative sum of all the fellow's profferings, he heard himself respond:

"Me? No, not *me*. *I'm* not the one with the problem, my friend. *I* don't beat up on little boys to get my kicks."

"'Unto the father is all earthly chastisement consigned.'—Discipline, brother; the term for what I do with my own begotten child is 'discipline.' And I fail to see how my own offspring's call for discipline is in any way related to you."

"I'm *making* it related to me. That mark on the child's face *requires* that it's related to me. It offends me, and I won't be subjected to it. As long as I'm on this bus you're going to leave that youngster alone."

"And if the Lord instructs me otherwise, which voice am I to listen to? To the Lord's—or yours? *Surely* not to *yours!*"

"If that 'lord' of yours objected to my protest, and if he had the wherewithal to stop it, he wouldn't have permitted my intervention in the first place, would he? While I'm here—while I'm back here watching—you're going to leave the child alone."

"Brother? What I do with my own begotten son is none of your concern. If I were you, I'd get my hind end off that seat right now and tiptoe back up front to where you came from."

"Ah yes, I appreciate that; but I've gotten rather fond of sitting here, you see—*brother*. It's a free country, as far as I've been told—I've been in some places, a long, long time ago, that weren't quite as free—I didn't like them very much—Oh, and I don't seem to remember hearing that the seats on this bus are reserved."

"Well *this* one is; I'm *making* it reserved—you hear me? Now be gone with you! I see Satan in your eyes, and I cast you forth like Satan himself. So arise this instant and be gone!"

The black-eyed fellow flung his hand out and up as though to exorcise some unseen evil spirit. And as he made this weird and histrionic sign, the woman sitting there compressed against the window looked up past her husband straight into his eyes, then down again forthwith. Her face, her whole demeanor, had the same pathetic, beaten-dog expression as the reddened face and frozen posture of the boy.

"Satan?" Glaring at the man, he forced a little laugh. "How can someone like *you* describe another living soul as 'Satan'? If there's such a thing as Satan in the world, my bet is, that you see him in the mirror every morning when you look in it to shave."

"I!—*I?! I* see Satan in the mirror?! *I?*" The man's black eyes turned hellfire red. "Listen to me, demon: The Lord speaks daily in my ear and it is *His* voice that tells me which things are holy and unholy. And the Lord's got quite a mouthful to say about you!"

"Oh he *does*, doe*s* he?—Well if that lord of yours decides to whisper in *my* ear and says to mind my business in his own authoritative voice, then maybe I'll consider doing what he says. But I see no reason to follow any directives if they're coming from a despicable, fanatical child abuser like *you!*"

He stared at the man, stared daggers, right at him, right smack into his red-black eyes. For ten seconds, or twelve, he stared—*they* stared, mutually unblinking—until the man finally, fitfully looked away. The compacted woman glanced up at him again, glanced briefly at the man again, sat back, and finally shut her eyes, shutting herself off entirely from the angst-filled scene. The boy, wide-eyed, blank-faced, looked up at him, imploringly. The little stream of blood running downward from his ear canal had clotted dry.

The man turned his face farther rightward and gazed out through the glass, where forested terrain flew by, featureless mostly, but with the occasional intervening farm. For five minutes it was quiet in their section of the bus, dead still. The scenery passed, the lowering sun flickered through the windows as it poked its amber daggers through the trees. Two women up near the driver chuckled briefly in their dull converse; then uninterrupted silence supervened again, all but for the engine's throaty churn, the tires' clip-clop-clopping on expansion joints, the whoosh of wind from the air vents overhead. The man stared vacantly out the window at a scene of quickly passing nothingness, the woman declined her head with shuttered eyes. All quiet and motionless, vacantly expectant....

Until the little boy stood up from his seat, put a tiny hand up to the slap mark on his cheek, and sidled across the aisle to the cushion beneath the protective stranger's outstretched arm.

A moment of delay, of quiet, and then—

THWACK!

This time it sounded proximate and loud—right smack dab in his ear! THWACK, it went!—Loud—LOUD! And with the blatant clap of slapping sound the wind displaced by the man's hand slapping blew harshly brisk against his face. Wind, sound—loud, immediate, as though it had been his *own* cheek that had been slapped. He turned around to look again. Reflexively he turned to look, on automatic pilot, so quickly that there was neither space nor time for thought; and he saw the man's hand raised a foot above, expectantly unbalanced there ... and poised to strike again.

None of this had been intended, of course. It wouldn't be at all appropriate to make a scene. He'd moved back here because he couldn't help but move back here. He'd thought—well, probably he'd thought too casually and way too optimistically that his simple presence here would have given some slight symbolic shelter to the boy, a sort of buffer, a gesture of protection, a transient feeling of community, of empathy, of someone actually caring that an infant cheek had been struck unjustly: a sort of bosom pal to share the suffering—if only for a while.

It had been so long since he'd been caught up in these cruelties of society, an immanent participant, a close observer. Twenty years in Stanleyville, living sheltered by the remoteness of his country home and Finotti's mindless ministrations: Twenty years now since he'd interacted with the outright evils of the world—not just *read* about the cruelty and injustice in the daily papers or in books; not just seen exaggerated evil portrayed cartoon-like in a film, or watched some actor feigning malice on TV; not just had his twice-monthly opportunity to avenge some heinous, unprosecuted wrong—

No, not known outrage secondhand; but actually *been* there, up from the bleachers, front-row seat, to witness villainy in one's own backyard, with one's own two disbelieving eyes. To feel the savagery an arm-stretch length away, watch the sadist gloat and the victim squirm....

No, no; he couldn't bide this sort of stark injustice passively. It was too much, too proximate and intimate, and way, way too much—So intolerably much, that reflex simply took over, his sympathetic nature simply did its thing:

He stood and grabbed that upraised hand—there was no preparatory thought, little willful intent. He simply stood and grabbed the upraised arm the way he'd grabbed that roughhouse boy's uplifted arm a day ago with clever little Linnie at his side. He grabbed the upraised hand of the black-eyed man, and their elbows somehow interlocked: so that when he held the hand firm and bent it backward. Back, then farther back, then more and more, not really thinking what might happen to the hand and arm in bending, but acting automatically—When he bent it back, then farther back, that hand went into … well, into what you might describe as an unnatural sort of angle, which then got bent a little farther still, inadvertently really, not really thinking about the strains and stresses on a human bone or what a radius or ulna's fracture point might be … until some taut structure suddenly gave a snap.

Crack! It went.

Pop!

And the man crumpled backward onto the seat where he'd been sitting just a little bit ago. And the woman looked up with the faintest sort of eerily complicit smile. And the boy clung to his side, face against his shirt front, sheltering tight, arms about his rigid athlete's waist.

And there was blood now soaking through the man's black sleeve where the compound fracture of the bones had torn a major vessel, as it seemed.

And a woman screamed two rows in back of him, behind his shoulder, frontward on the bus—LOUD—one quick shriek and then no more.

And the bus slowed quickly, jarringly, and swerved across two lanes of mostly vacant highway to the gravel shoulder of the road and slithered to a stop.

And the driver hollered wildly from the front:

"What the *hell*…! Hey, buddy! Hey! You!—YOU!—What the hell is going ON back there?! … You there—HEY! What the…!"

And the uniformed driver was up and out of his seat, and striding down the aisle toward where he was standing above the black-eyed man with the shattered arm and quickly seeping blood. And the child still clinging round his hips, face buried in his flank.

And once the driver got back there to the place where all the action was, and got himself a tolerable look, he stopped dead still and ceased his hollering just like that! and just backed off, his eyes agape in wonderment and probably a decent bit of fear as well....

And he knew at once that it was time to go. No option now but to go and go quickly. The boy would be all right now; that he knew. The man would be no danger for a while, not for quite a while until the arm got well; and after that, once the bleeding stopped and the bones were set and the arm had healed again—well, abuse would be unpalatable to a black-eyed man like him for many months or years to come, unpalatable the way a certain dish that makes one sick seems less than tasty for a lengthy while, once the sickness is long gone.

The boy would be all right; the woman too—for a decent while at least.

But it was time for him to get away, out the door and far away as fast as his soft-soled bargain shoes could carry him....

And for safety's sake, he proceeded to do precisely that.

14

It was an email from Gonzalez, and the instant Wilson clicked it open on the monitor, he knew.

And so he printed it out, along with the newspaper article Gonzalez had tacked on as an enclosure. And out of the library he rushed, across the hallway and down the dozen feet or so to Madam's sitting room.

The door was just an inch or two ajar, enough for him to see the TV's crimson radiance flickering dull against the draperies. The room was dark, of course. The lamps were generally off by day and all the curtains drawn up tight when Madam watched her films. One didn't dare disturb her when she had her movies on, not at inessential times; this Wilson knew quite well from all those gashes in his arms and broken bones. He wouldn't ordinarily have been so bold as to disturb her—But, considering the alternative, Madam would be positively livid if the information that he brought to her were very long delayed, and so....

He pushed the door a little farther in and tentatively probed one eye into the room, enough to see the image on the screen. Another film like all the rest: Horror films, slasher films, gore and violence, blood and guts: standard fare for her these past half dozen years. At first, ten years ago or so, she'd watched such films before the monthly kill, and only then, so as to get her dander up enough to do the deed herself. Her brother had recommended this at the beginning. "She has her mother's traits, Wilson. Sooner or later she'll be a slave to them; and when she gets to that degenerate stage, she'll need to kill; so let her do the act herself."

That was twenty years ago when Brother gave his admonition, back in the foggy weeks of his conditioning. There were signs of her derangement even then, of course—after all, look at what she'd done to Brother just a few weeks afterward— But after stabbing Brother, she'd grown—well, not what you'd call remorseful, no; but a whole lot less edgy, more tractable.

Back then, twenty years ago—why, back in those far less homicidal days, she'd been almost a companion to her Helper. Twenty years ago, before her spine had shrunk to such a hideous degree and all those grotesque changes in her face had gotten so much worse—back then she could be seen in public and not remarked with horror; ten or fifteen years ago, the two of them would go to restaurants occasionally or sometimes to a show— But *now*....

Wilson watched her dimly in the television's light as she raptly watched the screen: Poor Madam! Aged and shriveled up these latter days into a thing that children couldn't look on without screaming and trying helplessly to run away. No use, though: she'd catch them anyway on the days her blood was up and her strength at more than minimal; and then he'd have his messy cleanup work to do—and all too often need to smooth things up with the authorities once she'd had her bloody fun.

Yes, Madam was in sad shape now, regrettable; a far cry from her image in that picture up above the mantelpiece, that monumental oil done centuries ago. She looked middle-aged in that gilt-framed oil, tall and stately, rather handsome for her years, elegantly posed and swathed in silk and furs. Twenty years ago, when he'd been first brought on as her latest Helper, it had struck him how much older she looked back then than in the picture—Oh, but the decay since twenty years ago—both physical and mental—goodness me!—It had progressed beyond all comprehension; and she had morphed into the gnomish thing a viewer's eye could see right now—a veritable nightmare to behold. Possibly Brother had aged that way as well—who knew?—But Brother took his blood more frequently—And then the marrow, too, the stem cells: Those Madam had declined most vehemently since Brother had been stabbed: "He has something up his sleeve, Wilson. Ignore his directives from here on in. Henceforth I shall be my own physician. My brother is a fool—A fool who imagines he's the cleverest of doctors, yes; but still a blundering and meddlesome fool and traitor; a traitor one can never trust."

Ah well!—He shrugged and watched her play the scene again. Gore, screams, violence: luckily she always kept the volume low, and no one past the papered walls had ever heard a thing. An axe, a severed head; steel and crimson filled the screen: The bloody act she doted on this second time was brief enough, and when she'd played it through, then put the disc on pause, she turned her head and motioned with that taloned hand to let him know that it was safe for an intruder to approach.

"*What*, Wilson? What *is* it? Something urgent, I assume, for you to have the gall to bother me at such a time. So speak up, man, and tell me what you want."

"Yes, well ... excuse me, Madam, I wouldn't have taken the liberty, but ... this email.... It's him, Madam. I'm absolutely certain that it's him!"

'Him,' of course, referred to Brother. Both he and Madam understood the certainty of that. And Madam thus responded in accordance with that fact:

"Are you *sure*, Wilson? *Him*? You're *positive*? What do you have there? Bring it here. I need to see."

Her blood was up, all right, you could see it in the glitter of her eyes and hear it in the shrillness of her voice. The film had got her going; no doubt whatever about that; those gory pictures always did. But however much the film had got her mental furnace burning hot, the very mention of her brother had stoked it hotter still. His arm would bear the brunt of it, Wilson knew that all too well—But all right; no avoiding the inevitable: These were the necessary perils of the job.

He clicked a lamp on, as she'd ordered him to do, and stepped up to her chair, then handed her the crisp new printout, with Gonzalez's attachment right up top: *Pittsburgh Post-Gazette*, read the masthead in gothic lettering, and then in plain old Times New Roman print a little farther down below:

Lester Hazelton, Murder Suspect
Found Dead Near Office
Police Say Likely Homicide

She carefully read the rest, deliberately, mouthing the words with tiny movements of her lips, one spat letter at a time, digging those sharpened nails of hers into the paper as her jaws got clenched and her eyes got wide and crimson-black as burning coals:

"Two others, Wilson!—Do you see? Do you see here? Three in all—Three killed with their necks snapped just the way he snaps them—Criminals too, Wilson!—Just the type he likes to use—You must be right—It *is* my brother. It *has* to be—Get me a map, bring me the atlas over on the shelf there—the big one—No, no—wait; stop: Come over here again; I want to ask you....

Pennsylvania—Do you see here what it says? Pennsylvania—He must have been there all the while—Why ... we could have driven there, Wilson. All these twenty years we could have driven in the car...."

She reached a hand up from the tattered fabric of her chair and grasped his arm. Just as he'd expected, though nothing much he could have done to change a thing. He didn't wince— he never did—as a nail bit into the fat beneath his skin and drew a little blood. Not as much as usual, though: Since the index finger—that jagged raptor's claw of hers—bent so sharply at its outer joint, the nail would generally slice in sideways, more like a slit wound than a puncture. The slits healed faster than the punctures did, however, unless some dirt occasioned to get in; so incisions by her index fingers were much to be preferred. And as the hand contracted further and the nail bit deeper still, she said to Wilson, flinging motes of spittle as she spoke:

"We might have gone there and somehow got him in the car—You would have thought of something to tell him—or *I* might have—And once we'd got him in the car—Oh, Wilson, I so long to have revenge! Do you remember the traitorous things he did to me?—And to *you*?"

He gave his nod compliantly, it being vain to contradict. The nail bit deeper down into the tissues underneath the skin, but it wasn't all that bothersome as far as pain. What with all the scarring on his arm between the elbow and the wrist, the superficial nerves were pretty nearly dead by now. Such cuts and punctures were a minor inconvenience, nothing more: Part of the job, he'd always thought, like the calluses on the hands of a laborer who shovels coal or digs the earth to earn his pay. Those shoveler's calluses would be as numb as these scar-strewn forearms were after laboring for twenty years.

"One thing I can never understand, Wilson, is how that traitor managed to escape me in the end. How could he have gotten out past the lock on the door and through the gate? How could he have done that?—and with such a wound and so much blood lost—do you know?"

"*I*, Madam?—No; how ... how could *I* know? There's no possible way that *I* would know how the door became unlocked and the gate unlatched."

"You wanted him dead as much as I did—did you not? You told me that you did."

"Yes, Madam, of course. Certainly I wanted that. Your desires are my desires; always."

"Well, *this* time—THIS time I shall arrange things so he cannot *possibly* get away. *This* time, I intend to finish what I set my mind to finish twenty years ago. *This* time, I intend to see that despicable brother of mine DEAD! You hear me?—*DEAD!*"

"Yes, certainly, Madam, but—forgive my presumption, please—but we have no idea where he *is*, only where he was at the time of the events related in the paper. He might have gone anywhere from Pittsburgh; maybe back to Europe, for all we know—*anywhere*. So—How do you propose to find him?"

"*Find* him? What need is there to *find* him. If he abandoned his home when it was burning, he never can return *there*; can he?—No. Obviously no. And if he can never return to the place he left, there cannot be the slightest doubt that he must eventually turn up here."

"*Here*? In *Charleston*? But ... but Madam, why? Why would he dare come here? That is ... after all that happened to him the last time he was here...."

"Never mind all that. He will be here anyway—Mark my words, he will. Brother will come for his things—And for our father's things, as well. The gold and papers he always leaves for an emergency—he would come for those alone; he always has in such a case—And then that box as well. He would come for that if for nothing else. All these years it has been kept in a place where I could get to it; our father's wish; so I know the box is here in Charleston—Although I can scarce imagine why he would have left it here this time: He certainly knows by now that *I* will never put that foolish box to use."

"Box?—A box? But ... but what *kind* of box?—Pardon me for asking, Madam. I have no intent to pry. But if I knew a little more about the things your brother may have stored away, perhaps I could be of more assistance to your plans. Forgive me if...."

"Yes, yes; no apologies; you needn't give them. You may be right for once in what you say. Perhaps a little knowledge might do our preparations good. That box—He never told you anything about the box?"

"No, Madam, nothing at all. When would he have had the opportunity to tell me much of anything? We never saw him after the ... after his injury, I mean, and...."

"Yes, but you spent a fair amount of time with him *before* the injury, as I recall; during your conditioning—the surgery and conditioning, that is. That took several weeks, as I remember—did it not? And he never spoke to you about the box during all that time?"

"No, Madam; he never so much as mentioned a box, not that I recall."

"Well did he tell you anything?—About our father, for example, or about his early life?"

"A little about your father, I believe. A doctor, wasn't he?—your father?—your father and *his*, I mean."

"Yes, yes, a doctor; Father *was* a doctor, just as Brother was back then. They worked together for a time. But medicine was primitive in those days, Wilson. Witch doctors—that's all they were, really. Very little science to it then—therapeutic bloodletting, leeches, and herbs, for the most part; that sort of thing. A very primitive time in medicine it was—did he not explain all this to you?"

"I doubt he did. I was rather unreceptive during much of the time of my recovery; and I remember very little of those days. He spoke a little of his mother—that I do recall."

"His mother! A simpleton if ever there was one! His mother was a weakling, Wilson. With all her physical strength and cleverness, she was a weakling; nothing more. She was one of *them*, you know—one of the Originals, like our father, with all the special genes—She had our unique gift. *My* mother wasn't an Original, but she was strong enough in her ordinary way and clever enough, even without the special genes, to guard her interests and to see to mine. Brother inherited his mother's frailty; I inherited my mother's *strength*."

"Yes, Madam, I'm very sure you did."

"Yes, Wilson, yes. But don't presume to patronize me. I'm not the least susceptible to that sort of thing."

She let go his arm, as though to disengage from him entirely. This was the time of greatest risk—that he knew from past adventure. She could pick him up and fling him bodily across the room, hard against the wall, something she had done a hundred times and more these last ten years, once her will had grown ungovernable and her anger waxed so great. She was small, yes, and shrunken; but her strength—It was as though her extraordinary physical power had been compressed inside a smaller volume, spring-like, and had grown the greater for compression. A flick of her arm and off he'd go, like a ragdoll, like a little plastic toy flung by a willful child. Sometimes he'd break a bone against the plaster or the floor, but nothing really major up till now; the little bones that broke these several years—ribs, toes, fingers and the like—had never kept him down for long and always healed without a doctor's intervention.

A time of mortal danger, to be sure—but now, for some imponderable cause, her mood commenced to calm. She sat back in her chair and took a breath and turned to him with a gentle, almost sympathetic look. His arm was bleeding where her nail had bit into a scar—but it was a minimal bleed, a mere pinpoint of red; and when he held it to his side against his shirt, she didn't seem to notice. If she *had* noticed, and a drop had trickled to her Persian rug, Wilson was well aware there would be hell to pay!

"He will be here, Wilson, mark my words. He will come to Charleston for the box, if he comes for nothing else. Just wait and see. The box or the girl—one of the two will lure him back here soon enough. You are continuing to watch that former friend of his, I assume?"

"The lady doctor, you mean?—Yes, Madam, every three or four months, I go for an appointment. I saw her just the other day, in fact—I hope...."

"What? What is it that you hope?"

"The nice young doctor—She never caused you any harm."

"No, but *he* did. He hurt the both of us—remember? Have you forgotten what he did to you as well?"

"The surgery, you mean? The conditioning?"

"Yes, of *course* the surgery and conditioning. Look what he has made of you, Wilson. Do you enjoy being an automaton?"

"It isn't that much of an impediment now, Madam. I'm really quite content."

"And your family? Your girls? You've never regretted losing them?"

"My family is better off without me. Your brother saw to their welfare, I believe."

"My brother! My brother is a traitor and nothing else. He was a traitor to you and he was doubly a traitor to me. I can never forgive him for that—*Never!*"

"I understand, Madam. But the girl—the doctor. Certainly she never did anything to cause you harm."

"Perhaps she didn't; but *he* definitely did.... And if doing ill to her causes the least amount pain to that traitorous brother of mine, mark me well, Wilson, mark my statement well—the girl will not be spared."

15

He might have drifted off to sleep last night still thinking about the villainous murdered doctor.... But it was the image of the baby that eventually woke him up.

That baby!—That eight-month stillborn baby! Sidney was up at five a.m., wide-eyed, though weary, staring at those photographs on his condo desktop monitor yet again: the criminal Dr. Hazelton on one side of the screen, cleft and butchered like a reject side of beef, and on the other side the baby: all swathed in bandages—all reassembled, in a way, respectfully—almost what you might call lovingly. So peaceful and angelic in the cozy place the techs had stumbled on it yesterday, that you might have thought the poor thing was asleep.

But *why*? What on earth could be the reason? The motivation? And how in heaven did Jodi's file get mixed up in so lunatic a thing?!

Sidney didn't have a clue.

He sat at his computer and wondered mightily. No dearth of data, of course. Everything was available to him, here in his second bedroom-of-an-office, here in his downscale condo, a couple of miles from where he did his customary weekday work. The condo desktop was connected to the Bureau desktop, and through it to the Bureau files, and to the Federal files, and to the individual crime files of the various states and territories: photos, facts, the whole shebang. Sidney could work from home just as easily as he could work from the Bureau office two short miles away; and he regularly did—early mornings, late nights, weekends, holidays....

Just like *this* weekend early morning, this Saturday, now at nearly eight.... And now at eight precisely, once the minute hand had scrolled its way to twelve, he decided that—Oh damn it all—Enough!—He'd had a bellyful of sitting on his backside like an idiot and scratching his head and pretty nearly going *nuts*!

So at a couple of minutes *after* eight, he got himself washed and brushed and ran that ten-year-old Norelco down his darkly stubbled cheeks; he slipped on a J.C. Penney suit—clothing suitable to an agent of his electively humbled social class; he climbed into the shiny Cadillac that Papa Jacob had phoned and got delivered to his place two years earlier—This was a weekend, of course, and a conscientious agent didn't use the government-issued Chevy on a day not classified a working day—All combed and groomed and spiffy now, our Agent Sidney headed.... Well, after mulling the limited number of options in his head: Since the doctor and the baby were the riddles of the day, and since this recent business with the two of them had happened at the Hospital, and that just a matter of twenty-something hours ago, he headed, quite naturally.... Well ... *there.*

"Sidney! What's up, kiddo? C'mon in; take a load off; grab yourself a seat."

"I called your house, Phil—on the way here, on my cell—and Rose said you were in your office this morning, so...."

"*Sure* I'm in my office. Whaddya think? People don't get sick on Saturdays? Surgeons don't yank out organs and need the experts in the path lab to tell 'em if they took out the right goddam stuff?—*Sure* I'm here—What the hell are *you* doing here though? *What?*—The FBI don't give you a single goddam minute free on the weekend? Or maybe you came to see old Uncle Philip on a personal call, huh? You need maybe some doctorly counseling on your love life this time?"

Phil must have been dictating something. He set down a little hand recorder when Sidney stepped into the cubicle; then pointed to an adjacent chair and nodded approvingly when Sidney compliantly plopped in. The place was deadly still today, just one lazy-looking female tech in aqua-colored scrubs out front to let an unexpected visitor in—especially an unexpected visitor with FBI credentials—But that was pretty much it: no interns running to and fro, their lab coats trailing in the wake; no scurrying assistants with test tubes jingling in their metal trays chock-full of reddish yuck—No sign of that secretary next door, either—the frizzy-headed pudgy thing who'd peeked around the corner when Phil got into that laughing jag the prior afternoon. Basically the two of them alone in this isolated recess far in the innards of the Path Department wing. This was probably as quiet as the Path Lab ever got.

"So—Sid! What? Love life OK then?—Or you waiting on your Uncle Phil's romantic advice?"

"No, no; no romance to get advice *about*, Phil; not in the past ten years at any rate. Look, the reason I drove over to the hospital this morning is…. Remember what we were talking about yesterday afternoon?—That hypothetical business you came up with about the guy we're after?—You know: the fact that he maybe can't form blood cells on his own, and his being a universal recipient and all."

"*Sure* I remember? *What?*—You checking to see if I'm getting senile yet?"

"No, no, don't make fun; this is serious stuff—what with Jodi's file and all. Look, I've been up since five o'clock this morning trying to put some of these jigsaw puzzle pieces in a row—This case means a lot to me, as I'm sure you understand—and—I don't know—the whole damn business doesn't quite add up."

"So you need some more of my vampire meshuggas, huh? OK, sure—go ahead and ask. I'll give you all the meshuggas I've got to give."

Sidney nodded; he didn't smile: "That stuff that happened in the Eighth Floor Lab yesterday: Something about it just isn't right."

"*What!* Not *right?* A guy murdered by a vigilante vampire with his blood drained out and his bones split open? You think there's something not quite right about *that?*"

"No, that's not what I mean; you know that isn't what I mean at all. Look, this Hazelton guy—and then that business with the baby too…."

"Oh yeah, the baby. I shoulda known you were gonna ask about the baby. Your tech guys were the ones that found it, you know. We wouldna even bothered to open that cooler door till Monday when the autopsy was scheduled to get done; so it's lucky for everyone concerned that your FBI fellas dug out their fine-tooth combs and sifted through."

"Yeah, nothing much gets past the forensic techs once we turn them loose on a crime scene—So, about the baby: Did you examine it yet?"

"Just a visual only; nothing detailed so far. I prob'ly can't give you a whole lot more than your guys already figured out. Your vampire fella did a bang-up job, though, Sidney; I can tell you that. Didn't miss a thing. Didn't miss a goddam stem cell on that mamzer Hazelton either. Every goddam useful stem cell in both those bodies got exposed and suctioned out."

"The baby too, right? Just as thorough a harvesting of tissue on the baby?"

Phil rubbed his hands together and shook his head.

"Sidney?—if you took a team of surgeons and hematologists from Hopkins or Cleveland Clinic and gave them a fat old fifty-year-old criminal doctor and a stillborn infant in the cooler waiting for an autopsy to get done—if you gave them both those bodies and all the equipment in the world, they couldna extracted one more stem cell from the long bones and the iliac crests and the sternums than your genius-of-a-vampire did. The guy's an expert, believe you me. If he filled out an application for a harvester of tissue here at the University, I'd hire him myself."

Not a whit of hilarity this time: Phil—which was certainly atypical for him—looked as solemn as a newly widowed bride; and Sidney asked him, with commensurate solemnity:

"OK, so given that, you understand my problem then: When we talked about it yesterday, the operative hypothesis was that the guy needed lots and lots of blood with maybe a little chaser of stem cells added to the mix—right? We didn't talk too much about the stem cells, true; but I wasn't thinking about them too much then. But I *am* thinking *now*, Phil. That baby—since five o'clock this morning I've been staring at the photos, and they finally got me thinking: Why all of a sudden is our vampire murderer going after two whole bodies full of stem cells with only a little bitty chaser of blood?"

Phil sat forward in his chair and raised his eyebrows inquisitively: "A 'little chaser' you said? Why? How much blood did Lederer figure your thirsty vampire took this time?—From Hazelton, I mean—the baby's red cells wouldna been worth gornisht by the time he got to it."

"Half; he took half—maybe sixty percent—of the blood itself. Not much more than that."

"OK; well, that fits, kinda. He got his last fix—when?— A week ago? So maybe he just figured he needed a little topping off."

"*Why*, though, Phil? It seems opportunistic, doesn't it? Almost like he had some extra blood and went ahead and used it, so it wouldn't go to waste; but he wasn't really *after* that."

"So he was after the stem cells, is what you're saying—which sounds pretty logical, I guess, considering the tissue he harvested from that stillborn kid."

"Well that's all he could have *taken* from the stillborn baby, wasn't it? You said the blood itself wouldn't have been usable—right?"

"Sure, all the red cells were dead by then: clotted, hemolyzed, good for nothing—useless for a guy who needed functioning blood."

"But the baby's stem cells—they would have been alive?"

"Stem cells?—sure. Chilled the way they were, the tissues in the marrow woulda been viable for quite a while; persistent little devils those stem cells; they woulda prob'ly been in great shape; sure."

"So *why* then, Phil? That's what's been driving me absolutely up the wall since five today. Why all of a sudden does the guy need a gigantic dose of stem cells and nothing else? And why does he take a risk like that to get them?—Right there in the hospital, I mean—For all he might have known, any doctor or lab tech or, well, *any*body, might have happened in…. And then to put that tiny baby's body back together too—I mean, the way he set the skin in place and wrapped the baby's limbs with gauze—It wasn't as if he were trying to hide the stuff he'd done—you couldn't hide all that—It's more like he was treating the body with respect, getting it ready for burial—don't you think?"

"I know, Sid; that kinda struck me too—But…. You're asking *me* why?—*Me*?—Hey, I'm just a nickel-dime academic pathologist, kiddo. You're the zillionaire federal agent who gets paid to figure those things out, not *me*."

"No hypotheticals this time, Phil? Didn't you write about anything weird like this in your occult pathology book?"

"Hey, my book was realistic journalism compared to *this* meshuggas, Sidney my boy—But you want me to speculate?—OK, I'll speculate for you; I'll give you a little of my pathologic Yiddish speculation, how's that?—So maybe…. I don't know—Maybe your vampire's got the flu, or maybe an ugly cold sore, or maybe one of those Excedrin headaches that just won't quit. Hell, maybe he noticed his goddam hair is starting to turn gray like mine did just before it all fell out—Hey, stem cells can fix a multitude of bodily ills, Agent Sidney; a multitude of sins. Name a disease and they're a potential cure for it. So maybe your brilliant vampire's got some cockamamie vampire disease."

"That's it? That's your best shot? You're all out of brilliantly insightful hypotheticals then, I guess."

"Like I said, *you* get the megabucks for agenting, not me. Snoop around a little bit. You're pretty smart, Agent Sidney—a heck of a lot smarter than *I've* ever been, anyway. I'm confident you'll come up with a clue."

And truthfully, that was why he'd come to the hospital in the first place, wasn't it?—figuring—well, if you've got one off-the-wall crazy aspect of an investigation, there's usually another off-the-wall crazy aspect not too far removed from where the first crazy aspect turned up—Which meant the hospital, and specifically the patient tower of the hospital, up or down the elevators from that Eighth Floor Lab where poor dead, murderous Dr. Hazelton had just a day ago turned up.

So where to start then, seeing as Phil hadn't been a tremendous amount of help? A humungous hospital with lots of floors and several buildings—Tons of options, a thousand or more people he could talk to, certainly—but first of all how about…?

Yeah, that made the best sense, he figured: How about Admissions? Sure. Let him see the patient census for the past few days: That's what he'd told the clerk, having flashed his FBI credentials and his agent's badge—Let's start with—oh, maybe Wednesday, two full days before the doctor's corpse turned up.

So starting back on Wednesday, the lady handed him a couple of printout lists—Which got him heading up the elevator to the inpatient floors, ticking off the names on his census sheet one by one, talking to the nurses on the several wards one after the other—smiling amiably where an amiable smile would help him get the kinds of facts he thought he'd need, frowning ominously when it seemed appropriate to frown.

Up and down all four medical and all three surgical floors he wound his indefatigable way, back and forth through the corridors, looking for a potential find, asking about a potential clue, beating those proverbial bushes for something potentially useful—any noticeable random something grossly out of the ordinary that would help him solve the mystery of those curiously urgent *doctor's* stem cells and stillborn *baby's* stem cells and just that little bitty chaser of opportunistic blood, until....

In the pre-op area, Third Floor, East Wing, quarter-to-eleven on this gloomy Saturday morning, an hour and a half after he'd started his restless search....

"So you're saying—let me understand you properly, Miss ... um, Gardner—you're telling me that the woman cancelled her surgery, signed herself out, and just picked up and left?—Left? Just like that?—And she signed herself out on the morning that the body was found? Yesterday morning? Am I getting the chronology right?"

"You are, sir; that's correct," said the nice young nurse named Arabella Gardner, according to her name tag, with bright green eyes and a pleasant pudgy face and a shyly sympathetic smile. She'd asked for his ID, as she properly should have done, and he felt a whole lot better for her asking: A nice, careful, thorough nursing pro playing by the rules, who'd likely get her details straight and not embellish the things she told him one teeny-tiny bit. "There was a fellow with them when they left," sweet Nurse Gardner was percipient enough to add.

"A ... a *man*? There *was*?—With ... *them*? Did I hear you right? Did you really mean to say ... *them*?"

"Yes. Yes, sir; with the woman and her daughter. Didn't I mention that her daughter was in the room with her all night?—the man and her daughter both?"

"The night before the scheduled surgery, you mean?—The night before yesterday?—Thursday night? No, I don't think you *did* mention that, Nurse Gardner—nice, worth-your-weight-in-platinum Nurse Gardner. Tell me what you can about the man, though. Do you remember what he looked like?"

"Do I *remember*! I sure as heck *do*!— You don't forget a guy like *that*! Tall, muscular, handsome. He looked just like a movie star—Or really a whole lot *better* than the movie stars today—more like the old-time ones, you know?—the ones in the black and white oldies they show on TCM, when the men were handsome enough, all right, but also elegant and refined—Not foul-mouthed, muscle-bound yo-yo's like the dopey guys in those silly action films today."

"And *this* guy was elegant and refined?"

"I don't know for sure about refinement, Agent Braman. I didn't talk to him one on one; but he certainly *looked* that way. I don't know how to describe him exactly, but he looked like a really fantastic guy."

He shook her hand, told her (truthfully) what a terrific help she'd been, gave her his card—in case she recalled some pertinent little detail later on (a careful agent never really knew)—and circled the name on his printout sheet of the patient who'd flown the Friday morning pre-op coop. Then down to Billing for a phone number and address—Adrienne Hartman was the name, and the address a place in Paxton—Not all that surprising now that the jigsaw puzzle pieces began to slip in place.... Mrs. And *Miss* Hartman, eh? Hmmm. Hopefully the cops wouldn't find two bloodless female bodies missing stem cells in a dumpster someplace. After what some creep had done to Jodi—well, with an unknown quantity like *this* vampirish creature on the loose, a worried agent never knew!

But all right, anyway, doing his optimistic darnedest to think positive, and hoping to merciful heaven for the best—he went out to his Cadillac, clicked on his cell, and made the necessary call:

"Mrs. Hartman? Is this Mrs. Adrienne Hartman on the line?"

"Yes?" A guarded and dubious yes. You could hear the woman's caution on the phone. She was alive though: Cautious and dubious, admittedly, but possessed of all her stem cells and—alive!

"My name is...." He explained things briefly—at least a few of the many things he might be required to explain. Would she be home in—oh, say, a couple of hours or so? He'd like to drive out, speak to her and the girl—informally, of course; mostly off the record. All right, she told him; not particularly pleased about the meeting, from the sound of her voice, but compliant enough to agree—Few people failed to be compliant with the FBI—He glanced down at his watch again:

"How about we make it—oh, say, three o'clock, Mrs. Hartman?—Do you think that sounds OK?"

OK, she said—most reluctantly, he thought.

"It'll be best if your daughter's home too. I'll need to talk to her as well—OK?"

OK, the lady said, no less reluctantly. With which he fired up the car and headed out.

Terrific! Fantastic!—For here was a woman who actually *knew* something—she practically *had* to know *way* more than anyone else. The whole of Thursday night in her room with the fellow he was after, and on into Friday morning for who-knew-how-many hours more. The best eyewitness so far, by far—And the woman's daughter had reportedly been in on the whole thing too!

Great! Incredible!—A veritable goldmine of firsthand evidence if there ever *was* so plentiful a mine of gold! Hmm—Sidney clenched his jaw and thought a bit: Important—yes: Too important—WAY too important a witness—or *pair* of witnesses, actually—to be relegated to the incompetent drudges in the Bureau's general staff, *that* was for sure—especially after the mess that blithering idiot Kellerman had pretty nearly made with Mrs. Anthony.

Oh, he could run back in and write it up, of course—that's what all the Bureau manuals specified. But if he wrote it up—let's say he wrote it up—well, what exactly would those other agents do? First of all, they'd wait two days till Monday, when every detail in a person's memory decays dramatically with time. But they'd wait till Monday anyway, forty-eight hours farther into the mother and daughter's memory decay. And then at last on Monday they'd drive on out and haul the two scared ladies in, stick them in a room on Level Two with mirrored walls and blinding lights, spook the living daylights out of them!—and make damn sure they never said a word—Hell, threatening them would only guarantee they never said a *truthful* word.

That wasn't an option here. Not on a case as intractable as this—it *couldn't* be an option!—not with Jodi's file involved in it and all—No, Bureau protocol was out of the question now—He'd handle *this* one by himself, keep things pleasantly informal; keep the woman talking so she'd tell him what he absolutely had to know. She'd want to protect the suspect, certainly—All the people that they'd interviewed so far had wanted to protect him to a greater or lesser degree: the lady from the BP station, nice Mrs. Anthony, her husband George, and then those couple of dozen other folks whose lawns he'd raked of leaves. Everyone described the guy as sweet as pie, courteous, kindly, honorable, as humble and respectful as could be.

This Mrs. Hartman and her daughter—they'd no doubt feel the same. They would, of course—but he knew how to deal with adverse witnesses like that, didn't he?—Of course he did, he being the go-to interviewing expert in the place. So sure; he'd handle this urgent bit of fieldwork by himself—Who better?—

First of all, he'd head on over to the Bureau building—he still had lots of time—He'd grab enough recording stuff to document what the Hartmans had to say—for his protection as well as theirs, in case of later contradiction.

Nobody else would need to see or hear their statements; he could guarantee the privacy of that. The offices were open today—crime doesn't stop on weekends any more than Uncle Phil's pathologic duties do. There'd be a skeleton crew around—someone to fix him up with the equipment he would need—video, audio—whatever was available. Half an hour to get over to the building and put together the requisites and—lots of time, *loads* of time!—in thirty minutes he'd be merrily on his way.

So he headed straight downtown, and turned into the parking structure adjacent to the Bureau Offices, and pulled the Caddy into his regular designated space, then took the staircase up to Level Three. Then out the stairway when he got to Three, and down the corridor left, as usual—he could navigate the route there with a blindfold on—and through the office door leisurely, casually—it being two full hours now until he told the woman he'd be at her....

"Agent? Agent Braman, sir?—Is there a problem? What are *you* doing here?"

"Audrey! Well, but.... But what the devil are *you* doing here? I thought that...."

"It's my Saturday on duty, sir—We do one every month—just from seven to one, though, today. Rhonda Boyer comes in to replace me at one."

"But ... frankly, I didn't know you ladies ever worked on Saturdays."

"No, no reason that you *should* know, sir. They give us half a day off during the week once a month to make up for the extra time; and we try and schedule the off days to coincide with when our agents aren't here. I was off last Wednesday afternoon, when you were up in Stanleyville traipsing through the woods, looking for the murder suspect's tracks—That's how we usually work things."

"I never knew that—about your being off like that, I mean, and working weekends. So—how do you get all the incredible amount of work done that you manage to do for me when you take off on a weekday like that? How did you make up for last Wednesday, for example?"

"Wednesday?—Oh, that was easy; nothing to it—I'm doing it right now, in fact—I'm actually doing some majorly important stuff for you this minute, to tell the truth—Would you like to hear the latest update on our case?"

Sure he would; naturally he would; any information, at this unedifying point in his perplexity, would be a truly major plus. So he stepped over to nice Miss Hamblin's desk and plopped his wiry backside down on the only available corner that wasn't stacked with memos and files and charts—for busy Audrey had been working hard as usual, all right—Not too snugly seated there, but not all that uncomfortably either, on the worn and roughened wood; and Audrey looked up at him with those gentle Celtic eyes of hers and that pleasant Celtic smile—of mostly Irish parentage, he figured, factoring in the auburn hair and freckles on her pretty Celtic face—A sweet-as-honey care-giver of a female, if there ever was one, this shapely, knowledgeable secretary of his; she'd make some lucky fellow a splendid wife someday; and therefore:

"Sure," he told her. "I've got a bit of time to spare. So? What earth-shattering revelations has my clever Audrey got?"

"*Good* revelations, *fascinating* revelations. I'm glad you're sitting down, in fact—So, sir—Did you know there was a computer in the Hospital's Eighth Floor lab?—Where the cleaning lady found that doctor's body, I mean?—Did you happen to notice the computer when you went up there to check the crime scene yesterday?"

"I didn't notice one, Audrey; but they generally have computer terminals in those labs, so it's not that much of a surprise. But why do you ask? What about it?"

"Well, you know how compulsive our techs are here—You know they're pretty thorough when we send them out to a forensic site and turn them loose."

"I know that; sure; that's how they came across the baby—Why? What other wonders did they ferret out up in the lab?"

"Well, that computer that they came across? They dragged it in yesterday while you were at your meeting with Dr. Sniderman, and they went through the hard drive this morning—and guess what they found!"

Sidney shook his head: "Damn! I'm pretty sure I *can* guess, Audrey; I'm pretty sure I can—Our murder suspect probably used it—right?"

"He sure did. He used it to access—you know that file you found on the computer in Stanleyville—the lists of criminals and stuff?"

"Sure I know it. I wish to hell I could forget!"

"I know, sir; I'm sorry that I brought it up again. But anyway, our suspect apparently got into it. Through the cloud, they said. He didn't have everything in his files on it, but he did keep some, I guess—And guess what file he pulled up last from his search—Guess what file they found front and center, right at the top of the recent searches—I bet you're gonna guess that too."

"You'll probably tell me Lester Hazelton's file, right?" Sidney smacked his forehead in a whimsically demonstrative way. "So *that's* how he picked his victim out, is it?—Holy Moses, Audrey! He used that file of his to find the nearest appropriate donor!—And you know what for?—You know what he used the donor *for*, Audrey?—For *stem* cells, *that's* what. That's what he used that stillborn baby for too. Problem is, I haven't quite figured out exactly *why* he did that just yet—But the good news is: After snooping around a little bit and asking the right kinds of people the right kinds of questions—I came across a couple of witnesses who might just help me in the figuring. I'm on my way to Paxton to meet with them right now, as a matter of fact. And I ran up here to grab some monitoring stuff, since it's an impromptu interview in the field, and I haven't got a partner to sit *in* on an impromptu interview in the field, so I figured: well, respecting protocol, for the witnesses' protection, and my own protection too, I ought at least to get...."

"Well, sir; hold on a sec right there—If you need a second person to sit in on the interview—Well what about me?—I mean, what am I, sir—chopped liver?"

"*You*! But Audrey!—you're a ... you're only a...."

"I know, sir; I'm just a lowly little secretary here; but after nine long years of being your lowly little secretary every day on every kind of horrible felony known to man, don't you think I have a pretty good handle on what to do?"

"I'm *sure* you've got an *excellent* handle on what to do, Audrey; you're the cleverest staffer in the place—the best I've ever worked with, truthfully; I'd honestly be lost without you—Your being a secretary isn't the issue here at all, really—but...."

"But *what*? If you say that's not the issue, and you think I'm so darn smart and so darn helpful to the work you do, then

what's the problem? I'm done here in fifteen minutes—umm...."
She looked at her watch: "Well, fourteen now—or, actually, if
my minute hand is on the money, thirteen-and-a-half—and—
well, I'd *love* to see the famous Braman interview technique out in
the field. So—wait here a couple of minutes then, sir, if you don't
mind. I'll run back and get the video equipment that you'll need.
I'm sure I'm smart enough to figure out how to turn the camera
on and off."

16

The northeast part of Paxton, where Miss and Mrs. Hartman lived, was a lower-class section of town. Not a slum *per se*, for your smaller-type municipalities don't have slums *per se* in the same unsavory sense your bigger cities do. But they do have areas in the environs with less impressive homes in greater states of disrepair: porches where overhangs tend to sag a little downward; exteriors where paint is peeling from the wood in the occasional spot; where roofs look shabby with an asphalt shingle missing here and there; and a window or two might be broken out or boarded over if the home' s been vacant for a while. In such a slightly blighted neighborhood lived Mrs. Hartman and her daughter, according to the address on his hospital data sheet. And the moment he pulled up before the house in question, Sidney knew with a fair degree of certainty the sort of furnishings he'd likely find within.

"Mrs. Hartman?" he asked, when a pleasant-looking woman swung the inner door ajar, peering through the screen. "I called you earlier this afternoon. I'm Agent Braman, and this is my assistant, Miss Hamblin. Is it all right if we come inside?"

She didn't ask for ID—unlike Nurse Gardner at the hospital this morning—but he showed it to her anyway, as regulations required that he must. She looked tired and weak, this fiftyish-looking woman, but not frail or dramatically ill— Hardly at death's door, notwithstanding the surgical treatment she'd eschewed, and the dreadful diagnosis she'd been admitted with: a middle-aged woman with a patina of smile lines that made her sympathetically attractive in a way. It was nice to have found her with her stem cells present and her bones intact— *Exceptionally* nice; for she had a particularly engaging manner too, though cautious and guarded to a degree. Her fingers fidgeted and her eyes moved furtively as she ushered the two of them in, as gracious as the inward ushering seemed: Clearly, from her anxious tone and manner, there was something this pleasant Mrs. Hartman wasn't very eager to tell.

"I'll need to ask you some questions, ma'am, if I may. Miss Hamblin here will be taking notes—just to make sure we get your statements down correct. We may make a video recording as well, if we need to. But if we do, it'll be solely for my own personal reference, and won't be shown to anyone else at the Bureau without your signed permission, all right?—Does all that sound OK?"

She looked at him guardedly, neither agreeing nor refusing—At least for the moment, she seemed to go along. They followed her through a cheaply furnished little living room into an even smaller cheaply furnished little dining room, replete with scuffed wood table, an empty china chest, and four rather derelict chairs. She motioned to a couple of the seats toward one side of the table, and he and Audrey sat in them—sturdier to sit on than he'd thought—while she took a similarly weathered seat directly across from him. There was a dim light on above them, for she'd snapped the switch on entering; but the doorway to the kitchen was behind his back, and the woman had the brightness from a day-lit window in her face.

"Well, first of all, Mrs. Hartman," he began, not smiling—for a smile would have been inappropriate to the unsavory facts he had to tell. Not smiling, true, but he said it softly, almost sympathetically; hoping that the things he had to tell her were things she truly didn't know:

"It hasn't hit the papers yet, and probably won't get out in public till tomorrow, ma'am; but there was—well, there was a sort of incident at the hospital the night before you left. Do you, or might your daughter, have any knowledge of what I mean?"

Her face looked blankly cautious, and a little bit surprised. But there was no evidence of alarm there, and no palpable anxiety about some horrible revelation yet to come. Agent Braman read people very well, and what he read from this woman's reticent face and curious gaze was the relative certainty that if there'd been a person done to death upstairs of the room she'd spent the night in, she didn't know the slightest thing about it; he was confident of that—and rather glad about it, in fact— And she answered accordingly, just as he'd hoped she would:

"An *incident*? Umm, n-o-o…. I'm not *aware* of any incident that might have happened then…. What kind of incident do you mean?"

"Well, let me ask you something else then; something more specific: Is the name Lester Hazelton in any way familiar to you?"

She stared across the table, not directly at his eyes, but at a place a foot or so below—at his hands, perhaps, where they rested on the tabletop; or at the tabletop itself, just a little bit left of his stationary hands. There was a spot worn through the varnish on the wood beside his little finger, and perhaps her hazel eyes got fixed for some unfathomable reason on that.

"No, sir…. Um, I don't *remember* hearing it—What does that doctor—um, is it 'Hazelman'?—What does he look like?"

"It's 'Hazel*ton*', ma'am—But as to what he looks like—or *looked* like—I'm not a hundred percent sure, to be perfectly frank with you. The way I got to see him yesterday, I'm not really all that sure about his facial appearance. He was physically short—I can tell you that much; balding, overweight. He must have had a big belly, stocky legs, thin dark hair: Did you happen to run into anyone like that?"

"Umm, n-o-o." She shook her head and assumed a sort of look…. Well, best you could describe it was a mildly pleased expression of relief. Then she seemed to think a moment more, and the look got brighter, flashing into something very faintly like a smile. Then finally she took a breath, very deep and slow, and let it out with an almost audibly effusive gush—A thankful sigh of relief if there ever was one!

"No, *sir*! I didn't see *any* doctor like *that*—not anybody at *all* like the man you're describing—absolutely not."

"All right, that's good; I believe you, and I'm very glad to hear it, Mrs. Hartman; I genuinely am. But—I've got to ask you this then. We know about the man who spent the evening in your room with you: From anything he might have said or done, do you think that *he* might have run into the person I described? Did the man who was with you *say* anything, or *do* anything that might have…?"

She interrupted

"The man?—But … but *what* man?"

That 'what'—the fifth word in her question—leapt out at least an octave higher than the words that came before. And her hands, which had been resting on the tabletop, disappeared immediately onto her lap clean out of view. He didn't say a thing in answer to her query, but merely watched her closely as she squirmed beneath his gaze, until:

"Oh, OK—*I* see—You mean *him*—*that* man—Well, *that* man—he's just a sort of friend of my daughter's—of Linnie's. I don't really know that much about him, but ... but...."

"All right then, Mrs. Hartman; look, let me make this clear before we go any further: You're not under any sort of suspicion here; bear that in mind. All I need from you is a little bit of information about the man who was in your room that night. I can see you're reluctant about it, but let me explain to you why I need to ask: That doctor I mentioned before—He was found dead yesterday morning in the hospital. A cleaning lady found him...."

"*Dead!*—But.... Well, that doesn't necessarily mean anything *bad* happened to him, does it? Maybe he had a heart attack or.... Oh, you don't actually think that *I* ... or that my *daughter*...! But, well, that doctor that you said had died: Don't you think he might have had some medical condition that he died from, or...? I mean, you said he wasn't a young man, and that he was overweight and all, and...."

"No, ma'am; we *know* he didn't have a heart attack or die from some medical condition due to his weight or age. We know for certain he was killed. And we know for certain that he was killed for use as a sort of tissue donor. Someone killed him and harvested some of the cells in his body to use for...."

He stopped and stared across the table at the woman. For when he reached this juncture in his explanation, it struck him that her eyes had gotten wide and her lips compacted tightly in a thin straight bloodless line. The very look of horror on her face and terror in her eyes had destroyed his concentration utterly, so that, in beholding her frightened face and a subtle tremor of her lips, he altogether lost his train of thought. And before he managed to right that derailed train of thought again, the gape-eyed Mrs. Hartman asked, in halting words, and something of a frantic screech, pitched higher even than its treble of a minute or so before:

"Of *cells*?—But ... but ... what *kind* of cells?"

"Some of them were blood cells, ma'am; but the majority were ... stem cells."

The woman's mouth dropped open, suddenly and *literally*:

"*Stem* cells!—You said ... '*STEM* cells'?!—Oh *God*!"—She practically shrieked the loudest word—"Oh my GOD!" repeating this second phrase again in that shrilly shrieking voice—Oh, and that *face*! That angst-filled, fear-warped *face* of hers, wide eyed, white lipped, as the features looked *before* his revelation—at this weird point turned....

Green.

It's true of course: there isn't any fluid in the human body that can turn a person green. Pink, yes; purple, certainly; crimson in a livid fit of rage; and naturally many varied shades of sepia from the sun; then ashy gray when the blood deserts the skin from cold or shock: those are physiologic colors, biologically explicable, attributable to proven pigments in the skin or blood stream. One can readily relate to those.

But *green*? An unequivocal tint of *green*? No, there isn't any rhyme or reason to a person turning green. 'Green' is a descriptive term used in a purely literary sense to indicate envy or illness or disgust, without an actual basis in fact. Humans don't turn green; human skin can't actually turn green.

Nonetheless the woman's visage did just that—dramatically, unequivocally, just the way the pulpy novels paint it: "Oh GOD!" she repeated, getting greener still. And those hidden hands popped up from underneath the table; and she started to rub them, hand to forearm, hand to forearm, rubbing, rubbing, as if washing with imaginary soap. Then the motion got stronger, harsher, the hands scouring more and more emphatically, persistently, as though in vain attempt to scrub the green skin clean—as though this amazingly greenish woman sought to rub the very flesh and muscle of her forearms right clean off the bones, to rid her person of the vivid, otherworldly greenish hue. Rubbing, rubbing, and that ghastly greenish tint to her skin and ghastly-looking grimace on her face, and ghastly-sounding words she spoke, until....

Until it finally dawned on him!— OF COURSE! How could it *not* have dawned on him right from the very moment he stepped in?! But it finally registered, just now, this instant—BAM!—It finally rammed its obvious pathway through his brain:

"Oh my GOD, Mrs. HARTMAN!—It was for *you*, wasn't it? That man in your room killed the doctor and got those stem cells for *you*!—For YOU!"

"I ... I.... He didn't tell us.... We didn't know...."

Whereupon she got up from the table, popped up so abruptly that the chair she'd sat on fell backward with a thud against the wall and slipped down skittering with its back against the floor. She took no notice of the chair, made no move to right it, but rather stepped around its horizontal legs, turned absently, and scurried to the doorway of the little dining room and through it, and out beyond it, whimpering as she fled:

"Oh, *God*! I didn't.... We didn't.... I ... I'm going to be sick, I think. I'll get my daughter for you. Maybe she.... I can't.... I can't...."

Then she disappeared, and there were footsteps on the staircase going up; and then a moment later sounds of water running somewhere up above, and the distant sounds of retching—very faint but unequivocal: Aargh—Aargh, in the auditory distance overhead —And the flushing of a toilet—Glubb, hisss—And in the midst of all of this, Audrey turned her disbelieving gaze toward him to ask him:

"He gave the stem cells to *her*?—But ... but *why*?"

"Right—why?—That's the operative question, isn't it? And the answer is, I don't *know* why; I can't even *imagine* why. I can't imagine why he *did* it, and I can't imagine why any reasonable woman would have possibly *agreed* to it—although, maybe she didn't completely realize what he was giving her or where he got the stuff he gave. Actually, Audrey, from the sound of Mrs. Hartman's voice and the change in her color—Holy Moses! Did you see that amazing shade of *green*!?—Anyway, I'm pretty confident the woman *didn't* know where those stem cells came from. Maybe the daughter did, and maybe *she* can help clarify things some more. I'll go out and call her in a minute to try and get some answers to the...."

But before he finished his sentence, that funny look on Audrey's face, and a corresponding swivel of his head toward the spot where Audrey's eyes got all of a sudden fixed and fastened wide ...

Informed him that the daughter in question had just stepped in the room.

A feisty teenaged hellion if ever there was one! You could see that in the way she sauntered sternly toward her seat.

Around the table and over to the chair that lay collapsed on the floor was where she sauntered straightaway. She picked the flat chair up and set her narrow bottom in it, straight across the table from him, precisely where her mother had sat, elbows on the tabletop, peering steadily across and up at him, as though she'd been designated Grand Inquisitor and he some apostatic heretic of Holy Mother Church. For a minute she sat there mutely staring, then roused herself to tell him that she'd need to see his credentials—and requested Audrey's as well.

Audrey got a pass. A sort of stenographer, he explained, like the ones who sit below the judge's bench in court; and this steely-eyed Miss Hartman said OK.

But she didn't do as much with him—no way. She took the ID card he passed her, yanked it clean out of its acetate, and examined it the way you'd pore over a con man's million-dollar check, turning it around, holding it up to the light—maybe for a watermark, though the damn things didn't have watermarks now and never had them, far as expert Agent Sidney Braman knew. But she subjected the little card to every methodical scrutiny short of the use of a microscope. A simple power play, obviously: This, after all, was on the Hartman Family turf. The gesture didn't mean a lot; not on its own, it didn't—What it evidenced was that this Hartman kid was not a person lightly to be trifled with. And Sidney wrote such trifling off entirely before a minute in the room with her had passed.

She handed back the card, looked him up and down, peering past her nose; then sat stone silent for a minute more of dubious inspection before she asked him:

"So what did you guys say to my mother to get her so upset?"

"Not much, young lady. I told her about the doctor— that's about it—She didn't seem to know what happened to him that night."

"*What* doctor?—You mean...?—What doctor do you mean?"

Nonplussed, a t-e-e-n-s-y bit tentative; yet still entirely in control; and he answered her curtly and to the point:

"The *dead* one. Can you tell me anything about that?"

The girl's face suddenly grew ashen pale.

"*Dead*? He really *is* a doctor, and he's ... *dead*? Are you...?" She stopped and shook her head: "What happened to him then?—if you say he's dead."

"I was hoping *you* could tell *me* what happened to the doctor in that regard."

"*Me*! Why *me*? He was alive when.... *Wait* a minute, though: What doctor are we talking about exactly, huh?"

"Dr. Hazelton, Lester Hazelton. Can you tell me what you know about him? Look, I'm pretty well convinced that you and your mother weren't directly involved; but we're just as sure that the man who was with you in the room *was* directly involved, and we know the reason why he *got* himself involved, so...."

"Hold on, Mr.... Mr—*Berman*, is it?"

"'Braman,' actually, but people calling me 'Berman' seems to be a universal pastime these days—And *your* name, young lady, is—Linnie? Did I get that first name right?"

"Linnie, short for Lynette—right, Mr. Braman—So— Do I call you 'mister'?"

"That or 'Agent,' either one. I'm not too particular about what I get called."

"OK, 'Agent' it'll be—So what happened with the doctor then? You said some *man* with us might've been involved with what happened to the doctor, right? So that means that the man who was with us is OK, doesn't it?"

"Why? Is his welfare that much of a concern to you?— From all we know, this man we're looking for might well be a murderer—you understand that, don't you? That would be an odd sort of person for a girl like you to be concerned about, don't you think?"

"Yeah, OK; but he never...." She shook her head, by mighty force of will truncating the remainder of the sentence. Then after taking a moment to compose herself, and soften her expression, she continued: "OK, look, Agent Braman ... look, I'm not gonna tell you anything about him, no matter what you ask me and no matter what you threaten me with—OK? I made a promise, and I always keep my promises, so you can ask all you want, but you won't get a single other answer out of me at all."

"All right, fair enough, Miss Hartman—Linnie, if you don't mind me calling you that—I respect the fact that you're faithful to a friend, Linnie; I genuinely am. So let's do things a little differently, then, shall we? How about if *I* tell *you* some of the stuff about this friend of yours that we've learned so far, and you just listen to what I say and add anything to it if you like— and *only* if you like—How about that? Does that sound like a reasonable way for us to conduct our conversation?"

"Sure; why not? As long as you don't pressure me to tell you stuff—sure, go right ahead and talk."

"OK then; well, first of all, we know that this so-called friend of yours killed the doctor that I asked you about. He killed him Thursday night or early Friday morning...."

"Wait a minute, Agent," she interrupted, waving a hand five feet distant from his face. "How do you know the doctor guy you found was *killed*, huh? Maybe he just died from something natural. Just because you find a guy that's dead doesn't mean...."

He halted her mid-phrase with his own uplifted hand, saying: "I *know* the man was killed, young lady, because the murderer who killed him—by first snapping his neck at the third cervical vertebra down, incidentally—proceeded next to cut his body open and split his bones with a surgical chisel to extract a mega-dose of stem cells from the...."

"*Stem* cells!"

With *this* interjection—though less dramatic than the mother's change of countenance had been—the *girl's* face turned a definite shade of green as well: Anatomically inexplicable, just like her mother's greenish tinge—But there it was; seeing necessitates believing. Positively green—a subtlety of green, admittedly; but green for certain; and her green-hued face stridently exclaimed:

"*STEM* cells! Did you say—*stem* cells? Oh *man*! Oh *brother*! Then *that's* gotta be where he got...."

"That's where he harvested the cells he gave your mother—Right. *She* didn't know it—I'm positive of that—and I figured out even before you reacted the way you did that *you* didn't know it either, Linnie—I'm confident of that as well—So?—Are you still willing to protect a murderer like this fellow you consider a friend?"

"Was the dead doctor a nice man, Agent? Did he hurt people?"

"Oh, OK; great, terrific. You know that too, do you? Good; I'm glad; if you know that much, you probably know a whole lot more. Listen to me, young lady; listen carefully: We're on the same page here, you and I. I know he's trying to do some good in his—well, let's call it a very unorthodox way—But when you think about what's 'good,' you've got to factor in this business with your mother too. Do you think his getting her to cancel her treatment is likely to do *her* the slightest bit of good in any way?"

"Oh, but it *will*, though. It's only a couple of days now, but she's stronger already just in the past two days; I can see it. You don't know about the treatment; you don't understand. Did you ever hear of Lister?"

"Yeah, sure; I use his mouthwash every day. Why? Is your friend planning to treat your mom with mouthwash when the stem cells fail to work?"

"Oh man! There isn't any way to even *talk* to you! You don't understand *anything*. You guys'll *never* understand! He's *curing* my mom. She'll be back to normal a month from now; just wait and see!"

"OK, no point in arguing. I'll talk the stem cell issue over with your mother when I get the chance. But listen to me, Linnie. As I said, we're kind of on the same page here. I didn't get far enough with your mother to explain the things I wanted to explain, so I'll explain them to you now, OK? You promised that you'd listen, so here's the deal: As to your so-called friend—I know you're trying to protect him, and I respect you for that. But bottom line—and this is the crux of the matter here—it'll be much, much better for your friend in the long run if I'm the one who gets to him first. There's one little wrinkle in the case he needs to explain—about a certain very disconcerting file I found on his computer—But if he can get through that, and convince me that he wasn't a party to a certain deed in question, then I'm the only one who maybe has the concept down that he's basically a well-intentioned fellow in his distorted sort of way; and I really don't want to hurt him—Actually, to level with you, young lady, I'm not quite sure exactly what I *am* going to do once I've had a chance to talk to him about that file—But believe me, truthfully, you'll be doing this friend of yours an enormous service if you give me some information on how to find him, and help to let me talk to him before some not-as-sympathetic person finds him first—Do you follow what I'm saying, Linnie Hartman?—*Do* you?"

Despite the obvious composure and bravado, she rather sheepishly nodded yes.

"OK, then—well, what I need to know from you is what sort of issue I'm gonna have to deal with here. There's something very, very weird about this case, and even weirder about this good-guy–bad-guy friend of yours; but I've got to deal with the weirdness sooner or later, one way or another, since that's my job. I assume this man has given you at least some minimal vital information about himself—Am I correct in that assumption?— Just give me a yes or no to that; all you have to do is shake your head or nod."

She nodded, a trifle more definitive a gesturing than the last reluctant nod; and she vouchsafed a millisecond of eye contact before her gaze dropped down to the tabletop again where it had been directed since the sensitive topic of stem cells first arose.

"OK, good; great; I think you understand where I'm coming from then. So—You were with him for quite a while, and he talked to you at least part of that time, I'm sure. I'll need to know at least a couple of things about him; enough to understand what I'm getting myself into, both for my protection and his—So ... can you tell me just a little bit of what he said?"

The girl stared down at the tabletop, not looking up for even an instant this time; and he left her for the lengthening moment with her thoughts. A minute passed—or so it seemed—during which he said nothing and the girl said nothing, and during which gape-mouthed Audrey looked on, ratcheting her eyes between the two of them, a viewer of some schizophrenic ping-pong game played with illusory balls and imaginary paddles for million-dollar stakes on a dining room table entirely devoid of net. Silence; motionlessness, an infinitude of delay—then abruptly:

"He's—you don't understand, Agent Braman—He's not *from* here."

"From *here*?—You mean.... So you're saying he's not from the *area*?—from ... *Pittsburgh*? From ... *Pennsylvania*?—*What*? That may be true, Linnie, he may have come from out of state, but that doesn't even *begin* to explain...."

"No. No, that's not what I mean at *all*. He isn't from *here*. He isn't *from* here at all."

"So— you're saying he's—*what*?—a foreigner, right? He's not from *America*? Is he an *illegal* then? Even so, even if he *is* illegal, no matter *where* he came here from, that *still* doesn't explain...."

"No, sir—No! I *don't* mean he's from another country; I *don't* mean he's not a citizen. That's not what I'm saying at *all*! I'm telling you he isn't from *HERE*!—*They* aren't from here, is what I mean—That's what I'm trying to tell you. You can lock me up or whatever you want to do, but I promised him I wasn't going to tell anybody anything, and I won't say one word more than that!"

Wow! He wiped his face: All right, he figured; no reason to torment the kid any further; no way either she or her mother had been culpably involved. He let her go at that point—And no sooner did she leave the room than her no-longer-green-faced mother reappeared in the dining room doorway. Adrienne Hartman was calm now, placid and composed. One thing was clear as glass: she'd been out of the loop as far as any sort of aiding and abetting went—that was as obvious as the erstwhile greenness of her face—A nice, naïve, manifestly decent woman; far more an innocent bystander than any sort of active participant in an illegal act.

She offered to make them tea, and he accepted strictly out of cordiality—That and maybe the chance to convince her that the benevolent charlatan who'd talked her into those stem cells—OK, granted that he might have meant well in his own deluded way, but—at any rate, best if she went back to the hospital to get the treatment she would need before the hour got too late. An obviously kind lady, an obviously decent lady—too nice and gullible and trusting to have to die of cancer if there was even the slightest possibility of being saved. Their vigilante vampire might have tried to help her in his inmost heart. But if this kindly woman died from her disease, her death would be partly on his hands.

So they got their cups of tea and sat with Adrienne Hartman and talked a while. Now that her daughter had spilled some of the beans—or so she likely would have imagined—and now that the cat was partway out of the bag, the woman spoke more freely, telling what she knew, though she obviously didn't know an awful lot. And the little bit she knew, and essential facts she told them, were:

"The man who was with us in the hospital—He didn't tell us anything about that doctor—the dead one, I mean. If I'd known about the treatment coming from a dead man, I never would have…."

"It's all right; no one's ever likely to arrest you for being too trusting, Mrs. Hartman. I just want you to promise me you'll go back to your doctor in Pittsburgh and get the surgery you need."

"You really think that man—that handsome friend of Linnie's—was a fraud?"

"I can't say for sure that he *meant* to be misleading in what he tried to do—no. From everything I know about him, he tries to do good as he considers good to be. If I had to guess, I'd guess that he was honestly trying to help you in his misguided way, but—I'm pretty sure the doctors at the medical center would be a whole lot safer bet in treating your disease. He must have been persuasive, though, for you to trust him the way you did. He's a pretty engaging fellow, from what some of our other witnesses have said."

"Oh, he *is*; he really *is* a terrific person when you get to talk to him. To listen to him talk, he seems to understand every single thing there is to know. He's really brilliant—I'm sure of that. All that time I spent with him, all night Thursday and then part of Friday too—In all that time, I couldn't manage to follow more than a tenth of the complicated scientific things he said."

"When he was with you in the hospital, you mean?"

"No, he didn't talk too terribly much in the hospital. He left for quite a while from late in the afternoon till really late in the evening. Then he came in and gave me the treatment; so I guess while he was gone, that was when he...."

"Yes, I suppose that's when he went upstairs to get your cells. So—if you didn't talk to him very much in the hospital, and he said all those scientific things you couldn't understand, then...."

"It was in the car; that's when he talked the most. He talked to us for hours on end. We drove him—Linnie probably told you where we drove him, didn't she?"

"She probably mentioned it, but with all the other things she told us, I didn't catch exactly what she said about the place. It was.... Let's see: She said it was...."

"Morgantown; we drove him to Morgantown. I'm sure she told you that. He sat in the back and talked to us and...."

"In the back of your car, you said—right? He was in the back seat of your *car* while he was talking?"

"Yes, right. He sat back there and talked a lot, and explained a lot of complicated scientific things to Linnie, and...."

"And he was there for *how* long?—In your car, I mean—Total time?—What would you say as an estimate?"

"Oh let's see. We drove him to the terminal in Pittsburgh first—that took half an hour maybe; there was a lot of traffic that day. Then Linnie made me run back and pick him up again—she was pretty frantic about it—and we drove around a little bit more in the city. Then we took him to Morgantown. We stopped for lunch at a Burger King for twenty minutes or so, but total time, I'd guess—maybe four hours, probably closer to five if you add the whole thing up."

"Five hours in your car! Then there's got to be—he's got to have left some evidence back there then—some hair bulbs or…. Where *is* your car, Mrs. Hartman? Can I see it?"

"Sure; of course you can. It's outside—the ugly green Toyota with the rusty hood. But I didn't see anything back there where he sat, or…."

"Well, did you clean it at all? Did you sweep it out or vacuum? Or has anyone *else* sat in the back seat since yesterday when the man you took to Morgantown was sitting there?"

"No…. I…."

"Five hours in the back? He sat there for five whole hours!?—I need your car then. I need to take it. I'll make whatever arrangements you want, anything you ask for, but I absolutely need to take that car with me today."

"Yes, but—I can't get by without transportation, sir. I mean: if you think I should go back to the hospital in Pittsburgh pretty soon; if you take my car away…."

"All right, let me think a sec…."

He thought that agitated second, while Audrey watched with widening eyes and gaping mouth. Then finally he pursed his lips and offered:

"OK, how's this: I'll give you *my* car—Not just lend it, but I'll *give* it to you in exchange—how's that?—free and clear. Do you know a notary around here? I'll sign it over and get the signing notarized today; then I'll send you the title as soon as I get home. If you give me your car, I'll give you mine. It's a nice one, just like new. My father bought it for me, but I can get another one anytime I like. It's a couple of years old, I guess; but it runs perfectly, and everything works—the power windows and the seats and the cruise control and…."

"It has power windows and cruise control? I never drove a car that had cruise control."

"Great—Let's go to a notary, you and I, right now, and I'll give you a letter of intent to send you a signed title—I'll get it to you tomorrow, I promise you I will. Just give me your car; let me take it right now; and we'll call the even trade a deal."

Whew! A long and very pensive ride back to Pittsburgh—And a very rickety one as well, for the Hartman car didn't compare to the pretty couple-year-old Cadillac he'd so willingly given up.

Audrey said something about him being 'out of his mind *completely!*' to do what he'd just done—as to the vehicle swap, she meant—But he explained to her that this job was more a hobby than anything else, that cars were the merest of disposable items to him, subject to wrecks and dents at any time; and moreover, that the cost of doing business had never been an object of concern in his investigations. If he came up with even a single hair bulb with the tiniest trace of viable DNA—which, after the guy had sat back there for five whole rumbly-riding hours in this heap, was more likely than not that he would—the exchange would be the best he'd ever made—cost of replacing the Cadillac be damned!

For a while after their abbreviated little converse, neither he nor Audrey spoke more than a word or two. That dialogue with the girl had been quite an interview to witness on a secretary's first time out, so Audrey was probably a little shell-shocked—not that *he* wasn't a wee bit shell-shocked too—from the loony implications of what the girl had finally opened her clever mouth and said.

At any rate, half an hour into their ninety-minute ride, they both seemed to recover from the impact of Linnie's riveting words and their connotative import; and once they'd recovered enough to talk, he gave a silly sideways smile to Audrey beside him on the seat and asked her:

"That stuff she told us, Audrey; right at the end—I'm curious: You heard her same as I did: What do you make of it?"

"About the man not being *from* here, you mean?"

"Yes, that's what I mean *exactly*. Did you hear the way she said it the same as I did?"

"I think I *did* hear her the way you did, sir. What do you think she meant by that?"

"I'm a little reluctant to even *think* what she might have meant. But the kid seems like a bright enough girl, and sane enough, and…. But given all that cleverness and sanity, what *else* could she possibly have meant when she told us what she did?"

"I've been trying to think of something, sir, and I'm afraid I simply can't."

"I'm afraid I can't either, Audrey. She seems to have swallowed all the crazy stuff our vampire guy has fed her. One thing I'll give him—the guy's persuasive as hell. He talked the mother into getting stem cells for her cancer, and he seems to have talked the girl into believing that he's come from outer

space—or 'they' have—She *did* say 'they', didn't she?—I'm not
at all sure what she meant by that either—the 'they' part—Good
God, though, Audrey! I hope there aren't any *more* of these
vigilante vampires out there harvesting bad guy's cells! If there
are, though—I was thinking, back in the Hartmans' place, even
before the daughter told us what she did, that if there are...."

"Yes sir? If there are, then what?"

"If there *are* more of them, Audrey, then maybe that file
I found was something that got used not just by our suspect, but
by others of whatever the hell kind of thing he is. And if that's the
case, then it's a whole lot easier to reconcile his being the
benevolent kind of character everyone describes—and not the
guy who did that awful business to my wife."

"Uh-huh, that does sound a whole lot better than what
we kind of thought before, I suppose."

"It does, it really does—But *listen* to me, will you!?—I'm
starting to fall for some of this screwball business myself. The
whole thing's pretty goddam crazy, and it's getting crazier by the
minute—Sheesh! Alien vampires! Holy Moses! How in the world
did he manage to put that kind of foolishness in a clever young
girl's head?"

"It *does* sound pretty off the wall, sir, I agree. But none of
it is totally im*pos*sible, is it? Couldn't there be some even minimal
basis in fact?"

"In *fact*? Well, I guess you're right when it comes to the
theoretical—Everything *is* remotely possible in a far-fetched sort
of way. After all, we live in an incomprehensibly complex
universe, so who's to guarantee what's possible and what's not?
But we're talking *credible* now, Audrey, not merely '*possible.*' An
alien? From another planet? Do you understand the flat-out
absurdity of a concept like that?"

"I'm not sure that I do, sir; not really. If you really *do*
think the idea is ridiculous, would you mind explaining to me
why?"

"Sure I will. Easy as pie. Here's the way the science goes:
First of all, no other planet in our solar system could possibly
harbor intelligent life—the conditions just aren't conducive. So
when we're talking alien life forms, we're talking other stars
beyond our sun—OK? And you know where the closest star
beyond our sun is—how far away it is, I mean? From Earth?"

"No, sir, not exactly. Pretty far, I'd guess."

"Well you're right; it *is* pretty far. It's Proxima Centauri, which is something like five light years away—Do you know the meaning of that distance? How far away from Earth that distance represents, I mean?"

"Not exactly, I don't, sir. No."

"OK, well, from the astronomy stuff I took a million years ago in undergrad, I kind of remember that a light year is the distance that light travels in a year, OK? Light goes 180,000 miles per second; and if you multiply that figure by the number of seconds in a minute—sixty—and then the number of minutes in an hour—sixty as well—then by the number of hours in a day—twenty-four, of course—then by the number of days in a year—365: Anyway, it comes out something like six trillion miles that a light beam travels in a year—and the closest star is five times that six trillion miles away from us—like, thirty trillion—OK?"

Audrey said OK.

"Now nothing can travel at anything even remotely *close* to the speed of light—physics won't allow it. The closer a moving object gets to the speed of light, the more massive it gets, meaning much more energy is needed to propel it. Getting up to the speed of light—which would get you from the nearest star to Earth in five years if you could go that fast, right?—That would take an infinite amount of energy—you see? And if you increase the energy stores on a spaceship, you increase the mass even more.

"So no, nothing can go faster than even the tiniest fraction of the speed of light. It would take hundreds—probably thousands or millions or even billions—of years for anything we can conceive of to get from any worlds that might have life forms to here; so travel from another focus of life to the earth just simply cannot occur. Ever. This character coming from outer space would be a ridiculous concept in the extreme."

"So what did the woman's daughter mean then? Maybe he isn't from…."

"Well?—Where, Audrey?—*Where?*"

"Gosh, I just don't know."

"Nor do I; nor do I. First the daughter says we're dealing with an alien—which is crazy from the get-go—then she implies there may be lots of them. It's nuts—totally nuts! I can't make heads or tails out of this screwball case, you know?—I mean—

what?—Are there gonna be a thousand *more* of these lunatic mass murderers out there we need to watch for?"

"I don't know, sir, but it shouldn't be all that difficult to find out."

"No? How would you go about finding it out then?"

"Well, sir, if I were trying to find someone who'd killed a lot of criminals, I guess I'd look for a place where there's a measurable decrease in crime."

"All right, that makes sense, but…. But you're *right*! That's a *great* idea! How would we go about tracking something like that?"

"Oh, I can get that for you easy as pie, sir. I can get it for you by tomorrow if you like—or Monday, I mean, tomorrow being Sunday still. All I need to do is get the crime statistics for the past—well, how many years would you want me to check it for?"

"How many? I don't know—maybe twenty. That's how long the murderer was up in Stanleyville, so I'd say twenty as a start."

"OK then; I'll get us the crime statistics for the last twenty years, county by county in Pennsylvania. Then, if the theory pans out and Stanleyville shows the pattern we're looking for, what other states should we check out next? Are there any special ones you'd like me to work on first?"

"Well, let's see: Why don't we start with—oh say, the states *bordering* Pennsylvania—how long would *that* take?"

"No time at all, sir. With the computer it's quick. I'll color-code the counties by crime and print out some maps. I'll have the Pennsylvania map for you first thing Monday morning, and then if that looks promising, I can do the others by maybe Tuesday afternoon. It'll be really fast once I get the numbers programmed in—So—will Monday be soon enough?"

"Monday? You'll really have the Pennsylvania map by *Monday*!? How in the world are you going to have it done by Monday if it's Saturday now and you won't be back in the office till Monday morning yourself?"

"Oh the place never shuts down completely, you know. When we get back this evening, I'll get right on it, right away. I'll be done with all the counties in a couple of hours, I'd guess; then get it printed for you Monday morning first thing. You'll have it on your desk by…."

"Wait a minute, Audrey: I can't justify your working extra hours on a weekend like this if you're on a salary and aren't getting paid. That wouldn't be fair to you. The map can wait another day or two if it has to. I've got lots of other stuff to work on, and there's no pressing reason…."

"Oh but there *is*, sir; there *is*! If you can give away a pretty car for a jalopy like this, how can I complain about a couple of hours more work on a weekend? No, sir, I'll set the program up tonight. Monday morning early, we'll know for sure just how well our theory works."

"OK—sheesh!—if you insist on it—but if you do, I'm gonna owe you one, OK?"

"OK, Agent, but if you owe me one—you can pay me back right now, this minute, by answering a question then, how's that?"

"Sure, Audrey, if I can come up with an answer, the answer's all yours."

"Well then, I was wondering … how come you didn't mention the stillborn baby when you talked about the stem cells today?"

"Would *you* have, Audrey? Would *you* have mentioned it if you were me?"

"Umm, probably not, sir."

"Why not?"

"I don't know. The woman was upset about the idea of getting stem cells from the doctor, so…."

"So knowing about the baby would have thrown her over the edge completely, don't you think?"

"I suppose so. I suppose that's probably right."

"Well, there's your answer then. She's a decent woman, and she's got enough bad stuff on her plate, what with her sickness and all the rest going on; no point in burdening her with more. And the daughter too: A nice kid, don't you think? I mean, the way she put herself on the line to defend some passing stranger she scarcely knows. I've got a lot of respect for that, Audrey. She and her mother are both pretty decent folks. No point in either one of them knowing unpleasant stuff they don't really need to know."

"You know, sir, you're a whole lot nicer person than the image you like to project. I've seen it for a long time, working with you the way I have, but all the other people in the office think…."

"Well let's just let them keep on thinking what they're thinking, shall we? We don't want to ruin the curmudgeonly mystique I've managed to earn over the years. So between the two of us, Audrey, my best of all the secretaries in the world, about that dubious niceness you think Sidney Braman's got going for him—how's about we keep that nasty little secret to ourselves?"

17

Over the guardrail, up over the concrete abutment; then fast down the steep-sloping hillside he came; half a mile up the highway from where the bus sat idling on the gravel shoulder, waiting for the urgent response team to come.

Yes, that frazzled driver would have phoned into town for an ambulance by now—But phoned into Charleston not *only* for an ambulance: The medics would attend to this mean-eyed fellow's mangled arm, you see. But the dastardly fellow who'd mangled it—they'd need a *different* kind of response team for him. Forget the circumstances—looking into the circumstances would take a lot of time—time that no one would be all that eager to spare. So circumstances aside, just haul the crazy forearm-mangler in and lock him up; we'll look into the details anon—

Which concept simply wouldn't do, unfortunately; these details, when looked into, had a good bit of the devil in them.

And so he'd jumped out of the bus when the driver ran forward and sprang the door, helping the dastardly mangler-of-forearms to get the hell away! And once he'd been let out on the berm, he'd raced ahead this good half a mile or so, then leapt down deer-like off the Interstate at the first side road crossing underneath: now scrambling down the steep embankment's treacherous grade, half sliding, half plummeting; clinging here with a desperate handhold, braking there with a slippery toehold in the withering autumn weeds....

Ah, but neither braking nor grasping had served him quite enough; for most of the way he plain-and-simply fell; fell hard and fast down all the thirty-some-odd feet of quasi-vertical descent until....

Until in the end it was with a pretty jarring impact that he finally hit the ground.

A long and precipitate fall that brought him sprawling onto the roadside's tarry berm and spilled him headlong outward like the limberest of circus acrobats onto the nearer lane of the two-lane undercrossing road—Which heavy landing occurred, as fate would have it, just at the very instant that a pickup truck was winding underneath the overpass around the bend. It very nearly hit him; and *in* very nearly hitting him, the old battered vehicle swerved to the roadside, swung in the gravel a quarter-turn round, and finally came to a rattling … clattering … chattering … stop.

"Hey you thar, mister—y' OK?"

He clambered to his feet, deftly, as was his agile wont, dusted himself off, picked up the shoulder bag that had ended its own independent transit right at the junction of pavement and berm a yard or so behind, and answered the thin, gaunt, old driver of the truck, after a momentary effort to catch his breath:

"Yes, sir; thanks for asking, but I'm fine. Just had the wind knocked out of me for a second, is all. I'm perfectly fine, though. Thanks for stopping to check; but you needn't be the least bit concerned about me."

"You come down offa th' Interstate up thar?"

He sidled over to the open window of the vehicle to respond.

"I did. Um…. Car trouble. Say—sir—do you know if this road leads into Charleston?"

Slender as a reed, ashen as a ghost, with a wisp of backswept hair just as thin and gray and spectral as the rest of him; hollow cheeks indented by departed molars many years removed, sallow skin, deep-set eyes, bony arm out the driver's window raising a skeletal finger to point:

"Yep, straight up that-a-way, young feller; straight on ahead. You goin' thar now?"

"Planning on it. Hoping to."

"Howsabout I take ye then? I'm a headin' thar myseln."

He looked at the man, a long incisive look. Good vibes, trustworthy vibes. If there was one ability he'd acquired these past three hundred-some-odd years, it was the facility of reading human beings at a glance. So many telltale clues that it took the merest fraction of an instant to decipher: The fixity or wayward motion of a person's gaze; the dilation and constriction of his pupils when he looked you in the face; the set of the chin—up, down, dominant, submissive, or what-you-will—the timbre of his voice to gauge the quantity of calm or stress; the nature or motion of an arm's positioning or gesturing: Men, women, young, old, infantile, senile, or indeterminate: no more difficult than dumb domestic animals to observe and comprehend, once one learned the blatant cues that told their tales. The good folks stood out just as clearly as the bad ones did. He'd lived these all-too-many years by harvesting the very worst of humankind to keep himself alive. And recognizing the predominant bulk of not-so-bad, and the scarcer group of truly decent ones, was an inevitable corollary of that.

This man, old and feeble as he was, seemed ... well: ill, lonely, stoical, gregarious more than most—And he was, as to his nature, fundamentally good as well, genuinely good: a kindly man readily identifiable by crinkled eye and gentle gesture and soft-voiced intonation. A definitely decent man, for sure, no doubt in the least. And so, since riding in his truck right now would be a safe enough option, as to the driver's benevolent intent; and seeing further that a lift into town would be of enormous benefit, knowing that the law was likely coming soon—Well then: He shouldered up that bag of his and answered with a thankful smile:

"Yes, *great*! You *sure*? It wouldn't be an inconvenience? I could really use a ride to Charleston if you mean it and you're heading that way."

"Sure thing then, sonny—hop in."

The creaky door swung open, he climbed up on the seat, slammed the door shut once his feet were safely on the mat, and the old man started off. And as the rusty vehicle rattled up to speed, it was noteworthy—and rather curious as well—that the fellow shifted gears without once engaging the clutch; shifted pretty darn smoothly too, noiselessly, as though he blended into the machine and knew this old Ford Ranger pickup truck the way an introspective man might know his own familiar train of thoughts. And once the clutchless shifting was over with and done and high gear finally attained, the man reached down, grabbed one of the several soft drink cups lying on the floor, spat in it—tobacco juice from the looks of what went in—dropped the mangy cup down to the floorboard with an absentminded flick of the wrist, and asked:

"Whatcher gon' do about thet car?"

"Sorry?"

"Thet car, yor car. Ye gon' jes leave 'er set? Up on the freeway thar—leave 'er set up on the freeway by its lonesome?"

No, he said, taking a moment first to de-colloquialize the question, then half a moment more to frame an apt response: Major problem with the engine—which sounded about right—

He'd need to get the darn thing towed, he figured; find a shop in Charleston that could do the work, order the necessary parts, and so on, so forth—reasonable, plausible, intelligible to the man—He'd probably just rent another vehicle in the meantime, he supposed, and....

"Never seen nobody come down off'n no high-pitch grade like thet'n afore. You some kinda circus acrybat or somepin?—Or mebbe tryin' ta commit sueycide!"

"No, just lucky, I imagine. I had no idea the slope was so steep till I took that first misguided step. I guess I should be thankful I didn't kill myself."

"Sho nuff—You ain't f'om round hyar, I can tell thet f'om the way ye talk."

"No, I'm from ... well, out east of here originally."

Out far, *far* east, he mused, chuckling a little to himself at the stupendous irony of that gigantic understatement. The nice old man was navigating a bit of curvilinear road, which gave some quiet time to think, and his thoughts took him leisurely back to the place where he was born.

That place was east, all right—across the ocean sort of east, if you're talking continent of birth. Then east a good bit farther still across the nations that a backwoods pilot of a tatty truck might've heard tell of on some travelogue or other as he was channel-surfing through: East past England sort of east, then eastward further still past the old familiar standby states like Germany and France and Spain; past Switzerland and Tyrol too, and on beyond the Slavic region in its turn, clear eastward to the northern uplands of Romania—though the locals had no concept of a unified Romania back in those ancient days. They called their border region Transylvania, a lowly Turkish province till the Habsburgs muscled in.

His father was born there—'created,' one might better say—one of the Originals, the fifty or sixty—not even the Originals knew exactly how many of them there were—fewer than a hundred at any rate that arose spontaneously in their busy market town. Their knowledge of how and why—the biology, the physics—was tenuously sketchy at best—But what they knew was, that they were programmed for a purpose: a purpose that was instinctive in their minds and souls and bodies from their very birth.

They had been—not 'created' exactly—but rather modified in some fundamental way. Father himself had no real understanding of this—how could he have?—having been born in an age that knew nothing of genetics or genetic programming or how such modifications could be induced in a limited population from somewhere unimaginably far away.

No, Father couldn't have even conceived of how he and the others came to be; but now, three-hundred-odd years later, it was easy enough to speculate, extrapolate, reason out how the genetic engineering might possibly have been done. Not precisely where it came from or the specific task it was designed to do— that information was in the precious box and, by Father's orders, wasn't to be accessed until the time was ripe. But one day now, it *would* be ripe—a day now not too far away—and the mystery would finally be solved. In the meantime all the rest was guesswork, but the guesses were getting ever closer to the truth.

Like the anemia. That was something that Father had stumbled on by pure luck and happenstance. Father was a doctor by profession—Not that medical training in those benighted days meant an awful lot—But Father was a highly gifted doctor and a clever fellow too—a good bit cleverer, quite possibly, than the rest. And he was observant as well, and inquisitive, and able to think outside the box. Not long after *he* was born—when his father was a little over thirty—suddenly, out of nowhere, many of the Originals began to die. This too must have been programmed in, it now seemed evident: Complete the task you need to do within the allotted time, then simply cease to be. And they *would* have ceased to be—all of them would have—if Father hadn't happened on his magic cure.

He had doctored most of them; Father was the only medical practitioner among their special group, it seemed. And being wise and curious and adventurous of thought, he noticed something very odd about the strange new illness that had arisen among his flock: The sick ones as they progressively sickened showed progressively more watery-looking blood. A curious observation, undoubtedly; something he had never clinically observed before—Which prodded him to reason thus: All right, if watery-looking blood was a concomitant of this new disease.... Well?—might not the new and strange disease be treated by somehow thickening the thinning blood?

There were wars about the land aplenty, death and mayhem everywhere—what with Turks fighting Habsburgs, and Turks and Habsburgs fighting mutually among themselves—And with plenty of destructive war, there was an abundance of bloodshed in its wake. Blood—oceans of it, everywhere, spilled wholesale, free for the taking....

Ah, but how might human blood be harvested so as to keep its useful properties intact? And how might the useful blood be administered to the dying to ameliorate their strange disease? Those were knotty problems to be solved—leaving aside the unknown imponderables of blood type incompatibility and such—But without some treatment or other, all of the patients were doomed to die—so what was there to lose?

In the end, Father thought: no, there's nothing to lose whatever, so might as well experiment—as all good doctors do. He tried many things, went down many a dead-end passage till he reached his long-sought goal. Wood and metal didn't work, and so he had glass syringes fabricated by a local blower—they seemed to keep the blood from going bad—then learned empirically to purify the glass and needles he'd had fabricated with moderate amounts of heat. That helped a whole lot too.

Of blood compatibility, he hadn't the faintest clue, of course—medical science wouldn't arrive at *that* contemporary concept till three hundred years beyond Father's time. Many of his patients died, that was inevitable; but not all—not quite all. A number of them survived—whether from getting the correct type of blood by pure good fortune—they died a little later on, as might be expected—or from having the incredible luck of being universal recipients, AB positive blood types; in which case they lived healthily and long.

His father was probably a universal recipient—though none of them could even have conceived of that likelihood back then—and he and his sister inherited that invaluable trait as well. Sister was born two years after his mother died. *Her* mother—his criminally twisted stepmother—had worked with Father as a sort of nurse and occasional midwife. She had cared for Mother in her illness: a skilled associate of Father's, it seemed, so convincing in her trustworthiness and reliability that no one linked the death of his kindly mother—and later of his father too—with the lethal dose of arsenic she had secreted in their food. Her guilt would never have been known for sure, but for her madhouse ravings after she'd been locked away to spare her own young daughter from being poisoned too. The arsenic dosage hadn't quite been sufficient to fully do poor Sister in.

Stepmother raved out her last few lunatic years in London's infamous Bedlam madhouse. They'd ended up in

London fresh from Hanover. Father had ministered to the court there, then followed the dynasty to England when Elector George inherited his kingly throne. It was in England that he himself, newly come of age by then, matured as an apprentice to his father, attending the nobility for bulging bags of gold; learning the family trade, of course—And learning too the art of treating the disease that would have killed each one of them if they hadn't found the secret cure. It would have killed Sister too: she would have succumbed shortly after age thirty, like the rest, if he, in Father's absence, hadn't intervened: Not that she felt the least bit grateful for his help. He had promised Father that he would look after her, and whatever gratitude she felt was due, she felt it due to a generation earlier than that of the brother she had wanted to disown.

A fresh-cheeked girl in her twenties, was his not-yet-lunatic sister when he went off to the continental wars. His illness had just then commenced, but that mattered not a bit. For he was doctoring in wartime, and doctoring in wartime meant blood—abundant blood everywhere, come and get your fill. Dead Frenchmen, dead English, a polyglot of nations dying or dead: it didn't matter whence the blood had come—Spanish, French, whatever—for he could use it all. AB positive—though he hardly could have guessed that then—and you are lucky enough to use it all.

But there was more beside the blood: Father taught him much, but there was more to learn for the inquisitive, and wartime was a perfect time to learn such things. Father had experimented, and *he* experimented too. Blood got bad, it seemed. It needed to be fresh to be of use. But if a body wasn't fresh and its blood went bad—well, what do you know, but it turned out that marrow could be beneficial too. He didn't know the marrow that he used in lieu of blood held stem cells—how could he ever have imagined such a thing back then?—but....

"Sounds it," said the thin old man, having negotiated the last of his tricky curves and having done so clutchlessly downshifting and shifting up again. He spat some more into a Styrofoam cup, flicked it to the floor, and repeated: "The way you talk sho sounds it," remarking still the un-Virginian accent of the acrobatic fellow in the pickup's seat: No longer a Transylvanian accent, the nice man might remark—no longer British either, these last two-hundred-some-odd years—he'd lost that stuffy European mode of speaking long ago—But emphatically American these later days, Midwestern, the nondescript broadcaster-ese of the contemporary airwaves. Bland, plain, white-bread-and-mayonnaise American, through and through—Though to the thin, old man half a meter leftward, he probably sounded Ivy League New England sort of east:

"You out f'om *way* down east, I bet. So then, sonny— You got bidness hyar-'bouts?"

"Business?" he echoed. "Yes, actually I *do* have business of a sort. I'll probably be here a day or two to get it done—Two days probably, or at the outside maybe three."

"Got folks round hyar-'bouts then?"

"No, not really—But—Well, actually I guess I kind of do; I suppose I *do* have what you might call family, in a peculiar sort of way."

Family! Yes, by the strictest definition of heredity she was family—though not the kind of family one might think of in the slightest sentimental way. If the man had seen his face just then, he might have surmised the irony in the question he'd asked and the sarcasm in the answer he'd been given in return. But the snaky road required his attention once more, and the old man never looked aside.

"Family in a funny kind of way, I guess, but nobody here I'd look forward to ever running into again. She and I—we had a little falling out the last time I was in town."

"Figgers. Relations is gen'rally like thet; oft times they is, I guess—Well then, young feller, since ye ain't-a-visitin' no fambly, ye got some other place ta stay?"

"Me?—No, not yet. I'll get a room, I guess. That Holiday Inn still open downtown? I stayed there for a couple of weeks last time I was here—though that's been a good twenty years ago now."

"Twenty yearn? Ye musta been jus' a li'l un back then from the looks of ye now. But thet thar Holiday motel—Naw thet thar place been shut clean up these past ten yearn now—But lookee here: I got a nice cozy room if ye gotta mind ta use it."

"You? You live in town then, do you?"

"Near to. Fifteen mile ahead. Jus' now comin' back f'om takin' me baby brovver Lester to the doc. He live out 56—this hyar's 56 we drivin' on, 'case ye don' know the roads hyar-'bouts. His place jes' off 56 near twenny mile out o' town."

"You're a dutiful sort of brother to do it, sir—But about the room: That's a generous offer, it truly is, and I sincerely appreciate your making it, but...."

"What!—gen'rous offer heck!—I ain't a-*givin'* it away, sonny boy, I's a gonna charge ye fer it. Ten bucks is all. Lots cheaper 'n one a them dirty old *mo*-tels out on the highway. An' that Holiday place aint in bidness no mores anyways."

"Ten dollars, eh?—That sounds pretty reasonable even for a room that's *not* so nice and cozy the way you say yours is. So—how much do I owe you for the lift?"

"Ride's free. Heck, thet brovver o mine—he fill up the tank fer me when I drive 'im over ta thet thar doctor place he goes. He's a-got this hyar double pension, ya know, lorsa money. Army pension and miner's boff. Ten bucks fer the room's a goodly deal, young feller—I don' make no profit on it, y'know, I jes like some comp'ny oncet in a while, is all."

"And you're close enough to town that I can walk there if I need to? Close to the river, say?—Anywhere near the hospital?"

"Whar ye mean ta go?—The hospital? Ye took sick?"

"No, not the hospital itself; I'm healthy enough—But fairly near it. South of the river—Around half a mile south, down on Townsend Street—you know where Townsend is?"

"Naw, don' go rount thar much nohow, over crost th' river, I mean. I ain't from Charleston original-like; jes' moved there ten yearn back myseln to do some stuff fer Les. An' my place ain't thet close to the river neither—quarter-mile, 'bouts, I reckon; li'l more ta git over ta th' hospital, I s'pose. But ye can use the truck if ye list. I don' go nowheres 'ceptin' drivin' Lester to the doctor place, so I don' need no *ve*-hicle 'ceptin two dayn a week. Use it when ye list yerseln, whenever ye list. I'm includin' it with the room. Ten bucks fer 'em boff—room 'n truck togevver—thet's a mighty gen'rous offer there, son."

"OK, I guess—You're on—But, as far as the truck goes, sir, is that pedal working there?—I'm not sure if I can drive it without stepping on the clutch."

The old man's place was neat and tidy; quite a shock to find it so, having seen the innards of the truck. But the man—Nathan Hatter was his name—made a point of putting everything in its own designated place, rather like a ship-shape-savvy seaman used to stowing every item in a proper little cubby hole; and all the little cubby holes in his neat and tidy home were filled with appropriate and immaculate things.

Cozy room, fresh linen, separate bath down the hallway from the guest room in the little place. Ten bucks couldn't possibly have been better spent, not any more than the twelve he'd paid for those sneakers on his feet or the two-for-a-dollar hot dogs that had kept him from starvation at the green and gold BP. He had nothing of consequence to put away, just the handful of duds in his shoulder bag; so getting washed and combed and moving into the ten-buck room took just a matter of minutes, not a whole lot more. After which bit of time, he took Nathan Hatter up on his kindly offer … and asked to use the truck.

It was six-fifteen by now, still light enough to check the old place out and maybe formulate the sketchiest of working plans. 'Old place' was how he'd always thought of it—not in date of construction, no; for Meredith's home had been built in the mid-Fifties, a moderate-sized, moderately contemporary dwelling on a lazy residential block: one of those older tree-lined neighborhoods where each home occupied half an acre or more: spacious enough, *isolated* enough that one had no need to listen to the neighbors' music played too loud, or overhear more gossip than was healthy for a not-too-friendly neighbor to overhear. Back when he had stayed with them—for that happiest three months *ever* in his age-long life—back then the house seemed almost built to order for his needs. Between the spaciousness of the land and the density of the foliage all around, one could come and go unseen, and do what one was required to do with no real fear of others' intervention.

Those first depressing weeks when Meredith had nursed him: Wounded, weak—he could never have provided for himself without the motherly sustenance she gave. But she had given that sustenance selflessly, with not the slightest thought of a reward. Far from any sort of benefit to her, in fact, the woman would have lost her job for what she'd done if she'd been caught; forfeited her career, in fact, her name, her very livelihood—car, house, money in the bank: Everything the family owned, everything it ever aspired to, could have easily been swept away if anyone had learned the facts. If anyone had known the whole of it, of Meredith's full involvement in it, she would have likely gone to jail.

Yes, Meredith had been a saint, all right, in what she'd ventured for his sake. But with Meredith—Well, with a living saint like Meredith, the recipients of her beatitude just never got too close. Not the kind of woman who could accept a person's thanks or return the fervent warmth her debtor felt. And as for *money*—Oh sure, he could have made her a millionairess time and time again with a simple phone call or the click of a computer mouse. ...

But Meredith wasn't the least bit concerned with wealth. *For me, no thanks*, she'd told him in as glib a manner as could be, *but if you like, well, go ahead and give Jennifer a little something as a gift.* That was the kind of gift he'd given gladly: the cost of her education *carte blanche*, a decent home in a not too nearby state, her every creature need—as far as he'd been told what darling Jenny needed. Meredith forwarded the monthly bills to that anonymous box in Youngstown; and he wrote the checks out happily, faithfully, right up to that last and final parting letter she had sent.

Yes, Meredith had been the one who'd saved his life, no doubt; to her he'd owed much more than the relative pittance sent to raise and educate the girl. His debt was owing to the mother, if to anyone—But it was the wondrous daughter in the end—of all the many thousand people in his life—that he'd truly grown to love.

Those three long months, first rehabilitating his body to make it sound, then settling his affairs, then finally building up his finances again before finally setting off: Meredith was working day and night at the hospital, then spending after-hours evenings with a woman out on Pine Street with a fractured hip, or up on Grafton with another Mrs. Someone who'd been mourning a dead child. The best of Good Samaritans Meredith, instinctually giving, having given all a nearly hopeless creature had required of her gifts—now that he was finally convalescent, she was nowhere to be seen.

Jennifer was off from school, though, through the sunny summer season of his healing; and so it was with Jennifer he'd spent those three recuperative months; it was Jennifer he'd shared his age-long wisdom with; and it had been Jennifer, and Jennifer alone, who in that gorgeous, vibrant summer of delight had given him, and taken back from him, a soul-mate, best-friend's heartfelt love.

She'd been a child back then, in a strictly chronologic sense. But Jennifer, in a larger, greater sense, could never be regarded as a child. With Jennifer, with that incomparable mind and heart of hers—if she'd been eleven, or twenty-one, or eighty-one—a soul like hers would always be the same. What he had taught her, the girl absorbed just like a sponge: The human world and how it worked and all the phenomena within that made it wend one way or the other, mathematically, historically, philosophically: Jennifer had assimilated all of that and put it though her genius brain and spirit, and refined it even more. What he'd learned in three hundred years, he condensed for her in three exquisite months; and she took it in, all of it; and for those three joyous months, hand in hand, morn to night, day after captivating day, the two of them were one.

Meredith, Jennifer, and Sister's virulent hatred to start the whole thing off: the closest thing to death and the nearest thing to life and love he had ever in his three long centuries known:

So it was with a plethora of recollections, both pleasurable and sad, that he got in the old man's truck and headed to the site of those vivid times that invoked such grand and awful memories. The route was still familiar after more than twenty years: A quarter-mile to the bridge, down Thurston past the hospital he'd very nearly died in, then over the river on Elm Street Bridge and down to Oliver, and right from Oliver a couple of blocks to Humboldt, then down two more blocks to Pittston, and another right to Thompson, and....

He pulled the rusty Ford in snug against the curb two houses up from where his transient family once had lived. Yes, the place looked very much the same as in his memory. The trees had grown or disappeared, some here, some there, leaving the front yard pretty much as he remembered. A new door: nice, lacquered wood, multi-paneled glass; the old door wasn't half as fancy as this new one was. Fresh paint on the trim as well, neat and manicured lawn: still well maintained as it always had been in the three glad months he'd been around. Meredith was gone these lonely twenty years now, just as long as he'd been gone; but to judge from all appearances, this still might be her home.

He sat behind the steering wheel and watched. Lights on in the front room, car parked in the drive, so someone likely home. A nice place, worth living in: Some thoughtful individual had bought it and done a decent job to keep it up. Easier if it had been vacant, truthfully, but somehow he'd find a way to make do. It would take some planning, some sales talk, a bit of clever fabrication possibly, to get him access to the basement, then somehow gobble up the concrete and whittle through the inch-thick metal barrier to get his things. A bit of preparation time: a day of observation to get a feel for the present residents' comings and goings; then a plausible reason for him to be in the home, if that turned out to be a requirement too. Check up on the gas or electric; radon testing, maybe: He'd think of something when the time was ripe. Three-hundred-some-odd years of major challenges like this: He'd never lacked improvisation up to now.

But for now, for this evening at several minutes after seven, according to the old Ford pickup's clock, he merely sat and watched. For quite a little while he watched: A flicker of curtains in an upstairs window, a light snapped on around the side—that would be the kitchen, as he well remembered. One occurrence at a time, though: The curtains first, the light ten minutes afterward. So unless the whole darn family kept together room to room, there was only one person in the home.

The front door opened and a woman stepped out onto the porch. Too far away to catch her features with any definition; but she seemed to be a youngish sort: slender, long gilt-brown hair, clad in a stylish V-neck sweater and jeans. She slipped a letter into the mailbox, lifted the little red flag to let the postman know he had a pick-up going out, then stepped back in the house and closed the door.

He waited, watched.... Five minutes passed ... ten.... And then he thought: Why not? ... Sure, why not just walk right up and ring the bell? The woman would come to the door, and he could say to her.... What, for instance?—Oh, maybe that ... well, maybe that that he used to live there many, many years ago when he was just a kid. Or—yes! He could say that he knew the *girl* who used to live there when he was just a kid. That would be plausible, wouldn't it? He looked roughly thirty-five, or so the folks who saw him said; Jennifer would be: Well, she was eleven then, so she would be very early thirties now as well. Meredith had moved away twenty years ago, so there would be plenty of water under the bridge since then. The youngish woman who'd just slipped her letter into the mail wouldn't have even *heard* of the family who'd lived here twenty endless years ago. He could say practically anything and probably be believed.

Sure, why not? Walk right up and knock on the door or ring the bell. Meet the woman. Size up the situation. Tomorrow, or the next day, he'd figure out a way to get inside, get downstairs, hack through the concrete floor, drill or burn through the metal plate, get his father's box and the few important items of his own, replace the metal panel over the compartment he had made, pour another layer of cement, smooth the surface, feather-edge the junction; and no one—least of all that nice young woman on the porch with the gilt-brown hair who had carried out her mail—would ever suspect a thing.

That was it; that was exactly what he made up his mind to do. He stepped from the truck and headed toward the house. Nice clean walk, front lawn raked with a minimum of scattered leaves, porch floor with nice fresh paint, fashionable welcome mat, that top-quality multi-paned new door, the mailbox on the porch with the red flag up, bearing the name....

Finotti?!

Was it ... but was it *possible?*—Was it *logical?*—Was it even *conceivable?*—that this nice young woman had bought the place and never bothered to change the name of the house's long-departed occupant on the box? Hardly likely; scarcely even *credible* in fact, but....

Hmmm. He put his finger up and rang the bell.

Ten seconds passed: Some steps. A light went on in the vestibule. A bit of movement of the door. It swung. A face:

"Oh GOD!" the lovely gilt-haired woman said. "It's *you!* Oh, *God*, I can't *believe* it; you look the *same!* How could you possibly look the same as you did twenty years ago? How is that even *possible?!*"

"Jennifer? Is it ... *Jennifer?*"

"I've waited all this time hoping one day I'd see you again. Hoping you'd come back someday, somehow. That's why I moved back here, hoping someday, somehow, the man I've loved since childhood would finally come home."

18

Audrey was heading down the stairway just as he was heading up, and...

Man-oh-MAN—But didn't she look *different* today!—*Really* different—*Majorly* different—Wow!—what with her hair all down across her shoulders and her eyes particularly bright and brilliant green—Sheesh! A really striking looking woman; no point denying it. Pretty enough—*striking* enough—to take his mind off that junk-heap-of-a-car and the DNA evidence Lederer's crew just might have come across in checking it out this weekend, a subject that had kept him up half the night last night in anticipation.

But Audrey—Man! The image of a cover girl if there ever was one: Ten years now since Jodi's death, and in all that agonizing time, focused as he'd been on his work and his passion for revenge, he hadn't really paid much heed to the office staff around him. Hell, he hadn't paid a lot of heed to *anything* around him, here or anywhere, other than his grief and anger and his work. Ten vacant years of offering his brief no-thank-you-misses to the solemn-faced divorcees at his door with their casseroles in hand and the million-dollar twinkles in their eyes.

And in their voices too—You could always tell by what a woman said or asked what she was after: "Gee," they'd say, "what's it LIKE to be a Braman, huh?" "What's it LIKE to be so rich?" "Your dad's a LEGEND, you know?—practically a *zillionaire!*" Maids and maidens after megabucks, a cushy life with all the trimmings—Oh, not that they didn't like you for yourself—a little bit, at any rate—But you never knew how much of their eager-eyed devotion was personal and how much mercenary—one of the many penalties of wealth.

Jodi hadn't been like that; and as far as he could tell Audrey wasn't like the others either. And as he stood there looking at the striking, smiling face of this gorgeous, kindly office-mate of his, it suddenly dawned on Sidney that: Well, maybe Uncle Phil was right; maybe it *was* time for him to get on with his life—time for him to *have* a life again, more accurately speaking—Oh, not with someone from the workplace—no superior to a subordinate should even *dream* of conduct as unbecoming as that—But if he ever had the amazing luck of meeting some sweet and pretty woman just like Audrey who *wasn't* from the workplace—yes, if he ever got that blessed second chance again....

For she did look absolutely ravishing today—Man!—The auburn hair, the emerald eyes—and that nifty little pants suit too: a brand new outfit he didn't think he'd ever seen before—not that he'd been generally prone to notice ladies' garb and such on prior days—But she was dressed up to the nines today in creamy silky stuff with a perfect fit around the waistline—a tiny waist like Jodi's was—and a demurely open front that looked ab-so-lute-ly, po-si-tive-ly, *flat-out*....

"*Audrey*! Wow! *Look* at you—Sheesh!" he enthused. "I never knew you'd grown your hair as long as that—you usually wear it up, don't you? I mean ... it's nice, it's really pretty; don't get me wrong; I'm not complaining in the least; but.... What made you decide all of a sudden to...?"

She shook her head in a charmingly dismissive way.

"Oh *that*, sir! Well ... what happened was: I got home kind of late the other day—Saturday, it was, after we made it back from Paxton, you know?—And my roommate took one look at me as I was coming through the door, and she said: She told me: 'Audrey, you know you really ought to....'—Well, anyway; I'm amazed you even noticed, Agent Braman. You usually don't pay that much attention to my hair or anything like that—But thanks for saying something nice; you'd be the only person in the office I'd be wanting to impress—So anyway, I'm just heading down to Graphics, sir; be back in just a sec—That crime map that you wanted?—for Pennsylvania?—They just phoned up to tell me that it's done."

"It *is*—Wow, you've been super busy, haven't you?—So—anyway—that crime rate business you came up with—what did the mapping finally show?"

"Oh—well ... you'll see for yourself in a bit, sir; but right now—Oh gosh! I should have told you right away. You got me flustered with those compliments, I guess, and made me totally forget—You've got a visitor—I brought him in and set him in the chair beside your desk."

"A visitor? So who...?"

"Go take a look, Agent." She flashed a devilish little smile. "I bet you're gonna be surprised!"

So in he went and—Whoa! *Surprised*, she thought he'd be?—She sure got *that* right—No *wonder* she was smiling! Sheesh! Surprised? Hell, that was light years from the word for it. *Amazed* might have been a better term; or *astounded* maybe—Hey, if socks really could get knocked off by some unexpected fellow waiting in another person's office—Holy Moses!—a pair of argyles would be flying out the window right now!

For it was Lederer!—Yep; the reclusive Gordon Lederer himself—who never left the sanctuary of his precious Forensics Lab—*ever*—except to run down to his Porsche at closing time and head in a beeline home. It was stretching the imagination to think that Gordon even knew where Sidney's office *was*. Or how to get there on the elevator. Or—Man-oh-*man!*—that he'd discovered that there so much as *existed* another level to the building beside the Fourth, where Forensics did its gory work— And in the shock of Lederer even *being* there, *sitting* there— Sidney blurted out, with a perplexed-most expression on his face:

"Gordon!—Sheesh!—What the devil…?"

"Cripes, Sidney—about *time* you got here, ain't it? Lucky you're on a salary—Hey, buddy boy—You and me: we gotta talk."

"Talk? Sure, Gordon, go ahead and talk. Must be some cosmic revelation if it dragged you from your sanctum in the path lab after all these years."

"Cosmic? Yeah, it's bona-fide cosmic, all right." Lederer put that out there loud enough for half the traffic on the freeway to overhear, then got up and bent his back and mumbled quietly in Sidney's ear the directive issued next: "Let's go out in the corridor though, OK? Or maybe out to the stairwell where it's more private still—which'll be even better yet. I got some majorly interesting stuff to tell you, my clever agent friend, so…. C'mon." He jerked his head and winked. "Saddle up and kick your pony in the backside—and let's *git*."

So Sidney, shrugging, smiled and up and got. Past the entry desk, straight out the office door, down scurrying hurriedly along the corridor two full steps behind Lederer's rapidly advancing pace. Then sidewise through the stairwell exit to the landing, stopping there, the two of them an arm's-length away….

And when they'd made it there, and mutually turned each to the other, with their faces a couple of feet apart, wary-eye-to-very-very-curious-eye, Gordon paused and craned his head upwards up the upper steps onto the higher landing a dozen feet above ... then craned his head downwards down the lower steps onto the downward landing a dozen feet below, as though to make damn sure that they were empty, devoid of ears around to hear, or eyes to see, or lips to tell the most profound of cryptic secrets ... and finally told him:

"Sidney? You got some really crazy shit going on, my friend. The absolute nuttiest thing I've ever seen!"

"You mean with my bad-guy-killing vampire, Doc? Hey, I'm pretty much aware of that already. The whole damn *case* is all-out nuts, and it's *been* nuts; and I'm sure it's gonna *stay* nuts until we get things figured out—But what did you come up with that's convinced you it's all that crazy *now?*"

Lederer made an inquisitive sort of face and shook his head:

"That car, Sidney: That crummy little car you brought us in—Speaking of which, there's a screwy rumor going down that you gave up your nice new Cadillac to get it—So? Is the screwy rumor true?"

"It *is* true, Gordon." Sidney chuckled. "You know something?—I had to call one of my dad's notaries out of church to stamp the transfer papers yesterday—it being a Sunday, remember—And then I had to send the title over to Paxton with a cockamamie *courier*—three hundred goddam bucks, I had to pay the greedy bastard that ran it out. But I kind of promised this terrific lady Adrienne she'd have the documents in a day, and I always keep my promises, so...."

"OK, OK, enough about the cars, all right? I don't stay awake nights worrying about your vehicle transactions, Sidney; save it for the DMV. It's only that I thought you were nuts when I heard what happened, is all. But, bottom line: I don't think you're as nuts as I thought you were before."

"Yeah? Well that's pretty goddam comforting to know, Gordon. But why the change of heart all of a sudden—huh? That little junk heap turn out to be a collector classic or something?—Or did you come across a stash of gold bars under the seat?"

"Better. Better than gold from an investigative point of view, old buddy. Hey, you figured we'd maybe find a couple of hair bulbs, right?"

"Sure. The guy was in there for at least four hours, maybe a whole lot more; and I know the statistics on hair exfoliation almost as well as you do, Doc. A person sheds—what?—fifty hairs a day, maybe sixty?'

"More than that, if he's got a head of hair as healthy as the artist sketches of your window-jumper show. Maybe four or five an hour fall out of a bushy muff like that—so you figured...."

"Well, I figured we'd have a decent chance of getting some usable DNA, and maybe a definite ID from that. So? What did you find, anyway? Must have been pretty goddam fabulous to get you down here to the office out of your zillion-dollar showplace first time this millennium—huh?—What did your cockamamie lab team finally come up with? Something good, I hope?"

"*Good*—It's a friggin' *jackpot*, Sidney. You got your DNA, buddy, and I got maybe a Nobel prize for myself if the whole thing ever gets researched and written up."

"Come on, Gordon!—Nobel prize? Hey, cut me a break here, will you? Nobel prize for goddam *what*?"

"For that DNA you sent us, Sidney old pal, old chum, old buddy. Look, what I found was...."

Gordon stopped right there and then. He looked up the stairwell again, then leaned over the bannister peering down. Then he stood there silent for a good long thirty seconds or thereabouts listening ... listening. No footsteps, no creak or hiss of springing doors; basically a plenitude of unremitting quiet; and in the vacuity of steady silence all around them, he finally resumed:

"We came up with six nice matching hairs in all: Thirty-something age-wise, male, wavy brown—Four of the six had usable DNA-containing bulbs."

"Sounds good so far—*And*?"

"*And*, Sidney—I had Cynthia run one of them. She came in Sunday—yesterday, like you said—I figured you'd be kind of in a rush, what with all those bloodless corpses in your bin and all."

"OK, *a-n-d*—?"

"So she comes in at noon to run the sample—Cynthia, I mean, like I said—and at three I get a call."

"OK, you get a call at three—Come on, Gordon! Get to the goddam bottom line here, will you already? Come on, Doc; spit the damn thing out."

"I'm getting there, buddy; don't spoil the fun for me, OK?"

"*What* fun?—You telling me you traced it to someone in the data file? *Did* you? You got a definite ID for us?—Holy Moses, Gordon, I hardly expected that amazing kind of luck. I honestly never even hoped...."

"Wait, Sidney; wait; don't get your innards in an uproar and spoil my revelation, OK? Hold on a sec—So, anyway, she gives me her data, Cynthia does, and I say to her, 'WHAT?'— Just like that: 'WHAT?'—Betty asked me who the devil I was talking to like that on the phone; I don't think I even answered her, I was so flabbergasted—But that's what I say to Cynthia— You know Cynthia, right? My senior tech?"

"I think I know her, yeah; the lady with the funny hair?"

"That's her all right; it's like pink some days; then some other days it's orange. Anyway, she tells me what the reading shows and I think she's nuts, but I figure: OK, so maybe I'll run in myself to verify; so I do."

"OK, you do—*A-n-d?* Why the hell are you turning a cockamamie five-line limerick into the *Iliad*, Gordon? *Sheesh!* Get to the goddam punch-line, will you?"

"All in good time, Sidney, my best-of-agent friend; all in the best of all possible times. So, anyway, I tell Cynthia it's some kind of error, that the specimen was contaminated, that—I don't know; I make up all kinds of bullshit so she won't run out and spill the beans. But anyway, I send her home and I have one of the junior techs run another sample from the second bulb, and then a different junior tech run a third one—so now when they're finished I've got three. And they all agree, Sidney, old pal, old chum. All three of the goddam testing graphs agree."

"Agree to *what*, Gordon? Come on, man, you're keeping me hanging too long with this convoluted garbage—*Enough*, OK?—So what did you *find* already? *What?*—The guy doesn't have any DNA?"

"Oh he's got DNA, all right. He's got DNA coming out the ying yang! You know how many chromosomes a human being has, Sid? You remember your undergrad biology 101?"

"Yeah, forty-six, isn't it? Twenty-three pairs, with two of them the X or Y, right?—Why? Doesn't the guy have a normal set?"

"Oh yeah: A normal set and *then* some, pal. Each of those samples showed fifty chromosomes even. The extra four are way beyond the others in complexity; like fifty percent more base pairs in each.... You got yourself a different kind of life-form, Sidney, a super-hyper-duper one. Good luck on finding it and trying to bring the som-bitch in!"

"What *is* it, sir? You look kind of funny; kind of—I don't know—a little ... sort of ... *pale*?"

"*Do* I, Audrey? I suppose I *should* look shocked a bit. It's.... You know that DNA we wanted from the car?" Sidney shook his head. "Well, maybe I'll tell you later on, if you can keep it to yourself; but, umm.... There was something *else* we were gonna do today, wasn't there? Honest to God, old Lederer got me so messed up with all that craziness he dropped on me just now that I can hardly...."

"The crime map, sir, remember?—That's what we were getting set to do—the incidence of crime in all the Pennsylvania counties. I worked on it this weekend, and I've got the printout fresh from Graphics if you want to have a look—If you're not too messed up from what Dr. Lederer just told you, that is—Here; hold on a sec. I'll bring the paper over to your desk to look at if you'd like."

And so she did. And *as* she did, with that mischievous little grin on her face, pleased to no end that she was aiding the investigation in her charming Gaelic way, Sidney noticed that, yes, that silky hair of hers *was* definitely different—But there were other things noticeably different besides:

Her manner, for instance: More open, less guarded, as though that day they'd spent in Paxton together had opened some hitherto locked communicating door. Oh, Audrey had always been solicitous of him, whether fixing his typos or bringing lunch at her expense—A genuine sweetheart-of-a-helper if ever there was one.

She'd been a doll, all right, considerate to a fault—But what about *his* end of the bargain? If her hair looked especially nice or her clothes were becoming, why hadn't he ever given her a compliment before? Had he even noticed?—Oh OK, maybe he *had* noticed—sure he had—But a friendly word? The common courtesy of a smile at least?—No, he'd been dismissive, neglectfully dismissive; he really had. And he made a promise to himself, right there and then, goddam it! that: Yep, no matter what—however busy, however burdened with his caseload—he'd be more attentive to pretty Audrey Hamblin in the future. After all, with all the kindnesses she showed him on a daily—almost an hourly—basis; why, truthfully, his time here, the rigors of his work here, would be an infinitely greater drudgery without her; unimaginable really, and in a fundamental manner, very sad.

Invariably *sweet* Miss Hamblin, invariably *motherly* Miss Hamblin: he owed her at the very least a smidgeon more regard. And as she set the multi-colored printout sheet atop his desk, showing him that trademark cheerful grin she always seemed to have, he gave her a nice warm smile back in return—For after all, it didn't cost him the slightest twinge of pain or the tiniest bit of effort to return her cordial smile.

And so he smiled up at her face as she set the page down flat between his hands, and gave a little nod as he scanned its gaudy printing, trying to look appreciative of her efforts regardless of what the darn thing might chance or fail to show: A neat and tidy multicolored map of the state—for everything she did for him was neat and tidy, always—with the incidence of major felonies color-coded to each district and municipality, north to south, east to west—Accurate and meticulous as always; for everything that Audrey ever did for him was done in just that absolutely perfect way.

So first he smiled appreciatively, as he'd promised he would do; and then he glanced down dutifully, as seemed appropriate at the time; and then he looked a trifle curiously, for there was something somehow different there that…. Hmmm.

Then all at once put his head down low above the desk, inches from the printout, and studied … *pored*—Hmmm—*Hmmm!*—Though he didn't study very long before he popped bolt upright in his chair and stentoriously exclaimed:

"Holy *Moses!*—This *map*! Good *grief!* Audrey! Has anyone else in the office seen this yet?"

"No, sir. Fresh from Graphics. You're the first one in the place to get the scoop."

"This guy!—Look, Audrey!—I'll be *damned!*—This chart you made for me: It's *incredible!*—Do you see what's happening here? Do you understand the significance of this?"

"Yes, I suppose I ought to, sir; I plugged in all the numbers—remember?"

"You did, Audrey. You did a helluva job; and it's fantastic what your work turned up—I'm.... Man!—I'm totally blown *away*!—I mean: *Look* at this—Bend down here and take a *look*: Our murderer—whoever he is—or *what*ever he is—he's killing off the bad guys one by one! Look at the counties surrounding Stanleyville—*Look*! Holy Moses! You see the colors here?"

"I do, sir. I was amazed when I pulled the figures up on Saturday night. Major felonies down eighty percent over the past twenty years; isn't that what the crime map shows?"

"It is—*exactly*—Just in that five-county region, though. Everywhere else there's an *increase*, see?—and—Look—there's a gradual slope to it—you see that as well? In the middle of this circle, centering on Stanleyville, the number of crimes is almost nil; then a little more and a little more progressively as the area expands. I'm totally in awe of what you came up with here, Audrey. This crime map gives a whole new dimension to the case, you know? I can hardly decide whether we ought to lock the fellow up or give him a commendation—*Sheesh*! It's the looniest ethical problem I've ever dealt with in all the time I've been here at the Bureau—the craziest by a factor of ten! Between this vigilante business and what Lederer just told me out in the stairwell...."

Sidney got up from his seat, bent down, looked over the printout once again, and shook his head:

"I don't know, Audrey; I've got a major dilemma in this case, with a scientific mystery to boot. I probably ought to run this latest scoop by Uncle Phil again. Look, why don't you give him another call for me—Dr. Sniderman, I mean—get hold of his office staff at U of Pitt, and see if he can meet with me for lunch today. Umm, let's tell him...." Sidney paused a moment hand to cheek. "OK, let's tell him this: Tell him to meet me at the deli in Squirrel Hill where he usually meets my dad. It's not too crowded there on Mondays if you make it in by noon; I know he likes the place; and it's only a ten-minute drive for him to get there, so.... So tell him quarter-to, OK? Eleven forty-five? Tell him it's a matter of life and.... Well, just tell him his agent-nephew is going nuts about the vampire case; that's all. I'm sure he'll understand."

Audrey's big green eyes got wide and just a smidgeon downcast—at least that's what Sidney thought he saw in that attractive face—And so, having observed the hint of disappointment, and having made his resolution to be a whole lot nicer to kindly Audrey from here on in, he mused a little more and offered, as a gracious second thought:

"Oh, and—Audrey? You spent all weekend on that crime map, I'm sure you did; you couldn't possibly have done all that research in just one day...."

"Not all weekend, sir," she interrupted. "As I said, it was just an hour or two Saturday evening after we came back with the car; and then a couple of hours on Sunday afternoon—It wasn't all that big a deal."

"No? But you don't get paid a nickel extra for the extra time; I know you don't."

"It's not a problem though; the Bureau pays me very well."

"Maybe so—but I still owe you one. You do a lot for me, although I never really give you half the credit you deserve. Anyway—look—if you want to try an authentic deli lunch today—you and that beautiful long hair of yours—you're more than welcome to come along."

So once eleven-thirty came around, out she went with him compliantly, Sidney feeling not the slightest bit of reticence about a social interaction with this pretty secretary-friend. If there'd been an ounce of reticence about it, the reticence would have implied some even minimal consideration of Audrey Hamblin as a woman and Sidney Braman as a man on a sort of luncheon date together. Sidney felt nothing of the kind. Audrey was a co-worker; that was it: an adjunct to the office where he spent his working days. She might have been twenty-five or eighty-five, drop-dead gorgeous or outrageously deformed, and the difference between the alternate personae of Audrey Hamblin wouldn't have meant a goddam thing.

And therefore, whatever nice Miss Hamblin might have thought about their first time ever *tête-à-tête* that midday Monday, Sidney thought nothing the least bit un-businesslike at all. And so he led her to the car, slipped behind the wheel just at the moment that she slipped unaided into the passenger seat; checked to see that her safety belt was fastened prior to starting off (per federal regulations, *naturellement!*) and headed out the parking lot toward their designated place to eat.

Squirrel Hill, the quondam Jewish part of town: that's where the deli was. Ten minutes to get there, in the pre-noon dearth of city traffic, five minutes more to park, making them a smidgeon earlier than the appointed time: Out of the car, coins in the meter, wingtip loafers onto the blacktop of the parking lot, where the garlic brininess of corned beef filled the atmosphere a hundred yards away.

Phil was seated at a table near the front when they stepped in through the door, nursing a can of diet Dr. Brown's and eying the bowl of old dills parked in front of him, pickled cukes that held a ton more salt than any coronary sufferer could safely eat. Phil took a long, slow, top-to-bottom look at Audrey, pursed his lips in a 'snazzy-looking woman!' sort of way; winked at Sidney, most suggestively; and started to his feet.

"No, no, Phil. Sit tight. We can dispense with the formalities. This is Audrey Hamblin; my secretary. You spoke to her on the phone, I believe—or your office staff did—Audrey: This is the legendary Dr. Philip Sniderman, the Chief Pathologist at Pitt and a long-time family friend."

Audrey shook Phil's hand and sat, and Sidney set an open menu on the tabletop in front of her, then turned to Phil to ask:

"So, Phil—have you spoken to Gordon Lederer yet today?—Or maybe he might have even called you yesterday sometime late."

"Lederer? Once in a blue moon maybe I get a message from your buddy Lederer. He sends me specimens and I send him the reports—that's about the most intimate we ever get. I haven't said ten sentences to the guy since that course we gave together a million years ago. Why, Sidney? Why do you ask?"

"I'll tell you in a minute; it's *about* one of those specimens, in fact; and that's the reason I thought we ought to meet today. But first let me fill you in on the stuff that Audrey's been working on and that she just printed out for me in a truly fascinating map, OK?"

Phil cocked his head with interest, and he continued: "You know our murderer's been killing off a bunch of bad guys, right? Well, Audrey figured out all by her clever little self...," Sidney glanced at her thankfully and smiled, "that *if* he's killing off a bunch of bad guys, there ought to be a corresponding decrease in crime—Which makes sense, right?—And there *is*, Phil; there definitely *has* been. The map she made for me of crime in Pennsylvania shows—get this—an eighty percent decrease in major felonies in the counties surrounding Stanleyville where our suspect just happened to reside. It's about as perfect a validation of our theory of a vigilante vampire as I ever could have hoped to get. And my clever little secretary here came up with the idea on her own, then worked all weekend to get the printout done—On her own uncompensated time, is what I'm saying here—So I decided that...."

He glanced again at Audrey and winked. Audrey, quite charmingly, blushed.

"Well, the very least I could do to thank her was to take her to a genuine kosher deli and show her what high-test corned beef does for a person's soul—And I wanted her to meet you too, Uncle Phil—which I'm sure she's gonna enjoy every bit as much as the food."

"Well good for you, Sidney! It's about time you took a pretty lady on an outing for a change. Haven't I been telling you it's time?"

"OK, let's not get into that again, Phil. It's just a business lunch, a kind of *quid pro quo*—Audrey and I are colleagues, just that; so when it comes to all your matchmaking business, let's...."

But at that antecedent 'let's', the straw-coiffed sixty-something waitress sashayed over, order book in hand, and they severally ordered lunch: Phil got his customary tuna sans mayo, Sidney a standard sort of not-too-fatty sandwich for himself—and for Audrey:

"Yeah, just try it. It's probably a whole lot different from the kind of corned beef you might have had before. Let me order for you, OK? If you don't like it, no problem; we'll get you something else."

Sure, smiled Audrey with a shrug; and the waitress took the menus, came back with their drinks, and in the calmness-amid-the-clatter that supervened, Sidney proceeded to the ultimate reason for their meeting that day:

"All right, Phil; well, I haven't said anything to Audrey yet, so.... Audrey? You're gonna see it in the report anyway when you scan it in the file, but you need to promise me you won't let anything about this information get out; OK? Not now, not ever, to *anyone*, unless I specifically give you the go-ahead—Agreed?"

Audrey nodded her agreement and he went on.

216

"OK then—Look, Phil, here's the thing: There was this car the suspect spent some time in, and.... Well, in short, we managed to get some DNA from the back seat—hair samples with viable bulbs, you see. And, to abbreviate the story that Lederer dragged out practically forever, the guy—or whatever other designation we'll have to use for him from here on in.... OK, bottom line: human beings have forty-six chromosomes in their genetic make-up, right?"

"Yeah, generally, although in some conditions—certain congenital anomalies, for example—there can be one less or one more."

"There *can*? Well—like what?"

"Down's is the commonest, Sidney, and that'd be the most familiar to you; but there are other trisomies and deletions where a chromosome gets doubled or eliminated—Turner's Syndrome, Klinefelter's, things like that—Why? Does your vampire happen to have an extra one?'

"Try four."

"Four *what*? Four *chromosomes*?" Uncle Philip shook his head most dubiously and crinkled up his eyes.

"Four *extra* chromosomes, yeah. Lederer ran three separate samples done by three different techs, and they all showed fifty on the nose."

"Impossible! No human being can have fifty chromosomes. They ran the samples wrong."

"All *three* of them wrong?"

"If they came out fifty, they're wrong—Unless it wasn't human material they were testing."

"I think that might just be the point I'm trying to make."

"*What*?!—Oh, come on now, Sid! You think your vampire has a different genetic make-up than the rest of us? I got lots of DNA from folks with aplastic anemia, buddy; and other than a gene or two or three—not a whole chromosome, is what I'm saying here, but just a misplaced gene here and there—they're pretty much like you and me."

"I hear what you're telling me, Phil. But what if this turns out *not* to be a simple aplastic anemia. What if it's *more* than that? Look, there's something else we've come up with in the last few days that you need to know about too. There were a couple of witnesses who spent some time with the guy—the ones who had that car—and I tracked them down, and...."

Sidney explained about the Hartman girl and mom; how he interviewed them, with Audrey's help; what they said; how he asked to take the car (He didn't say a word about the Cadillac, however; which was something Phil would never understand). He mentioned how the stem cells from the doctor and the baby got used to treat the woman's cancer … whereupon Phil excitedly exclaimed:

"He really *did*, huh? He actually injected her with that mega-dose of stem cells he got from Hazelton and the kid?"

"Yeah; a regular *shitload*-full, from what you said he managed to extract, right?"

"Right. Enough to kill an elephant—or *cure* one."

"So—what you said just now: You think that stem cells actually *can* cure something as horrible as cancer?"

"Didn't I tell you that the other day?"

"You told me stem cells could *treat* things, yeah; but we were talking about headaches and baldness the other day, not cancer. We weren't even *considering* serious conditions like *that*."

"No maybe we weren't, Sid, but…."

At which point their dialogue got interrupted once again by the arrival of the food. Everyone was hungry, what with all that tallow and garlic in the air; so they took their respective bites and sips and second bites and second sips in silence. Audrey's Reuben really hit the spot; the meat knish and gravy seemed to too. She gave out some lovely 'mmm!'s and 'oh, yum!'s from her side of the table. Nice, naïve gentile kid, mused Sidney: Once she got some decent deli in her, there'd be no going back to bologna and mayo ever again!

So they ate uninterruptedly for a good five minutes or more, before Phil set down his remaining portion of tuna on rye and resumed:

"Sidney? As to this cancer stuff you asked about: For years I've been trying to get the medical community to look at cancer in a totally different way. The therapy they give: The radiation, the chemo, and all that other crap—All those treatments do is damage the body's protective cells. Cancer is a disorder of immunity, simple immunity. If we could administer healthy immune cells to a person with cancer—even the most advanced forms of cancer—we'd have a good chance at a cure. This guy—your benevolent vampire or whatever the hell he turns out to be—not only is he cleaning up the human garbage off the streets; he's trying to help the good folks too. Like I said, he should get a medal instead of a jail cell. The guy's a regular genius—and a regular *ethical* kind of genius to boot! If I was you, and I had the authority to do it, I'd drop the investigation right now, today, and let your benevolent vampire keep doing the kind of mitzvas he does so well."

"You know I can't do that, Phil. I mean—even if I agreed with you—and I can't say that I *don't* agree at least a little bit—I'm sworn to do my duty. His ultimate guilt or innocence isn't my decision to make."

"So? Do your duty then. Find him; arrest him; lock him up. He won't make it long in a prison cell if he needs a regular infusion of blood—So your problem gets solved then, right? A month in jail and your nice-guy murderer goes poof! Dead and gone, case closed, game over, huh?"

"Well, there's a l-i-t-t-l-e bit of a problem with that one too, frankly, Phil. One of the witnesses—the cancer patient's daughter that I mentioned before—I guess she had a pretty decent chance to talk with our guy at length; and according to what she said—and what he must have said to her—there may be more guys like him out there. Maybe a lot of them; maybe a *whole* lot—we don't actually know."

"Yeah? A lot? Well good. Terrific! The more guys there are like that the better, as far as I'm concerned."

"She said something else too, though, Phil; something kind of spooky, especially with this chromosome thing that's come to light. She said—I wish to God we'd turned our video thingamajig on so I could remember the exact wording—But anyway, what she said was, as near as I can remember—and correct me if I'm wrong here, Audrey; feel free to jump on in at will—What the daughter said was this: She said that the guy we're looking for wasn't ... '*from* here'."

Sidney curled up two fingers of each hand to make a pair of air quotation marks encapsulating those last two cryptic words.

"She said '*from* here', like that. So I asked her—Audrey was sitting at the table with us and can verify what I say—I asked the kid what *here* meant, Phil—whether she meant—oh, you know, like 'Pennsylvania' or 'America' or what? And she left me with the impression that *here* meant—well, like *everywhere* here— the whole *world* seems to be what she's referring to as *here*—which sort of indicates that she believes the guy we're looking for is...."

"What?—A *spaceman*? Ha!—You make a date for her with a shrink?"

"No, that's just it. She's a nice, clever girl. Smart, poised; definitely credible in everything else we talked about. But as for this—I don't know what to make of it. Especially with the chromosome stuff we've got and…. But let me ask you one more thing about the chromosomes, OK?"

"Fine with me. I'm not sure I'll know the answer if it's Martian DNA you're asking, but go ahead and ask."

"OK. Let's try this then. Let's suppose for a minute that the guy really *does* have fifty chromosomes, OK?"

"It's OK to *suppose* he does, I guess—I'll go along with that."

"So if you wanted to take a normal human being and give him four extra chromosomes, how would you go about doing it?"

"How, huh?" Phil paused in deepest meditation for half a minute or so; took another bite of his half remaining sandwich; chewed half a minute more; then: "OK, here's how: I'd put the other chromosomal material into a virus and infect him with it."

"And that would transfer the extra four chromosomes to all his cells?"

"Theoretically—maybe. If it's a fetus in a newly pregnant woman it pretty likely would."

"OK, assuming the 'maybe' to be possible then, and assuming the pregnant women were available, what would it take to program a virus like that?"

"Genetic engineering? Genetics is only information, Sid. Genes have a quaternary code: four different nucleotide bases in different combinations. Once you figure the information you want to stick in, all you need is the raw material—carbon and hydrogen and oxygen with a dab of nitrogen tossed into the mix. Then it's just a matter of chemical reactions. Information plus chemicals plus energy…."

"OK, hold on a sec: You said energy, right? What if the energy came from a different place—If the energy and information weren't 'from here'?" Sidney raised those four quoting fingers again, gesturing grammatically. "I mean, *matter* can't be transported from distant parts of the universe—that's impossible, considering distance and scientific laws—But *energy* can—energy travels at the speed of light. You see what I'm getting at, Phil? I'm trying to think this nutty business through, you understand? So—Does that sort of theory make any sense?"

"I see what you're getting at, all right. But as for sense, it's a pretty distant stretch."

"So how do I put all this stuff together then? I've got some interesting evidence, and fascinating theories, but I've got to put the pieces into a reasonably coherent whole—Any idea how I can do that?"

"Hey, if you're asking *me*, I think the whole thing's totally bonkers. You got spacemen and vampires and dead guys and stem cells all stirred into the same meshuginer pot—Sidney, look—listen to me, boychik—I can handle the werewolves and the vampires—maybe even the occasional zombie now and then. But when you get into aliens from outer space—And not only that—oy!—but you're talking about *vampires* from outer space harvesting stem cells to treat nice girls' mothers with cancer: Sidney my boy, go back to the board room at Bramancorp. When you start chasing after vampires from outer space harvesting stem cells for mothers with cancer—you need to find a new line of work."

Phil didn't laugh, but Sidney did. But since Phil didn't respond to the little bit of laughter on his part, he didn't maintain the laughter very long. At any rate, the waitress came back and he ordered some dessert—Audrey just *had* to try the cheesecake, he urged; it was the signature offering of the place. And while the sandwich plates were being cleared, and the soft drinks topped off again, and the chocolate cheesecake delivered posthaste, two strawberries resting alluringly on top, Phil started up with his matchmaking craziness again:

"So—Audrey: Tell me something: Your boss here never took you out for deli food before?"

Audrey very tenuously shook her head.

"So? Where does he *usually* take you for lunch?"

"This is the first time Audrey and I have *gone* to lunch, Phil. I usually bring a sandwich in, or she picks me something up—and won't take any money in return. We always argue over that."

"So, when you bring your sandwich in, you usually bring one for Audrey too? She's a big girl, ain't she? She's gotta eat just like you do. She shouldn't buy your lunch all the time and you never pay for hers."

"Come on, Phil. Turn it off, will you? We both know what you're trying to do."

"*Me!* Hey, *I* didn't ask the lady to come to lunch, did I? *You* did. I'm just saying ... what I'm saying is—maybe you two nice kids oughta make a habit of deli lunches out."

"Come on, Phil—*Please?*"

"Whaddya say, Audrey? Don't you think Sidney here is a pretty damn attractive kinda guy?"

Audrey took a strawberry from the top of her chocolate cheesecake and blushed again.

"Well? We're all too long out of junior high these days to just sit around and look silly, ain't we now? Tell me, Audrey, honestly, don't you think this boss of yours is a quite a major catch?"

Audrey looked at Phil, then looked at Sidney, directly, imploringly.

"Look, Phil: Audrey and I—we're colleagues; we work together. A professional office stays professional all the time. I know you mean well, and I'm sure Audrey knows it too, but...."

He stopped. Phil was looking at him in an uncomfortably penetrating way. Then Phil's eyes moved across to Audrey, bringing his own eyes in their train. Audrey was crying. Not just wet eyed, but dripping down voluminously in long mascara-tinted streaks. Then she looked up at him, right smack into the epicenter of his gaze. Just that one long lingering black-teared look ...

And he knew.

19

They hadn't talked too long the night before. The girl—for he still thought of his darling little Jennifer as a girl—was so nonplussed at seeing him again, and he so outright flabbergasted at finding her in the most unlikely place in the whole wide universe he would have ever expected her to be…. Well, in short, he had given her a hug and a kiss on the cheek, in lieu of further explanation, then gone back to the old man's place to think things out and maybe get some sleep.

But the next day, bright and early, before she would have likely left the house, he drove over in Nathan Hatter's rusty truck, and knocked just seconds on the door before the multi-paneled glass swung in and:

"I hope I didn't wake you, Jen, but…."

"*Wake* me? You honestly think that I could sleep?"

"I didn't sleep much either. We'll need to talk."

She led him in and over to a kitchen table similar to the table they had sat at for dinner with the rest of the Finotti family twenty years before. Jennifer was eleven then, Meredith thirty-nine, Anthony—though he hadn't been around much till the very end—poor Anthony Finotti had been forty-two all those many years ago; he'd made it up to sixty-two, give or take a month or so, one week back in time from this piquant Tuesday morning, when he'd burned himself to death in a Pennsylvania bed.

Jennifer sat and stared and nervously wrung her hands: Did he want some tea? she asked. Some breakfast? Anything? That loving look in her sleepless eyes: No one but little Jennifer had ever looked at him—not ever!—in just that bright-eyed captivating way. It was a look that made him feel a little strange; back then it did a lot, and now a little, too. He wasn't certain exactly *why* back then, but now….

"Do you have to be somewhere this morning?" he asked.

"Just rounds. I canceled the office today except for emergencies—oh, and one nice lady with congestive failure who won't respond to meds; I'll see her in the office in a bit."

"So you finished, did you? Residency and everything?"

"Uh-huh, I did: three years of internal medicine at Hopkins, then a fellowship at Yale. You knew I was in med school, didn't you—at U of M? Mom must have written that before she…. Anyway, I started my practice here a year ago."

He looked at her. It wasn't all that easy for him to look at her, not with those bright green eyes reflecting in his face; and that adoring look about them that he didn't completely understand—or maybe didn't *want* to understand. But he *did* look, partially avoiding the epicenter of her gaze for comfort's sake.

She'd turned into a truly lovely woman, certainly; with abundant gold-brown hair above a peasant's shallow brow, luxuriant eyelashes, classically high cheek bones with elegant hollowing underneath—the quintessential cover-model look. Tall and slender as a model too, and with graceful hands and sensual lips and neck. Prettier and less careworn by far than Meredith had been; but Meredith had been older when he'd known her than Jennifer was now, so maybe that was part of the explanation for Jen's physical perfection: terrific genes admixed with rosy youth.

Anthony had been a handsome fellow too, back when he was younger and before the lobotomy had stamped that bland expression on his face. So between the two of them, Meredith and Anthony—yes, they could have produced a genetic gem like this. And they *had*—here was living proof of it: Knowing the sanctitude of Meredith, there could be no questioning the paternity of her kid. A hereditary beauty, sure enough—and a graduated doctor to boot—The pretty, sultry daughter had her saintly mom's initiative and brains. She'd been living here in Charleston for a year in safety; that was true. But the safety here in Charleston was fragile at the very best: Doctor or not, lovely or brilliant or otherwise, he'd need to get her far away from here—And do it pretty quick!

And so they sat and examined one another cautiously, met each other's eyes a little sheepishly, and talked:

"I … I can't stay in town for very long, Jen. I've come to get some things."

"Things? From here, you mean? Oh, but there's nothing left from when we lived here before, you know. Someone else was living in the house—Mom had sold it; I'm sure she wrote and told you that—But I wanted it—I *needed* it. So I paid the man who'd bought it a whole lot more than it was worth, and gave him what he asked to move his family out."

"What time are your rounds?"

"Whenever. The patients aren't going anywhere; and none of them are critical or anything. I mostly need to check their chemistries and smile at the nurses and say hello. And the nice old lady with congestive failure can wait a little too; she's stable now; my office staff knows what to do."

"So we've got some time?"

"Time? Now? What does *time* mean to me? If you asked me to go away with you right now—this instant—I'd get in the car without a momentary thought—in that old truck, I mean, or whatever—and leave everything behind without a single glance back. I wouldn't ask you why or where or really much of anything. I'd just go. Don't you understand what happened with us?—or with *me* at least? Don't you understand *anything*?"

"Jennifer, you were just a little girl back then. What you're saying...."

"A little *girl*?—A little *GIRL*?! Don't you think a little girl has feelings? Weren't you ever a little boy?—Oh, but you were— you *were*!—It's just been so many centuries since then that you forgot."

"Jennifer...."

"No, don't talk to me, just listen. I've been thinking for the last twenty years what I'd say to you if I ever saw you again. Some of it I've forgotten, but the rest is graven in my mind. What happened with us—or with me at least—was a once in a lifetime connection—Or no, that's wrong—it was a once in a *hundred* lifetimes connection—once in a *thousand* lifetimes, maybe. Those months we spent together—didn't you feel any kind of bond with *me* during those amazing months?"

"Jennifer, I...."

"*What*? Did you or didn't you? I need to know."

"What difference does it make? You know what I am and what my life is like. You were a little girl back then. If you hadn't been a little girl...."

"*What*? If I hadn't been a little girl—then *what*?"

"If you hadn't been a little girl, and if I could have made myself a normal kind of man: if you'd been older and I'd been younger—then things might have been different, I suppose."

"Well I'm not a little girl now, am I? Do I fit your definition of a woman?"

"What difference does it make?"

"All the difference in the world to me."

"You know what my life is like. You know that more than anyone—Except maybe your mother. She's the only other one who knew."

"She's gone—did you know? She died two years ago."

"It's painful for me to hear that. Do you realize how painful that is to me?"

"I do. You two were close."

"All *three* of us were close. That summer we spent together was the closest human contact of my life."

"Was it?—*Really*?"

"Yes, it was. You ought to know it was."

"So why did you have to go then?—*Why*?"

"Jennifer! Did you forget what happened? We *all* had to go. It isn't safe for either of us to be here—even *now*. How could you have been so careless as to come back here alone? She's still alive and still as vengeful as she ever was; I'm positive of that. And there's no predicting her behavior. There never was, even as a child. She inherited it from her mother, no doubt about that; but even her mother didn't have the thirst for blood that my sister seems to have. She always loved to kill—*always*: As a child she would torture little animals, and later she had some male friends back in London that—But anyway, you get the picture, I'd imagine. As for my being here, I came back to get some things, and *only* to get some things, and once I have them—listen to me—once I have them, you and I have got to *leave*!"

"You'll take me with you then?"

"How can I? I have no idea where I'm going, or where to get another Helper, or…. Your father—I suppose you still remember him—He's dead."

"All right. I wouldn't have wished him dead, truthfully; but I can't really grieve for him now, not after all that happened when I was a kid."

"No, I wouldn't have expected you to grieve. He lived until a week or so ago, though; and wasn't unhappy or ill-provided-for these past twenty years."

"You know? Those things you told me about yourself—I kind of half-believed them all these years—But when I saw you again last night, it really registered. You look exactly the way you looked before you left. I haven't seen you in twenty years, and after twenty years you still look exactly the same. This is like a fairy tale for me. Like a dream. It's hard to even describe what the feeling's like."

"All right, look: I suppose it's reasonably safe for us to stay in Charleston for a little while. She couldn't possibly know I'm here, and she wouldn't be likely to drive around looking for me, even if she did. That gives us a little time. I'll need to go and get some tools and a concrete saw and—have you got some cash on hand? I doubt I've got enough, and I'm sure you know I'll pay you back."

"Pay me *back*! Don't you realize you paid every penny for my undergrad and med school education? And expenses too? And clothes? And a nice apartment, and food, and Mom's house, and...?"

"I didn't know for sure that it was paying for you to be a doctor, no. That was money better spent than I'd hoped; I'm glad you went that route, though; I truly am, and.... Oh, and— back to what I was saying—I'll need access to a computer too."

"Sure; you can take my laptop. And as far as money goes, I've got...."

She got up off her chair and left the kitchen; then came back a couple of minutes later with a purse in one hand and a computer case in the other.

"Here—here's the laptop, and.... OK, I've got a few hundred in cash—let's see, two hundred, three, three-fifty, four—here; take the envelope to put it in. And here's a VISA card too. Just tell them I'm your wife or something, though I doubt that anyone'll ask—Or go to an ATM: The pin number's—Here, I'll write it down on the envelope for you. If you need more, I can go to the bank later. Just tell me how much and...."

"I'll pay you back, you know."

"Come on! This is Jennifer you're talking to, remember? I don't care about the money. Just don't run off again, OK? Promise?—Say you promise."

She took his hand and held it softly between her two smooth temperate palms.

"Promise. Say it. Promise me. Don't leave here now until you promise me you're coming back."

He gave the promise she demanded, and hugged her tight, and left; vowing that he'd be back in the afternoon to talk.

His darling little Jennifer! Older, wiser, a tiny bit more beautiful as a grown-up woman than she'd been as a precocious child—

But just as absolutely wonderful as ever, in every other way.

20

Audrey was a different woman today entirely.

Not her pretty eyes and silken hair—which were the same bright eyes and glistening hair as yesterday—But something about her manner, her tone, the way she interacted with him from the moment that he stepped in through the door—that's where the striking difference lay.

That plate of cookies that she'd plopped down on his desk with a benignant little smile—Now there!—That was different, definitely!

And the flick of her hand across his shoulder when she'd sauntered past his chair on her way out for the interoffice mail—Hardly the sort of frank and outright chumminess the two of them had ever shared before today.

Oh, nothing all that flat-out brash in either instance, it's true; nothing the prissiest of office-mates would dare to call objectionable: The touch was merely friendly, and those cookies: Well, you could write the cookies off as more or less a caring colleague's kindly thought, like all those gratis lunches that she'd carried in.

But something made him feel the s-l-i-g-h-test bit uncomfortable in a circumspect kind of way. And once she dropped that sheaf of papers on his desk, then scooted off to Graphics for the crime maps of the adjoining states—Once she'd cleared the exit door and headed toward the staircase out of view, Sidney grabbed the phone, and scrolled its list of numbers for the Medical Center Lab, and made his frantic call to Uncle Phil.

"Can of worms!" ejaculated Philip, once apprised of what the heck was going on. "Whaddya mean *I* opened up a can of worms, huh? *You* were the one who asked her out to lunch, weren't you?—And you wanna dump the whole farkakte blame for it on *me*?!"

"All right, maybe taking her for lunch was a minor lapse of judgment on my part—I'll admit to the validity of that—But those comments that you made: That was the crack in the dyke that really loosed the flood, Phil. You shouldn't have egged her on the way you did. You know what she went and did for me this morning? She brought me in a plate of *cookies*, for heaven's sake!—Sweets!—I *never* eat sweets!—Honest to God: it's just not like her, you know? Sheesh! This is even *worse* than a can of worms; you've gone ahead and kicked a goddam *hornet's* nest— And it's right in my back yard!"

"Oh yeah? You know what an alte cocker like me would give to have a hornet's nest like that in *my* back yard—huh? And what if I *did* egg her on a little bit—What if I *did*? Maybe the cookies she baked you are *terrific*—did you bother to taste 'em yet?—And besides: Forget the goddam cookies, boychik: You think it'd be so terrible for you to go out with a girl again after ten goddam years?"

"She's not a *girl*, Phil, she's an *employee*—someone I've got to work with; a *subordinate*. You don't have relationships with subordinates."

"*Me*? *I* don't? You mean *you* don't. *I* sure as hell would if I had the slightest chance and was as young and dashing as you are, kiddo. You need to lighten up a little bit, Sid. Really; after all this time, there's no reason for you to be a monk."

"I'm *not* a monk—why do you keep saying that?—It's only…."

"Only *what*? Jodi's been gone for over a decade now—a goddam *decade*, Sidney, for crying out loud! So I'm asking you: Only *what*?"

"Let me ask *you* something, Phil—and tell the truth for once, OK? Did Dad put you up to all this foolishness?"

"What foolishness do you mean, buddy boy?"

"You know exactly what I mean; don't play games, OK? Answer the question honestly: Did Dad put you up to it?"

"I can't say that he put me up to it in so many words, no—but I know he's worried about you. You know that as well as I do, Sidney. Let's not pretend you don't."

"So? What's he so upset about, huh? Am I getting leprosy? Have I got the plague? Is being without a woman bad for a person's health?"

"Physically, I don't know. Mentally—that's a different ballgame totally. Look, think back to what happened with you and Jodi. Try and think back to the old days, OK?"

"I'm not sure what you mean by that."

"No? Don't you think I knew the story of you and Jodi right from the start? Don't you think Jacob talked to me every goddam golf game and filled me in on the whole shebang?"

"On *what*? What did he fill you in on?"

"All of it. How you two kids met; how hard it was for you to open up at first; and how she won your heart once you finally let her in. I got the scoop from first to last every couple weeks through eight long holes of looking like a goddam sand-trap schmeckel. That's half the reason Jacob paid my membership at the club, 'cause I sat in the cart and listened to him kvetch till he got through. Listen to me, Sidney; you're a tough nut to crack, my friend. Once you let someone in your life, you're a saint to them—to her—but getting in there: There's the rub. All I'm saying to you, boychik, is open up once in a while. This girl Audrey—she likes you; she really, truly likes you, I can tell. Remember how nice it used to be for a girl to like you? Forget she's an employee for a little while and let her in the way you once let Jodi in. You need that as much as she does."

"I appreciate your concern, Phil, but.... Oh, hell; here she is again. She just ran down to get those other maps for me and it looks like.... Yeah, from that look of exaltation on her face, it's a decent bet we got another drastic plunge in crime out in Maryland or Ohio or.... Anyway, I gotta go. But look, let's keep our focus on the vampire stuff from here on in, OK? That's where I need your input; not with the matchmaking. I'll get back to you later about our vampire spaceman and his extra chromosome insanity—But as for Audrey; she's off the list of topics now, forever, you hear?—Over and out!"

He clicked off the phone, and no sooner did he click off the phone, than there she was again, hovering at his desk with the sheaf of multicolor printouts in her hand, and a big enthusiastic smile across her face, and a cheerful voice that requested him to:

"Look, sir, look! You won't believe it! Look at *this* one. It's just like the Pennsylvania map from yesterday. The other states were pretty normal, but look at the West Virginia map—It's got to mean the girl was right, doesn't it?—There *isn't* only one."

She spread the paper gently on the desk in front of him. The other sheets of paper in her hand—the less revelatory maps, from what she'd told him—Ohio, New Jersey, Maryland, and the like—those she casually set aside. But *this* one—the one she smoothed down knowingly, lovingly, like a million-dollar Rembrandt print extracted from its frame: *This* particular sheet of colored paper that she handled with devotional respect, was a highly detailed map of West Virginia, as she'd said. Like the Pennsylvania map of yesterday, this West Virginia map showed each municipality of the state color-coded to reflect an increase or decrease in major crime in the period from twenty years ago to the present day. As in the Pennsylvania map, the West Virginia colors were fairly uniform throughout—reds, oranges, yellows, corresponding to large, medium, or minimal increases in major felonies over the past twenty years: All the numbers would likely have increased at least a bit, of course, owing to two decades' corresponding increase in population—more folks in general, so more bad folks in particular, just as any thoughtful person might expect.

In West Virginia, as in Pennsylvania, bright warmish colors were predominant throughout—red, orange, and yellow alternately stippled north to south, east to west across the page. That's what the Pennsylvania map had shown; brilliant high-crime coloring all across—All but for the singular exception of that one circular five-county area centering on Stanleyville, which had progressively tended toward its central region of a coolish, crime free, pastel powder blue.

This West Virginia map, now that he looked at it attentively, was just as remarkable as the Pennsylvania map had been: Red, orange, yellow all across, top to bottom, right to left—EXCEPT: Yes, there was the same singular phenomenon again, that curious exception to the rule: Just as in Pennsylvania, another pale blue area, this time in the far-west corner of the state, right near its double-sided border with Ohio and Kentucky—indicative, when he looked down at the actual numbers for confirmation, of a nearly seventy percent reduction in serious crimes over the past two decades—*seventy percent!*—pretty nearly the exact same level of decreased crime as the statistics for Stanleyville and vicinity had shown—Less than a third the crime expected, in just that one particular area of Western West Virginia, and absolutely nowhere else!

"Is this second map accurate, Audrey? You double-checked the figures to make sure we got them right?"

"I did. It's right—*exactly* right—Which means the girl was right in what she said. She told us 'they'; and the West

Virginia map confirms her statement, doesn't it? There *must* be more than one."

"It *does* confirm it, Audrey. It looks like there's a second one of these—well, whatever you want to call them—And there may be a million more besides these two for all we know! Sheesh! We've got—what? Six states now or seven that you've plotted out so far?—Which leaves—what? Forty-something more to go? And then every other country in the world outside the US, and—Holy Moses! Who knows how many if these cockamamie vampire weirdoes might be out there! So first we'll focus on these two guys now, and then the next thing after that'll have to be...."

"You want me to get started on the remaining states today? Plug the figures in and...?"

"Umm, no; hold off on that for now. It might be better if we restrict things to these two guys first, then get to any others who might be out there once we have a handle on these first two. Let me just take a closer look at this West Virginia map, to see if...."

Sidney bent low above the map, looking, studying, tracing the azure-colored pattern with a finger....

"Umm—Audrey—Hey, Audrey—Bend down and take a look at this."

He reached out for her elbow and found it immediately to his left. Then he pulled it, pulling her along behind him: Around the swivel chair in back and over to his right where there was room for her to position her head beside his directly above the map. Then he drew the elbow lower, and lower still, until her eyes got down to just about a foot above the paper, her face just inches from his own. And when he'd got her there, properly positioned there, right above the map, he told her—in way too loud a voice for that delicate little ear of hers, close as it was to the sounds that issued forth:

"Look!—Sheesh!—Look at this map again! You see the boundary here?" He indicated with a finger. "You see how straight it is? Look how it.... Here—Find me the Pennsylvania map for comparison. What did we do with it?—Do you remember?"

"Sure, sir. Here; underneath the cookies. Hold on a sec; I'll dig it out."

Which she did, expeditiously, setting the map of Pennsylvania right beside the West Virginia one, edge to edge, so that comparison would be a breeze.

Whereupon Sidney bent lower still, mere inches from the print, peering intently at the pair of maps, alternately one, then the other, running an index finger around the bluish zones of either map, each of them in turn, until....

"My *God*, Audrey, look! Ho-ly Moses! Look at this border here—Good grief!—you see it?" He jerked her elbow down again, for she had half-way straightened up; then got her head positioned in the proper place to see the thing in question best. "Holy Moses! Look at this straight-line border! You see how straight it is?—Amazing! Unbelievable!—You know what this amazing straight-line border *means*, Audrey?—What it *represents*?"

"Umm...." Audrey waggled her head, signifying, Sidney assumed—'Umm, well ... not exactly; n-o-o-o?'

"OK, look. Look here—You see the Pennsylvania map? Look at the circular zone around Stanleyville."

"Around the blue?"

"*Yes*, the blue—of *course* the blue—but look at the *outline* of the blue."

"The outline, sir?"

"Yes, *outline*— the OUTLINE! You see the difference between the outline of the blue on the Pennsylvania map and the outline of the blue on the West Virginia one? You see it?—*Do* you?"

"I.... I'm not sure, sir. Other than the transition in the colors, I mean...."

Blank again; impenetrably. She met him with a clueless sort of look.

"No, no, *not* the colors—Well, the colors are relevant too, of course; that confirms what we said before about another killer being out there; so it *is* significant, of course—But look at the border *between* the colors—You see? Look here: That narrow border tells us something a whole lot different than the colors themselves. Look. Look real closely here." He pointed. "You see how gradual the transition is from blue to red?"

He ran his finger around the very hazy blue-to-reddish junction of the Pennsylvania map.

"And see how razor sharp it is here?"

He did the same with the much more linear junction on the West Virginia map.

"*Now* you see?"

"Umm...."

"OK, look." Sidney got up off his chair, placed his hands, one on each shoulder, and bent her downward to a perfect vantage point immediately overlooking where the two map edges joined. "Here. Look: The blurry border around Stanleyville tells us—what? That the suspect from Stanleyville fanned out to find his victims, right? The farther away the area gets from Stanleyville, the more criminals are left; the closer the fewer—but the transition is gradual. You see how gradually the blue color blends into red here? Look: blue, then mauve, then this real pale ocher-orange, then a little redder, then…. You see?"

He made a semicircle with his index finger indicating, in the region to the north of Stanleyville, exactly what he wanted her to see.

"And then to a lightish shade of orange over here—on the other side of Stanleyville, toward the south." This was down toward Pittsburgh, diametrically opposite the semicircle he'd indicated up above: "See? Blue here—right?—hardly any crime. Then kind of purplish over here—a little bit more crime—you see? Then orangish down here—another little more—You see it, Audrey—*do* you?"

"I *do*. I *do* see it, sir. A gradual transition. That makes perfect sense."

"It does, doesn't it? It makes sense that a killer of bad folks looking for victims *every*where would find more of them closer to home than farther away—right? But he'd probably find a *few* farther away; so farther away there's *some* crime reduction, but not as *much* reduction in crime as very close to home—you understand?"

Audrey definitively nodded that she *did*, in fact, fully understand.

"So around Stanleyville, the border's blurry—right?—Got it?"

She agreed that that was right and that she'd got it.

"OK, so bearing that in mind: look over here now." He pointed. "What do you see on the West Virginia map?—God, this is *incredible!*—Who came up with the program for these crime maps, Audrey—did *you?* Did you think of plotting it by municipality all by yourself, without the programmers' input?"

"Yes; well, it wasn't all that complicated, sir. I just arranged the colors to reflect the crime statistics, and used the local district and township numbers for the entries; it wasn't anything all that difficult to program in. All I did was...."

"All you did was solve this whole damn case all by your brilliant little self, young lady; *that's* all you did!"

"I *did?*"

"You sure did. Here, look real closely at the West Virginia map you made for me—you see?"

"Yes, sir, I *do* see; I *do*! The border isn't blurry at all—It's sharp!"

"Right; straight-line, razor-edge sharp, all around—Which means...?"

"Umm ... W-e-l-l ... I'm not exactly sure what it *does* mean, sir. Does it mean something important?"

"I think an impartial arbiter of vigilante vampire statistical data would consider it important, yes: It means, my genius-of-a-secretary, incredible Miss Hamblin, that the selection of victims around Charleston, West Virginia conforms to jurisdiction! The victims end abruptly at the county line— BANG!—here—right here—smack dab *here!*—you see? Blue on this side of the border, just like the ocean—OK? And then a pretty shade of red—red as a nice ripe cherry—practically a block away past the border!—Which for the West Virginia fellow involved is the next best thing to a fingerprint ID! This super-detailed little map on the desk that you were clever enough to make for me, my darling little Audrey, means we've got our West Virginia vampire practically in the bag!"

An enormous smile, an *outrageous* smile—which looked quite odd on Sidney, who had never, within Bureau memory, been observed to wear so radiant a smile before. But a big, broad, white-toothed smile, bright and effervescent—A smile huge enough, transmissible enough, to make Audrey Hamblin break out in a nice cute smile all on her own.

Then Sidney almost did a little dance, a stumbling Semitic jig of sorts. He moved his feet around a bit, at any rate. And since he was standing at the time, popped up straight from his prior attitude of bending toward the desk, taut vertical in his ecstasy of joy—well, those jig-like steps of his made his torso move a little too. And whether it was for tensional relief, or plain old enthusiasm-of-discovery, or even so noncommittal a factor as transient loss of balance from the dance step he so ineptly tried to take: he put his arms straight out and gave the wide-eyed Miss Hamblin a great big grateful hug!

"Audrey," he smiled. "You're a regular little genius—you know that, girl? And I'll tell you something else: You're gonna solve this whole damn crazy riddle today all by your brilliant little self; that I can practically guarantee!"

"I *am*? You *can*?—But *how*?"

"Jurisdictional authority, my dear Miss Hamblin; jurisdictional authority. There's a public official involved in this West Virginia crime map business, I can tell you that for sure. I'd look into the county people first—sheriff's department, legal personnel, that sort of thing—That's what I'd recommend if I were suggesting your next computer-savvy move....

"But if you do your usual exemplary work with that telephone of yours and the Internet you're so good at navigating—I'm absolutely positive you'll have a name for me by the end of office hours today!"

But he was wrong about that—wrong by a couple of hours, actually, as to his initial estimate of time. The county rolls were long, the information slow to trickle in: Even electronically, the data stream was maddeningly slow. And add to that the many other impediments to Audrey's daunting task: The numerous phone calls she had to make, the many figures to tabulate, the voluminous texts and files and images she was required to download.

At six o'clock, an hour into her unpaid overtime, Sidney ran out for a couple of dinners-in-a-box: a five-star Italian bistro three blocks down that had to scramble through some closets for carry-out containers to put the goodies in. They ate together at his desk; ate their veal and pasta hurriedly, impatiently; for the final names were just now coming in. He gathered the boxes and Styrofoam cups while Audrey clicked and printed and made some final after-hours calls.... And by seven-twenty; by late enough in the evening that it was getting pretty dark:

"Here they are, sir. I'd make a bet it's one of these guys here—Well, there's one woman on the list as well, but she's a long shot; I put her way down toward the bottom of the batch."

"Let me see, Audrey. Just one page? How many have you got on there in all?"

"Nine total, but the first one is the likeliest, I'd guess."

She passed him the printout: Nine banal-enough-looking names in a two-inch vertical row.

"Gonzalez? Is that the guy you mean? OK, we'll start with him then—So, tell me—what's the story there?"

"*Great* story, sir; fascinating. We couldn't have found a more likely candidate if I'd done the research for a year."

"No? OK—So: tell me—*what?*"

"OK, well first of all, I did that statewide missing persons search before I did anything else—the way we did with Pennsylvania, remember?"

"Yeah, right. And in Pennsylvania, half the missing persons were concentrated near Stanleyville, so that was in agreement with what we'd thought."

"Right; and it agreed here too—A little more than half the missing persons from West Virginia came from Kanawha County."

"Which is Charleston, of course—the area in blue on our map."

"Right, exactly, but there's more. Here's the interesting part, sir: You know how the missing persons from the area around Stanleyville were mostly people suspected of crimes but never arrested?—Oh, some of them were felons too, I guess, but only maybe twenty percent, if I remember right. Only twenty percent were ever actually listed as having been in jail."

"Right. I remember that. The Stanleyville suspect seemed to go after really evil people who were sort of under the radar, didn't he? Really bad guys, for sure; but sort of bad guys who'd managed to slip through the cracks."

"That's what we figured, sir, for Stanleyville, right—But the figures from Charleston show a completely different trend. The missing persons from Kanawha County were almost all in the system when I looked them up. Actually, something like eighty percent of the Charleston area missing persons were listed as—here's the really weird part, Agent Braman—They were on the books as having skipped out of their parole."

"Their *parole!*" Sidney's jaw dropped palpably. "Holy Moses!—They skipped their damn *parole?*—So then—we need to look into the parole system for Kanawha county, right?—Have you got a way to check that out?"

"Top name on the list, sir. That Gonzalez fellow, first one there—He's the senior parole supervisor. And when I looked into the histories carefully, most of the missing parole violators were on at least one occasion released to his custody—mostly the last time they were accounted for, in fact."

"They *were*!? They actually *were*?—Incredible! Fantastic! That's gotta be our guy then! OK, so—we're gonna need to find him next. And right away! Have you got a number we can call?—His cell? Or residence maybe? Or...."

"Already done, sir; I dialed it a little while ago, in fact."

"OK, great—A-n-d?"

"And nothing, Agent. He picked up the phone. I asked him if he was Mr. Gonzalez—Thomas Gonzalez, that is—He said he was. I asked if he had any information about the parolees who'd gone missing; and he hung up without another word. And when I called him back, a minute later, the line was busy; and when I called again five minutes after *that*—just a little while ago in fact—his wife answered the phone—I assumed it was his wife—and she told me that he'd left."

"*Left*? She said he *left*? Well ... but did she say where he was going, or tell you anything more than simply that he left. Did she say...?"

"She sounded pretty frantic, actually. She was crying, I think, judging by the sniffly kind of sounds she made; and then she hung up too; and when I called the number back again, just a minute or so ago, nobody answered at all."

"*Really*—*Honestly*—Well, that's pretty much a wrap then, Audrey—That's gotta be our Charleston guy for sure. Fantastic work, young lady. Fabulous! I'll put out a bulletin to get the guy picked up ASAP, and then we'll have to get our team inside his house somehow—That'll be next on the agenda—We'll get a warrant—maybe tonight if we can get the judge up out of bed—and see if this Gonzalez has a crematory oven in his basement or whatever—You've got a current address, I assume? Is it on the page here?"

"Sure is, sir. But you're not likely to find a crematory oven when you get there, I'll bet. The place he lives: I checked it out on the realty site: He's got the whole top floor of a downtown luxury condo—Fanciest residence in Charleston, I'd guess—It sold for three-million-six, five years ago...."

Audrey paused a couple of seconds, smiling knowingly, then continued:

"Now ... I didn't see that Mr. Gonzalez had ever won the lottery or anything, and he doesn't seem to have inherited a fortune from a favorite aunt—But, with that three-and-a-half-million-dollar place he bought: Interesting thing is, Agent Braman, the top salary a parole supervisor gets paid is something like eighty grand a year."

21

If he had been capable of feeling anything, he would have been shocked.

But being incapable of feeling shock—being, actually, incapable of *any* significant emotional reaction *whatever*—it wasn't exactly shock that Wilson felt when he got the phone call from Gonzalez, but rather a sense of concern and deep inadequacy. For he had never been called on to perform the sort of function that would be required of him over the forthcoming months. And lacking the hands-on experience—lacking, at this late date, any real experience at *all*—well, how the devil was he supposed to hone the skills he'd need in just the next few weeks?

One thing was certain: Madam must be told. She'd need to be alerted right away—*now*! And so up the hallway to Madam's TV chamber, pushing in the door as unobtrusively as ever he could, but....

But, hmmm ... peculiar—Madam wasn't there; she'd *been* there only half an hour ago, watching those horrendous scenes of hers again, churning her blood into an uproar; and Wilson knew from past experience that when she got like that, when she got her blood to churning up like that—boiling, frenzied—she would be ... there would be.... Oh my!

So up the stairs he scurried, up to her bedroom, hoping against all likelihood that he might find her there—She generally wouldn't nap at such a time; but just on the optimistic happenstance that....

But no, not in her bed either—not on the first floor or the second—Which left—Ah yes: the place she'd often wander off to after a three-day bout of watching films and getting frenzied: He'd likely find her another level up.

So up he ambled, up a narrow stairway to the topmost level of the house, and over to the dormer window giving access to the roof. Peering, prowling, that's what Madam generally got into when her blood was at a boil and her strength was at its fullest. And then those horror films to get her hungry for a kill, like romance movies to a teenage girl....

But—Goodness gracious! No sign of her here either, neither standing at a window staring out, nor crouched on the roof, as often, nor perched atop a chimney peering down.

And so.... Wilson leaned w-a-y out the window, holding on for dear life, and scanned across the grounds. Hmmm—nothing on the lawn, no; no rustling in the bushes; no fluttering of leaves ... except....

There! Over near the wall, beneath the copse of trees; some fallen leaves were scattering in the darkening evening air, though there was not the faintest sniff of wind about, and.... Wilson watched a moment more until....

Yes, there!—She was down there, all right; you couldn't make her out, not for certain with the shadows deep and the sun just due to set; but you could sense a bit of movement underneath the branches of the trees. She'd managed to snag something; that was for sure: another dog—hopefully a dog and not another child. That business with the little girl a couple of months ago: Good lord!—If he hadn't come up with an ingenious plan and managed to divert the authorities: If they'd brought a warrant and gotten in the house—Oh my!—They would have had to see her; and if anyone had stepped inside and *seen* her....

No, Madam was in no condition to be seen these days. Shrunken as she was, hideous as a gargoyle on a gothic roof: the puckered face, the strangely bulging muscles underneath her skin: Whew!—One look at her and anyone would know at once that something was amiss. A snapshot—or worse than that, a video—if it got out, and got broadcast—Good lord! They'd have a regular media circus on their hands: TV crews with telephoto lenses, news reporters gathering on the street outside—Oh, and there'd have to be an inquiry too; a court, a judge—And the last thing they could tolerate would be public inquiry—So hopefully, *mercifully*, Wilson prayed the thing she'd snatched out on the lawn was *not* another child.

So fretting, worrying—to the extent that such a man as he was capable of those things—down went Alexander Wilson, scrambling just as quickly as those sturdy, stocky legs could carry him, down the narrow flight of steps, and then the wider one, out the front door, scurrying across the lawn, over to the trees where the leaves were stirring underfoot....

But it was a cat—whew!—nothing but a measly little cat. Wilson took a breath and gushed a long, exhaustive sigh— Madam was busy with nothing but a silly little fur-ball-of-a-cat. The neighbors wouldn't go and knock on people's doors for missing cats; a missing cat wasn't something that would summon the authorities—So they were safe, the situation was containable—at least for now.

Wilson stood aside and watched. There it was, poor thing; Madam had it in her claws—the little that was left of it— black and white fur, an awful lot of blood for such a puny thing. Now that she'd had her bit of fun, she'd leave it to be tossed into the hopper; he'd do the cleanup in a while, hose down the lawn and such. She'd be a whole lot calmer now that she had got some of the frenzy out. Those movies got her dander up, and catching something for a kill: That generally got it down. At the moment, thank heavens, she seemed relatively calm, sated: The absolutely perfect time to tell her what he had the need to say.

"Madam?—Would you please accompany me into the house?"

"What is it, Wilson? You see I'm busy, don't you?"

"It looks as though you've finished, Madam. Would you kindly accompany me in?"

"All right; you're right, I *have* finished; that is true. You can dispose of this a little later on; before morning sometime, I would hope. So?—What is it that you wish to say?"

"An important matter to discuss with you. We received a phone call, just this minute, in fact. Would you please accompany me in? It would be best if we discuss the subject of the telephone message inside."

A great deal calmer—yes—practically compliant, one might say. She took his arm and let him lead her past the open door, through the entryway, down the hall, and over to the Queen Anne wing chair in her sitting room. She didn't ask him for the remote to her TV; of her grisly films she'd had enough for now. Once he was finished telling what he had to tell, he'd get a basin and a cloth to sanitize those nasty nails.

"All right, Wilson, what is it you have to say? Speak up, man—*What*?"

"The phone call, Madam: It's…. It has to do with Mr. Gonzalez."

"*Him*? Well?" Yes, she was calm, all right, fatigued from her exertion: A little cat, perhaps, but swift enough to lead her quite a chase.

"What *of* him? What *of* Gonzalez? He wants more money, I suppose—Well, give him what he asks for if he has to make a fuss. Find out what he wants and send it. We can ill afford to get the man upset."

"Oh, but … it isn't money though. He called a little while ago; but it wasn't money that he called about."

"So *what* then? What else does he ever want but money? Whatever it is, give it to him. Don't argue or debate, just give. Buy him another car if he wants one, or a bigger home if that penthouse doesn't suit him anymore; I don't care. Don't bother *me* with it—just see what the man requires and write him out a check."

"But Madam: it isn't what you think at all. Mr. Gonzalez phoned and told me that he's leaving. He's going away. He's on his way right now. He got a call, and someone must have learned about the arrangements that we've made; and he said he's leaving right away, tonight; and that we'd have to make some alternate arrangements to meet your future needs."

"*What!*—Alternate *arrangements!*—*What* alternate arrangements?—You're saying *now*? How can we make any alternate arrangements *now*?"

Oh my! That upset the hornet's nest—Her blood was up again. The cat had calmed her for a bit, but this business with Gonzalez was riling her once more. Wilson might have known— And in a way, he *had* known, hadn't he? But had there been another choice? One had to break the news, and pretty quickly too; delaying it would only stoke her anger more.

"This abruptly!" she wheezed, now in a really frenzied voice, piercing to the ear. "How can he…? How can *we*…?— Wilson, tell me: What did he say? Tell me what he said. Word for word. Exactly what Gonzales said. *Tell* me!"

"Yes, Madam; excuse me, Madam, but I was *about* to tell you what he said. Mr. Gonzalez said that someone had called him. From the FBI, he said. Someone from the FBI called him just a little while ago on the phone, at his home—a woman, he said, from … from—Pittsburgh, I think it was—And she asked him about the parolee cases he had handled over the years, and asked him why so many of them went missing, and where they might have gone, and…."

"The FBI! But ... how could they have known anything at the FBI?—The FBI! But ... but.... He must have said something. He must have talked to someone—Gonzalez must have done something foolish, Wilson.... Get him for me—do you hear? Bring him to me. I shall extract it from him; I'll find out—Believe you me, I'll find out—And if he did something foolish—if he said something foolish, Wilson—I will have my revenge!—You know me well enough to understand I mean the things I tell you; and you know as well as I do that I will make him pay for what he told them if he told them anything at all. So go right now and fetch him for me, Wilson—you hear me? Bring him to me—*Now*."

"He's gone though, Madam. He was in his vehicle when he called, and he must be on his way by now. Going overseas, I imagine. He has plenty of money to go wherever he likes, you know. You've paid him a great deal of money over the years."

"I *have* paid him—very generously too. And if he *has* told someone—anyone! ... But what would he have said? Think now, Wilson: Can you think of anything Gonzalez might have said?"

"He knows where the parolees were delivered, Madam; and he knows the kind of car I picked them up in."

"Yes, but no more than that—was there? He never knew exactly what we did with them—Do you think he realized what we did?"

"I think he didn't *want* to realize those things, Madam. He never asked more than I volunteered to tell. And even then...."

"You told him it was—what? What did you tell him they were for?—Some sort of charitable purpose, was it not?"

"I told him it was a project to rehabilitate the prisoners. That it was an experimental program to send the parolees out of state to be reformed."

"And he never asked you more? You think that he believed you?"

"I suppose he *wanted* to believe and didn't dare to ask. I think he was glad to get them out of Charleston, frankly, Madam. Many of the law enforcement people likely feel that way."

"Well, we have to know, Wilson—It is imperative that we know—So find him—do you hear me?! Bring him to me!—You hear me, Wilson?—Go find him and bring him to me *now*!"

She grasped at Wilson's arm, and squeezed, and twisted as the claws went in; and blood oozed out from beneath the thumb nail, though Wilson didn't flinch.

"I can look for him, Madam, if you wish; I can go to his home to look, but I'm sure he won't be there."

"How can this have *happened*?!—Do you know?"

"No, Madam. I can't think of *any* way it might have happened. Gonzalez has always been reliable; for twenty years he's been reliable to a fault. I can't think why he would be other than reliable now."

"*You* can't think—*you*! You aren't *here* to think. It has never been your *role* to think. Your role is to *obey*; to listen and obey. I demand answers and you're here to *give* me answers. Now find out precisely what happened and report back to me."

"Yes, Madam; of course; as you wish, but.... How would you propose that I find that out?"

She pushed up from the armchair and stood. Fragile as a child when the blood ran thin, but she had ample blood cells now; copious blood in tortuous veins. Each month or so, after the fresh new blood went in, for many days thereafter, the purple veins beneath her skin bulged full. And when the veins bulged full like that, Madam was as quick and powerful of arm as she had ever been these recent twenty years.

And so today, her quick arm moved, and the veins bulged wide; and Wilson's forearm got jerked up and sideways, then out. And he flew across the room; flew quick like some flattened stone a playful child has skipped across a pond. And when he hit, his fellow arm hit hard, striking the far wall with a considerable-sounding thud. He was resilient, though, and rugged, and had been thrown across the various rooms, against the various walls, of this antiquated residence innumerable times before. The impact of his body against the plaster was hard, judging by the sound it made; but he got up quickly, limping only minimally, and returned like a faithful puppy to her side.

And once he got there, to the right arm of her chair, she reached up—for she was sitting again—and touched his macerated forearm skin—though gently now—and explained to him calmly, quietly, as though he'd never been flung against the wall and never been required to return:

"It's him, Wilson. It can only have been him. Just like the last time twenty years ago. Someone has made an attempt to destroy me, and I'm certain it can only have been him!"

"Your brother, you mean?"

"Yes, who else but Brother? He's on the move again; I knew it; I told you so. That fire in Pennsylvania—that got him moving, and he'll be here, mark my words. His things are here, and our father's things are here—I told you that before—and he'll come to get them rather soon. And to destroy me before he feels the sharpness of my knife again, I'm certain that he did something to Gonzalez to interdict my flow of blood. But I shall destroy him first; somehow I WILL find means to destroy him first—We shall catch him—the way we did it last time, Wilson— The same way—do you remember?"

"Yes, Madam; my memory is very vivid of that day."

"Remind me then. I have a tendency to forget these past few years. You got him to my room—Can you remember how you got him to my room?"

"Yes, Madam. I told him—you instructed me to tell him—that you were ill—having trouble breathing, I believe. He asked for Larkins, and I told him that Larkins had gone out to get some medicine for you, so...."

"Larkins was his Helper at the time, was he not? A thin man with graying hair?"

"Yes, Madam. You had stabbed him earlier before Brother arrived. I put his body in the cellar."

"Yes, I recall that now. The man was downstairs and he was facing you, and I came up behind him—He didn't resist, did he? I have no memory of a struggle."

"No, Helpers lack the ability to resist. You left the dagger in, so there was very little blood. Your brother noticed nothing to alert him on entering."

"Yes, yes; and Brother came upstairs—you sent him up—and he leaned over me to check my breathing—I had the dagger in my hand beneath the covers—a new dagger, a fresh one; and that was when I.... Yes, yes; tell me, Wilson, do you think it would be possible to employ a ruse like that again?"

"I very much doubt it, Madam. Your brother is very smart."

"All right; let it be for now; you and I will think of something. Together we.... But—What about the daughter? The doctor?—She is living in that home, is she not?"

"Yes, I believe she bought the old Finotti residence last year."

"Good, then, very good—You know the address, I assume?—So go and watch the place; begin tomorrow morning. Keep a lookout for him, Wilson. If he goes there—if you see him there, and he meets with the girl—she's not a girl, I know, but I still think of her as one—if he goes to her, he will do whatever he must do to protect her—He will or old Finotti will if he remains alive. Brother has always tried to protect those two, you know, the nurse and her daughter both. I should have killed them back at the beginning, twenty years ago; I would have done so if they hadn't run away. But now...."

"All right, but Madam—Pardon me for asking you again, Madam, but *can* you? Can you harm her? I know what you said the other day, but.... The doctor—unless she's done some evil act or hurt another person in some way...."

"Silence, Wilson! You tell me that I *can't?*—*You?* Who are *you* to tell me what I can and cannot do? I can do what I like. I killed that little girl who came here with her cookies, did I not?—And was she evil? And the other one, the skinny one whose ball bounced on my land across the wall. Was she evil in any way? And did you not dispose of them as you always do? Those girls had never done evil, as far as you and I have ever been aware—had they? And ... and those two Jehovah's Witnesses two years ago: Had *they* done evil, so far as you know? When I ordered you to dispose of them, you did that too. When the mood strikes me, I do what I like. This is my property, and anyone or anything that invades my property is *mine*—you hear me?— MINE! Who is there to stop me doing what I like and what I must to protect my privacy and my land?—Will *you* prevent me, Wilson? Are you *able* to?"

"I am conditioned to obey, Madam; but we are specifically programmed—I and you as well, from what your brother said—never to harm the innocent to satisfy your normal monthly needs. That is part of my conditioning that cannot ever be changed."

"You say it cannot, do you?—So what are *you* then, Wilson? You were evil once. Whether you admit it or not, you were. I could use *you* as a donor if I chose—do you understand? And if I ordered you to be a donor, to supply the blood I need, what would you do? Have you ever thought of that?"

"I haven't, Madam, but it is mandatory that I obey."

"It is; I fully realize that it is. So do what I ordered then: Go to the daughter's house and watch. If Brother turns up there to see the girl, then bring her here to me. Wait until he goes away and bring her here to me. If he knows we have her here, he will come here to protect her—I know he will—And when he comes—*this* time!—I intend to finish what I should have finished long ago. Go and watch the house, and if he comes, bring the daughter here the moment that he goes away....

"And sharpen another knife, Wilson. Good and sharp this time. I want to make sure the job is well and truly done....

"And—Wilson?—listen to me, Wilson—even if he doesn't turn up at the house—heed what I am saying, Wilson; listen carefully: Even if he doesn't show up there, tomorrow or the next day or the next day after that, bring the daughter to me anyway. If nothing else, now that Gonzalez refuses to get us any donors—while we try to find another source, I can keep her for another couple of weeks and use her for her blood."

22

"This is like dream for me; you know? Being here with you again is like the fondest, sweetest dream I've ever known.

Jennifer sat on the bench with him: *Their* bench, the one they'd lounged in and talked in and watched the summer bloom and ebb for hours and hours on end. *Their* bench, true—but it wasn't quite the same as it had been twenty years ago. The keepers of the park had replaced the old bench with a new one— no longer weathered wood alone, but weathered *iron* and wood combined: though the rust spots on the iron and the fading of the wood weren't all that commendable a change.

Twenty years now since the two of them had been here last, but the scents and sounds seemed very much the same. The ancient maple trees were taller—just a bit—wider—just a bit— sparser, yellower, now that fall had come to stand in for the sunny summer of his memories.

But the odors of the grass; the vapors of the nearby stream; the pudgy infants plodding on the lawn: Those were part and parcel of his memories. Jennifer sensed the reminiscence just as much as he did; and she told him so, once they'd made it to the bench from where he'd parked the beat-up pickup truck over near the ball field. And once they'd sat down close together on the new replacement bench, and turned to one another hand in hand: Once they'd settled in, and sniffed the verdant air, and nestled warmly in their memories, she held his hand in both of hers and told him of her dream of him; and to that vivid fantasy he answered truthfully:

"Yes, for me too. I've thought of you and Meredith every day of my life since then; some days every hour; every minute, waking and asleep."

"And you never thought of even calling me? Or writing? Even a note to say you were alive and that you remembered me? In twenty years, you never had the urge to even call?"

"How could I, though? It would have been impossible for me to see you—you understand *that*, don't you? You understand that he was with me all the while, and all the time that he was with me, I couldn't let him anywhere near the two of you, ever again. Keep that fact in mind, and I know you'll understand."

"My father, you mean? Mama said he would have died if you hadn't taken him along."

"He would have *had* to die, wouldn't he? You and Meredith could never have lived in any reasonable comfort or security if he'd been around. And even if you'd gone away—far away—he would have turned up eventually and done his best to wreck your lives again. He didn't deserve to live, that's true; but I couldn't bring myself to kill him, not after knowing him as your father and Meredith's husband, so I...."

"So you kept him as a Helper—yes; that I understand. Mama told me that you did. It's better that you found some beneficial use for him, I guess. He wasn't much good for anything else."

"Your mother almost died from one of the beatings—did she ever tell you that?"

"Not that exactly, no; but.... All I remember of the man is those beatings: Mama screaming in the night, then black and blue next morning, with her eyes puffed shut: I remember them taking her to the hospital a couple of times—And as for what he did to me, I still have scars on my shoulders from the burns; I don't think he even lit those cigarettes for anything other than to make the burns—But you remember those burns, don't you? You were with us then. That's the night you took him away, and I never saw him again after that dreadful night."

"OK, no need to think about those bad times anymore. They're over and done with now; you're grown and happy and a lovely woman—and a practicing doctor too! I can hardly believe my little Jennifer is a graduate physician—You were always a brilliant girl, but...."

"I was a brilliant girl because of *you*—don't you realize that? You taught me everything in those three amazing months—absolutely everything I ever had to know."

"Did I? I didn't teach you *things* exactly; I taught you how to *look* at things, how to *analyze* things, how to learn the things you had to learn and how to remember them. What I taught you was the art of remembering and thinking. You know, when I was a child...."

"A million years ago—right?"

"Not quite a million, but sometimes it seems that long."

"So *how* long exactly? Three hundred? That's the number I sort of recall."

He nodded tentatively. "It's about that; yes. I was born—near as I can figure it—not long after the siege of Vienna. That was in 1683, so add it up from there."

"It's hard to imagine—you know? You told me some of it when I was a kid, but what you told me has always been more or less a childish memory. I suppose I believed it, in a way—kind of in the same way a child from ancient Greece might have believed the tales of Hercules. You were almost a kind of Hercules to me, but a Hercules that I'd actually met and talked to and...."

"And learned how to learn from; that's what you ought to say. That's what your Herculean friend taught you: The secret of how to learn. When I was a child—that's where our conversation got derailed, remember; so I'll put it back on track—When I was a child, printing was only—what?—a couple of hundred years old? People still had hand-copied manuscripts and treasured them. And paper wasn't cheap yet either. Even by the time I was growing up, books were still expensive and relatively scarce.

"What that meant was, Jen: it meant that a person didn't just pick up an iPad or go out to the local library to look some interesting topic up. People used their memory much more back then than they do today. There were men in those days—some of them were teachers, but many of them were just ordinary common folks—there were men who had whole vast compendia of knowledge in their heads. I learned from some of them myself—Back in Padua I did, when I studied medicine there, and then at Leiden later: This fellow Liberius—they Latinized the names sometimes; Liberius came from Freiburg, so they Latinized the German word for 'free'—Anyway, he taught us anatomy, and he had the whole human body in his head—everything, mind you, every nerve and vein and facet on a bone.

"And there was a botanist too, Fabricius Filius was his name—We student doctors learned plants back then for medicinal use—Well, old Fabricius's massive memory held *every* plant—thousands of them; tens of thousands, possibly—names and habitats and properties—Men like that—Liberius and Fabricius and all those other geniuses in Pavia—and in Leiden, and in Paris too when I went there later on—they taught us some of their tricks of memory and recall—And that's some of the nifty stuff that I taught you."

"You did; you really did. That way of pigeonholing facts, encoding them in visual imagery—You know I still remember every bit of the history you showed me how to learn? I still remember all the presidents and vice presidents and all the cabinet secretaries just the way you showed me how to stick them in my head."

"I'm sure you *do* remember: people don't forget things when they learn them properly."

"Yes, but those learning tricks of yours!—Did you know I finished at the top of all my classes every year in school?— Every year, every subject, no exception."

"I'm not surprised. You were a smart kid going in."

"Maybe. Anyway, between the memory tricks I'd learned, and that way of analyzing facts, and understanding science and math and the cyclical patterns of history, and....."

"I know; I know. When you've had three hundred years to learn things properly yourself, you can boil them down to the essentials and teach them to another person pretty easily in three intensive months."

"Which you did. And I've never forgotten a bit of it to this day."

"Good. I'm glad. I'm proud of what you've done. And to see you a doctor now—But, speaking of your being a doctor— what time do you need to get to work?"

"I go to the hospital first, for rounds; then the office afterward. I'll probably leave pretty soon. It's eight-fifteen now, so—maybe we ought to head on back. Did you get your urgent shopping done?"

"Some of it. I got the drill and concrete saw. There's still the metal; and I'll need a plasma cutter for that. They don't keep those things in stock—not for inch-thick steel—so I had them order one; and it'll be in by tomorrow possibly—If not, then maybe one day more."

"When did you do all that burying back then?—Hide away your precious stash, I mean?"

"The day that you and Meredith left. It wasn't safe to take it along, not knowing exactly where I'd finally wind up; and in case something happened to me, it was important that my sister could get to it, just in case I no longer could. My father

made me promise I would always keep that option open—
Although now...."

"So—what was it that you left there? Can you tell me
that?"

"I can, I guess; you know everything else by now. I left
some safeguards—ID and Social Security numbers in case I had
to transfer funds—which I really do right now; I can't access a
penny of my brokerage accounts—And I stashed away some
gold—I always store a lot of gold, just for safety's sake—I've got
gold buried in a couple of dozen places I'll probably never get
back to now.

"And that paper of my father's too, that's the main thing.
Time to take it with me now: Sister's out of the picture as far as
that's concerned—That box with my father's instructions is a
deep, dark mystery even to me; but one of these days I'll explain
to you the little bit I know."

"You have no idea what's in it?"

"In the box? No, I promised not to open it until the time
was right, and I've always kept my word. For three hundred
years now I've always kept my word."

"But there are instructions in there? Something you need
to do?"

"Yes, some task we were *all* meant to do. A message we
need to send, I gather—I have no idea what it is or where it's
supposed to go. The paper in the box will tell me that."

"So—how many of you are there—do you know? Are
there very many left?"

"No, not like an army or anything, but some, a number.
Maybe hundred maybe a thousand at the present day. None of
us know for sure, I'd imagine. Only a fraction of the Originals
survived to reproduce—the ones Father taught the secret of
harvesting blood and who had the right blood type to begin with.
And of the second generation and the ones after that, most of the
major countries have just a handful, maybe a dozen—
whatever—though I have no idea where they are and their exact
number. I met two of them—of *us*, I ought to say—back in
Vienna when I was one of the court physicians to Charles VI,
and I showed...."

"Wait. Stop. Charles VI? That would be..."

"1730 or so. The Emperor died in 1740, and this must
have been a decade or so before his daughter succeeded and the
succession wars began. But anyway, as I was saying, I showed the

two men I met how to use stem cells—marrow, actually: I had no idea about stem cells then—and that helped keep a lot of the other ones alive and healthy. But it's not like we have family reunions or anything—Other than Sister, I guess I'm out of the loop as far as the rest of them are concerned. There are some other minor details I can tell you, but not a lot. I'll explain a little more when we have more time, but for now...."

"All right; well, if there's something else you plan to explain to me, that means you won't run off again for another twenty years, at least. So—I'll see you later on today?"

"Sure. What time do you finish at the office?"

"I've cancelled most of it. Drop me off at home now, then come back around two o'clock—OK? Then you can tell me more about what life was like in 1683."

Wilson was parked there closely watching as the truck drove up: an old, decrepit pickup, not the kind of vehicle a wealthy man like Brother would customarily drive. But when it stopped in front of the house, and the pretty, youthful doctor got out, and went inside; and when the beat-up, tatty pickup pulled away and rumbled by the place he was sitting in the Lincoln parked against the curb ... a glancing look through the pickup's windshield as it passed, informed him that—

Yes! Brother certainly—It *was*! It absolutely *was*! Twenty years since he had seen him last, and yet the handsome fellow looked the same.

So Brother in the truck drove past, and headed down the street, and turned right at the corner—you could see him in the side-view mirror as the truck slid out of sight—And Wilson sat in patient obedience and watched—for that's what Madam had instructed him to do, and of course he sat and did it.

And in twenty minutes time, out the daughter came again, and got into what he logically assumed to be her own car, a later-model pearl-white Buick, and drove straight off. Madam hadn't ordered him to follow *her*, and so he sat, obediently waiting.

And he would sit obediently waiting until just before one, when Madam would be ready for her lunch, and it was therefore requisite for him to drive back home and do the preparation, and put the food he'd cooked up in the blender so she could swallow

STEVEN M. GREENBERG

without chewing, past those broken stumps of long-departed teeth.

Whoosh! Screeee!

The engines were screaming in frustration when the door swung open inward once again and two men stepped aboard. They wore business suits, both of them did, and the suits on both the silent men looked snug around the upper chest and shoulders, and their collars looked constricted on the neck, the way dress clothes look constricting on excessively muscular men.

They stopped and spoke to the flight attendant up front, spoke very briefly, very quietly—too soft in their mumbled burble for even the passengers up near the entry door to overhear.

Then the attendant went forward toward the cockpit, while the two men started slowly down the aisle. Down they came, through first class, and past it, scanning the passengers as they walked. Through the first few rows of economy, scanning sideways still ... until they pulled up midway through the cabin at the twenty-second row.

And there, at the twenty-second row, one of the men, a tall, clean-cut, youngish-looking fellow with a vested, striped gray suit, bulging laterally, as from a hidden gun: This brawny man leaned over past the passenger in the aisle seat on the left, inclining toward the passenger in the middle seat beside him, and barked out curtly to the middle-seated passenger:

"Mr. Gonzalez? Are you ... Thomas Gonzalez?"

The passenger thus questioned was a pale man, with marbled hair and a high receded brow. He was mid-fifties, maybe more, casually dressed, but with expensive kinds of clothes: a cashmere sweater, designer-style jeans, an ostrich-leather briefcase on his lap. He said nothing, but it was evident to his seat-mates, right and left, that his hands were trembling, and his brow was moist, and his darting eyes searched furiously for something—perhaps an exit path—though what he sought specifically was very hard to tell.

And after twenty wrenching seconds of inexorable silence and darting of eyes and sweating of brow on the part of the middle-seated passenger in the twenty-second row, the tall, strong, gray-clad man who had addressed him took a photograph out of his inside jacket pocket near the gun and looked at it for a little while and said:

"Mr. Gonzalez? This photograph identifies you as Mr. Thomas Gonzalez of Charleston, West Virginia—Are you in agreement, Agent Benson?"

Agent Benson evidently was the fellow standing next to the gray-suited questioner—the second man who'd come aboard—dressed in solemn pin-striped black. And he took the photo and looked at it carefully, and then at the middle-seated passenger in turn; and finally indicated with a nod and a basso 'yes' that he did, in fact, agree.

"You'll need to come with us, Mr. Gonzalez. We have a ninety-minute drive to Pittsburgh, and there's a fellow there named Braman who'd like to talk to you right away."

23

"Hey—Sidney?"

"Phil! Yeah, uh…. Look, Phil, I'm right in the middle of something really, really big right now. Could I maybe call you back?"

"Sure, you can call me anytime, kiddo; but you're gonna wanna hear this stunning revelation first—So? You wanna listen now and get it over with?—Or you wanna sit there for an hour pondering your kishkas out before you finally make the call?"

"OK, I give. You've managed to get my interest sufficiently aroused. So?—What the hell is up?"

Phil chuckled genially—you could hear his genial laughter on the line.

"Sidney?—You were right about the fifty chromosomes your fella's got."

"I was?—Well, I mean, I *know* I was, but … why do you *say* I was? What did you all of a sudden find out?"

"I been doing a little research, Sid, and…. You know what you said about more than one of your vampire creatures maybe being out there?"

"*Sure* I know. I'm breathing up the tuchas of a second one right now, as we speak—Audrey found him with another one of those brilliant little crime maps she designed. She showed it to me yesterday, and after she dug a little more, we zeroed in on some guy in West Virginia, then put out a bulletin late last night—around ten, it was. And they just now picked him up in Youngstown at eight this morning at the airport on the way to…. Well, out of the country someplace, I forget exactly where— Mexico, Panama, wherever—Anyway: *I* got another suspect I'm gonna question—But how did *you* know a second one was out there, huh? You must've done some fancy research to find that out."

"Not so fancy, boychik, as it was persistent. You got old Uncle Phil to wondering the other day; so I ran up to the med school library here at Pitt and did a search—That fifty chromosome craziness got rattling in my head, you know—And ... well, what I did was: I plugged in 'fifty chromosomes' cross-indexed to 'anemia'—The medical librarian did it for me; she's a regular goddam maven with that research crap—And, anyway, whaddya think turned up?"

"Another vampire, right?" Sidney puffed a little laugh out through his nose: "Wait, lemme guess; don't tell me, Phil: A regular Dracula type with fangs and wings and a casket to go to sleep in—Did I manage to guess it right?"

"Not quite, kiddo, but relatively close. Turns out there's this cockamamie syndrome—I never heard of it before, 'cause it's been reported mostly in the Eastern European medical journals—Romania especially, and Hungary, and ... and—Transylvania, believe it or not, just like in the books—But I finally got the abstracts in English and—They do that, you know?—Simultaneous translation from any goddam language in the world—What an amazing age we live in!"

"OK, OK, I know about the Internet capabilities, Phil. What about the research you did? Finish up, 'cause I really gotta go."

"Yeah, Sidney, sure. Sorry about that. So anyways, there's this syndrome, Bratianu Syndrome, after the guy who wrote it up the first time—There's maybe twenty cases reported total; that's it—just twenty, which is why most of us never heard of the damn thing. It's a fatal aplastic anemia in patients with fifty chromosomes, mostly related to advanced parental age and—get this—it's only been reported in the prison population. Bratianu's original article—back in the fifties—reported three cases—Actually, it's more a case report than a regular article, but the first guy that describes something generally gets it named after him—Poor Dr. Alzheimer, huh? Anyway, Bratianu thought it was something the patients caught in jail, and he did a lot of microbiologic studies which came up with zilch, as you'd expect.

"But the syndrome, as they describe it in the other, more scholarly reports, goes like this: Usually the father's old, like nearly a hundred kind of old. The case that got reported last—maybe twenty-some-odd years ago—the patient's dad was ninety-some years old when the affected kid was born—pretty amazing when you think that these were pre-Viagra days back then—The old man might have been even more than that—nobody kept good records, so they didn't know the father's actual age a hundred percent for sure."

"So what happened to them?—The patients with the syndrome, I mean—not the fathers."

"What happened? To the anemics?—They died; all of them died—They were all in prison, remember?—No way to get blood—None of them actually went to the doctor to get diagnosed—You see? You see the pattern here?—There were a couple of posts done on the bodies in the more recent cases— that's when they did the chromosomal studies too—and—you ready for this? You sitting down? You sure you wanna hear the rest of this meshuginer BS?"

"*Sure* I want to hear. After all this vampire lunacy I've got sitting on my desk, I'm ready for any goddam thing your librarian dug up—So what do I need to be ready for? Tell me what you found."

"All of the Bratianu Syndrome patients that were written up were smart—I mean *really* smart—IQ's off the chart, OK?"

"OK, that's interesting to know. Not a total revelation, frankly, but interesting, at any rate."

"And something else besides: They were strong too—all of them were. I mean really, *really* strong—Their muscle fibers were different from the normal kind. A different form of protein—actin, myosin, yeah, but in a different form. The last patient that died—the one from twenty-something years ago?— They did a protein analysis on the muscle tissue—you hear me, Sid?—and it was weird, a total redesign of the molecular structure to make the contraction twice as powerful as normal— maybe three times, maybe four—who knows? It was postmortem, so they couldn't estimate the strength all that well— Anyway: They all died from the anemia, though. All of the patients with the syndrome died: It comes on when they're thirty-some, from what the reports say, and they die from it, a hundred percent of 'em die. Once they're in captivity they die. Like I told you in the deli, go ahead and lock your nice-guy vampire up and he'll die too."

"Yeah, well, *our* suspect—the Stanleyville one, I mean, seems like a decent person, I agree; but I'm not so sure all of them are as nice as our guy is. This second fellow that we're after seems to be far less socially benign."

"No? Why *not* benign? What did she find out, your pretty Irish girlfriend? The second vampire bump off a coupla good guys by mistake?"

"Not by mistake, Phil—Don't misunderstand me, though, I'm not saying all of the second suspect's victims were fine upstanding citizens exactly. But the missing folks from West Virginia—we've been looking through the records—the profiles and court reports, and—Well, nearly all of them were offenders on parole within the county where the suspect lived. A few of them were murderers and all-around thugs, that's true—we don't need to waste a lot of tears on them—But not all the parolees were violent criminal types. Half the missing victims' names we traced were just young kids caught with a little marijuana in their pockets, or a couple pills of ecstasy at a party with the girls, or picked up for driving drunk a second time, or unpaid tickets, or....

"Anyway, Phil—This West Virginia suspect seems to be a really truly bad guy just out prowling for his blood. He's a killer, Phil—a cold-blooded murderer who doesn't give a damn how good or bad his victims are—Good news is, though, the guy our fellows arrested at the airport—He's in custody and on his way here now. I'll get first crack at him in the interview room, and we'll know in an hour or so a whole lot more about these Bratianu creatures that Romania churned out—whatever the hell they are."

24

Sidney's brow was sopping wet and his shirt stuck down to his chest when he ran up from the interview with Gonzalez and hollered:

"Finotti, Audrey!—Tell me everything you've learned about Finotti: What did the people who knew him say about him when you called?"

Audrey looked up from her keypad with those big green eyes drooped inquisitively low:

"What did they say? Well, the description pretty much conformed to what the driver's license photo showed, sir—But why...?"

"No, no; not the *physical* description; I *know* what Finotti looked like. I mean his demeanor, his personality. Wasn't there something about him being ... I don't know—a little weird?— Didn't somebody describe him as a sort of weirdo? Kind of robot-like or something?—I seem to remember...."

"Oh *sure*. You're *right*. A couple of them *did*. Two people did—or maybe three—The man who sold him the cars in Stanleyville—He said that—And the lady in Cleveland he bought that fifty-thousand-dollar watch from—both of them described him the same exact way, sir: kind of robot-like, just the way you said, with, um, a kind of flat expression and a monotone voice. They both made a point of that, the man at the dealership and the lady at the jeweler's both. And there were others too, I think. It's all in the file, Agent Braman. Do you want me to...?"

"No, no, not now; I just wanted you to confirm what I remembered having heard—So *great*, then. That's it! First Finotti; and then this new guy Wilson—they're both pretty much the same: mask-faced, robotic—which means...."

"Wilson! Who's *Wilson*?—if you don't mind my asking, sir—Umm, what did that Gonzalez fellow down in Interview *say*?"

"He said everything, Audrey—everything a scrupulous interrogator might ever want to know! The guy's terrified of going down for a zillion cases of murder one, and he opened up like a clam shell in a pot. Hell, he was practically begging me to ask for more—But bottom line, what he gave us was this: He—this guy Gonzalez—definitely isn't the principal here. Oh, he handled the parolees, all right; but he was an intermediary—He picked them up from prison and passed them on. And the man he passed them onto—he doesn't strike me as the principal either, the one who actually needs the blood. This Wilson guy I mentioned—he's the one who *took* the parolees from our blabbermouth downstairs—he's the next link in the chain—And he seems to be another robot character like Finotti—Gonzalez described him in that exact same way—Somebody messes with the brains of these lackeys, I guess—whether they drug them or...."

"That's what the lady at the watch place said, sir—that Finotti talked like he'd been drugged."

"Right—Well, drugged or something worse, maybe—Anyway: we'll have to start with this Wilson character first—since he's the next step up the ladder toward the one who gets the blood—So—you want to check him out ASAP? Alexander Wilson is the name. Gonzalez said he dropped the parolees in a lot near the river in Charleston, and Wilson picked them up there, one a month—not to the day exactly, but roughly on that schedule. Picked them up in a dark blue Lincoln, fairly new, Gonzalez told me—we're getting some pictures of Lincolns so he can identify the year. So, meantime, try and correlate the name Alexander Wilson with a description of that type car. We're gonna get these guys before long, Audrey, and that map you came up with gets the credit for it all."

"Well thank you sir, and—I'll get on it right away: Alexander Wilson in Charleston, right? With a blue-colored Lincoln. If it's anywhere obtainable on the Net, you'll have it in just a sec."

Not *quite* a 'sec,' no; but not too much longer, either. In under twenty minutes' time, up popped Audrey from her desk, and she was over to his side with a crisp new printout in her hands, exulting in an effervescent voice:

"Got it, sir! Eighteen blue Lincolns between one and four years old in Kanawha County—where Charleston is—and only one is registered to a Wilson; and it's an *Alexander* Wilson, just like you said, so...."

"Terrific, Audrey! That's great!—You've got an address for me, I hope?"

"I do, but it's a dummy address, I'm pretty sure. A cheap apartment, from what the satellite view shows on Google Maps—here, look at the printout—But nobody's actually been living there. The manager says some middle-aged, bald guy comes and gets the mail a couple of times a week, but never spends the night. He almost never sees the guy go in or out or to the mailbox, but he pretty regularly spots the car."

"And that's the dark blue Lincoln—right? So great; we'll start from there. How about a license for the car—you get me that as well?"

"The number?—Sure. It's on the second page. Umm—do you want me to alert the locals to pick that fellow Wilson up?"

"No, no. Whoa! No locals, Audrey: We don't want to tip our hand just yet. Last thing we'd want is for our vampire guy to get alerted that we're on his trail. So no; no Keystone Cops this time. *This* time, what I'm gonna do is: It's—what?—A couple hundred miles to Charleston from here; say, three-four hours? If I head out now, I can be there by—oh, maybe two; maybe a little *before* two. So ... I'm gonna take off then. If I can find this fellow Wilson and follow him myself, he'll lead me smack dab to the vampire guy we want—And not just him, Audrey—the other one, the Stanleyville nice-guy murderer—he'll be there by now as well. From what the Hartman ladies said and the report we got on the incident outside Charleston on that bus yesterday afternoon...."

"The guy who broke that phony preacher's arm, you mean?"

"Yeah; that's our guy from Stanleyville for sure—I mean, running down the highway at ninety miles an hour like that—who else? So—OK, I'm heading out then; tell the Chief. I'll check in every hour or so for any updates that come in, and...."

"Yes, but—sir—wouldn't it be easier if you didn't have to call?"

"Not call? How do you mean?"

"Well, wouldn't it be easier if I went there with you—to Charleston, I mean? Then I could give you all the data you need in real time, with no delays. Wouldn't that be of help?"

"No. I mean—well *sure*, it'd be a help; real-time input is terrific. But you couldn't do your work like that, could you? I need you to keep up with the latest data on the investigation— check out this fellow Wilson and so on, so forth. And in a moving car out on the highway—You wouldn't have the resources in a car, or get a decent Internet connection, or have the computing power, or.... *Would* you?"

"Oh, but I *would* though, sir; I *definitely* would: If I had your laptop and a telephone link-up through a cell, I'd have everything I'd need—It's pretty much as fast as in the office. And if I'm right there with you, I can tell you what's happening exactly as it happens. And whenever you want something new, you won't have to call in and wait; I'll have it for you on the spot, hot off the presses. There won't be even an instant's delay."

"Yeah, that sounds great, fantastic; but...."

"But *what*? I can't see any downside to it at all—can *you*? And if I go with you, you can buy me something to eat along the way, so I won't have to starve to death sitting at the computer or eat those old, stale cookies on your desk—They're not that tasty anyway, frankly—I'm not that great a baker, as you probably discovered if you tried them out—So how about it, sir? You said I was a help to you before, with your interview and all, so why not let me be a help to you today? And if we stop along the way to grab a bite, I won't order anything expensive, I promise."

"Well what if we get tied up there and need to stay the night?—Or maybe more than just one night—it could be a couple days or even three. I mean, I'd get you a decent room if you came along, but—Well, wouldn't you need to call your roommate at least, to let her know?"

"Oh, don't worry about my roommate, sir, she'll be happy to have the privacy for a day or two—No, sir; I'm suited up and ready. Let's get on the road."

It was a dark blue Lincoln, the latest model, expensive. A car like that stood out, especially in a neighborhood like this: not a poor neighborhood exactly, but not a fancy one, either. The Finottis couldn't have bought a home in a fancy neighborhood twenty years ago, and even though Jennifer might have afforded a luxury residence now, she'd chosen to come back to her decidedly un-fancy childhood home.

But there it was: the expensive new car, a car he hadn't noticed this morning, although, truthfully, he hadn't paid too terribly much attention until now. Not there when he'd come this morning early to pick her up, he was pretty sure of that. But when he'd dropped her off.... Yes, he might have seen it then; it seemed to him he might have. And now, looking faintly through the Lincoln's windshield halfway down the block, he got the feeling that—hmmm—that there was someone there behind the light reflection in the glass; not a hundred percent positive, but pretty probable that someone was sitting there motionless and watching.

And so he climbed out of the old man's truck and headed down along the curb toward the Lincoln fifty yards away. Started slowly, but then, when he saw for certain that there really *was* someone there behind the wheel—a roundish face, maybe balding, looking out in his direction—he started speeding up, walking faster....

But not quite fast enough to make it there in time, no: For the dark blue Lincoln fired up and got in quick reverse. It spun into a driveway, trunk-end first, then jerked out forward, its tires spewing lots of smoke; until it turned the other way and sped off fast down Thompson to the corner, then right there, until it disappeared at top speed out of view.

It was nearly two o'clock now; Jennifer would be here anytime; and he walked back to her porch, sat there on a step, and waited, antsy, pensive, pondering. He thought in taut anxiety for a minute or two or three; and in that matter of a minute or two or three, as Jen had promised earlier, her car drove up, pulled in, parked; and she was standing with him at the porch's bottom step. And it was with a cartload of agitation that he informed her:

"Jen, listen to me; this is important. There's something's going on. Run in and grab the things you absolutely have to have—and then we're getting out of here. We're getting out *right now!*"

"*Now?* But ... *why?* What *happened?* Did you hear something or...?"

"It's her. It's her for sure. There was a car there—down the block there—watching. Wilson maybe, or whoever she got to replace poor Wilson if he isn't with her anymore—She might have killed him for all I know—although she wouldn't know how to make another Helper if Wilson's weren't around, so.... But anyway—whatever—there was someone out there watching the house, parked down the street. I think I noticed the car parked there when I dropped you off—I'm not positive, but I think so— And when I got back here a little while ago, it was still in the spot where it probably was before. So I headed over to check things out; but whoever was in there backed quick into a driveway and just took off. Fast, though, *really* fast—the tires were squealing. I'm sure there's something up."

"And you think it's *her*? Your *sister*? But ... it's been so long now; and how would she even know you're here? How would she know *I'm* here, even? It isn't like I might have had any contact with her as a patient, or...."

"It doesn't matter *how* she knows, only *that* she knows. And I'm positive she *does* know. Which means it isn't safe for you to stay here, not for a minute; so you're coming with me. We'll go to Mr. Hatter's place for now. She won't find us there—not in a day; there isn't time for her to look. Tomorrow I'll have the equipment I need to come and get my things, and we can be out of here for good. You'll have to arrange the schedule with your office and the hospital—it's short notice, I realize that; but we haven't any choice. Once we're even a few miles out of Charleston, she won't be able to follow. It's only right in the immediate area that she's a threat; so once I get you just a mile or two away...."

"*Me* away? You mean *us* away, don't you? If I leave this place, I leave with you—to *stay* with you—whatever the conditions, however we have to live. If I don't stay with you, I won't go with you. If you're planning to live without me, then you'll have to leave alone."

She passed him on the step, and he followed her inside through the open door. And once they were in and the door was shut behind them, she took him by the arm, turned him face to face toward her, put her arms around his waist, and told him:

"Those are the conditions. If I leave here, it's to be with you. And to be with you forever. No exceptions, no excuses; that's it!"

"It isn't possible, though. You know it isn't possible."

"Why? Because of your needs, right?—Your requirements?—Isn't that what you used to call them?"

"Of *course* because of my requirements."

"My father's dead, you said—right?"

"Yes, I told you he was dead. It wasn't anything I did, though. There was a fire. It started in his room, I think; and...."

"That doesn't matter. What happened to him isn't really my concern anymore. What I'm getting at is—you made him into a Helper, you said."

"Yes, and a really good one too, one of the best I've had. He was loyal and dependable—and smart as well, in his unobtrusive way. I could trust him to make decisions that some of my other Helpers in the past couldn't possibly have made. He handled all my personal affairs—shopping, banking, registering the cars and real estate in his name—everything I couldn't do myself out in the open with no legitimate ID. Your father was a really perfect Helper. He won't be easy to replace."

"No? So how are you planning to replace him then?"

"I can't say just yet. Once I get settled, in whatever place I finally wind up, I'll try to find someone who fits the profile. Usually some felon who ought to die, but has some minor spark of virtue to his life. He's got to be smart enough, physically fit, have a presentable but not particularly striking appearance—a ham-on-white-bread sort of guy—I think you probably get the picture. Some anonymous John Doe fellow who can take my place in public and transact whatever daily business I need to do; someone with valid papers, ID and such—since all the properties I own outright have got to be in his name—But there can't be any pending charges that might lead to his arrest. It's tough to find a suitable candidate, but eventually I discover someone close to what I need—I always have; for the last fifty years or so, I've always come up with someone...."

"*Fifty* years! But I thought.... Didn't you tell me—But you *did*; you just said this morning—Three *hundred* years, you said."

"I did; that's right, but until fifty years ago, I didn't need that kind of aid. It's only these last fifty years, with all the credit cards and electronic data and security cameras around—The security cameras have really been a nightmare, as you might imagine. There's not a bit of privacy anymore."

"Oh right! I get you now; I understand. You know, it's hard to think this whole thing through for someone who hasn't lived it: Anyway—you need a Helper to be your public self— that's what you mean—right?"

"Exactly. Yes."

"And the position's open right now—You're saying that's right too?"

"Yes it is, and you can stop making your idiotic plans right there; I see exactly where you're going; and that's as far as I'm going to let you get—Are you telling me...? You're not actually saying you want to be lobotomized like that monster-of-a-father I rescued you and your mother from?"

"I wouldn't need that if I did it voluntarily, would I?—Or don't you think I'm smart enough? Or personable enough?—And by the way—How *do* you do those lobotomies anyway without a surgery suite? And besides that: I thought those operations were outmoded nowadays; no reputable surgeons even do them anymore.

"You're right, they don't. Actually the procedure is quite effective and predictable if the surgeon does it properly and takes his time. I tried like hell to teach that Freeman fellow, but he couldn't get it down."

"*Freeman?*—You're saying ... *Walter* Freeman? The guy who did lobotomies on half the inmates in the psych wards back in the Fifties? You're telling me you *knew* him?"

"For a while I did, yes: He was too much in a rush to do things properly, though. A dozen in a day, old Walter did. But to do them so they work and get predictable outcomes, you've got to take a week or more to do just one."

"That's ... that's *incredible*! You actually knew the infamous...! So tell me something *else*, Mr. done-it-all: What other famous doctors did you know?"

"Oh lots. I met Muniz too—he's the one who started open-skull lobotomies in Lisbon before Freeman's day. A nice enough fellow, I guess, but he wouldn't take direction any more than....

"But all right, Jennifer, look: We don't have the many years it takes to catalogue the cast of famous characters in my life. Go get your things ready. Once we make it over to nice old Mr. Hatter's place, we'll sit and talk and I'll tell you a lot more interesting stuff you might not really want to know. Like Henry Ford, for example—When I lived in Detroit back in the 1890s, he and I and this fabulous machinist named Leland...."

25

Clicking, typing. Audrey sat in the center of the back seat, laptop spread beside her to the left, iPad on her knee, clicking and typing and muttering quiet little mumbles to herself in that charmingly efficient manner of hers, as sweet as apple pie.

And Sidney? Well, as for Sidney—Agent Sidney merely thought and drove. Slumped behind the wheel, the seat-back set as close to horizontal as a Chevy's seat would go, permitting him to think. Not as comfy and conducive to such thought as the Cadillac had been, no doubt. But the Caddy was a memory now, days beyond regret; and the Bureau-issue Chevy would simply have to do. And Sidney could think with the best of them anyway, reclined or arrow straight or what you will; think powerfully and usefully under the least ideal conditions—And that's precisely what he did.

Vampires! he thought. *Spacemen*! for crying out loud! Sheesh! How does a relatively bright guy, a grounded-in-reality sort of guy, educated by the best, experienced to the max, make sense of the absolutely senseless?

It's tough!—But the facts were starting to link up together in a row, coherently—if not entirely credibly. There was a logical explanation to this riddle—there *had* to be—And if he thought the thing out as carefully as he always did, the explanation would pop into his head in time.

And so he drove and thought:

That robotic pair of front men, he thought: Mentally modified in some exotic way: Automatons, actually, with mask-like faces and compliant brains: No official records on Finotti, except for a couple of bank accounts and a driver's license from the DMV; and that was during—what?—his final twenty years of life? Twenty years of near-complete obscurity—and so far, according to the records on this Wilson guy—just like Finotti—Audrey had come across nothing meaningful for....

"How are you doing on the Wilson business, Audrey? Find anything yet?"

"Just his driver's license, sir; and a couple of bank accounts. Nothing in the court records or newspaper archives for, ummm—ten years back now. I'm still looking, though."

"OK, keep it up. Go back twenty or more if you have to. With Finotti it was twenty years, remember? Let me know if you come up with anything at all—and right away, OK?"

"Sure thing, sir. Anything else I can get for you right now?"

"Not just yet, Audrey; if I think of something, I'll let you know."

He *would* let her know; but just at the moment he slumped back in his seat and thought some more. He thought: Hmmm: Two men made into quasi-robots by—what? By supermen with fifty chromosomes who were cleverer than Einstein and strong as grizzly moms with little cubbies in their wake—And maybe *deadlier* than mama grizzlies too! Anemic, though, needing their periodic dosages of dead men's blood. Hmmm....

'Not *from* here,' the Hartman girl had said. Which meant they were from somewhere else; somewhere other than—Well? *What?*—Other than the earth?—Sheesh! And Phil had said—what had Phil said exactly? How do you go about getting those four more chromosomes added to your cells? A virus, right? Energy altering a virus that plants the supplemental chromosomes in human cells. So maybe it was the *energy* that wasn't originally 'from here'—*that* might make sense. Phil had scoffed at the suggestion, but it really *did* make pretty decent sense: Extraterrestrial energy, programming a virus to go and do its thing. Hmmm: Plausible, wasn't it? The energy— electromagnetic energy: Now *that* would travel at light speed, getting around the impossibility of matter doing so, permitting data transfer through interstellar space. Well? Why not? Pretty far-fetched, pretty hard to swallow, certainly, but maybe, just maybe....

"Hey, Audrey?"

"Yes, sir?"

"The girl—the Hartman kid: Do you think you could give her a call on your cell and ask her something else?"

"I suppose so, sir. What do you want me to ask?"

"I don't know—maybe more of what she started to tell us at her place—About that 'not from here' craziness. Do you think she'd tell us anymore now that we know the stuff we do?"

STEVEN M. GREENBERG

"Well she told *me* a little when I called this morning."

"This *morning*? When did you call this morning?—You're saying the girl, right? Linnie Hartman? You spoke to her today?"

"I did, sir. When I was checking on Gonzalez and the connection to Charleston; I wanted to know if her handsome friend had ever mentioned the place."

"And? *Had* he mentioned the place?"

"No, just the state; not any cities specifically; but we got to talking for a while, and once the kid got started—wow!—she talked my ear off, just about."

"She *did*? So how did you get through to her finally? *I* sure didn't have much luck."

"Oh, you know us girls, sir. Girls say things to other girls that they'd never tell the boys."

"So—what did she tell you then? Anything pertinent? Did she happen to mention viruses or energy or any crazy stuff like that?"

"Not viruses, no. But she *did* say something about energy—'Beams,' I think she said. It was pretty confusing, though, and it didn't really make a lot of sense."

"Well, what *did* she say? Can you remember?"

"I can remember some of it, I guess. I was scrolling through some data on the Net when I called her, and I didn't pay that much attention when she started rambling on. But what she said, the best I can remember it, was that our suspect's father was—how did she put it exactly?—Um, he was affected by some kind of beam, before he was born, I guess, as an embryo or fetus—that's what she said; I don't know what kind of beam she meant exactly, but.... Anyway, he had a kind of inner need to send a message somewhere—I guess from the beam or whatever—but he didn't have the means to send it yet. So I guess the son's supposed to send it when he has the means—'means' I guess is the technology or whatever; we don't have it now, I suppose, so.... Honestly, sir, I would have typed the things she said while she was talking if I'd've thought you'd have the slightest interest in the crazy stuff she said, but it sounded so ridiculous to me...."

"It does, I know, the whole idea sounds ridiculous—But I've been thinking.... Well, the stuff that I've been thinking kind of goes along with what she said. So—when did our vampire suspect tell her all this stuff?—When they were with her mother in the car?"

272

"No, before, I think. In the bus station before the mother picked them up."

"Well, that's good anyway. The mother didn't hear it, so she was telling us the truth when she said she didn't know about the guy—So great, Audrey; the stuff you got from Linnie Hartman *does* make a little bit of sense; I kind of get the picture now—You follow the science-fiction logic of this lunacy so far?"

"Not really. The whole thing sounds so...."

"Off the wall; right. It *does* sound pretty off the wall, I admit. But—Hey, remember that guy a couple of years ago who was trying to collect sunlight to build a bomb?"

"The PhD from Pakistan at Pitt?—That math and physics whiz? Yeah, I remember, sure. The other agents were amazed when you figured *that* one out—they really were!"

"Were they?—Well, what I did was: I figured it out by being flexible—*mentally* flexible, I mean. You've got to start with the assumption that nothing's beyond the realm of possibility— Like that screwy bomb of his. You know something, Audrey? I showed the plan we found on his computer to a couple of physicists at a conference in Cleveland a year or so ago—and you know what they said? They both said it actually might have worked!

"So you see? What you've gotta do with these Looney Tunes cases sometimes is discard the scientifically impossible— like *travelers* from outer space—your flying saucer spacemen, that means—But the scientifically *not* impossible—energy from outer space creating vampires—however weird it seems from a realistic point of view?—That you sometimes gotta keep."

A dump. Wilson's condo was a dump and nothing more.

If Alexander Wilson had paid out all those mega-millions to Parole Supervisor Gonzalez to buy the guy a super-duper home, Wilson's *own* humble dwelling was—well, suffice to say, it was a mail drop only—unfit to be actually lived in by a man with that much dough.

Sidney had turned off the Interstate to center-city Charleston right at two-fifteen and headed for Wilson's address first. The GPS directed him into a pockmarked parking lot half-filled with a scattering of aging, inexpensive cars. He and Audrey did the obligatory look-through—the manager let him into the unit with his pass-key—But there was nothing in the place whatever: bare walls, not a stick of furniture, nary a glass or spoon or can of beans in the musty cupboards—or, more to the point, not a scrap of paper with the slightest bit of information as to the whereabouts their suspect Wilson might be found.

The manager had caught a glimpse of this Wilson guy from time to time, he'd said: A blank-faced, middle-aged, balding man who came around once a week or so to fetch his mail. He wasn't all that easy to be seen on the days that he appeared; but his car was, a nice new dark blue Lincoln that parked in its appointed space fifty feet from the manager's window. Other than those periodic mail runs, the only contact anyone seemed ever to have had with the elusive Mr. Wilson was the checks he sent for maintenance fees. Which checks, as Sidney had anticipated, bore the address of the empty condo up the steps on Level Three.

All right, pretty much as they'd predicted from the start: a skittish sort of front man, and cautious to the nth degree, just the way Finotti had been. Not quite landed in their net just yet; but they were getting close: A little input from the local branch might be in order; so next on the agenda was a stop at the offices of the Charleston FBI—a pretty flimsy operation compared to Pittsburgh, sparsely staffed, as it turned out—But hey!—how much staffing would the Charleston office need, when you considered that...?

"So tell me, Agent Krystowiak," Krystowiak was the duty officer; the guy in charge this afternoon while the Chief was out politicizing over a leisurely late-day lunch. "You guys didn't notice that your crime rate dropped off by seventy percent over the past twenty years?"

"We kinda noticed, yeah; but the Chief just figured it was down like that 'cause the boys had done their jobs."

Sidney shrugged. No point explaining the incredible to the incredulous; so all he told Krystowiak was that there was a local case they needed to investigate, he and his computer whiz Miss Hamblin, out of the Pittsburgh branch. What they needed—if he'd be kind enough to help them out—was an open station in the place, computer time, and total access to the local files; verify it with the Pittsburgh office if you must—which Edwin D. Krystowiak did, and apparently got enough of an earful to let Sidney and Audrey do their thing.

Which was mostly Audrey's thing, quite naturally. So while she went ahead and did it, Sidney ran downstairs and got himself a Diet Coke and Audrey a cup of cocoa from the machines. By the time he made it up again, ten minutes from the time he'd left, she had the whole scoop on Wilson glowing brightly on her screen.

"Here, sir, I've got it. Here's the stuff on Wilson we were looking for. Sit down and have a look."

And so he dropped into the swivel chair beside Audrey's at the monitor and had the requested look—And *wow*! Holy Moses! What a fascinating look it *was*!

"Alexander Wilson," said the document on the screen, "Released on a legal technicality." For what? asked Sidney, and Audrey scrolled back through the records she had sifted through before and eventually brought it up. Back through April, but … um, no, it wasn't April…. So maybe it was March? But, well, no, Audrey thought it probably was earlier than March, so—Uh, February?

"Umm—here!—Here, I've got it now—Look, sir: 'Alexander Wilson, indicted for third degree murder for….'—Here! Listen to this; this is the part I was looking for to show you. 'Alexander Wilson indicted for distribution of tainted blood to hospitalized patients.' Let me scroll back a little farther for a second and…."

And there it was—Incredible! Alexander Wilson, director of the Kanawha County Blood Bank, indicted for supplying damaged blood to twenty-seven patients—Old blood, deadly blood, months past the printed date of expiration on the bag. Six people wound up dying, damaged kidneys, damaged lungs, and so forth, so on.

And what about the good blood, the unexpired blood that Wilson must have taken in exchange? Stolen from the Blood Bank for some illicit purpose, the indictment said—although no one ventured a theory at the time, close to twenty years ago, almost to the week, as to what that cryptic purpose might have been.

"So—that's got to be the thing then, right?" asked Audrey. "There's got to be a relationship between this business with stolen blood and all the other facts we know. That's what we were looking for, wasn't it? That's the last thing I could find on Alexander Wilson before his records totally disappear."

The office was deserted this late into the afternoon, the other agents out on the few investigations the dearth of county crime had left them to pursue. It was a little after three, and they had the use of the facilities for the duration—Like Uncle Philip's path lab, the Bureau office never totally shut down at night or over weekends; not any more than crime itself shuts down. And so Sidney slumped down in that chair right next to Audrey's in mental solitude, and thought a bit in deepest quietude, and finally, clearing his throat and straightening a bit, said to the cute and bright Miss Hamblin:

"All right then, Audrey, this Wilson guy's the one we're after—Wherever we're going to find him, we'll likely find our perpetrator too—So, next on our agenda is to come up with a place, and since we're at an impasse as to locating the place— short of staking out the condo and hoping he'll turn up—what we ought to do first, is to shuffle through those potential victim files again, now that we've got access to the local feed from Charleston. Start running through those missing persons and parolee lists one more time, using the local data we just got, and maybe something will turn up—And if we get lucky, it'll turn up fairly soon."

Fine, said Audrey, she'd be glad to have a look ... but— what exactly should she look for? After all, she'd been through these case files more than once by now, so....

"Yeah, I realize you have, but—when I get a bugger of a bind like this, what I generally do is, I snoop around for something out of the ordinary, something that doesn't quite fit into the general pattern of the case. That pretty often works. So think back through the files you went through earlier, OK?— The majority of the missing persons in the Kanawha County files were parolees, right?"

"Way more than half were, sure; but the rest were mostly domestic sorts of things—missing wives and husbands, and a couple dozen teenage kids—who usually turn out to be runaways, don't they?—Which isn't the kind of case file that we want."

"No, that's right; I wouldn't bother with the probable runaways for now, but—well, were there any *other* cases you can think of? Think back: Anything out of the ordinary in the missing persons lists? Or maybe parolees that somehow stood out?"

"I don't know; let me glance back through the names again to see...."

Which she did, clicking, typing, scrolling at breakneck speed, until in fifteen minutes' time she finally came up with:

"All right sir, here's something: I don't know how unusual or relevant you'll think it is, but—A couple of little girls went missing right in the exact same neighborhood near downtown Charleston, and they've never been seen again— *They're* on the missing persons list—And there's a reporter too— I'll check the files on him in a sec. But other than those two young kids and the reporter, it's pretty much all parolees and spouses and juvenile runaways, so...."

"All right; well, I'm not too sure those little girls would be related to the case, though, Audrey. Young kids don't seem to fit our suspects' victim type—not enough blood, I'd guess. I'd probably skip the little girls for now and look for something else. Probably the reporter wouldn't be related either, so...."

"That's all, though, sir. Like I said, there really isn't anything else on the list that looks the least little bit suspicious. Just the parolees and that one reporter and the girls."

"Well, what about the parolees, then? Run through those again and see if you can find anything different in *that* group that doesn't quite add up."

And so she did that too, and in fifteen minutes more:

"OK, here, sir. One of the parolees—here's his picture on the monitor—He's listed as a missing person, but it looks as if he's still around—I'd say he's *definitely* around, in fact, 'cause he's the prime suspect in a murder case that happened after he went missing—Now *that's* pretty darned unusual, isn't it?—Doesn't that fit the bill for the sort of not-quite-normal pattern we've been looking for?"

"Maybe, Audrey; maybe just possibly it does. What else have you got on him? Does it say what the murder charge entailed, and when and where and...?"

"Uh-huh. Here's the whole Charleston Bureau file. It's a little girl he might have killed, and she.... Oh gosh! Hold on a minute, sir—Wow!" Have a look at this!

He rolled his swivel chair a little leftward and scanned the printing on the screen. Leonard Dworski—that was the parolee's name. And the girl he might have killed? The pretty little thing whose picture sat there on the left-hand side beside the text: She was the second of the two little girls who'd gone missing! A bloody dress, identified as hers, was found several miles away in a dumpster, with Dworski's fingerprints—in blood—like boldface printing, writ large for all to see.

"And the other missing little girl came from the same neighborhood, you said?"

"Uh-huh, just a few houses down. That was two years ago, though, sir—Do you think there's a relationship?"

"Oh, there's a relationship, all right. That dress—the bloody dress—can you dig me up a picture of it?"

Audrey clicked and typed and quickly brought it up.

"Planted!" said Sidney. "I'll ... be ... *damned!*"

"*What*, sir? What are you thinking?"

"First of all, it's a hell of a lot easier to hide a dress than it is a body—no reason for a killer to leave a dress to be discovered when the body can't be found. And second, these are all left-hand prints, and they're on the opposite side of the garment—the place a killer's right hand ought to be. They're planted, Audrey. That stupid, sneaky bastard used the other fellow's hand."

"*What* other fellow's hand? I don't quite follow what you're getting at?"

"That fellow Dworski—Our murderer cut him up and used his hand to leave those prints—just the left one, I suppose. Sheesh! A sneaky bastard, but pretty goddamned dumb!"

"And he killed the little girl too?"

"Yeah, sure: Our main guy did, not that Dworski character. I'm not quite sure why he killed the girl—*both* girls, actually—they don't fit the victim profile. But that's it for sure. We're getting close now, Audrey. The girls were neighbors, and little girls can't travel very far. That neighborhood is the place we need to look, so.... But wait a minute; you said there was a reporter missing too? Let's go ahead and check that case file out as well, just for completeness' sake—Look back through and see if he disappeared in the same general area as the girls."

More clicking, more typing, and finally:

"Right again, sir. His car was found half a mile from where the two girls lived."

"Can you show me where it was exactly? Can you get it on a map?"

"Sure. Let's see.... Umm—OK, here's the location. Do you want a satellite view?"

"No, the streets—I need to see the names.... There! Bingo! That's where his car was?—There?"

"Uh-huh."

"Anything in the files about the circumstances of his disappearance?"

"Umm." Audrey clicked and scrolled. "Here it is: A man named David Corwin from the local paper here—He was working on—Oh my goodness!—He was working on a story about the missing parolees when his wife called in and reported that he hadn't come home."

"And they found his car in that lot on Ferry Street? Where the arrow is?—You're sure?"

"Uh-huh, that's what the report says."

Sidney shook his head: "You know what *else* happened there Audrey?—can you guess?"

Audrey shrugged.

"That's where Gonzalez dropped the parolees off—in that same exact lot off Ferry.... And those little girls? They lived close to there, you said?—half a mile; didn't you tell me that?"

Audrey moved the map around and pointed to the place. Half a mile exactly, almost to the inch.

"Newman Road? Both of them lived on Newman Road? Both of the girls?"

"Uh-huh."

"OK, great, that's where we'll find our vampire—or whatever the hell he is. Shut down the computer, grab your stuff, and let's go check out Newman Road."

26

"He's a really decent man, you know?"

They were sitting on the bed in the tidy little room that Nathan had assigned to him. Jennifer would sleep in it tonight, while he had tossed his bedclothes and his pillow on Nathan's living room couch.

"*Sure* I know he's decent. He charges me ten bucks a day for the accommodations and then spends double that on groceries to cook me three terrific meals a day—And he won't take a penny more in payment—says he's grateful for the company. One of the nicest, kindest men I've ever known."

"So—how did you happen to meet him, anyway?"

"He gave me a lift into town the other day. It's a long story, Jen."

"*Another* long story, huh? I guess you accumulate quite a lot of them after three hundred years."

"Uh-huh, *quite* a lot, and quite a few of *those* quite-a-lot are pretty downright weird; one of these days maybe I'll tell you some of the high points. But it's been a decent life, all things considered. I guess I've done some good in a microcosmic way. Someday maybe I'll finally get to finish up what we were sent for—or not exactly *sent*, but—but that's another long, long story that isn't ready to be told."

"A man of infinite mystery if ever there was one."

"True enough; a mystery even to myself, sometimes— But, anyway, I'm glad you like Nathan. He said we could stay as long as we like, and when I told him we were pretty certain to be out of here tomorrow, he seemed a little crestfallen. I almost wish we could take him along."

"Me too; he *is* a genuinely benevolent guy—They're hard to find these days—Oh, by the way, did you know his brother is a patient of mine? I didn't realize it till he told me. He must have seen me through the reception window or at the door while he was sitting in the waiting room. His brother talks about him a lot. I guess his wife died a while ago—Nathan, I mean, not his brother—She was sick and he spent a long time nursing her, then when she died, he came to Charleston to nurse his brother Les. He's a kind of natural care-giver, I guess—not enough of those folks around."

"No, you're right, there aren't—So—is his brother Les as hard to understand as Nathan is? I have to concentrate on every word he says, then translate it in my head. It's a major challenge every time we have a conversation."

"A challenge for *you* maybe. I grew up here, remember? Half my schoolmates talked that way. It's really kind of charming, I think."

"Yes, I can't argue with that. I'm really going to miss him when we leave. But I've decided: Before we head out tomorrow, I'm going to arrange a little thank-you gift. I think our buddy Nathan will be pleased."

"A gift?—What is it? Can you give me a clue?"

"Nope, no clue; not yet. Wait until tomorrow and you'll see."

Wilson was on foot now, standing on those sturdy, stocky legs.

Not in the car this afternoon; for Brother had spotted the car and would recognize it now: And so afoot since after lunchtime, having parked the too-familiar car a block away, past two backyards, one neatly tended, the other overgrown. This house, this porch he stood on peering down the block, was the home with the weed-strewn lawn; and he stood there in the shadow of an overhang, fifteen feet from a diminutive FOR SALE sign out on the unkempt grass—Stood there watching, as he had sat there watching from the car this morning too. Not impatient in the least these past two hours or so, for these were his instructions, and impatience wasn't one of them—Madam hadn't specified that—So here he stood, content enough, six lots down from the pretty doctor's house—the one he went to for his kidneys....

And finally right around three-fifteen—it said so on his watch—around the corner came that ratty old truck again, with two heads eminently visible in the windshield as it turned onto Thompson. And it stopped briefly at the house the doctor lived in, and out she climbed, and in she went for several minutes while the truck stood idling at the curb, waiting to see that she was safe. And when she stepped through the door again, with a little carrycase in hand, she went off to her own car—that whitish Buick in the drive—and fired it up; and the truck drove off in front, with her Buick not too very far behind.

So off ran Wilson, fast as ever he could run on those sturdy stocky legs; through the two adjoining backyard lawns, one neat, one not, and over to the Lincoln tethered at the curb. And he cranked it up and headed off, his tires squealing protest in their wake: down to the corner and sharp left there, and left again, until…. Yes! He could just make out the doctor's Buick down the block a hundred yards ahead. The truck was immediately in front of her; and when the traffic cleared on Jefferson, it turned off right. But the doctor's car waited for some more traffic to clear, allowing him to get a whole lot closer up. Waiting … waiting … and she put her signal on … pointing … to the left it was! … and….

And yes! She turned that way: left, exactly opposite to where the truck had gone. So Wilson did the same, turned left, and followed: Out Jefferson to Caldwell and right there toward the bridge. Her car passed slowly over the bridge, in moderate traffic, not at all hurried or on alert—She hadn't seen him, or didn't even realize she ought to look—And she led him, block by unintending block, to…. Where was she headed exactly?—Oh yes—*sure*! The area of the hospital; finally turning into a parking structure adjacent to—what was that building next to it? Ah yes—of course! The Medical Office Complex. That was where her suite was, and this was probably the lot the doctors parked in, though the patient lot was half a block away. He lost her when she drove in past the gate, of course, not having a card to enter there. But he drove along past the entrance and parked outside, out along the street, where there were places in the two-hour metered zone. She would come out this way; she had to. So he put a quarter in the slot and waited for a while, not impatient in the least. Half an hour he sat, getting into Madam's snack time, true; but Madam had specifically instructed him that finding the woman was much more important than her food.

But in half an hour, perhaps a little more—there she was again, the Buick exiting right where it had driven in. And of course he followed—easily, of course, for this nice, smart doctor was utterly unaware: down Hungerford to—what was the street name? J-something: It started with a J. And down that J-beginning street to Arbogast, a couple of blocks on down—he

behind her by a good full fifty yards to preclude recognition—
and veering left on—oh, something or other, he hadn't quite
made out the name—Then left again to....

There; down the block: The old rusty pickup truck was
parked there, the one he'd seen Brother in; and she pulled in just
in front of it, nearly touching bumpers, and got out, and went up
to the little house and right inside—Apparently the people living
there didn't think to keep it locked....

So she was here! If she didn't go home later, he would
find her here—Here!

He would head right back, right now, this very minute,
and tell Madam the address. And she would be glad and pat him
on the arm without the talons digging in, before he finally cooked
and pureed her late-day meal.

Then they would have all evening if needed to get the
things they'd have to have all dusted off and tested out to see if
they were strong enough to handle a set of muscles as powerful as
Brother's were.

How appreciative Madam would be!

27

The concrete—that was the easy part.

Once he'd drilled down to the metal plate and slipped the diamond saw blade in—well, other than the noise and dust, that part of the operation went effortlessly enough. Fifteen minutes cutting and the plug was free—along with a three-inch notch to get a handhold—a two-by-two-foot block of concrete as massive as a granite boulder—And once he'd wrestled *that* unmanageable impediment up and onto the basement floor and finally out of the way—whew!—he was down at last to the surface of the steel.

A challenge *there*, though, that massive metal plate—as he'd realized it would be. That last sad day, after Meredith had started up the car and she and Jen had grimly headed off, he'd run out to the foundry and bought himself an inch-thick slab of steel, three feet square, three-hundred-plus pounds, going on four. An enormous effort at the time for him to drag the damn thing down the steps and slide it into place—But that was more than twenty years ago. And twenty years ago, still weakened by the stabbing and recovery, he hadn't honed his body into the tip-top shape he'd got in in today.

Now, though, cutting a nice-sized hole would be the toughest part, hoisting the metal out a breeze. A window in the center would do the trick: Eighteen-inch diameter, say, centered—he ran a finger around the area in question—yes, just about here; nothing would be damaged if he centered the severed section here.

And so he fired up the special-order torch for inch-thick steel: the plasma cutter plugged upstairs into a higher-voltage outlet for the stove. Nothing to clip the ground wire to—just a flat, unbroken plate without protrusions—and so he held the ground against the metal with his left hand while he did his measured cutting with the right. Smoke, hiss, molten iron flowing down the slow-advancing edge as he snaked his way around, cutting … ninety degrees … then a hundred and twenty … then a hundred and eighty—halfway there now, slow and deliberate because of the full-inch thickness and having to use one hand to cut, the other to hold the ground clip tight against—but steadily and carefully arching in a smooth advancing curve, until... three quarters of the way around now, and ... and....

And there! Down with a thud the metal circle fell into the cavity below: A hidden cavity, as he remembered forming it, three feet square, a foot-and-a-half deep, fashioned of the heaviest duty concrete, like the overlying surface he had labored through to get down to the plate. Trapped inside the cavity twenty some-odd years ago, the air that wafted from the opening smelled mildewed when he caught the first stale breath. But the odor dissipated quickly in the basement's fresher damp as he worked the heavy metal from the new-cut hole: Shifting till he got a handhold, then ... up ... out ... and—whew!—finally flat with a heavy rolling clangor onto the concrete surface to his left.

There! Quite a piece of work, *that* was! But ... good. At last! The decades-hidden cavity was gaping widely open now, lighted for the first time in over twenty years: And the first thing the overhead fluorescents shone in on was—

The gold.

There right below, smack in the center of the cavity, stashed right where he had stashed them in the boxes that he'd bought them in: cardboard boxes of four by six by four inches tall—Two of them—each with—if he remembered right—five hundred one-ounce Krugerrands in twenty-item plastic tubes. So a thousand times.... Somewhere roughly between a million and a million-five at current spot, which would get him on the road and settled comfortably in some decent place—yet to be determined, of course—and would get Jennifer settled somewhere safely too: Enough of a stake to set her up in a nice new office suite and cover the first few months of overhead and rent. Oh—and buy old Nathan his thank-you present too—that could be ordered right away.

He pulled out the coins and set them on the basement floor, right beside the metal circle and the concrete square, then reached in for the rest: Off to the side, out in the recess of the cubic space: Yes, there it was, safe and sound—the box—THE box, his father's box, which he lifted from the opening carefully, lovingly, the way he'd held his father's hand after the poison had nearly done its work—though only Father had realized the malady was due to poison at the time. If it had happened today, and they had diagnosed the cause, there might have been an antidote to save his father's life—to save it pretty easily, what with life support and artificial means to get a patient past the crucial stage. But way back then, with the incompetence of 1715 treatment to rely on: Yes, those were the dark days of the healing art; exorcising demons from the hopelessly insane, hoping to treat anemia by draining vital blood.

Ah well!—water over the dam, underneath the bridge!— Still, each time he thought of it, however faint the memory had grown, it got his blood to boiling yet again—A demon-of-a-stepmother; and then a half-sister who was congenitally very much the same.

All right, no point in dwelling on the past; there was a future to consider, and lots of work to do—So he set the precious box aside, beside his memories, beside the coins, beside the metal, beside the concrete ... and reached in for the sheaf of documents:

They were there—*Everything* was there!—No paper-munching microbes had been at their destructive work. Wonderful! Terrific!—Here was everything he'd need: all the names and numbers he'd require to get accounts set up to let him transfer sufficient off-shore funds to make him rich again. A couple of million to start things off, and he'd be on his feet once more, buy himself an isolated residence out in the boonies of some distant countryside somewhere. He'd find himself a Helper to handle the title transfer and such—that was the foremost need of all: pick an appropriate sinner out, get his forebrain cut and his compliance reconditioned—A couple of weeks or so to arrange for Jennifer's comfort and safety—that would, of course, come first—someplace far enough away from Charleston that Sister couldn't possibly venture there. That done, the rest would come as easily as it always had in years long past. Yes, all the iffy fragments of his future were falling into place; things were beginning to look up again.

He slid the steel plate back into the hole—which fell in all the way, for a quarter-inch of metal had been melted from the edge—Then he poured the water in the tub of concrete to his right: Mix it to the proper consistency, shovel it in around the block of concrete back in place, fill the fissure, smooth the surface, feathering the telltale edge, spread some charcoal dust around the floor to make the color uniform, and he'd be on his way again. Jennifer should be done with all her obligations at the hospital and the requisites of shutting down the practice, in—What was it now? Ten-forty-five?—So by noon or a little afterward, they could be on their way, heading west in Jen's nice car until he got one of his own and a Helper to get it bought and registered in the brand new Helper's name.

An hour or so to spare, then—time enough and more: Thirty minutes at the dealership to order Nathan's truck—If they wouldn't take the gold in payment, maybe another ten minutes or so to stop at a precious metals buyer and turn a couple dozen ounces in. Yes, sure, he'd need to cash some of the coins in anyway—they wouldn't be too thrilled in taking thousand-dollar Krugerrands at some truck stop for a twenty-dollar check—So he'd get—oh, maybe ten or fifteen thousand in ready cash beyond what Nathan's truck would cost. That would take a quarter of an hour maximum. Still loads of time. Fast-drying concrete, worth the extra cost; so not much longer waiting here.

He sat cross-legged on the floor beside the drying patch and reached out for his father's box: It was a sacred thing to him—the aim and purpose of his life. Carved three centuries ago from a block of Asian sandalwood, yet still as fresh and fragrant as when his father passed it, dying stoically, into his hands.

"Radu," Papa had said—for they'd named him Radomir at birth, though he'd had a hundred other less exotic names since then, none of them the least indicative of who or what he was. "The box: What you must do is written in the box. It must not be opened until the time is right."

Then Father's pulse had waned and ceased, and the hand had fallen limp. *A message to the stars*, he'd said—but what had Father meant by that? The stars? The heavens? Three hundred years now and the words were still a mystery. The very nature of the Originals, the aim of their existence—his own, his father's, and all that yet were living of their kind—a mystery as cryptic as the universe itself. For three long centuries he had pondered, philosophized; made every attempt to learn what he could learn, to reason the unreasonable through, to fathom the unfathomable—Why? How? When?—Beyond imagination utterly, till just these last few dozen years, with the newfound scientific revelations, the analytic equipment just now coming into play, the mass of data on the Internet—Now, at last, the enigmatic pieces had begun to fit into place.

A message to the stars, but what *kind* of message and to *which* among the stars? Some distant civilization seeking other life that had somehow modified his own? Perhaps. One day, within a generation likely, Father's requisites might be met, his precious box opened at last, and that ancient paper would reveal it all. What more was needed, actually? An X-ray laser of forty or fifty terawatts would do the trick; and soon such power might just be available—But where to aim it? What specific message must be sent? In the not-too-distant future, the contents of that box would tell it all.

The floor had gotten dry and smooth, the color uniform enough, the junction between new and old indistinguishable what with the charcoal dust embedded in the mix. The plasma cutter and cords linked to the outlet behind the stove upstairs— they were of no further use to him; so he left them there— Whoever bought the place from Jennifer could sell them for a tenth of what he'd paid.

He picked up Father's box and the sheaf of papers and the sixty precious pounds of coins and headed up the basement steps. A stop at one of those gold and silver buyers out on the highway, then half an hour longer at the dealership down the road a little more, then finally back to Nathan's in a bit. Jen would be there by noon if not before.

Then out the door, and in her nice new Buick with abundant cash in hand, and merrily on their way.

Not so terrible a stop in Charleston after all.

She snarled. It wasn't often nowadays that Madam snarled, but she definitely snarled today, this morning, when he balked at bringing her the doctor if it might cause the doctor any harm:

"We can't, Madam," he had told her, just like that—for the doctor wasn't evil in the slightest sense he knew of, and his programming from Brother had forbidden him from injuring those who weren't evil in some flagrant, toxic way. The little girls, the two young fellows at the door—and all of the parolees from Gonzalez who weren't outright fiends: Killing them had never been his doing. Madam and that knife of hers—it was they who'd done the work. But the doctor? For him to bring the doctor here if bringing her meant death—No, that act was impermissible; and he had summoned up the nerve to tell her so—

And so she snarled. Toothlessly of course—At least she couldn't bite him anymore: The scratches weren't bad, all things considered, the punctures not that slow to heal, the fractures always knit in time—Ah but the bites!—Those jagged bites had often got infected in the old days, what with the sharp, decaying teeth. Those miserable bites had been a burden, certainly; but now—thank the stars in heaven!—all the jagged teeth were gone: So snarling far less fearfully than she'd snarled ten years ago, she told him, albeit in a grumble filled with anger:

"You will do what I ordered you to do!"

"But.... It isn't in my program, Madam. I cannot physically perform requested duties that have not been programmed in."

She snarled again, snapping: "Well, get the car then, Wilson. Get it ready and keep it idling by the pantry door."

"The car, Madam? Ready?"

"Yes, get it ready—can you hear? Get the car for me and I shall do what I need to do myself. I can see to this necessary business with or without you—And I will!"

"But—*You*, Madam? You haven't ridden in a car in several years now. You haven't been out of the house, and—you've never even *sat* in our current car."

"The current car has opaque windows—has it not?"

"Of course, Madam; certainly. All the cars we've ever purchased since I started have had mirrored windows. The current one has mirrored windows as well, just as you specified on the order sheet."

"Good. I like my privacy—Then do what I say: Start the car and drive it over to the pantry door—Oh, and fetch my shawl and a long black lightweight coat. I shall need to cover up."

"You seriously intend to go out then, Madam? It's been many years, and ... and your appearance these recent days, if I might venture to say so...."

"What? You no longer find me beautiful? How critical my Wilson has become! Now listen to me Wilson, listen and obey," she hissed. "Go and start the car. Do as I say. And get the shawl and coat I asked you for. If you refuse to do my bidding, I am fully capable of doing everything myself. This business will be over with today. That daughter—and her meddlesome mother too—I should have killed them both twenty years ago.

"But better twenty years late than not at all."

28

Sidney piloted the car while Audrey waxed effusive:

"Comfortable! Oh, sir—it was *beyond* comfortable! I never even *dreamed* there were places to stay as nice as that till now."

"Well good, Audrey; terrific. I'm glad the hotel met your needs. Me personally, I don't care all that much about the place I spend the night. I can sleep in the back seat of a rent-a-car if I have to—and I've had to more than once, believe you me. But my dad always told me: 'Sidney,' he says, 'if you invite a lady guest someplace, make sure you treat her like a queen.' So that's the way you get treated when you drive to Charleston with a Braman, Audrey—just like a queen. I'm glad the suite I got you was OK."

"*OK!*" she gushed, then went on with the grateful verbiage for a good long bubbly while. A sweet appreciative kid, *really* sweet. Not like the glitzy damsels at the country club that Dad's rich buddies tried to fix him up with on the occasional weekend night. Unlike those pampered princess-types, for pretty Audrey Hamblin here, this luxury provisioning was a new adventure; and it was loads of fun to show her some of the 'finer' things in life: Even if they weren't all that fine to him, he got a kick out of letting her experience how the other half—and not necessarily the *better* half, truthfully—got on with their platinum-plated lives.

"Here, sir. This is the street, fifty yards up. See the sign there? That's the place we turn; go right, then straight ahead." She broke off from her litany of gratitude just in time to tell him when the turnoff toward Newman Road came up on the right. Not the route they'd come last evening for their initial quick drive through, no; but a different way entirely, leading from the river; the way that fellow Wilson must have come from Ferry Street where Gonzalez dropped the doomed parolees off.

So they'd been in the vicinity last night as well. Not quite able to identify a specific house of interest in the dusk; for there were several close at hand that met the rough criteria of being large enough and secluded enough to hide nefarious goings-on. This was a rich man's neighborhood, with its gated lots of copious acreage luxuriantly forested between the scattered mansions, homes replete with eight-foot walls and football-field-length driveways leading though the sculpted grounds to colonnaded fronts. Jodi's family lived in just this kind of residence; and when he went to Maryland to see them once a year to reminisce and to commiserate, their neighborhood felt very much the same.

"Here, sir. Left here, then right at the first cross street down."

Which directions he followed obediently, ushered along by Audrey's graphics on the iPad on her knee; turning onto Newman Road right smack dab where the house of the second missing little girl rose majestically to the right. On Audrey's side he passed it, and as he slowly idled by, Sidney asked his pretty navigator:

"So—she was eight, right?—the little girl whose bloody dress you showed me on the monitor? She couldn't have made it far from home if she was only eight—unless somebody snatched her in a car, of course—But if we're going by the theory that these missing kids are related from a geographic point of view, then we're figuring it's got to be a house in this neighborhood someplace. Chances are, we'll be driving past it sometime today."

The house next down from the second little girl's place was a less impressive home, not walled, not particularly private, set on half an acre or less: they'd pretty much ruled that one out last night. Then the next succeeding—he drifted past it at a crawl—Big enough all right, walled high enough, blocked off sufficiently from the road. But Audrey had checked the records out last evening on the laptop from their rooms, and discovered that an elderly couple lived there these past ten years or more, the husband a retired neurosurgeon, the wife a homebound invalid—so not the homicidal type at all. And anyway, beside all that, the police had interviewed the nice old folks at length, the records said, and cleared them fully of involvement. According to the interview, they'd seen the little girl on the day she disappeared, walking down the street in that pretty floral dress, bouncing a ball—A big, blue plastic ball, they remembered; a lovely little girl who was never to be seen again.

The Larrimers owned the next house up the block, a ranch-style home with a low wood fence and a big front door eminently visible from the road—a venue less than suitable to serial murdering for sure—And the house across the street: Tenanted by another doctor, an orthopedic surgeon with a spotless record and a homebound wife and infant kids, clearly not an anemic killer in search of blood; so *that* was off their checklist too.

At the corner they turned, then turned again on Barrett, heading north once more toward the river in the direction of Ferry Street where the parolee donors got exchanged. The first two homes on the left, they'd ruled out with a fair degree of certainty; another on the right as well, and then a second little bungalow on the right—too small, too visible....

Until a couple of hundred yards up from where they turned, a block from Newman Road and running parallel, was another mansion meriting attention, one where they had parked a while and looked around with interest at dusk the night before. Its back yard wasn't very far from the second little girl's back yard—a distance easily handled by an eight-year-old kid—It had a massive gate as well, and a high enclosure wall—both made to order for keeping prying eyes at bay. It was owned, said Audrey's sources on the Net, by a man named Helverson—though there seemed to be no record of a man named Helverson in the public files for ten years back—Aha!—a lot like Wilson and Finotti— But even *more* so.

Not so much as a driver's license or a bank account did Audrey's research ferret out for mysterious Mr. Helverson— Incredible! Not a single parking violation, or moving violation, or, in fact, any documentation *whatever* in the public domain for that entire decade back. She could search back ten years farther still when they finished for the afternoon. But in the meantime, there was enough about this big, decaying mansion and its documentless owner to justify a later second look; and so they placed it at the very summit of their list.

So this Helverson residence was number one as a place of interest, and then a couple of other cloistered houses up the street that satisfied the general criteria in a way, though hardly quite as well: Three big homes in all worth watching on the immediate streets around; and then another one or two less likely long shots one block farther to the west, out on Grantland Road: Two little girls of eight and ten might take a stroll that far, concluded Sidney, in a pinch. He made a mental note of each place they were considering, then turned the Chevy northward toward the river, heading back.

All right then, best thing right now would be to freshen up and get a bite to eat—Audrey hadn't had a decent breakfast yet, just a donut and some juice—Then back here after lunch again—say, maybe one-thirty, maybe two—to prowl around some more. No million-dollar jackpot as of yet—but they were close.

By nightfall, Sidney felt reasonably confident, they'd have the house in question pretty well identified—And their murderer most likely in the bag.

Jennifer's Buick was parked against the curb a yard or so behind the neighbor's car. And when he pulled up to the house, he left Nathan's battered truck a foot or two in back of the Buick's bumper, and grabbed his little stash of vital things.

Jen had left her doors unlocked—she always did, the trusting soul—and he stowed the sixty pounds of coins on the floor behind the driver's seat and the box with his father's precious paper partway under the passenger seat beside.

He couldn't lock the car, since he didn't have the fob to lock it. But Nathan's street was safe enough; and with nobody around, and the minute or two he'd be inside—time enough to say goodbye to Nathan and tell him that his gift was on the way. A shame they couldn't stay to see his face light up when the brand new truck arrived....

Ah well!—Content about the present, way less anxious for the future, he stepped up on the curb, heading toward the door....

And then he saw the shoe.

There on the grass beside the sidewalk: A woman's shoe that looked a lot like Jen's!—A woman's shoe that—Oh my God!—It *was* Jen's! It really WAS!

So up to the porch, grabbing for the knob, but.... But the door was.... Nathan NEVER left it open like this— NEVER!

So inside—quick, quick!—not really thinking, but reacting; turning leftward once inside the vestibule, and seeing....

BLOOD!

There on the carpeting beside the kitchen opening! Tracks of blood, little bloody footprints, thicker by the kitchen, then growing thinner, fainter coming forward toward the door.

So over to the kitchen—in an instant, in a heartbeat— seeing there flat in the middle of the kitchen floor, sprawled out on his back, eyes frozen wide in death—Oh my *God*! Nathan!— Poor Nathan, unoffending Nathan, his shirt front soaked in blood, exactly the way his *own* shirtfront had been soaked in blood twenty years ago. Nathan—Poor, poor Nathan! Stabbed as *he'd* been stabbed, *exactly* as he'd been stabbed—Which meant….

Oh my GOD! But where was JEN?! Oh GOD—Good GOD! Jen! JEN! Time to weep for Nathan later, time to *avenge* Nathan later—And he *would*—But JEN! Where the hell was JEN!?

So down the hallway in a frantic rush and into the room she'd slept in the night before—Silent, empty, no sign of disorder here; Jen's purse lying on the bed, her car keys alongside. No blood, no sign of a scuffle—good, good—The closet—no, nothing there. The next room down the hallway—Nathan's room—vacant, neat.

All right: think—THINK: She might have gotten out in time—Yes: No sign of a scuffle, no blood anywhere but in the kitchen and on the carpeting outside it, those, tiny short-paced tracks—so…. Jen didn't have her car keys; they were on the bed, so outside on foot, quite possibly, losing a shoe in the hastiness of flight, somewhere nearby hiding out, maybe in a yard or at a neighbor's house—But she would have seen him drive up in the truck if her hiding place were close enough—she'd certainly be watching if she were hiding anyplace nearby—so….

So back into the kitchen kneeling beside Nathan's body, just outside the pool of blood, touching the forehead skin—not yet fully cooled, so not much time had passed—closing the gaping eyes—Poor man! Poor kindly, generous man!—He clenched his teeth—There would be retribution for this kindly man. There would be *punishment* for this: That lunatic sister of his—Yes—oh yes!—it was time for her to make amends for such as this; to pay, to suffer condign retribution for this and all her evil doings of the past as well—It was definitely time!

He went back to the bedroom for Jen's purse and keys— she'd need them when he found her, and there was no way she'd ever come back inside this place again—no possible way! Her purse in his hand, her car keys in his pocket, he headed out. He'd cruise around the neighborhood and find her if she'd stayed close, or figure where she might have run to if she'd fled....

But halfway to the door ... he saw it—THERE—On the wall!

He hadn't seen it till just this very instant, since his back was toward it when he'd first rushed in—But there scribbled on the plaster right beside the vestibule, as prominent as a beacon in the night—he saw the bloody script: two lines of lettering fashioned by an old familiar hand with a crooked finger that stopped him dead in his tracks.

Sister's hand—Yes, *Sister's obviously*—No mistaking it— The words were written with a finger dipped in blood—in *Nathan's* blood—it had to be—for it was Nathan's body that had been bled that way. Hard to read the jagged letters individually, what with the smears and runs and frenzy of the script—Oh, but clear enough to comprehend the whole in its totality and import—She'd *left* it there for him to comprehend in its totality and import, after all, despite the crooked-fingered penmanship: There in garish red against the off-white plaster wall, the bloody writing read:

IF YOU WANT HER, COME FOR HER. YOU AND I CAN TRADE.

He froze. He dropped down to his knees on the bloodstained rug and plain and simply *froze*—

No!— GOD no! Sister had taken *Jennifer*! She had come here—shriveled as she was—She herself had somehow left the sanctuary of that cloistered home, traveled here, regardless of the risk involved if anyone had seen her; come here on the public roads in broad daylight—And she'd gone away with Jen!

But *how*? *Why*? How could she have justified killing Nathan?—How?—HOW?!—'Harm only the evil'—their genetic make-up demanded that. And Sister had fundamentally the same genetic make-up they all had, passed down from the Originals fully intact; he had tested her himself and verified the profile of her DNA. A lunatic mother, all too true—but could a single group of twisted genes eradicate the mandate of their entire race? It certainly hadn't done so as to intellect or strength.

She had the right genetics in her make-up, that was a proven fact—But looking at it from another point of view: Could

Nathan have been evil in some unapparent way? That was doubtful—certainly it was; all these many centuries of life, he'd been a foolproof judge of humankind: Nathan had given off the very best of vibes—Clearly he had—But a hidden trace of evil lurking somewhere deep within? No, that wasn't entirely out of the realm of possibility.

But what about *Jen*? Not a drop, not a trace, not an atom or scintilla of anything even *remotely* approaching evil in Jen— That was absolute—But Sister had taken her as well with the manifest threat of harm. Could she carry out the threat? Was so flagrant a violation of their code even *possible*?

She had used her celebrated dagger on *him* twenty years ago, no denying that; but there'd been bad blood between the two of them for ages back—that he could accept and understand—And besides, he *himself* had killed; *he* might be classified as evil in a legalistic way—But with a person such as *Jen*...?

No; no excusing that; no casuistic argument to paper over that. Sister was different from the rest of them. Her chromosomes were just like theirs, her strength, her intellect—all those inheritances were intact; but something had misfired badly in her genes. She'd always had a lust for blood, that's true, ever since her earliest years of life. But those were little animals she'd tortured and done to death—an aberrance certainly, but not specifically forbidden by their genetic code.

His poor pathetic sister!—how she'd maddened first, then shriveled up and shrunk with age! She'd refused to use the stem cells these past thirty-some-odd years—never quite trusted his judgment and abilities that far. From the days of their youth, she'd habitually slighted him, derided him, tried her best to undermine whatever good he'd tried to do—she and that malignant mother of hers. "Keep peace," Father had ordered, and he'd obeyed; but Sister and her mother had made a point of countermanding all his efforts to unite the four of them and bridge the gap. Whatever he said was wrong; whatever he did was misdirected.

Making helpers, though—that was a different thing entirely. Every twenty years or so, he'd get the frantic call: "Canaday is dead," she'd say. Or "Neckerman" or "Grosvenor." "I'll need you to make another for me. You'll have to be here soon." And he'd go; of course he would—she'd only have a month of red cells at the outermost. He'd head right off to

Ottawa or Tampa or to the suburbs of L.A., and snoop around a bit; and there would always be a candidate available: some malignant sociopath, if the fellow's traits were bad enough and he was strong enough and lived near enough for his services to be obtained.

Like Lionel Helverson, cut and programmed forty years ago; a derelict and viper to beat the band; he'd probably killed as well—that, they didn't know for sure. Twenty years of service as a Helper for Sister. But he'd been devious and lazy, and took a shortcut that was impermissible by their moral laws. "Helverson's dying," came the sudden phone call twenty years ago; and he, of course, had run.

It was time for him to relocate anyway. Twenty years of mysteriously disappearing criminals and the authorities begin to suspect that something is amiss. So he'd picked up and taken off; burned down the palatial residence outside of Omaha with everything left inside—books and clothes and everything of value—to be sure and leave no trace—then got in the car with Helper Edward Larkins at the wheel and driven off. Two days drive to West Virginia, mostly pedal-to-the-metal; but by the time they finally pulled up to her big old house in Charleston, poor Helper Helverson was dead.

But there was Wilson readily available—the quintessential sociopath if there ever was one. Some terrific blood bank the larcenous fellow ran! Pass expired red cells off on the unsuspecting public, and sell the fresher stuff to some guy named Helverson to be used for God-knew-what. A lot of patients died—more than got reported in the papers or cited in the judicial inquiry—but Sister paid the crooked lawyers tens of thousands and funneled additional tens of thousands to the presiding judge—and got good old Wilson off. He didn't quite deserve to live, considering his misdeeds, but being a Helper was the closest thing to death just marginally short of death itself. A plain old, ordinary sociopath like all the rest—the easiest ones to modify if you knew just what to do: A few tracts severed in the frontal lobe, slipping the pointed probe above the eye; then a little behavior therapy for a final aperitif—stimulate the pleasure and pain centers at the appropriate times—zap here—zap there—and voila! Alexander Wilson at your service, milady! From all appearances, he had served her pretty well.

Served *him* well too, leaving the door unlocked, and the gate agape that fateful painful night. He would have never made it out into the street if not for Wilson—maybe there was a residual drop of decency in the fellow after all. If it was Wilson that he'd caught a glimpse of in that car down the block from Jen's place, the fellow hadn't changed too awfully much; still slow and stocky, still balding with that big round inexpressive head.

He wouldn't be too helpful *this* time. Jennifer was in Sister's clutches, and Wilson, though he'd been merciful once, had no reason to be merciful again. If Jen life could still be saved, it would be up to him to save her, whatever it took. An even exchange—his life for hers? Was that so terrible a deal?

That box, that precious, sacred box! All his life he had lived to complete the duty required by it. "Do not open it until the time is right," his father had admonished, and he'd abided by that steadfast rule. But inside him, inside all of them, graven in their very chromosomes, was a compulsion, an obsession, to complete the designated task before their deaths, whatever that mysterious task turned out to be. It was like a hunger in their souls to perform something never fully specified, an all-embracing love without an object to consign it to. "When the time is right, when Mankind can communicate with the stars, then open the box and...." The time would be right soon enough—but would he survive to do what he had lived to do? That was supremely doubtful now.

At any rate, he'd lived a good, eventful life these three long centuries and more. Many others had a paper just like the one in Father's box—Thanks to the stem cells he had shown the men in Austria, there were lots of others still alive and healthy. They could do what needed to be done when the time was ripe—which it likely would be fairly soon.

Yes, and he was tired of this endless burden anyway....

Not the least appropriate time for him to die.

29

"Look, sir—Look! You see that man down there?"

He did; of *course* he did. You couldn't really *help* but see him, what with that party-colored outfit he had on: A tall, slim veritable peacock-of-a-man, all dolled up for the fairway, judging by the golfing duds he wore: lime green slacks, sunset orange sweater, crimson baseball cap pretty nearly glowing like a searchlight in the dark: Why, the guy was obvious from a hundred yards away; from way up *here*, in fact, where Sidney made his customary right-hand turn onto the street a block from Newman Road: No attempt at camouflage on *that* man's part! If he'd set himself in that specific spot—as garishly outlandish as he looked—he probably wanted someone to *see* that he had set himself in that specific spot. And it was the specific *place* where he stood watching, so overt and obvious, that Audrey had remarked.

For he stood there watching the selfsame house that they'd noticed yesterday at dusk, then idled by this morning before their hasty luncheon at the Marriott: the Helverson house—or deeded, at any rate, to a recordless nonentity who happened to bear that name. Their foremost focus of suspicion for sure, this place, what with its massive gate, its eight-foot wall around the premises, its multi-acre land engorged with trees, as remote and inaccessible as a hilltop cabin in the woods. Nefarious deeds could readily be done here in confident obscurity, and quite possibly *had* been. 'Helverson' said the ownership documents on record; but if they could link the home to Alexander Wilson, then find the person he was working for, their mystery, at least the one in Charleston, was pretty neatly solved.

So the man who stood outside the iron gate, overtly looking in, was—well, about the most striking observation of the whole damn morning this morning or the whole damn night last night. And as Sidney cruised on up the street, a little closer to the man each second that elapsed, both he and Audrey held their gaze with wide-eyed fascination as they neared.

From fifty yards away (and closing), they could see that... No, it wasn't Wilson—no chance of that—Not the Alexander Wilson they were looking for, at any rate: the stubby, dull-eyed bald man depicted in that full-face photo from the West Virginia DMV—Not him for sure. No how; no way!

Not the Wilson in their photo—but if not Wilson, then *who*? And to find out who, Sidney rolled on up to the gate, and to the man, and to the house in question; and Audrey zipped her window down, stuck out her hand in a salutatory wave, cleared her throat to get attention, and queried in a friendly voice:

"Umm, excuse me, sir: Is this your house?"

"Who wants to know?" growled the man, turning full-face toward the car. He had a high-mag pair of binoculars in his hands; the sorts of things an ornithologist might use for scoping out exotic birds.

"Oh yes, well, sorry to disturb you, sir, but, umm, my husband and I—we've been sort of cruising through the neighborhood to check if there's a place around for sale. Do you know if this place happens to be for sale?"

"*This* place?" the tall man questioned, cocking his head. "Hey, I don't think you'd even want to *consider this* place, lady. This place is creepy as hell. If you ask me, the whole damn *street's* that way, tell you the truth—But if you're serious about buying here, I might be open to an offer if you want to throw one out. The wife and I have been thinking pretty seriously about tossing in the towel as far as *this* part of Charleston is concerned. And we'd kind of like to toss it pretty quick."

"Oh? But ... *why*?" asked Audrey, in that maple syrup voice again. "Have there been any problems in the neighborhood?"

"Problems? Well, that depends on what you'd consider problems." He leaned down toward her window with a condescending smile. "Just some missing dogs and cats and other minor inconveniences—Oh, and a couple of little kids as well—that's all; not much. Us, we lost a dog—damn nice one too. My kids are still crying every goddam night for him—with little kids it really takes its toll. Two weeks and a half now Pete's been gone and they're still sobbing every night. Ten years we had old Pete; same time my Ellen had the oldest kid. Big dogs don't usually live as long as that; but Ellen—she took care of that big old Shepherd like it was another of her precious little babes. *Health* food she gave it!—Jesus!—You believe *that?!*—Vegetables! Tofu! You ever hear of a German Shepherd that put its feet up on the table begging for a plate of *tofu?*"

"No sir, never did, but—*Missing* did you say? *Pets* missing, and *kids?* Little *kids?* So—do they know what happened to them? Is there a suspicion of foul play?"

"Hey, if there *was* foul play like you asked just now, my bet is, it was here, right here in this spooky goddam house behind the gate. Whatever else, I'm pretty sure they took my dog."

"They *took* it? You're saying that the people in the house just came and *took* it? It's a Mr. Helverson living here, according to what the deed says at the Registrar's. So you think that Mr. Helverson came over to your home and took your dog?"

"I don't know about a Helverson, lady. Guy I talked to the other day gave the name of Wilson. And I'm not saying that he came over to my place and took the dog himself, no—I'm not saying that. But there's a break in the wall out around the side." The golf-attired fellow pointed where he meant, past the iron gate, across the thickly wooded property where the broken wall, regrettably, was hidden from their view. "And my guess is, that a lot of pets, and maybe those two young kids as well, might've wandered in through where the wall's been crumbling down—and most of them just never wandered out."

"Oh my! I see why you're suspicious then—But … you said *Wilson?*—Did you say the man who lives here gave his name as *Wilson?*"

"That's what he said, yeah. Not that I'd believe *everything* he said, though. He's a pretty spooky guy?"

"Spooky?—Well—in what way?"

"In *every* goddam way. No expression on his face or in his voice. Flat, monotone—you know? Like I told you, lady: really, really *weird.*"

"Umm—One more thing, sir: Sorry, but…. Do you happen to know if he drives a Lincoln? Did you ever see him driving in or out through the gate here in a dark blue late-model Lincoln?"

"Aha! So you *do* know him, don't you?—I figured you maybe did, with all those snoopy questions you've been asking me. So? You already talk to him about the house?"

"No; I haven't talked to him directly; I haven't really met him yet—but…. So then you're saying that he *does* drive a dark blue Lincoln? Have you ever actually *seen* him driving in that kind of car?"

"Well hell, lady, it's parked right there next to the entrance on the side—can't you see it yourself?—Or no, maybe you can't make it out from where you're sitting down low in the seat like that. Here, get out of the car and come over to the gate and you can see it plain as day. He just drove in a little while ago—Wilson and a couple of people with him—which is why I came to have a look—I plan on keeping tabs on all the stuff that's going on in there."

OK; enough; both of them had heard quite enough. Audrey thanked the golfing guy for his time and trouble and the information he'd been kind enough to give. Sidney smiled and thanked him too, leaning across the console to shake the fellow's hand and ask him where he lived.

Which seemed to wrap things up. The golfer gave a conclusive sort of wave, then turned and walked away—directly toward the house he'd pointed to: A couple of live ones in the car, he'd probably figured; maybe they'd have a look at his place and take it off his hands.

So he walked off jauntily and left them alone, idling at the curb in front of the Helverson estate—Ah, but it *wasn't* the Helverson estate; it was *Wilson's*. Whatever those papers as to ownership had said, this was Wilson's residence, with Wilson's name properly identified by his snoopy neighbor as to occupancy, and with Wilson's car parked at the side door in ready view. Case pretty nearly closed now for sure, forever. All they'd need to do to tie things up with a fancy ribbon and a bow, was take a look around, scope the situation out, find out exactly who was home—what unsuspecting catch was trapped inside their net—Then once the presence of the proper little fishies was assured, they'd make their phone call to the Bureau office here in Charleston, get the troopers mounted up, yank the net up tight around the bad guys who were in it—and their work in Charleston would be done: Home by midnight, then tomorrow a celebratory lunch—Way better than the deli, he take his helpmate Audrey to a top-notch restaurant—lobster and caviar—the works! And so he nodded that darkly handsome head of his and said to sweet Miss Hamblin, conclusively and with determination:

"OK, Audrey, here's the way we're gonna handle things: I'm gonna drive on down the block and around the corner. Then I'll hop on out, and you can...."

Whoa! Audrey stopped him then and there with a palm extension and a resolute shaking of her head: "Get out there for *what*? What in the world are you planning to do?"

"Hey, we've got to check the place out, you know. I can't just call for Bureau backup until I know what I'm calling the Bureau backup *for*."

With which explanation, he slipped the car in gear and did what he'd just said: Down the street, around the corner, and fifty-odd yards farther on, where he slowed and idled to the curb, then pulled up there. And as the gearshift slid into Park and the ignition key clicked off, Audrey resumed their interrupted conversation with:

"So ... what you're saying is...." She shook her head in a manifest medley of disagreement and disbelief. "You want to go and check it out your*self*, you mean? Inside that gate? Just you alone?"

"Sure—Why not? We need to know, don't we? Whoever's in there, we've got to find out who it is."

"Yes, but we *know* that, don't we? We know that Wilson's there—we're sure of that. And the man we talked to said that two other people were with him in the car when he went in. So that's probably got to be...."

"Got to be *what*? *Who*? We don't really *know* who it's got to be. Maybe it's the killer that Wilson works for and maybe not. Maybe the Stanleyville suspect made it to Charleston and wound up in there too—We just don't know. Hell, maybe *none* of them are in there, not even Wilson—he could have snuck out the back for all we know: Or if it *is* Wilson in the place, then maybe there's another victim with him ready to be hung upside down and drained of blood. What we've got is an unknown quantity, Audrey; and unknown quantities can bite you in the backside if something you don't know about goes wrong. We've got to spring a trap today—that's what we're doing here—And if we don't know what's *in* the trap, it isn't safe to spring it yet—You understand? So what I've got to do is...."

"No! You're not going in that place yourself! You're not! I'm not going to let you!"

"Look, no point in arguing with me; this is my job. You know what my job entails better than practically anyone by now.

I've been in a whole lot dicier situations than this a hundred times. Now listen to me:" He took her by the hand, and she squeezed back warmly—much more warmly than he'd been expecting, to tell the truth. "Hey, I'm a big strong fellow, and I've never been considered particularly dumb. I can take care of myself, OK?—So just sit here for a while and wait—And stop your worrying; old Agent Braman will be fine."

"No! NO!—You're *not* going! I won't *let* you go!"

"All right, calm down. Don't cry, OK?" He put up a knuckle and wiped her eyes. "I can't stand to see a woman cry."

"It's … it's not the first time, is it?—that you've seen me cry?"

"No, maybe not; I suppose it's not…."

"It didn't bother you all that much when it happened the last time, did it? When we went to lunch with Uncle Phil?"

"It did, though. I can't say I wasn't touched that other time. It's only that…."

"Your wife, right? The stuff that happened to your wife: Is that the reason you don't seem…?"

"Uh-huh; it's mostly that, I guess. That business ten years ago—that's why I joined the Bureau in the first place, you know; it's hardly for the salary—And I'm not that big a fan of violent crime."

"I know that. I know you better than you think I do."

"And I know *you* better than *you* think too. I'm not a fool, you know. I realize we've got a connection; It's only that…." He paused.

"That what—Your wife, you mean?"

"No, that's been ten years now. It's time I got over it."

"So what then?"

"The ethics of it, I guess. The fact we work together—me being kind of a boss and you being…."

"What—an underling?"

"No, not an underling; I'd never think of you as an underling—What I mean is: Sometimes there's a kind of transference between a boss and a subordinate—A boss can sometimes take advantage of his position; and I'd never want to take advantage like that."

"OK, so what if I just quit?"

"Quit!—No! What would I do without you there? Your being there is the only…."

"Me too. You're the only reason I've stayed at the Bureau the past nine some-odd years."

"OK, OK. I've gotta get in there and do what I've gotta do. We'll continue this discussion later on—OK? I guess there's a lot for us to say. And we'll sit and say it, I promise. But now I've gotta go—Really—Whether you want me to or not, I've gotta go. I'll be fine; don't worry, just trust me on that. Now—open up the glove box and take out what's inside. Here; here's the key and...."

He slipped it in her hand, and she put it in the slot and turned the key a quarter turn around, then reached into the cavity, coming out with:

"This? The 45?" She put her index finger on the handle. "Good. I'll feel a whole lot better if you're carrying a 45."

"You know a little about firearms, do you, Audrey?"

"A little bit, sir, uh-huh. I grew up on a farm, and— Didn't I ever tell you that I grew up on a farm?"

"I don't think so; no. And, by the way, after the little conversation we just got through having, do you still want to call me 'sir'?"

"I don't exactly know. What do you think I ought to call you then?"

"Well, 'Sid' or 'Sidney'—one of the two. 'Sid' is probably better; most of my bosom buddies call me 'Sid.'"

"OK, if that's what you'd like, it's fine with me. It'll take a little while getting used to, though."

"No rush; we've got the next forty or fifty years."

He smiled, and she smiled back, more warmly than he'd ever seen her smile before; more warmly, truth be told, than he'd ever seen *anyone* smile back at him before. *Ever.*

But then his face turned serious again, and hers did too, following his lead: "So—about the farm: You ever fire a gun when you did your farming chores?"

"Me? Sure. I've been shooting since I was ten. Heck, I've been known to plug a groundhog at fifty yards with my daddy's target 22. But I've handled bigger calibers than that lots of times before."

"Good; terrific; my kind of girl; I should have known it all along—Well there's a gun in there for you too, just in case you need it. Look under the owner's manual and stuff, and underneath you'll find a holster—see it?"

She did, and nodded that she did, and took it in her hands, holding it the way a woman familiar with a pistol would likely hold one.

"All right, now unclip the strap and take it out."

Which she did as well, pretty darn deftly for an office secretary: Yep, no question, she was his kind of girl.

"OK, Audrey—well, that, young lady, is a 9mm automatic—you probably know that already if you've handled a few guns—It's not too heavy, just perfect for those pretty little hands. So—here—you know how to lock and load? Just pull back on the slide all the way to put one in the chamber—you see?—Nice easy mechanism; nice and smooth. And here's the safety, up here by your thumb—see? Push it up and down a couple of times to get the feel if you haven't done it before. You know which way is off?"

"Sure, sir—uh, Sid, I mean—Sure thing. I've got one at home just like it: Smith and Wesson Automatic Nine. I've got a carry permit, actually, and I bring a sidearm with me on all my dates."

"You—*what*?!"

"Just kidding, sir—uh, Sid—Just a little gallows humor to lighten things up—And things *do* need lightening up right now, you know: I'm not too happy about this Lone Ranger scheme of yours without a Tonto to tag along."

"I'll be fine, I guarantee—So—anyway, here goes: I'll head on out and work my way around the property to where the wall is broken on the far side, the way the golf guy said it was. Then when I get there, once I'm sure I can pick my way through, I'll dial your number on my cell. When you hear it ring, drive back front outside the gate, and stop there, and lean on the horn like crazy. Keep it going for a minute or so—a ton of noise—OK?—That'll get whoever's in the place up to the windows near the front to see what's going on; and while they're up there looking, I can sneak up to the side of the house without a lot of prying eyes. Then once you finish with the horn, go pull the car around the corner again—back to where we are right now—And keep the doors locked tight and the weapon on your lap. Keep it in your grasp, keep a bullet in the chamber, and point and click if you have the slightest doubt about a potential threat. If you feel you have to fire though, empty the whole twelve rounds into whatever you're pointing at. It's got hollow point bullets the same as mine does, so it'll stop most anything short of a rhino in a Kevlar vest—OK?"

Sidney tapped her on the arm, not without affection, and concluded:

"Now hand me the 45 and wish me luck. I should be back within ten minutes of the time I call. If I'm not, there's trouble—big time—and you're a smart enough farmer's daughter to know what you'll have to do."

Sister wouldn't kill him right away; that he knew for sure.

No, first he'd be shackled to a metal bench or chair, the way she'd done it with those victims that he'd brought her while Helper Wilson was healing up. A couple of genuine monsters, those two slimy donors he'd furnished for her needs—He'd practically caught them in the act, and got them bound and gagged and on the way to Sister's place before the law showed up.

And once he'd got them there, well hadn't Sister had her *fun*! *Fun*, yes—*ocean-loads* of fun! The look in her eyes, the drooling from her saggy lips: No sedation for those two sinners, no indeed! For the first poor victim she'd been strong—the anemia hadn't weakened her as yet—Monster that the fellow was, he almost made you pity him, almost made you wish he'd had his neck snapped with a dose of propofol in his veins—Ah, but Sister wouldn't hear of such a thing. She wanted her enjoyment, her sport, her several pounds of living flesh—with a cautery at hand for fear she'd waste too much of the victim's precious blood.

That had been a preview—He could anticipate the same: Shackled to an iron bench in the basement—unless she had a stronger thing to use these days—it would take him hours to die; hell, maybe *days*. Oh first she'd taunt him with a flimsy ray of hope. She'd feed him, give him something cold to drink, let him sleep the night—if he could sleep sitting up chained to a bench that way. A day or two afterward—that would be the time; she'd let him know when it was coming in advance. All this killing was a game of cat and mouse to her, the mental torture not the least delightful part. When the ending finally came, not a very easy exit for the sufferer; he'd been a witness to the way she feasted on the pain. For Sister savored death the way a smoker savors fine cigars: slow, luxuriantly slow; anticipate that final inhalation, then take it in with leisure and delight—And so he'd have a day or two to wait before the end came slow and painful in the basement with the knife; he had a little bit of time.

Time to watch Jen leave the house and know she was safely out of Charleston, at any rate: That would be a consolation, certainly. For it was certain she'd be safe once he arrived. Sister wasn't sound of mind by any means—not fully competent twenty years ago, and likely steeply downhill ever since—But that offer that she'd made—a bargain signed in blood—that would be sacred to her; symbolic gestures like that always had been. And his surrender to her will would set the seal on the agreement they had made. All well and good then: Jennifer would be out and in her car as soon as he came meekly through the door and got the shackles on. On that they'd made a tacit deal.

And as for him—Well, it had been a long and fascinating life, it truly had. He'd done and seen and sampled all that life could show a man; every trial, every possible adventure any human being could experience and survive, good and bad, pleasurable and agonizing to the nth degree. Everything there ever was to hope for and regret; he'd done it all—absolutely everything—or pretty *nearly* absolutely everything: there being still the regrettable exception of ... love.

Yes, love, a beloved woman's love—that he hadn't had the pleasure of knowing in its highest form—not once, not *ever*— For what sort of woman could he have brought into the life he had to lead? Free your mind and try to imagine that; not a pleasant task.

And to be with a woman briefly, fleetingly, outside the closeness of a home; to enter into a relationship as intense as it was transient—Well, that would eventuate sooner or later in some kindly woman's pain—no alternative to that, was there? And since he couldn't be the *cause* of a decent person's pain— being not just *averse* to causing pain to the benevolent, but absolutely *interdicted* from it, engraved in his genetic code—That being the case, a genuine kind of tender love—a truly heartfelt love—that much-desired thing had passed him by these past three hundred years and more; and would be gone forever with the passing of another several days.

Oh sure, he'd felt a powerful love for Jennifer as a child; and she had loved him back in her own pre-adolescent way; and they'd been together day and night in that happy home for the whole of one splendid summer. But love back then had been paternal, not romantic: a love of age-old man for budding child. Now that she was grown into a woman, and genuine co-equal love was capable of blossoming into its proper form, full-blown— now that there was a chance for actual love, first time in his over-ripened lifetime—the first time *ever* ... he would have to leave her. But to give his life so she could live her own—not a decision that took too much time or required too much thought. Yes, a life too long was better over now. It was time for him to die, so that Jennifer had her turn to live.

It took ten minutes, more or less, to drive to Sister's gate from Nathan's house. Coming up to it, there was another car pulled against the curb with its horn blaring like a freighter in the fog, and he pulled around the vehicle to get himself a look: A woman in the driver's seat, young enough, attractive enough, secretarial in her prim and proper dress—Picking up the boss, he figured, or waiting for a little child to come out of the house across the street to take to school; the little brick house with emerald trim where those nice young honeymooners moved in twenty years ago.

No matter, no problem; honking horns and waiting drivers weren't his concern right now—*Jen* was; *death* was, and *only* Jen and death. He cruised on past the silver Chevy without a lot more thought, turned around, and pulled Jen's Buick over near the wall ten yards beyond the iron gate.

He left the power window halfway down and tossed the keys into the console's drink cup—Jen would have no problem finding them there when Sister let her out—then popped the door and trotted in his lithe and cat-like manner to the gate. When he approached it, the woman in the silver car had started off—no boss, no child, poor thing, so she'd driven there and honked her horn in vain. Off she went, regardless of his presence, backing into the drive across the street, then out around the corner at an idle speed, until her car passed finally from his line of view.

So here he stood alone in as eerie and uncomfortable a scene as any he had ever witnessed, just as grim and uninviting as he remembered the house and its surroundings from twenty years ago: a mental picture recreated right down to the uncut weeds and the looming shapes of overhanging trees: Nothing had changed a bit; everything just the same, as though it had been frozen twenty years ago in time. Twenty years ago, practically to the month, he'd been sprawled out on the pavement bleeding out his stolen blood, until that kindly driver of the van had picked him up and brought him to the hospital that Meredith had ultimately saved him from.

Today there would be no passing van, however, and no open doors from Sister's stodgy mansion to stagger out of. Today, tomorrow, possibly the next day after that, he would be nothing but a mass of gritty liquid run out through the hopper he and Wilson had modified and installed. It was an outcome he accepted: After all the lives cut short to save his own, it would be an apt and proper end.

The gate was closed—Sister wasn't expecting him this soon—and so he came in over the wall. He scaled it neatly, deftly, as was his agile wont. The door would be unlocked, no doubt, and Wilson on alert. They'd bind his hands and chain him to a wall, or maybe shackle him first thing to that iron bench she kept down in the basement. But once he was chained or bound or shackled, Jen would be released.

The car was waiting for her, a million-plus in gold behind the driver's seat.

—Oh, and the box—his father's box—Maybe one day Jennifer would look inside and find the paper written out so long ago. And maybe when the time was ripe—if there ever came a technological breakthrough to *make* it ripe—she'd carry out his father's wishes in loving memory of her one-time childhood friend.

She put a talon up to separate the curtains just enough to see.

The silver car—that's where it was coming from. That horn! Half a minute of it now; enough to rattle *any* woman's nerves—And now, particularly now when she was waiting, listening, wondering if that traitorous brother of hers would come, wondering if his simple nature made him gullible enough to trade his life for the life of a woman who was as good as dead anyway. Did he honestly believe his brilliant sister could possibly be naive enough to let the nurse's daughter go? Free her merely because of a bargain he thought they might have made? Send her out into the world with all the things she'd seen and heard, as though she hadn't seen and heard too much?

310

Was Brother foolish enough not to realize the daughter had to die? Not today perhaps, or tomorrow—But in another couple of weeks fresh blood would be required, and the daughter could serve in that regard as well as any other source. If Brother hadn't interfered with Gonzalez, there might have been no pressing need so soon. But now there was, and he only had himself to blame.

That horn, that maddening, infuriating HORN! She could hardly hear her thoughts for the infernal noise! If Brother *did* come, if he *had* come, she wouldn't have known about his presence for that cursed, never-ending horn!

Why, she'd barely heard the cheep of the motion sensor over to the east through the sound of that idiotic beeping. 'Cheep' it went, when there was a movement to her left as she stood here at the window facing toward the gate. That meant movement past the break in the wall—generally a neighborhood pet slipping through, though twice she'd been lucky enough to catch a little girl—On any other, less important day, she would hear that alluring 'cheep' and climb up to the roof, scan the grounds, find the source of the signal. Little animals were best left alone—squirrels, rabbits: what fun were they? Ah, but the big ones—the dogs especially—Now they made hunting *fun*.

Ah!—at last!—The noise cut off abruptly, and the car that had been making it backed into a driveway, turned west and disappeared. She could think again; she could listen again most carefully in the hopes of hearing Brother....

But would he come? Was he that insanely trusting?—that absurdly credulous of a bargain that no rational being would deign to keep? If he *did* come (Ah! If only Brother did!), she would have her long-delayed revenge at last, twenty years late, no doubt; but the delay had only whetted her appetite for what was now two decades overdue.

Bzzz—There! That was the motion sensor straight out to the *south*, sensing something directly out front. She pried the curtain very slightly open with her taloned finger, peering with one eye, seeing—What? *Another* car, a shiny white one this time, pulled up tight against the curb, most of it hidden by the wall.... And there! A tiny bit of movement up along the wall—A hand! A sleeve! Someone climbing over, hidden by the branches of a tree; not quite visible. Was it...? Could it be...? Could it possibly....?

Bzzz—the southward motion sensor again, and with it, piping over the buzzing from down the staircase calling upwards, Wilson's voice, loud and eager, proclaiming:

"He's *here*, Madam—your brother! Shall I take him down and chain him to the bench?"

"Yes!" She smiled and clenched her fists so tightly that a talon made a puncture in her skin. "Yes—Yes, Wilson—*Yes*! Take him down and shackle him. Use the heaviest shackles, the new ones you brought me yesterday. Remember: Brother is strong; no one we have ever bound was as strong as he. And those bolts fastened to the concrete—are you certain they will hold?"

"Four thousand pounds, Madam; the hardware store assured me of that. And the shackles and chains can contain even more."

"Good, then. Secure his arms and legs to leave a minimal amount of movement—just be sure to make the shackles tight!"

Five minutes to get to the break in the wall. Enormous acreage first of all, so halfway round it couldn't possibly be quick. And then there was the overgrown vegetation to contend with, and the critters—thorny bushes, spiky weeds; gnats, vines, spider webs getting in your eyes and hair: all that to impede a fellow's transit. Yech!

So five minutes wasn't all that bad, all things considered. And once it had elapsed and the ambit had been accomplished, Sidney saw the crumbled masonry littering the ground, just where the golf guy told them it would be, and he stopped and crouched beside the opening well out of view of the house beyond. He'd need to move carefully now, deliberately. For these weren't stupid people in the place; they were pretty damn clever from what Phil had said. They'd know the wall was broken in this spot, and they'd have some kind of signaling device quite likely, a trip-wire probably, or some sort of light sensor with a laser beam.

So Sidney stopped at the nearer edge of the opening for a minute or so and looked; looked as carefully as though his life depended on his looking carefully. But no, no sign of a wire, no sign of a laser that he could identify, after meticulous inspecting, probing, feeling with a finger; and therefore....

Whew! He waited a minute more, peeking an eye around the raggedy concrete block, through the bushes and the trees adjacent to the wall, barely seeing the house for all the abundant greenery; just a window here and there, some ivy on the bricks: no sign of life, no lights, no movement....

And so he made the call to Audrey's cell. OK then, wait ... wait: Ten seconds passed ... fifteen ... twenty.... And then the horn—Terrific! thought Sidney. Exactly on cue—That Audrey: Sheesh! Tell her something and the sweet kid got it done, invariably; his kind of girl for sure!

So ten seconds more in antsy wait while the horn was drawing every eye's attention to the front of the house. Then up, and through the gap, past the trees, past the briars, over the bushes, and quick as hell for the near side of the house, getting there in a flash—Once he hit the ground-cover on the lawn, there was nothing to delay him.

So good! Flat against the brick, brushing through the ivy, he sidled to the nearest window up closest to the front. Probing an eye up to the edge, peeking around it, he saw: What was it? A dining room it looked like, though the lighting inside was pretty dim, just the daylight coming through the two windows opposite, facing out the front. But no one was in there, and the horn was still going like crazy, so they must have been looking through some other windows, which was great: his lucky day. A perfect plan so far.

Whew! A ghastly-smelling odor to the place!—the scent of death, decaying matter, rising from the soil.... And as he wondered about the scent, and crinkled up his nose in repugnance, and glance again through the window of the dining room, or whatever, he noticed.... What was that? The horn had stopped now, and pretty soon after the horn cut off, he thought he caught a glimpse of something moving out past the windows facing the front. And when he peeked around to look again....

Yes. There! What was that? A movement just beyond the outside window passing rightward: a person seemingly, heading toward the entrance door....

So slowly, gingerly, crouching lower, kneeling in the smelly soil to keep beneath the windows, he crept up toward the angle of the house—the junction of the side wall with the front—

and peeking round the corner v-e-r-y carefully with the pupil of one eye, he saw:

A man. Tall and muscular, with finely chiseled features, moving like an athlete, graceful, catlike—So—yes! It was—it had to be....

The Stanleyville suspect for sure—Terrific! With Wilson inside and presumably the murderer he worked for as well; and now with the last of their oddball cast of characters showing up: Well, how could you top *this* for a successful investigation?! They'd have the lot of the weirdoes they'd been after in the can before you knew it, and be heading home by sunset today—F-a-n-*tas*tic!

All right, not a whole lot more to do from here on in; just a little final wrapping up. So here's the plan: Once he could be absolutely certain who was trapped inside their net, he'd run back through the broken wall and summon in the troops. Fifteen minutes for the posse to gallop out with all their fireworks— twenty at the most—and he and Audrey would be sleeping in their beds tonight. He'd take her for a real nice thank-you dinner first.

So back along the ivy toward the rear end of the house, creeping tight against the brick; coming to the window of—he stuck his head up, v-e-r-y cautiously: It was a kitchen—just as empty as that dining room had been....

And then a little farther on, he made it to the window of a.... This one was a sort of pantry, situated just before the angle between the side wall and the back, empty and dark like all the rest, and so....

He rounded the corner of the house, creeping, trying his darnedest to keep off of that nasty-smelling soil, and when he made it to the edge, *this* time, he clearly saw....

A light!

There!

Coming from a lower window: A cellar window, obviously; halfway down along the rear wall of the house.

Good!—Finally!—A likely sign of life at last!

He'd shuffle over v-e-r-y, v-e-r-y carefully and have himself a look.

30

Whew!—Bright in there, thought Sidney; so dazzlingly bright after the darkness of the shadows he'd been creeping in, it took a couple of seconds for him to make the details out.

And when he finally *did* make the details out—at last!— he got the image of an empty cellar space with a mottled concrete floor, stained with something indefinably offensive— Could that ruddy coloration of the concrete be ... blood?

Maybe. He wouldn't bet against it; for there were more strange things besides: There—right in the geometric center of the space, he saw a metal bench, thick, firm, heavy-duty, bound tight to the concrete with heavy-duty bolts, shiny brand new hex-bolts with heads that that looked a full inch thick. Then to the metal bench, in turn, was fixed a set of shackles held by chains— And not just plain old prison handcuffs either—hell no!—But high-test, full-strength shackles, thick enough to hold a gorilla with an aching tooth that needed yanking out—Ouch!

And as he watched the empty basement and the shackles and the bench ... suddenly he noticed a bit of movement over to the left: some steps there with their risers minimally visible; and a pair of feet and legs proceeding down—which was the movement that he'd seen....

And stepping onto the mottled floor came the handsome man he'd observed through the dining-room window moving deftly toward the house—The man from Stanleyville, he figured—Of course it was the Stanleyville suspect—who else could it be?

So onto the concrete floor the handsome fellow stepped; and right behind him came more feet; more legs; and ... There!—*another* man: stocky, balding, a face without expression entirely—hell, you could make that out even through a dirty basement window twenty feet away—An oddball kind of face, sluggish, mask-like—which must be Wilson! Yes! The very spitting image of that DMV photo in the folder in the car— Wilson!—Right here in the basement: the two of them together in one place—Great!—Fantastic!—So at least a couple of their perpetrating cast of characters were present on the stage. And—what's to rule against it?—Maybe a couple more would turn up pretty soon!

And so he watched a little longer, holding very still and keeping his fascinated eyeball to the farthest outside margin of the glass. He watched in rampant curiosity as the man who must be Wilson led the man who likely was from Stanleyville over to the metal bench; and the Stanleyville fellow sat there, voluntarily, for all a guy could tell, not visibly objecting to the choice of seat, though it looked pretty hard and uncomfortable, judging from appearances—a surface no self-respecting tuchas could find much pleasure in.

And once the guy was seated—what was Wilson doing back there anyway?! Tough to see, because his hands were blocked from view, but.... He was.... He was—Sheesh! Was he chaining the handsome fellow to the bench with those shackles fit for some achy-toothed King Kong? Holy Moses, but he *was!*—Man! Four strong shackles, arms and legs chained tight, though the shackles on the hands didn't look as tight as the shackles on the feet—at least they didn't look too tight from out beyond the window peeking in. Hmmm: There had to be a reason for *that*, although the whole damn thing seemed pretty devoid of reason from a federal agent's point of view.

So he watched with waxing curiosity; and as he watched a little more, there came some movement again, off to the left just like the last time, over at the foot of the stairs, and....

And what was *this!*—Sheesh! Ho-ly *Moses!* A little tiny woman, bent double and nearly bald, and with such shriveled skin and so puckered-up a face that she looked almost dead herself, as though she herself might be the cause of the rancid odor on the property out among the weeds. He couldn't smell her though the window, of course; but she sure did look that way; she definitely did: dead flesh, a moldy, rotting carcass on the hoof!

She stepped up to the man chained to the bench and said something briefly, angrily. You could see her saggy mouth move in profile and some spittle issue from her lips, although you couldn't hope to hear—And then the man said something back, not very angrily, it seemed. And then the woman turned away and went rightward toward, then through, a door across the room from where the steps came down, twenty feet or so across from there.

Beyond the door she went, and in maybe thirty seconds, maybe forty (he wasn't looking at his watch), out she came with another woman—her diametric opposite as to youth and physical attractiveness: a very pretty woman—or really *more* than pretty: a tall and shapely light-haired woman who might have been a model or an actress: really gorgeous in a leading lady sort of way—though not as alluring as Audrey, frankly, once that spunky farm-girl personality got factored in.

And in they came, the gorgeous woman just in front, the little tiny gnomish woman just behind, with the little tiny gnomish woman's hand reached up onto the gorgeous woman's waist, sort of leading her from behind; directing her over to the metal bench where the Stanleyville fellow sat in shackles and chains. And once they got up closer, given the alteration in perspective, you could see that in her hand—Holy Moses! The little woman held a dagger in her hand!—Not a knife at all, but what you'd have to call a dagger, so long and pointed at the tip and curvilinear of blade, that it could only be referred to as a dagger—vicious-looking, fit to maim or kill and nothing else. And she pulled the gorgeous woman lower and brought the dagger to her throat, then held it there while she inspected....

It was the shackles she was inspecting, their lack of tightness on the fellow's hands; she seemed to notice that, as he himself had noticed when they first got placed. And she motioned to the man who was likely Wilson, the dull-faced fellow standing behind and to her right—gestured to him with one hand while she kept the other with the dagger at the gorgeous woman's throat. And she said something as inaudible as all the rest, said it angrily, expelling the spittle again: With which comment or directive, he bent down—Wilson did—and tightened the shackles properly. And the little woman moved her arm abruptly and....

Ho-ly *Moses!*—She up and flung the gorgeous woman halfway across the room against the wall where the steps came down, flung her with a hollow thud as though the gorgeous woman's hundred-some-odd human pounds were so many dozen feathery ounces—like a spiteful child tossing a little rag doll in its rage. Man-oh-MAN! It was something incredible to see!

And the gorgeous woman hit the wall and collapsed there, unconscious—which you'd pretty much expect, given the force of her impact. Then the tiny woman turned to the man who was likely Wilson, turned *on* him rather than *to* him, as you'd best describe it, and....

Oh good *grief*! She stabbed him with the dagger! There—just like that! Right in the chest, right where the heart lay underneath the ribs. You could see the blade go in and the blood spurt out onto her black dress, and on her hands and a spray up to her face, reddening her visibly. And she looked at the wounded man ferociously, and licked the blood spots off her lip ... and ... and ... *smiled*!

The little woman *smiled*!

Ho-ly Moses! That was pretty much enough!—*Enough*! So Sidney yanked the gun from where he'd stuck it underneath his belt—But by the time he'd pulled it out, and got it cocked and ready, and taken proper aim—the little woman was over where the gorgeous woman lay unconscious: No clean shot from here. And being very small, the little woman was mostly hidden by the gorgeous woman as she dragged her back into the other room, across the cellar from the staircase. A minute or a little longer than a minute elapsed while she was in there, and when she came out again, she scurried across the cellar, moving so quickly, with such unearthly speed, no marksman could have hit her through the glass. Uncannily the woman moved across the cellar to the stairs—and disappeared immediately up them.

And Sidney shook his head and figured—whew!— Enough of *this* incredible mishugas! Time to put a call in for the troops!

She ground her gums together furiously: Wilson had betrayed her. But *worse* than that: Wilson had considered her a fool!

And in a way she'd actually *been* a fool in Wilson's eyes; she *must* have been. *Trusting* the man—trusting *anyone*!—Twenty years ago she should have realized that such a man as Wilson was not the type of Helper one could trust. Brother would never have made it to the street outside the property without a bit of help—a door unlocked, a gate intentionally agape—He never could have done so on his own: a fact she should have seen back then—And now: those shackles—so negligently loose, he might have wriggled out an arm, reached out, and done her serious harm.

No more of that—no more dependence on a Helper—ever!—never in her life again! She'd made a bargain with Gonzalez—or Wilson had, compliant to her will—But from here on in, for the duration, no more intermediaries; she'd make her own arrangements starting now. Mercenary lackeys like Gonzalez were out there for the asking, merely waiting for some payment to supply her with her blood. What did it matter whence the donors came? Prisons, shelters, youth homes—even senior residences would do—so long as the seniors were not too thin of blood or had transmissible disease. All one needed for the bargain and the victims, was abundant financing. And she *had* abundant financing—unlimited, actually. She could buy whatever, whenever—*whomever*—she liked.

Up the cellar steps she went, plotting, planning, grinding those toothless gums in frenzied thought. She was as fleet as a famished tiger from the rush of watching death; as exultant as a champion from the taste of salty blood.

Blood! *Fresh* blood! *Thick* blood! On her normal refill days she was weakened when she got her monthly chance to kill—But *today*! Today she was *far* from weak; and the blood—Wilson's last delicious spurt—That had brought her spirits up and piqued her appetite for....

MORE!

That chirp from the motion sensor—She'd hardly heard it for the cursed horn. But a chirp had sounded, she was sure of that: something slipping through that blessed opening in the wall.

Too soon to butcher Brother—he'd need to stew on his mortality for another couple of days. And as for the girl, no need to drain *her* blood for another several weeks—with muscles at their strongest now, a couple of weeks would be a more appropriate time.

Ah, but a nice warm animal! What *fun* to catch some animal—a cat or dog or what you will—now *that* would be a tasty aperitif after a less than satisfying snack. Wilson's death was nothing but a tease for her: a bit of Chinese dim sum that had merely piqued her appetite at best. So a cat or dog out on the lawn just now: the pursuit, the capture, the execution with her knife! The cats were not much fun, of course—not clever enough to sense that brandished knives meant imminent demise; you never saw the glint of terror in their eyes.

Oh, but the dogs!—the bright-eyed, cogitative dogs!—yes—big ones especially!—Now they were cleverer sorts of beasts; almost prescient in a way. They saw the blade and cringed abjectly, comprehending what it meant. If it were a dog out there that made that single 'cheep'—another great big brown one like the furry thing two weeks or so ago—How full of blood *it* was! What joyous fun to catch and kill it right out on the lawn! Yes, yes—Another one like that would be a special treat, a glass of brandy after lunch. A big brown dog like that with fur that sopped up half the bloody spill: She'd kill it on the lawn and drag it down the cellar steps and toss it in the hopper with Brother two or three days hence. What fun! What joy! A big brown furry dog at large among the bushes!—She simply had to look.

So up the cellar steps into the hallway, then up the steps again to the second floor, and then once more ascending to the third. The dormer window in the back: That was the one she always used to climb out on the roof. And she did just that, crouching on her haunches on the slate in front, and then behind, to peer about the property: She did this often with superb results: People never bothered to look up: the little children, the door-to-door religious fools: no one ever saw her on the roof.

The big dumb animals as well. Your people and your larger creatures never fear destruction from above: Rodents do: they get snatched by hawks and owls and other flying things. They look up habitually, the squeamish little fools. But humans and cats and dogs?—Virtually never; they always look down or straight ahead. But up above they never look.

So she crouched low on her haunches forty feet above the lawn, peering down and outward high atop the slate, scanning her acreage hungrily; looking eagerly for a dog—that would be her preference of course; a cat mere consolation. She scanned the lawn and the section of the woods that could be seen; she looked out toward the gate; she squinted toward the bushes where the wall had crumbled down:

No dogs though. No movement at all, regretfully, except a couple of songbirds fluttering about, and—but wait!—what was that across there in the weeds?—A rat perhaps, too small to be a cat or dog: The fluids from the hopper strewn across the ground each filling time—such residue attracted rats.

No movement at all just now, however; a false alarm— But wait!—What was that there—down along the side wall of the house? Was there a scattering of leaves? Was it a *man*? Hard to see for the three-foot overhang, but she heard a bit of rustling down there too—her ears were very sharp—And leaning over, squinting downward in the dowsing sun....

Yes! She could see a hazy shadow move, slinking around the side of the house in the direction of the broken wall. A man! An invader of her property!—Imagine that! No measly dog, no inconsequential cat—but a full-grown, blood-filled *man*! What unexpected luck! What splendid, unanticipated *fun*!

So down she went, shimmying down the drainpipe in the back like a frisky chimpanzee. She was light, shrunken down to pretty nearly nothing these recent days, just skin, developed musculature, and collapsing bone, so the drain would easily hold her weight. Down she went, and at his back and coming up to him mostly unaware, halfway across the lawn in the direction of the broken wall. She grabbed him by a shoulder and threw him down, and she was on his chest with her legs across his arms, pinning him there; and with a blow to the head she knocked him out, unconscious as the dead.

Mmmm! She'd haul him down and chain him in the basement next to Brother; and Brother could sit enchained and watch the stranger die tonight—Not a measly dog, this time, but a man, full-grown: A full-grown, blood-filled, darkly handsome man!

That would be a preview. Tomorrow maybe Brother's turn; then in two weeks more, or three, she could get her nice fresh fill of red cells from the girl.

What fun! What happy, unanticipated FUN!

31

Ten minutes had passed by now and Audrey was getting a l-i-t-t-l-e bit concerned.

So out of the car and around the corner to the massive iron gate again to get herself a look. And when she turned the corner and reached the gate … that was when she saw the other car:

The one that had passed her by before. The man in it—she hadn't seen him very well, but he had stopped for an instant while she was making all that noise, and briefly stared at her, then proceeded up the block a bit, going who knew where—

But it was *here* that he had gone, after all, turned around, come back, and not just *stopped* here, but *stayed* here; left his shiny white Buick here. This was unexpected certainly: another unexpected player in the piece. Sid might be in trouble—her kindly, handsome Sid might be in desperate need of help. Good Lord! Something pretty quickly needed to be done.

So first of all she took a sec to look: The window of the car was open wide and she had a look inside there first. Then, noticing something on the floor behind the seat, she opened the door to check it out.

A box: A small but heavy cardboard box; and then another box beside it, same size, same shape. She pulled the top off; it wasn't sealed:

Oh my goodness! Gold! It was *gold*! Gold coins in heavy plastic packets—*hundreds* of them in dozens of heavy packets, twenty or so in each! Something strange, all right! A million dollars on the back floor of a car? Sitting there unlocked? Yep—something really strange was going on for sure.

And so she looked some more. On the other side, beneath the passenger seat slightly sticking out, an ornate wooden case: antique, elegantly carved in an intricate design—ancient-looking, truthfully. She knelt atop one box of coins and reached across to pick the carved box up: Light, fragrant—it smelled like sandalwood.

No coins in there, not much weight to it, but precious and exotic, judging by the way it looked. No lock on the box, no one to prevent her, her curiosity now piqued, and so she opened it and looked inside: Nothing in there but an ancient folded note, hand-printed on crinkled yellowed paper, though fresh enough and fairly well preserved.

Which, when she examined it, first one page, and then another, and then the third and last, had antique text, complex diagrams.

Curious. Interesting. Arcane kind of script, but in plain old English anyway—And so she took the moment more required and quickly read.

His head was sore; it ached.

And when he began to come around, he felt the warmth of flesh beside him, pressed tight against his shoulder and the left side of his back. And then he tried to move, but wasn't able. And it was when he *realized* he wasn't able that he felt the shackles on his legs and arms.

Which made him come awake more fully now. And once he did, he heard the warmth beside him and behind, against his shoulder, ask:

"Do they know you're here?"

"Who?" he mumbled foggily. "Does *who* know I'm here?" Sidney wasn't quite himself as yet.

"She saw the ID in your wallet. It says you're from the FBI."

"*Who* saw it? Was it the little woman?"

"Do they know you're here? I hope you told someone you're here. Does anybody know?"

"Someone does. Yes; they'll know if I'm not back before too long."

"Will they bring help?"

"They'll call for some. I'm sure they'll call when I don't get back—Uh, how long have I *been* here?—And who the hell are *you*?" He asked this latter question because he couldn't see the body he was talking to, since he was shackled facing away from the face of the man who owned the body, side to side and cattycorner back to back on the rigid metal bench.

"You don't *know* who I am?"

"I probably can make a pretty decent guess. I think I saw you through the window. Are you the guy from Stanleyville?"

"Not from there originally, no; but recently, yes. How much do you know about me?—About *us*?"

"A lot, I think. Although a lot of it is guesswork."

"All right, then, tell me what you've guessed."

"First you tell *me* something, will you? How much trouble are we in?"

"An awful lot if no one comes to look for you—Look, I don't care all that much for myself, truthfully; but there's a woman here...."

"I think I saw her. Through the window. She's a special friend, is she?"

"Special, yes—So tell me: How much do you know? Tell me about that guesswork you've been doing these last few days."

"None of it is from the girl, though. It's important that you know that. She wouldn't tell us anything."

"No, I didn't think she would—You mean Linnie, right?—I didn't think she'd tell you very much."

"Most of what I know is just putting two and two together. So: tell me this: What did she mean when she said you weren't 'from here'?—That's all she really told us, by the way. So what exactly does it mean?"

"What do you *think* it means?"

"Hey, you're a regular fount of information, buddy—aren't you? If we're in that tight a bind, you might as well tell me at least a little of what I've asked."

"Fair enough; I see your point. I wasn't born here; that's the first thing. I was born in a little town in what is now Romania. So that's the 'not from here' Linnie might have meant."

"I don't think it *is*, though."

"No? Then tell me what you think. Tell me a little about all that guesswork you federal agent guys have done."

"Not 'guys'; not plural. It's been my investigation totally from the first. I'm the only one who knows a thing. Fact is: I've got a sort of special interest in the case."

"And what would that sort of special interest be?"

Sidney pulled against the shackles, futilely, growling: "A file of yours. A file I came across on your computer."

"OK—And how does that...?"

"I'll *tell* you how it sparks my interest, buddy. My dead *wife's* name was on it—OK? Jodi Braman—Does the name Jodi Braman ring a bell?"

"Not offhand it doesn't. Which of the computer files did you find it in?"

"The list for Pennsylvania—One of the thousand-odd case files you stored in there—Jodi Braman—You don't remember entering it in?"

"Not exactly, but…. 'Braman', is it? Was she—are you—related to the Braman clan from Pittsburgh? The rich and famous ones?"

"I am. I'm Jacob Braman's son."

"All right then, I remember. I remember the case reasonably well, in fact. Ten or twelve years ago, wasn't it? Your wife was killed by a couple of kidnap pros from out of state—Ohio, I think they came from. I remember the details now."

"Out of state? How did you know they were from out of state? You sure you weren't involved in some way? What the hell was that file doing on your computer if you weren't somehow involved?"

"If you're asking that, you don't know much about me, do you?—Which is good; which is a whole lot better than the alternative. Your guesswork leaves a lot to be desired, Mr. Braman—Or should I call you *Agent* Braman?—Which do you prefer?"

"Hey, I don't care. I don't think we're in a position to get all that caught up in the fine points of formality just now."

"You're right; we're not. And *since* we're not, I'll go ahead and tell you a little of what you asked me as a sort of parting gift in case we….. Well, it can't do too much damage now anyway, I suppose—whatever supervenes.

"As to where I'm from—you asked where I was from—the answer I gave you was correct; I was born in what is now Romania. As to where *we're* from—ultimately and fundamentally—that I honestly don't know. There's someplace out there that wants a certain message sent. I don't think any of us know exactly where that is or what the message required consists of; all I know—all our whole population knows, I'd imagine—is that we have an inborn need—more of a compulsion than a need, actually—to finish the task assigned long ago to our forebears. And in the process of doing that, we—all of us—are genetically prohibited from doing any collective injury to the population at large—Which makes us pretty beneficial citizens, when you look at things objectively.

"I've done a lot of reading, Agent Braman, and I've run a lot of tests; and I believe I understand our condition fairly well. The anemia—you know about the aplastic anemia, I assume?"

"I do."

"Well it's part of the program—stamped in our genetic code. The population—our ancestors, I mean—they were engineered to complete a certain task within thirty years, and then die out. But since the task couldn't be completed in that time, technology being what it was back then—and still remains a bit short of the goal today—a few of us—*enough* of us—managed to keep ourselves alive.

"So that's our story—as much as I know and have been able to discover with a lot of thought and digging. But as for your wife—your primary interest is your wife, I gather, and I don't want this stimulating dialogue to end with you thinking that I—or *we*—had any part in her murder—So as I say, as for your wife, she was in that file because it was a horrid case and it hasn't yet been solved. It wasn't your *wife* I would have targeted if I ever got around to working on the file you found—It was her murderers—And, as I remember, I had the case pretty well narrowed down to those two professional killers in Ohio—in Akron, if memory serves me right. But there are thousands of bad guys out there, and only so much time."

"So you didn't...."

"No; haven't you been listening? Not only *didn't* I harm her, but I am completely incapable—*constitutionally* incapable—of harming her or anyone else who isn't an outright villain—Don't you understand?"

"Yeah—Yeah, I think I do now: I'm glad I finally do. Sorry for my tone before; I'm not too cheerful at the present time, given the circumstances—So—as to our problem: that little woman: She would be...?"

"My sister—half-sister, actually—different mothers, father the same. Long story there, Agent—which we don't have time for, I sincerely regret to say. But in a nutshell, her mother was a lunatic—paranoiac at first, catatonic at the end—and I suppose Sister inherited the trait. That mother of hers—she tormented my poor sister when she was a little child—tortured her, actually: burns, needles, those sorts of things—helped to shape her character, such as it is. Then when my father found

out about the torture and tried to intervene, she poisoned him."
A momentary pause with a long and pensive sigh. "I think—I
keep thinking—my father might be alive today—even today—if
that crazy, cursed woman hadn't killed him."

"I see; that must have been a horrible thing for you; I
can relate to your loss; believe me I can—So—Your sister—the
way she looks...?"

"Stem cells—You know about the stem cells? Well, you
talked to the Hartmans, so...."

"So your sister doesn't get them?—the stem cells? Is that
the difference?"

"In how she's aged? It is. She wouldn't listen—she'd *never*
listen, ever since we were little kids. Once a month blood to stay
alive; twice a month blood and stem cells if you want to be fit
and trim—Besides, twice a month eliminates a lot more bad guys
from the earth—But don't complain; I save you fellows lots of
work. Pity that my work is over and done with for the future,
but....

"But Listen: Hold on. I think I heard something. She
might be coming back. I've got a little time, Agent—she'll
torment me for a couple of days before the coup de grace—But
for your sake, and yours primarily: Let's hope your friends will be
here soon."

Audrey took the other way around the property; not the way that
Sidney had gone, but rightward from the gate along the wall. A
high wall—higher than she could reach up to the top, tiptoe to
fingertip—so her pacing along the outside of the wall would be
invisible to anyone within. She could get to where the wall was
broken totally unperceived.

Just beyond the gate she stopped and made her call. A
secretary answered, and gave her to the Supervisor—all that
happened pretty quick: So far, so good. But then the impasse
came: Twenty minutes, maybe thirty, till anyone could get to
where they were—That was the way bureaucracies worked; she
might have known as much.

All right, they'd be coming anyway; that was a
consolation. But meanwhile, what was she to do? If Sidney was
in trouble, half an hour would be an awful lot of time to sit and
wait. She had that Smith and Wesson Nine, and maybe she

could be of at least a little help: help to delay things anyway; help to prevent some tragic outcome if another gun could do that much. She'd never be able to live with herself if she didn't even try.

So quick along the stuccoed wall, out from the gate to the angle where the wall turned left, then left at the angle, and back along the wall—OK, no one could possibly see her from inside; the wall was big enough—until....

There—That was where the crumbled section was, ten feet across, or maybe twelve. A tiny rivulet of drainage had undermined the wall's foundation, and it had fallen down—Just like that washout at her father's farm when the fence was caught in the runoff from the hillside and swept clean away. Practically overnight it happened; after a night of heavy rain, the whole darn section had been swept away.

So in she went, holding the loaded pistol in her hand— the right hand—so that the left was free to push aside the branches lest they poke her in the eyes. The ground was wet and sticky with mud and clingy with undergrowth, vines, nettles, that sort of pesky thing; a lot of it scratched her legs. And it was smelly too; a deadly smell, like the farm when a cow died and they didn't find it right away. Something was really rotten in the ground.

It took a while for her to scramble through the foliage and get where she could see the house. Maybe not too safe to go right up to the house immediately. And so she crouched there a while to watch, hidden in the bushes.

Sidney, her kindly, handsome Sidney might be in trouble, and the Bureau people half an hour away. Once she got the situation sized up a little, she'd do whatever a former farm girl could do to get the situation fixed.

What a fun-packed, stimulating day!

She'd started down the steps to finish off the agent in front of Brother's eyes, that bloody knife in hand, but then...

The motion sensor chirped again! The little yellow light flicked on a couple of inches down the panel—saying *what* this time? Ah—same as the first chirp of the day—near the break in the wall again!

More fun—more chasing! But *what?*—What silly creature was it this *time?* Another agent? A cat? A dog? Whatever it was, it meant more blood, quarts and quarts of tasty blood to be spurted out and spilled—Yet *another* execution for Brother's sake, to show him right before his eyes what he had coming soon—

So up she went again, up the two long flights to the dormer window on the topmost floor, and out onto the slate, and crouching low on her haunches, first in front, and then behind, and finally off to the side where the wall had broken down. That was where the alarm had read, telling her that something near there moved.   So good. *More* fun. Whatever it was, she'd see it pretty well from here—man, woman, or beast—Lucky the fool things never bothered to look up!

Audrey looked up.

The farm had taught her to look up. Hawks after the chickens; that eagle in the woods that had once picked off one of the fluffy newborn sheep. She didn't like to shoot them, but a shepherdess's duty is to the welfare of her flock. One time three of her little ducklings had been snatched—tiny chicks her dad had given her to raise when she was ten. She hit the hawk at ninety yards with a target 22. No other hawks had ever flown back to the hatchery again.

So, reacting to the instinct, up she looked, as she always did—and noticed something strange: A sort of dwarfish woman on the roof crouching very low. At first she thought: They have those—what do you call them exactly?—Ah yes! Gargoyles: That's it. They have those gargoyles on the roofs of some of the fancy buildings in Europe. Pictures she'd seen, of course, never the actual thing. People like Sidney got to see the actual thing, but as for her, she could do without it. Europe, palaces, places to stay like the suites at the Marriott they'd slept in—Nice enough for rich folks, sure, but not for her. If Sid got through this scary mess OK—Oh God! She hoped he would!—She'd love to take him to her daddy's farm. He'd really like it, she knew he would; and Mom and Dad would come to love him like their own if things worked out the way she prayed.

But that awful thing up there: Gosh! no gargoyle, but a deformed little woman, sure as anything. No hideous statue, for she moved. Not too much movement, true; but you could tell she moved when you watched real close. Mostly, though, she just sat stone still and squatted on the tiles, looking all around—looking for *her* maybe, though she stayed way low in the bushes and would be impossible for anyone up high like that to see.

Ten minutes or so she sat like that—she sat and the woman sat, both pretty darn hold-your-breathing kind of still. Then finally, the little woman stood straight up—or actually, she didn't really stand; she kind of bent, looking old as the hills, the oldest, weirdest, puckeredest-looking person she'd ever seen or ever even *imagined* ever seeing. Gosh!

So the little woman kind of stood, pretty crookedly bent like the letter C shrunken down to minor case, and walked away across the roof, over back behind where you couldn't see her anymore. When five minutes more had passed and the little woman didn't reappear, Audrey worked her way on over to the house. Carefully past the weedy lawn and along the wall toward the back she went, creeping her wary way around.

At the junction of the side with the rear end of the house she turned leftward. There, down low: a glow of light seeping through a basement window. There! That was where she'd creep r-e-a-l slow and try to sneak a look.

No dog, no cat, no other government men out there—too bad. But there was fun enough to be had with what she'd caught already. Yes, fun—lots of fun!—No need to wait; she'd head on down and do it right away!

So down she went, down the two long stairways to the big main floor and over to the steps leading to the cellar. She had her knife in hand and brought a plastic bag along as well—she'd gone and got it from the kitchen. What she would do—this would be a new experience entirely, all right, and she had thought it up while crouching on the roof—What she was going to do today was this: She was going to put the plastic bag over the government agent's head. It would take—oh, maybe a couple of minutes for him to go into unconsciousness for lack of air, struggling all the while. Then, once she took the bag off and he came around again—pretty nearly died then had the miserable luck to come around—she'd disconnect the chains and drag him over right in front of Brother and do it there: stick the knife in so that the spray hit *Brother* in the face—Hah! Right in that sickeningly handsome face of his!—show him how much fun he'd missed in life, putting people down with that clever little neck-snap trick of his, missing all the joy of spurting blood.

So down the cellar stairs she went, and when she stepped onto the concrete she could see Brother's wide-eyed stare at the vastly different things she was holding in her hands. He was used to the knife—he'd seen that memorably enough twenty years before—But the plastic bag: Now *that* was what had made his eyes gape so hysterically wide. Was it for *him*? That's the curious thing that left him wondering.

Not fearing, though—for Brother was a man who seemed immune to fear. A fatalist about himself—But as for others: Yes, that was where he turned a bit too soft. The girl, for example—the doctor: Ah!—so *that* had caused his eyeball bulging then: He likely thought the plastic bag was for the *girl*— That would never do though. Asphyxiating some perfectly useful blood cells one might need oneself would never, ever do.

But Brother had no clue to that. All right, she'd let him stew a while, worrying, wondering; then while he was wondering, she'd slip the plastic over the government agent's head. Some muffled screams, a lot of thrashing—and then the knife, the blood.

What an unexpected, fascinating day!

Light. Bright light, so bright after the darkness of the bushes she'd been crouching in, that it was hard for her to see at first, until....

There. Good! Audrey's eyes adjusted, and she could tell through the outer angle of the window that—Oh my! That was Sid down there, all chained up, and another fellow with him, chained together on the same long metal bench.

And the little woman—looking less like a woman, now that you could see her in the light—and more like—what?—Like one of those evil witches in a fairy tale—but not a very pleasant fairy tale, honestly—a fairy tale not all that suitable for little children to read at night and try to sleep afterward. A fairy-tale villain who would get you looking in the closets and keep you trembling on your pillow wide awake; that was the kind of fairy-tale person *she* was.

She had something in her hand—There!—A knife!—Or no: not so much a knife as what you'd call a *dagger!*—long and curved in the middle and pointy at the end—a vicious-looking thing, fashioned for murder and nothing else. And in her other hand—what was that? It looked like a plastic trash bag, one of those big black jobbies with a floral scent to keep your garbage smelling sweet.

The little woman stood there looking toward the bench—you'd probably better say she *bent* there, looking toward the bench—with her withered skin and her angled back and a toothless kind of smile. And then she fluffed the bag—jerked it downward through the air so that it opened widely at its mouth and narrowly through the rest of it. And she stepped toward Sid; around the edge of the bench, past the other man toward Sid, and opened the bag a little wider with the point of the knife, and started to put it....

Oh my goodness! That was it! Audrey couldn't wait a single second more; she simply couldn't. Half an hour till the troops arrived? Sidney didn't *have* half an hour till the stupid troops arrived! He didn't have any fractions of an hour at *all*—none; zero—This was show time!—Good golly! It was now—or it was never, so better, *way* better, make it ... NOW!

The Smith and Wesson Nine was in her hand primed for use, cocked and set to go with one in the chamber and eleven more in wait; and she broke the pane with its handle—Clash! Tinkle!—the lower, outer pane of the six small panes in the window; it was pretty thin and shattered right away.

And when it did, the woman turned and raised her knife. It wouldn't help to raise a knife, though; no reason at all to raise a knife. Not to counteract a gun—Even a crazy tiny little woman should have realized that!—Jeez!

Bang! Whew—the darn thing was loud!—way louder than her daddy's 22. Of course the brick wall threw the sound waves back, so that it seemed much louder than right out in an open field, let's say. Not a lot of kick, though, for the mess it made when the hollow points hit home. Sid had been right about the handling of the gun: just perfect for a little female hand. When she took it from the glove box, he told her right at first: if you point that thing at somebody, go ahead and empty the clip. Which she did; a dozen shots in all, loud as dynamite echoing against the brick.

When the Bureau people got there, she and Sid were sitting on the front porch steps with his arm around her back. "What took you so long?" her handsome Agent Braman asked the guys. The Swat team in their riot gear looked pretty darn foolish, truthfully; totally useless in a way, as though it took them all that time to put their equipment on, then never had to use it anyway.

There was another lady in a room downstairs, and when Audrey let her out and unshackled Sid and the other fellow from the bench—the keys were in the little lady's pocket soaked with little lady's blood—the handsome man and the pretty woman got in the car out front and left. Sid said to let them go and didn't say a word to the authorities when they finally arrived.

On the long drive home, he'd tell her why, he promised; and she'd tell him all about the letter in the antique box. Kind of funny and ironic when you thought about the stuff she'd read in there, though it would take a while before the shock of all this meshuggas wore off (as Sidney aptly called it—he had some really nifty words), and they could sit down and chat about the irony of that letter and have themselves a pleasant little laugh.

ADDENDUM: DINNER AT THE SNIDERMANS'

"Hi there, Sweetie!"

"Hi. Audrey. What's up?"

"Have you got a minute? Are you swamped?"

"Always time for you, my darling girl. What's going on?"

"A couple of things—Oh, did your deal go through? I know there was a problem with the negotiations on that one."

"I think so; I think we'll go ahead with it. They want a bundle for the tech firm, but Dad wanted us to pick it up, so I think it's gonna be a go."

"Jeez! I bet you miss the cases at the Bureau with all those zillions of dollars on the line every day."

"I don't miss them any more than you do—Truthfully, honey: aren't you happier hanging out at home?"

"When the baby comes I will be, sure—So—why I called…."

"Uh-huh?"

"Two things, like I said. First, your Uncle Phil left a message on the machine—*our* Uncle Phil, I ought to say—he tells me I'm his favorite shiksa, which I probably am. I'm the only shiksa in the clan, right?"

"You are. You're *my* favorite shiksa too, you know. So what did Phil want?"

"Dinner. He and Rose want us Saturday for dinner."

"Oh boy! I hope she isn't making matzo balls!"

"They weren't as bad as you said they were—Come on! You guys can be mean, you know? Rose is nice and she does her best. She tries."

"OK, OK, you haven't tried her brisket yet—So what was the other thing?—You told me there were two."

"Oh yeah—yeah. That guy called again—from the court, I think."

"The court? What did they say from the court?"

"He didn't say 'court' actually—He said something about the bench—I took it to mean like a judges' bench, so I wrote his message down to get it straight."

"OK, and what does this urgent message say exactly—this judge you talked to from the bench?"

"He said—here I'll read it, OK? I wrote it out on the pad here on the desk…. Umm, he said, 'Tell your husband that the file he was concerned about has been terminated in a satisfactory way.'"

"The file? Terminated? What the hell does *that* mean?"

"*I* don't know; I thought that maybe *you* would."

"Well—did he say anything else? The bench—what did he say about the bench? I can't think of any bench he might have been referring to."

"Oh let's see: He said something about you two being on some bench together and he said some stuff about 'guesswork'—that's the term he used. He said that if your guesswork had improved from in the past, you'd know exactly what he meant."

"*Guesswork*!—Ho-ly Moses! The *bench*!—the *metal* bench!—Sheesh, Audrey!—'The case is terminated,' did he say? You know what that means?—It means he got the guys!"

"*What* guys? What are you talking about?—So—you know the man who called and what he meant?"

"I sure do. He's still doing his thing, I guess. That's good to know. The world's a better place for vampire guys like him who do those kinds of things."

"So—You think it was the vampire guy from Stanleyville—you really do?"

"I'm *sure* it was, and I'm sure that Jodi's case is closed. She was a sweetheart, and now that those murderers got caught and drained and vaporized, may her spirit rest in peace."

"If it was really him, he sounded pretty upbeat—really happy, I mean. I don't think he ever looked inside that pretty antique box of his."

"Well if he ever calls back, don't dare and tell him what you read in there. You wouldn't tell him, would you, hon?"

"Me? Heck no! If he knew that his lifework and his father's lifework was just to be a pen-pal for some extraterrestrial schoolkid's science project, he'd probably be crushed."

"*Anyone* would be, wouldn't they? I mean—the message probably took ten thousand years to get here and it'd take ten thousand more to get it back; so the kid'll be long gone and probably the whole civilization he lived in will be too. If our vampire ever actually manages to send the thing, it'll be a total waste."

"Yep: It's funny, Sid: People tend to do the stuff they're told to do, even if it doesn't make a lot of sense."

"It's the story of humanity, hon. Probably the story of the whole damn universe these last ten billion years. We do things just to do them. Other than living out your life, and doing a little good for others, and having a bit of harmless pleasure every day, most things we think are the most important duties in the world don't amount to much of *any*thing in...."

"The End."

AFTERWORD

If you're reading this, there's a pretty decent chance you made it through the book—which is terrific; I'll take it as a compliment. If you made it through and kinda, sorta liked it, dear reader, you have absolutely done me proud!

If you took the time to read the Foreword before delving into the story, you may recall that I promised to give a further justification for writing such an offbeat novel in a bit more detail. Well, here's that further justification I promised I would give:

Why a novel about vampires? you ask? Fair enough, but: Why a novel about *anything*? In my currently four-book literary career, I've discovered that inventing a plot is far and away the easiest part of writing a novel. I've got a hundred interesting concepts in my head.

The plot invention takes all of an hour or so; give me a topic and I'll come up with an interesting plot. It's basically, as I said before, a concept, rather like a rough sketch as an underlayment for a monumental oil. What the initial sketch is *of*—whether landscape, figure, historical tableau, etc.—has surprisingly little to do with the quality of the completed work. A Rembrandt self-portrait, a Vermeer domestic scene, a Rubens classical study—all of them are superb works of art. We admire them, not because we think Rembrandt's face is particularly handsome, or Vermeer's airy room in the painting is artfully arranged, or Rubens's pudgy nudes are amorously enticing: Tastes change over time; and what looked beautiful in Rembrandt's day, or Rubens's day—or even in Picasso's day, scarcely half a century ago—may not appeal to our senses as much at the present as it did in the past. What makes their art enduring is less the subject than the manner in which the recreation of that subject is performed.

And so it is in literature. A story about vampires? How much different is that than a story about ghosts? Or witches? Or sorcery? … As in, say … Hamlet? Macbeth? The Tempest?

See what I mean? It's not the *subject* as much as the *execution* that determines greatness in a work of art—Which brings us to the inevitable question: How are we to *judge* the quality of a work of art? What factors in a novel, for example, merit the golden stamp of excellence? Why is Faulkner great? Why is Proust great? Or Tolstoy? Or Melville? Or my personal favorite, Henry Fielding?

To examine that question, maybe we ought to digress a bit and consider the nature and structure of a novel, its types, its good and bad characteristics, what makes us want to read it, and, more importantly—*much* more importantly—why we might want to read it a second time, or a third, or fourth, or....

Well, let's start with the two basic novel types—for all novels—contemporary ones at least—can be pretty well pigeonholed into those two fundamental types. And those—for the majority of readers who are not Lit majors or at least autodidactic literati (the preceding phrase, of course, written for those who ARE Lit majors or autodidactic literati)—those novelistic types, dear average reader, are: (1) Plot-driven novels, and (2) Character-driven novels.

What's the difference you ask? (if you're not a Lit major or auto-whatever-the-hell that pentasyllabic term was). For those of you who are neither, and proud of it, the distinction is this: Plot-based novels are, as you'd expect, driven by the generally interesting progress of narrated events with relatively little development of the characters *involved* in those events. The type is exemplified by the action novel: the superhero, the secret agent, your Airport book that keeps you going through its pages, wondering what might happen to the potential victim or victims; to civilization itself if the happenings are on a greater stage. As to character development in such books—why the secret agent thinks the way he does, how the agent's past experience, his childhood, his prior trials and tribulations, shaped his actions and worldview; how the events in the fast-paced narrative turn him into a better man—or a worse—there is little space or time devoted to that. If there were, the attention diverted from plot events would misdirect the reader from the bomb about to go off or the shoot-out about to occur, lessening the tension that propels the book relentlessly forward. A good action novelist knows that any loss of tension just won't work, and he therefore keeps his characters more or less standard types—typical heroes or anti-heroes, vulnerable maidens, pleading moms needing to be helped, nasty blackguards—that sort of mold-made folk.

So there's your plot-driven novel in a nutshell—But how about its character-driven counterpart? What's a typical example of that? Well, again in the confines of a nut, look at the novels that win awards—*Big* awards, we're talking—National Book Awards, Nobels, and the like. The people who *give* those statuettes and medals usually want to immerse themselves in a character, to get to know him, to understand the innermost workings of his mind. They want to see him grow and change and develop in response to whatever events occur in the story line, trivial though they may be. They want a book they can think about, mull over; they want characters in the novel who are real, believable, men and women just like us—like *them*—human in a credible and heartfelt way; characters who aren't just good guys or bad guys with their white and black hats, but individuals who are BOTH good and bad, in variable measure, just as everyone else is who is REAL; imperfect folks, in many ways flawed but wanting to be better than they are—or maybe worse, depending on the character involved.

Those character-driven books are the ones that win the golden palm, serious books written by authors who are often academics writing largely for other academics. They all-too-often aren't best-sellers, though in many cases they ought to be. But such books require effort from the reader; they require thought, and the occasional visit to a dictionary, and the periodic deciphering of a complicated passage here and there. Not quick reads, but rather books to be pored over, scrutinized, discussed with others. Not an effortless task, but works that will reward the reader greatly for the effort he invests.

Now at this point you should be asking: Why can't a book be BOTH plot- and character-driven? —A terrific question that leads us to the concept of the 'hook'. The hook, my patient reader (if you've made it this far into my tiresome self-justifying essay), is the initial device that sucks you in and makes you want to read the rest. In the old days—the olde, olde days of Richardson and Fielding, and the less old days of the lionized but often tedious Henry James—readers were more like you: They were patient, sophisticated, desirous of getting something from a book other than cheap thrills and entertainment. They were willing to put some effort into what they were reading in order to be enriched by it. Like you, they were the kinds of readers a serious author adores.

No more. Today's patrons of the literary arts want a quick thrill without the work. No time for introductions, no intellectual foreplay—give 'em the story and drag 'em into it by the scruff of their necks—BANG! A shot— BOOM! An explosion! —Fire in the house, body in the basement (sound familiar?)— Villain sends a notice that the world will blow up—NOW!!

Same with a character-driven story in this recent impatient age. Get the reader into the character ASAP: A kind, sweet girl who just saved a little puppy from being flattened by a car—Oh, but *what?*— WHAT? Her poor old mom just died? Her father beat her? Oh my! What will happen to her? Will she learn from her misadventure? Will she grow? Will she be a better person in the end for her travails? Read on, those of you who've gotten suckered in past the first paragraphs, and eventually you'll find out.

You see? You get the picture? It's one or the other. Either hook the jaded reader on rapid-fire events or do it with a sympathetic character, and quick! Modern-day literary patrons don't have time to wait for for both.

And so we're left with the action story, pure and simple, or, alternately, the often-tedious tale of a life-change or coming-of-age. Either get us riveted in a narrative of fist-clenching adventure, which is ultimately meaningless; or bore us to death with the enlightening story of how poor Edith dealt with her loss—a loss from which we'll grow and ultimately learn.

And so I wrote about vampires—can you blame me? I wanted to give you a story that was (1) interesting, (2) at least somewhat original, (3) logical—you can't refute the medicine and physics incorporated in the plot, (4) populated by believable and multi-dimensional characters speaking (5) realistic dialogue individualized to their roles, and—finally and most important— dah-ta-da-dah!—(6) carefully written. That last factor in my list of virtues will lead me to the main point I want to make (be patient); but first a few words about character portrayal and dialogue.

As I noted earlier in this already overlong apologetic essay, an author cannot possibly hook his reader on plot development AND character development at the same time. It's one or the other. This book makes the necessary concession to plot from the very outset— BUT, I have tried my best to develop the primary characters as the story goes along. Because of the dictates of a fast-paced, event-driven narrative, the players in the piece are necessarily pushed somewhat into the background, being shaped by the events in the drama far more than shaping them. Still, there is room for the characters to grow a bit as they interact with the plot events and with each other. Can extensive character definition exist in a book of this type? A crucial question. I think it can, for the same reason it exists in some of the offerings of the better writers of the past.

Examples, you ask? Economic character definition in a limited number of words? Shakespeare did it in almost all of his plays. Look at the portrayal of Polonius in *Hamlet*: We get to know the man nearly as well as we know Hamlet himself, and we do so after a stingy few lines spoken before Hamlet bumps him off early in the play. And Dickens too: A plethora of minor characters defined in a handful of paragraphs—and defined memorably too, like the convict in *Great Expectations* and Micawber in *David Copperfield*.

So it can be done; I've provided evidence of that, at least by reference. And as for me, I've tried mightily to do it—to what success you'll have to be the judge. Does the vampire come across as a unique personality with a voice of his own? Does Sidney? Do Linnie and Jen and Audrey? I did my best to breathe life into each of them; and if I failed—well, at any rate, my heart was in the right place when I tried to give you a book worth your time and effort. If I succeeded to any degree in plot and character and especially in my next and most important factor of a worthwhile book, then the time I put into the project, at least in my humble estimation, has been eminently worthwhile.

And so we come to the main point I want to make, the most important factor in making or breaking a piece of writing of any kind—and if you have the ear for it, I have no doubt that it will be your chief quality too: A really, truly good book—the *sine qua non* of a really worthwhile, keeper-of-a-book—is that it be carefully written.

What do I mean by carefully written? If you read the book and it spoke to you in a musical voice, an emotive voice, and you HEARD that musical voice, and felt the emotive drumbeat of the sound, then stop right here: You get it, you totally, absolutely get it, and need read no further on. If you didn't hear the music and the rhythm in the prose, and didn't quite feel the language's emotion, well, that's all right too. It's in there as a sort of bonus for readers who DO hear and feel it. But I did my best to make the story interesting for those who lack the ear.

I wrote the book for the same exact reason and in the same exact manner that I wrote all my previous books. There's a common denominator in all my fiction thus far: and that's the meticulous attention to language. My primary love is words; the ferreting out and setting neatly into the text the precisely appropriate word in the precisely appropriate place. To me, writing a novel is very much like doing a 127,000-clue crossword puzzle. Like the puzzle, a perfectly written book—a *correctly* written book—has only one specific word (or letter) that will fit ideally into each potential space. Changing any word or any sequence—the least, most insignificant-seeming change—will only diminish the cumulative whole. Each word must be selected for denotation, for connotation, for sound, for rhythm, for texture—The very 'a's and 'the's and 'hmm's and 'umm's must be set in place to fit into the cadence and eliminate undue repetition. The intent in doing so is to produce a text that reads smoothly when spoken aloud—that's a given—but also has the proper meter and melody to enhance the specific passage it describes.

At this point, the best thing I can do is to give you an example. You've just read the present story, so let me offer something from my prior book, *Flocking*. Here's the description of the protagonist, Jeremy Lipton getting his first unpleasant, and wholly accidental, inhalational exposure to the mind-reading drug he's been developing. It's not intended to be a pretty sight:

> O-o-o-h SHIT! That DID it—*BIG* time! An impenetrable cloud of miasmatic powder rose and hung and wafted toward his face, enveloping it, etching at the lining of his nose unmercifully. He sneezed again—and again--with double, triple, *quadruple* the effect. His tears sprang forth like faucets at full flow, his nostrils poured like gutters in the rain. The smell and taste provoked an immanence of suffocation, the powder seeped like noxious vapor through his nose and throat and lungs: Acrid, bitter, *sickening*! Lemony-garlic, turpentine and vinegar! He retched: Once. Twice; then managed to suppress the abominable reflex, forcing himself bolt upright, knocking his head:

Bang!
Ow!
Shit!

Hard on the strut supports, rattling the overhanging cages once again ... having gathered to the best of his ability what he could of the vile, intolerable spillage. The jar, at any rate, was ninety-five percent full, the rest an irrecoverable monolayer bound like quickening plaster to the unremitting floor. He screwed the bottle tight—tighter than he probably had the need to (a whole lot tighter, to be honest with you, folks, for Teddy could hardly pry it open later in the morning)— thrust it onto the countertop an arm's-length to his right, right beside the box of sealed Velveeta cheese, and scurried to the bathroom down the aisleway to shower off his face.

Just a few explanatory words as to what I've done here: "immanence of suffocation"—Say that in one breath and it will induce in you—well, an immanence of suffocation. "Acrid, bitter, sickening! Lemony-garlic, turpentine and vinegar!" Does that convey the quality of the stuff poor Jeremy is breathing in? I hope so; that's what I tried for, and tried by picking words and sounds and cadence that would convey the sensations that such an exposure would invoke. The passage works for me on many levels and perhaps it works for you. Perhaps some passages in the present novel worked that way for you as well. If at least some of them did, my work was a success.

So if you made it through this overlong and mildly pompous essay, you have a rough idea what I tried to do in my story about vampires. Why did I write it? I wrote it because I HAD to. After a wonderful career as a very busy surgeon, God knows, I don't need the bucks. I write because I love the process; I *need* the process, which makes my life, at this stage of it, more fulfilling and complete. My goal was to produce a novel that rewards not just a reading, but a *re*reading and maybe a *re*-re- reading after that. We don't read Shakespeare for his plots, do we? I mean—a drama where a 'ghost and a prince meet and everything ends in mince-meat?'—The story is beside the point entirely; it's the language that draws us back and sings to us its imperishable and melodious song. It's the music of the language that has drawn me back to Melville and Faulkner and Catullus and Wilfred Owen—and, yes, even to old Abe Lincoln, the poet laureate of presidents—more times than I have fingers and toes to tally them up.

If I've succeeded in my task, this book and my others will draw some of you back as well for a second read; and if any of my writings accomplish that, not one micro-millisecond of my labor at the keypad has been in vain.

Steven M. Greenberg, M.D.